BOW STREET SOCIETY:
The Case of The Pugilist's Ploy
By
T.G. Campbell

Cover illustration by Peter Spells
Bow Street Society Logo by Heather Curtis

Text & artwork copyright © -
2022 Tahnee Anne Georgina Campbell

Edited by Susan Soares
All Rights Reserved

Printed by KDP

ALSO BY THE AUTHOR

The Case of The Curious Client
The Case of The Lonesome Lushington
The Case of The Spectral Shot
The Case of The Toxic Tonic
The Case of The Maxwell Murder

The Case of The Shrinking Shopkeeper & Other Stories
The Case of The Peculiar Portrait & Other Stories
The Case of The Russian Rose & Other Stories
The Case of The Gentleman's Gambit & Other Stories
The Case of The Fearful Father & Other Stories

The Case of The Devil's Dare
in
Criminal Shorts
a
UK Crime Book Club anthology sold for the benefit of
The Red Kite Academy in Corby, Northamptonshire, UK.

Dedicated to Mum

ACKNOWLEDGEMENTS

Thank you to all my readers, including my beta team, for your unerring enthusiasm and support. It keeps me going in moments of self-doubt and pushes me to be the best writer I can. Also, thank you to my sister for her faith in me and unconditional support, and to my editor, Susan Soares, for her professionalism and keen eye for detail. I wouldn't be where I am without you all, and I want you to know I appreciate you all from the bottom of my heart.

I'd also like to thank Pam Mills [MA], author of *Prevention, Detection & Keepers of the Peace: Policing Tonbridge, a Division of Kent County Constabulary. The first 50 years and more.* (Tunbridge Wells; Heronswood press Ltd, 2022). The research sources and knowledge she gave me about late nineteenth century Tonbridge in Kent were invaluable. I highly recommend her book to history enthusiasts, as she truly has an encyclopaedic knowledge of Tonbridge.

I'd also like to thank Fiona Orsini, curator of the Drawings & Archives Collections at the Royal Institute of British Architects (RIBA). She kindly provided photographs of Norman Shaw's original 1888 floorplans of the New Scotland Yard building for me to use as references whilst writing my descriptions.

Finally, I'd like to thank ex-Champion Lightweight of America and England, William "Billy" Edwards, for writing his comprehensive *Art of Boxing and Manual of Training Illustrated* way back in 1888. I'd also like to thank Peter Lovesey for writing the second Sergeant Cribb mystery, *The Detective Wore Silk Drawers*, and W. Russel Gray for writing his essay *For Whom the Bell Tolled: The Decline of British Prize Fighting in the Victorian Era*. You were all tremendous sources of inspiration to me.

TABLE OF CONTENTS

Acknowledgements 6
Prologue 9
One 18
Two 24
Three 33
Four 48
Five 58
Six 67
Seven 78
Eight 90
Nine 97
Ten 105
Eleven 114
Twelve 121
Thirteen 130
Fourteen 136
Fifteen 142
Sixteen 146
Seventeen 161
Eighteen 174
Nineteen 178
Twenty 185
Twenty-One 194
Twenty-Two 204
Twenty-Three 214
Twenty-Four 225
Twenty-Five 231
Twenty-Six 242
Twenty-Seven 250
Twenty-Eight 257
Twenty-Nine 269
Thirty 274
Thirty-One 278
Thirty-Two 287
Thirty-Three 300

Thirty-Four 308
Thirty-Five 316
Thirty-Six 327
Thirty-Seven 335
Thirty-Eight 340
Thirty-Nine 346
Forty 355
Forty-One 367
Forty-Two 371
Forty-Three 374
Forty-Four 380
Forty-Five 386
Forty-Six 391
Forty-Seven 395
Forty-Eight 404
Forty-Nine 410
Fifty 415
Epilogue 422
Notes from the author 431
Gaslight Gazette 441
More Bow Street Society 442
Sources of Reference 447

PROLOGUE

Mr Joseph Maxwell's dark-green, bloodshot eyes tracked a snowflake as it drifted past his window and landed upon its ledge. Others followed suit as the bleak sky unleashed its flurry upon Bow Street. The din of passing carriages and pedestrians soon waned in response to the heavy snowfall until only the occasional whinnying of a horse broke through the hush. At the same time, the distant, muffled voices of Miss Trent, Mr Snyder, and Miss Dexter came from the kitchen downstairs.

Reluctant to join them, Joseph lay upon his side on a narrow brass bed in the middle of the room. Located on the first floor of the Society's house, directly over the parlour, its interior had been untouched since Thaddeus Dorsey's day. Light-green wallpaper, embossed with dark-green swirling leaves, had faded in the sun. Patches above the wall-mounted gas lamps had also been blackened by the flames. The exposed floorboards would creak unforgivingly under foot, whilst their old varnish had been scratched and thinned in several places.

A few days had passed since Oliver's arrest. During that time, Mr Snyder had been kind enough to retrieve Joseph's typewriter and clothes from the house on Duncan Terrace. These, along with some ornaments and prints, had helped him to settle in when he'd first arrived. Yet, now, he regretted his decision to have them brought to Bow Street. They weren't comforting reminders of home, but instead representations of the happy future Poppy had been denied by him and Oliver. As a result, their presence had only served to heighten his guilt.

Attired in an off-white nightshirt beneath the many woollen blankets, Joseph's slender form exuded the strong scents of bodily odour and unwashed linen. His dark-auburn hair rested in a tangled mess upon his head, whilst his jaw and high cheekbones were covered in stubble. Having not had anything to eat since the previous day, his stomach complained with a growl. The thought of seeing the others filled him with a dread so nauseating, though, his hunger pains vanished in an instant.

It wasn't as if they were unsympathetic—quite the opposite. Yet, each expression of condolence, offer of assistance, and gentle embrace had felt like a lie. Those giving them were sincere, of course, but he wasn't sincere in his gratitude. He'd spent hours going over what had happened in his mind and, no matter how he'd looked at it, there remained one inescapable truth: he should've done more.

"It's sickening," Dermid Maxwell sneered.

Dragged from his thoughts, Joseph looked at his brother holding the *Gaslight Gazette*. He'd just finished reading Joseph's article about their mother's suicide and Poppy's murder. "How you could bring yourself to write this is beyond me."

Joseph eased himself into a sitting position but remained under the blankets. "I had no choice. If I hadn't, Mr Baldwin would've, and he…" He frowned. "It would've been lies."

Dermid hmphed.

At thirty, he was the elder by nine years, but the shorter at only five feet four. Although his wavy, black hair and vivid dark-green eyes made him handsome, his large nose and pointed jaw were repulsive reminders of their father. His attire consisted of a knee-length black overcoat, waistcoat, suit, and tie teamed with a white shirt. All of it, except for the tie, had been tailor made for him. Unlike Joseph, a hint of lavender soap lingered about him.

Dermid folded the newspaper and tossed it onto the writing desk. "When are you due to give evidence?"

"In a f-few days," Joseph mumbled, bowing his head as the nausea returned.

"You'll need to bathe before then." Dermid glanced over him in disgust.

"I-I will."

The burgeoning reputation of the Bow Street Society had encouraged the sensationalist press to portray the group as the genius sleuths who had exposed Oliver whilst the police had stumbled around in the dark. As a result, the flames of public outrage had been fanned into a frenzy, thereby compelling the courts to hasten the process. The looming festivities of Christmas had also added an extra degree of pressure. No one wanted to sup their mulled wine between hearings after all.

Dermid hmphed again and went over to the window. Clasping his hands behind his back and knitting his brow, he gazed out at the horizon. After a few moments had passed, he turned to Joseph. "Have you thought about what you will do once this is all over?"

Joseph lay on his opposite side. "I-I don't know when that w-will be." Hearing his brother approach, he brought his knees up to his chest and clutched the blankets tightly beneath his chin. "P-Please … I want to b-be alone."

Dermid released a sad sigh, and Joseph felt the bed shift as he sat on its end.

"As you know, Father has wrote a new will, leaving everything to me," Dermid began in a gentle tone. "Both houses on Duncan Terrace, the business, his financial assets—everything. Once he has been found guilty, and his inevitable sentence carried out, I intend to liquidise it all and divide it equally between me, you, and Frazier." With a sideways glance, he mumbled in disgust, "The second Mrs Oliver Maxwell will also receive a small yearly allowance."

"I don't want it."

Dermid pinched the bridge of his nose. "*Don't* be *foolish*. It would give you financial independence." He paused as a thought occurred to him. "You could finally marry Miss Dexter."

"N-No, I couldn't." Joseph frowned, and his eyes glistened with unshed tears. "N-Not now."

Dermid's lips formed a hard line as he exhaled through his nose. Taking a moment to reassess the situation, he decided a change of tact was required. "I've booked passage to New York City in January. I have to close the business there. I want you to come with me."

Joseph turned over and stared at him, wide eyed. "*Me?*"

"The change would do you good, and I'd appreciate the company."

Joseph sat up. "B-But New York City is in America."

"It is."

"Y-You want to sail t-to America … t-to be *in* America … with *me?*"

Dermid gave a small chuckle. "You're acting as if it would be a disaster."

"It-it would be."

Dermid smiled. "Whyever for?"

"B-Because it's me." Joseph's eyes became downcast. "I always make a m-mess of things."

Taking a firm grip of Joseph's shoulder, Dermid waited for their eyes to meet. "Don't worry. I'll look after you." Joseph's eyes became downcast once more. "You don't have to decide now. Give it some thought and let me know what you decide once this whole business with Father is finished. Agreed?"

"Agreed," Joseph mumbled, unconvinced.

"Good." Dermid stood. "In the meantime, try to eat and get some rest."

* * *

Dearest, darling Lynnie,
I hope this letter finds you and Percy well. The news in your last was most saddening to your father and me, for it will be the first Christmas Day we have not made merry together. Naturally, we appreciate the pressures of Percy's schedule—and yours, of course—have made it quite impossible. Nevertheless, we

*are disappointed it will be just the two of
us this year. Your father has been utterly
morose over it, even if he tries to be strong
for my sake. We shall simply have to make
arrangements for you both to visit us here
in Cheshire come January. Does Percy
still perform those delightful card tricks?*

Dr Lynette Locke discarded her mother's letter and,
plonking her elbows down with a thud, rubbed her
forehead with both hands. Closing her eyes at the same
time, she reminded herself that her parents knew nothing
of what was happening with Percy. Nevertheless, her
mother's blatant attempt to make her feel guilty had
initially caused her body to tense and quiver from the rush
of anger.

Plucking the letter from the bureau at which she sat,
she scanned the remainder of its contents with dark-blue
green eyes blemished by dark circles. A grey tinge had
also settled upon her fair complexion, making it look
washed out. The rest of her appearance was just as
haggard. Her once meticulously styled dark-blond hair was
scraped into a tight bun at the back of her head, whilst her
bright, fitted clothing had become a loose, dark-brown
woollen dress. Although only thirty, the heaviness of her
fatigued limbs made her feel much older. The burden of
her husband's round-the-clock care had also caused her
shoulders to droop and her posture to slouch, thereby
superficially shortening her six-foot height.

She returned to the start of the letter and read; *it will
be the first Christmas Day we have not made merry
together.* Her eyes glazed over as she watched the events
of the previous Christmas Day unfold in her mind. Percy
had impressed her parents with expensive gifts, charmed
them with compliments, and entertained them with his wit
and sleight of hand. He'd also waited until they'd retired
for the night, and he'd been intimate with her, to ask for
some heroin. A bitter taste seeped into her mouth as she

recalled what he'd said: *I only need one dose to help me sleep.* He'd only ever ask for 'one dose,' but it was still 'one dose' of many. She lifted her gaze, knowing he was asleep upstairs. It was all he did these days.

From the moment his attendant, Claude, had brought him back from the opium den, he'd been undergoing a sodium bromide treatment to help him through the worst of the withdrawals. Outlined in Dr J. B. Mattison's plan for the treatment of opium addiction, it consisted of administering sodium bromide to Percy every twelve hours. She'd started him on the minimum dose of sixty grains in sixty drachms of cooled, boiled water. Now, she was giving him the maximum dose of one hundred and twenty grains in the same number of drachms of water. By the third day of the treatment, Percy had become drowsy. By the fourth, he'd descended into a profound slumber.

Although it had meant he was unaware of his body's fevered reaction to the loss of the opium, it had also caused him to be unaware of other things, too. Namely, the need for him to stay awake long enough to exercise, wash, or converse. Even eating had lost all interest for him, and every mealtime had become a battle of wills. When he'd begun to lose weight, she'd had no option but to implement a regime of force feeding.

A pained expression fell upon her face as she recalled that morning's breakfast. Percy's struggles were difficult enough to witness, but it was his whimpering after each forced swallow that had truly grieved her. Closing her eyes, she swallowed the lump forming in her throat and took a deep, shuddering breath. Opening her eyes, she took out her writing things and, with a trembling hand, began her response.

* * *

Sitting at the table in the Society's kitchen, Miss Dexter planned to draw Miss Trent as she rolled out some pastry for a batch of mince pies. Unfortunately, the more she stared at the blank page, the more her mind was filled with the events of a few days' ago. She still couldn't believe it; it was so horrible, and yet, so tragic. Neither Poppy nor Sybil Maxwell had deserved what had befallen them. Joseph hadn't, either. She felt her heart ache.

Attired in midnight-blue bustle skirts and blouse, the eighteen-year-old artist's auburn hair was neatly wrapped in a bun at the base of her skull and adorned with plain, silver pins. They, and the silver brooch pinned to the collar of her blouse, sparkled in the lamplight.

A full decade older than her friend, Miss Trent was also three inches taller at five foot seven. Her attire consisted of plum bustle skirts with a lilac panel at their front, a plum jacket with silk lapels, a cream blouse with ruffled detailing, and a broad, black belt with brass buckle. An apron was also tied around her waist. Like Miss Dexter's, the gold and ivory brooch pinned to her blouse's high neck occasionally caught the lamp's light. Finally, aside from a few loose curls against her back, her chestnut-brown hair was pinned atop her head in an elaborately sculpted mass.

Setting aside her rolling pin, Miss Trent looked to Miss Dexter with the intention of enquiring after the progress of her sketch. The sight of the artist's green eyes staring, unblinkingly, through the page at something unseen beneath made her frown, however. It had been hard on them all, but Miss Dexter had taken the news of Oliver's deeds to heart.

"Red shirt's in the livery," Mr Snyder's rough, East End of London-accented voice remarked from the doorway. With a calloused and cracked thumb pointing over his shoulder, his brown, beady eyes looked between his friends. Broad in build, his black bushy sideburns and short hair appeared more unkempt than usual. His brown jacket, dark-brown trousers, and worn, black leather boots were also damp in places. At forty-eight, he was the most senior in the group.

"Is it still snowing?" Miss Trent enquired.

"Yeah, but not as heavy," Mr Snyder replied, taking a seat opposite Miss Dexter.

"Good." Miss Trent carefully cut circles out of the pastry and scooped a spoonful of filling into the centre of each. "Am I moving too much?"

"Hmm?" Miss Dexter lifted her head. Realising what she'd said, she offered a polite smile. "Not at all." With a melancholic expression, she set down her sketchbook and pencil. "I haven't been able to draw anything."

"Inspiration will come, lass," Mr Snyder gently encouraged.

Miss Trent cut out smaller circles from her pastry and, placing them upon her filling, carefully pinched the two edges to form a seal. Putting them in the oven to cook, she wiped her hands upon her apron and put some tea things upon the table.

"The water should be boiled now," Miss Trent said as the sound of knocking took her from the room.

Miss Dexter stood and, using a towel to grip its handle, lifted the kettle from the stove and poured the boiling water through the tea strainer, into the pot. Next, she used a spoon to drive the remaining tea leaves through the strainer before setting it aside and sliding the lid into place. As she returned to her seat and waited for the tea to fully permeate the water, she added sugar and cream to her cup in readiness.

Mr Snyder watched her with concerned eyes. "How've you been holdin' up, lass?"

Miss Dexter stilled, partway, in returning the sugar bowl. Lifting the lid of the teapot and inspecting its contents, she slowly stirred the dark brew within. "Well. Thank you."

Mr Snyder added his own sugar and cream once she'd replaced the lid and poured the tea. "It's been a terrible business, all this."

Miss Dexter hid her sadness with a bowed head as she sipped her tea.

"Have you talked to 'im since—?"

"*No.*" Miss Dexter simultaneously lifted her head and lowered her cup. "I …" She felt her cheeks warm as she realised how rude she must've sounded. "I'm sorry, Sam." She offered a weak smile that failed to reach her eyes. "No, I haven't." Sitting up straight, she arranged her spoon upon the saucer. "I… I think it's best that way."

"It's *incorrigible*!" a woman suddenly cried from the hallway.

Exchanging glances, Mr Snyder and Miss Dexter rose to their feet. With the latter following, Mr Snyder opened the door and looked past the stairs to Miss Trent and the middle-class woman in a tall hat, red bustle dress, and dark-red jacket. From Miss Trent, Mr Snyder enquired, "Everythin' okay?"

"Yes, thank you, Sam," Miss Trent replied. To the visitor, she said, "This is Mr Snyder and Miss Dexter, members of the Bow Street Society." Her gaze shifted back to them. "Mrs Gove is here to ask for the Society's help. Miss Dexter, could you bring us some tea in the parlour and take my pies from the oven?"

"Of course," Miss Dexter replied with a small nod.

"Thank you," Miss Trent said.

As she indicated the open doorway, Miss Dexter and Mr Snyder returned to the kitchen. Whilst she removed the pies from the oven and prepared a fresh pot of tea, he gathered up the jug of cream and sugar bowl and put them onto a tray. When she added the teapot to it, he placed a gentle hand upon her arm. "Let me know if there's owt I can do."

"I will." She smiled. "Thank you, Sam."

ONE

"Two cups, Charlie," Inspector John Conway said, his breath turning to steam in the freezing night air. Lowering the brim of his trilby hat over his tired, dark-blue eyes, he dropped the coins into Charlie's waiting hand. A three-foot-high, three-legged urn with silver finish stood on the far right of the coffee stall's narrow, wooden bar. Red-hot coals housed within a grate at its base emitted warmth that, although meagre, was welcomed by Inspector Conway as he held his numb hands over it. Having spent the latter half of the night meeting undercover officers in dank alleyways, he felt every one of his forty-three years. Giving a loud sniff, followed by a harsh cough, he winced at the pain shooting through his chest. It had only been a little over a week since he'd fractured his ribs in the *Key & Lion's* bareknuckle boxing ring.

"Them ribs, still?" Charlie enquired, filling the first of two earthenware cups with a dark-brown liquid from the urn. The coffee—if it could be called that—had been so adulterated with chicory, its intense sweet tobacco-smoke aroma was the first he'd smelt, followed by a whiff of caffeine.

Charlie was similar to Inspector Conway in both age and build. Bundled up in a thick, brown woollen scarf, coat, and fingerless gloves, his brown eyes twinkled in the light of a lantern hanging from a hook to his right. The hook being attached to a low set of shelves, similar to a bookcase, nailed to a box that served as a driver's seat on the horse-drawn, two-wheeler wagon.

"Yeah." Inspector Conway hunched his shoulders, held his elbows against his sides, and slipped his hands into the pockets of his knee-length, black overcoat. An icy gust of wind blew across his back, causing him to take a step closer to the stall. Pitched beneath a streetlamp at the entrance to Westminster Bridge, it was as familiar to the grizzled policeman as his own home.

Running perpendicular to the bridge was a low wall made of stone. Beside this was a deserted thoroughfare lined by the buildings of St. Thomas' Hospital. Lamps burned in several of its windows as doctors cared for the sick and dying housed within its walls. On the opposite side of the river, the Houses of Parliament's clock tower chimed six. The first ship of the day also sounded its horn in the far distance, the reverberation of its deep boom drowned out by the bongs of Big Ben.

Inspector Conway preferred to visit the stall at this time as he was practically guaranteed to be Charlie's sole customer, bar the odd doctor. The drunken fast gents and women selling pleasure for a few coins would've come by around midnight, whilst the working men were closer to three. There was also the strong chance of a cheaper cup of coffee since Charlie, nearing the end of the night's tenure, was keen to sell the last few drops before going home.

Pointing to the remnants of meat upon the shelf, Inspector Conway ordered two ham sandwiches. In the short time he'd been standing there, the heat from the stall had warmed the reddened cheeks and nose of his weathered face. It had also dried his dark-red beard and moustache which had been dampened by the earlier snowfall. Tucking the sandwiches under his arm and picking up the cups, he thanked Charlie and left the stall. Hearing the snow crunch beneath his feet as he went, he took his time and finally put everything down upon the wall's icy top.

"Here." Inspector Conway passed a cup to a man in his mid-twenties with matted brown hair, a fair complexion blackened by grime, and hazel eyes. Approximately five foot eight inches tall, he wore a green overcoat with frayed edges, tattered brown trousers, a dark-blue neckerchief, and a pair of old boots. Gulping down most of the coffee, the man snatched the sandwich as soon as it was offered and devoured it in a few bites.

"What've you got for me, Sergeant?" Inspector Conway enquired, taking a bite from his sandwich. He barely noticed the thinness of its meat or the inferior quality of its bread.

"It's what we thought, sir."

Inspector Conway took a mouthful of coffee. "When?"

"Tomorrow. After the shop's been shuttered for the night."

"Is their bloke still workin' there?"

The man nodded. "He's gonna let 'em in."

"We'll do as we said, then." Inspector Conway ate some more of his sandwich. "You'll be nicked with the gang, but don't make it easy for the lads."

The man smiled broadly with a mischievous glint in his eyes. "Yes, sir."

Inspector Conway took a final mouthful of coffee before passing it to his sergeant who drained both cups in a matter of moments. "Best be off with you." Inspector Conway took back his cup. "Don't want 'em wonderin' where you've got to."

The man wiped his mouth with the back of his sleeve. "They think I've gone to see my old mum."

"At six in the mornin'?"

"I left 'em last night, sir."

Inspector Conway gave a grunt of acknowledgement. Nevertheless, a hint of concern penetrated his otherwise hard gaze. "Watch your doings, lad. I don't want to bury another copper."

"No fear of that, sir." The man shook his hand. "Goodnight."

Inspector Conway watched his sergeant hurry away into the darkness. Eating the last of his sandwich, he returned the cups to Charlie and bid him a goodnight before carefully making his way across Westminster Bridge. Glancing up at the clock tower as he passed, he compared the time to his pocket watch and adjusted the latter.

A wind had picked up on this side of the river, prompting Inspector Conway to cross the road and walk in the shelter of the buildings there. His gaze soon fell upon one in particular—the imposing edifice of New Scotland Yard. Standing separately from its neighbours, its many windows shone with lamplight, whilst its four turrets gave it the appearance of a castle silhouetted against the night sky.

As he neared its main door, a figure emerged from the shadow of the building and held a lantern aloft between them. The moment its light illuminated Inspector Conway's face, though, the constable's dark-brown eyes cooled, and his lips contorted into a sneer. Lowering the lantern, he muttered a flat "sir" and returned to his post as Inspector Conway strode past and climbed the stone steps. With a backward glance, he opened the door at the top and went inside.

Walking across the hard floor beyond, he heard his footsteps bounce off the white-washed walls. A gas-lit corridor straight ahead was lined by solid wooden doors belonging to the offices of the Metropolitan Police's Receiver and Pension Clerk, amongst others. At this end of the corridor, on the right and left respectively, was a lift and the main stairwell to the upper and lower ground floors. A uniformed attendant stood outside the open doorway of the lift, waiting for a passenger.

Inspector Conway's early days of being a detective inspector at A Division had coincided with those of the building. He could vividly recall his first time travelling to the first floor in the lift. His sergeant at the time, who'd held an unerring fascination with new technologies had persuaded him to give the contraption a try. With them and the attendant, its narrow interior was more cramped than Inspector Conway would've liked. Its concertina gates also had to be dragged across and secured with a loud scraping of metal and clang. Finally, the dragging sensation upon his stomach as the lift moved upward had been far from pleasant. He hadn't travelled in it since.

Taking a sharp left and passing under an archway, Inspector Conway entered a second corridor that ran horizontally to the first. Along its right-hand side were windows overlooking a cobbled courtyard. Doors lining its left led to interview rooms and the offices of an Assistant Commissioner and Chief Constable. Beyond these was another stairwell leading to the upper and lower ground floors.

Passing them all, Inspector Conway took a sharp right into a third corridor that ran vertically to the second and parallel to the first. The doors here led to the sergeants' room, a clerks' office, and Chief Inspector Jones' office. Knowing it was too early for his friend and senior officer to be there, Inspector Conway instead went past his door and into the next, leading to the inspectors' room.

Inspector George Pilker, a slim man in his mid-forties with a long face, protruding ears, and blond hair, narrow sideburns, and thin moustache was the sole occupant. He looked up from his desk with parted smiling lips as he heard Inspector Conway enter. Yet, the moment he saw his face, his smile vanished. Pinching his lips instead as a tightness entered his jaw, Inspector Pilker stood and tidied some papers into a pile. Picking it up, he looked past Inspector Conway as, with a defined stiffness to his back and shoulders, he walked around him and left.

Inspector Conway stayed put until his colleague had passed before removing his hat and, crossing over to his own desk in the far right-hand corner, tossed it onto its top. Easing his overcoat off his shoulders, he winced as a sharp pain shot through his chest. Taking a couple of deep breaths, he nevertheless relieved himself of the garment and draped it over the back of his chair. Intending to stay there for as short a time as possible, he remained standing as he went through the documents which had been thrown onto his desk. These consisted of daily bulletins, handwritten reports from Mob Squad detectives, and typed memorandums issued by the chief inspectors. One memorandum caught his eye. It read:

> With immediate effect, all Metropolitan Police officers are forbidden from summoning Dr Percy Weeks to any location for the purposes of seeking his medical assistance. This applies to all cases of homicide, suicide, and accidental death regardless of their location and circumstances. Any officers found to be in breach of this order will be disciplined.
> — *Chief Inspector Richard Jones*

An intense heat flushed through Inspector Conway's body, causing his face to turn red. Snatching the piece of paper from his desk, his other hand slowly clenched into a fist as he read it through a second time. The thought of Dr Weeks losing a substantial part of his income only served to heighten his anger further. Crumpling the paper into a tight ball, he tossed it into a nearby bin and kicked his chair into the wall behind his desk.

TWO

The fire snapped and crackled in the hearth as the hiss of gas emanated from the wall lamps on either side. Dense condensation covered the window, blocking the barren yard from view. With the dull, early morning light behind, it seemed almost ethereal to Dr Neal Colbert. Sitting on a worn-out wooden chair in front of Miss Trent's desk, he shifted his gaze to study his surroundings further. The dark olive of the wallpaper flooded his vision in all directions. He knew that without the fragmenting influence of pictures or furniture, it could trick him into thinking the walls were closing in. To guard against this, he returned his gaze to the window and noted the frozen snow upon its ledge. Movement in the corner of his eye soon drew his attention to Miss Trent, however.

Sitting behind the desk in a chair far superior to his own, she held her shoulders back and her spine rigid as she read the contents of a file. Aside from the usual signs of concentration—a sweeping gaze with the occasional blink and closed yet relaxed lips—her face was expressionless. It made reading her incredibly difficult, something Dr Colbert found unnerving. For physiognomy was all about finding the 'mind' in the face, and hers was hiding her thoughts well.

In contrast, Miss Trent had garnered much from their greeting a few minutes prior. Since their last meeting, Dr Colbert's dark-blond hair, eyebrows, and split moustache had become unkempt, whilst puffiness beneath his chocolate-brown eyes had dulled their vitality. The haphazard fastening of his waistcoat, crooked tie, and crumpled shirt also hinted at a sleepless night spent tending to the sick of mind at Bethlehem Hospital.

She put down the file as she met his gaze. With strength in her voice, she said, "I've now completed my evaluation of your application and interview and concluded the answers you gave were both comprehensive and truthful."

Dr Colbert's body stilled, but he darted his gaze from her face, to the file, and back again. "I don't understand. Did I give you cause to doubt me?"

"Not at all."

Dr Colbert furrowed his brow and, with a small shake of his head, gave a half smile. "Then why question the integrity of my answers?"

"It wasn't intended as an affront to you or your reputation, Doctor. You were a stranger when we first met and, as such, had the potential to use deception to secure your membership. As the Society's clerk, it's my responsibility to ensure its integrity is preserved."

Dr Colbert slowly sat back in his chair. "I see." He looked to the window as he imagined Miss Trent exposing him as Inspector Woolfe's informant. The thought alone was enough to make him feel a little lightheaded. Sensing her eyes boring into him, he pushed the visions aside to rally his courage. "H-How did you test the integrity of my answers?"

The corner of Miss Trent's mouth lifted. "By researching physiognomy in the British Museum's reading room."

Dr Colbert stared blankly at her for a moment before the weak laughter of relief creased his features and relaxed his shoulders. "Thank goodness!" He shook his head with a smile. "I thought you might've questioned my colleagues at the hospital."

"That wasn't necessary. Besides, there was no guarantee they knew of your application, despite you mentioning it was Dr Charles McWilliams who recommended us." Miss Trent unlocked a drawer in her desk and took out a small red hardback book and envelope. Placing the items between them, she indicated the former. "These are the Bow Street Society's Rules of Conduct and Membership. Please make it a priority to familiarise yourself with them, as members are expected to abide by them without exception." She slid the book toward him. As she indicated the envelope, Dr Colbert saw it had a distinctive red 'B' in its top-right corner. "Formal requests for members to investigate a case will be delivered via messenger in envelopes like this. A summary of the case will also be included. You're free to reject a request if you don't have the time or find the details of the case too distressing."

Dr Colbert gave a dismissive grunt at the last as he leafed through the rule book. Stopping on a page, he read the first few lines. "It states here members must cooperate with Metropolitan Police officers at all times."

"Do you object?"

Dr Colbert looked up sharply. "No, of course not."

"Good."

"Why would I?"

"Why, indeed."

Dr Colbert studied her expression but again, it was giving little away. Shifting uncomfortably in his chair, he turned the page and stopped as another rule caught his eye. He read aloud: "Members are forbidden from committing a crime unless there is a sufficiently justifiable reason to do so, such as a person's life being in danger if one fails to act." He met her gaze. "In that case, wouldn't I be obliged to notify the police of my fellow member's criminality—if I'm to cooperate with the police at all times, that is?"

"It would depend upon the circumstances."

"But doesn't such a contradiction in the rules undermine the Society's integrity?"

Miss Trent's mouth twitched, but her expression remained emotionless.

"Doesn't it, in fact, portray your members as nothing more than vigilantes in frockcoats and petticoats?"

Looking him straight in the eye, she replied in a resolute tone, "The cases we investigate are rarely straightforward. They often involve the most heinous of crimes. Under such conditions, we must overcome the obstacles presented by the deceit of those involved and the police's resistance to our presence to uncover the truth. On rare occasions, it may be necessary for us to take calculated risks—"

Dr Colbert parted his lips.

"And, yes, the law into our own hands to allow us to do that," Miss Trent swiftly added.

Dr Colbert closed his lips and stared past her ear for a prolonged moment.

"If you've changed your mind—" Miss Trent began.

"No." Dr Colbert's eyes snapped back to her face. "Not at all." Feeling his resolve to abolish the Society grow in light of their so-called 'rules,' he relaxed into his chair and smiled. "Actually, I'm rather keen to begin."

* * *

Inspector Conway looked from the clock to the door and back again. Shifting his weight and elbow from one armrest of his chair to the other, he winced at the discomfort in his chest. Holding his breath until it had passed, he exhaled through his nose and tried to focus on the report in his hand. Within the reading of a few sentences, though, his mind had wandered back to the memo. He glanced at the clock again.

Only a few of the desks were occupied, with those closest to him standing vacant. Nevertheless, his hearing was assaulted by the collective noise of rustled papers, scratching pens, slammed drawers, and numerous conversations. Running alongside this, albeit on the fringes, were the echoing footfall and voices in the corridor. All of it kept his concentration at bay and his head pounding. Squeezing his eyes shut and rubbing their lids with his thumb and forefinger, he dropped his hand into his lap and opened them wide.

"A long night, was it?" an unexpected voice enquired in a sardonic tone.

Inspector Conway looked up into the probing dark-blue eyes of Inspector Gideon Lee. The six-foot, lean frame of the fifty-eight-year-old policeman from T (or Kensington) Division loomed over his desk as he stood before it. Fresh snowflakes dotted the shoulders of his black ankle-length fur coat whilst the tips of his salt-and-pepper hair were damp from the same. His black leather-clad hand held the silver handle of an ebony cane at his side as he continued to look down at Inspector Conway with an emotionless expression.

Putting the report face down upon his desk, Inspector Conway sat back in his chair and folded his arms without breaking eye contact. In a low, firm voice, he enquired, "What are you doin' 'ere?"

Inspector Lee turned and, strolling over to the hat stand by the door, relieved himself of his coat, gloves, and cane. Beneath, he wore a tailored midnight-blue suit with matching waistcoat and tie, and white shirt with starched Eaton collar. Straightening his cuffs, he returned to Inspector Conway's desk and looked to their colleague. "Meeting Inspector Pilker." He returned cold eyes to Inspector Conway. "What are *you* doing here?"

"My duty."

Inspector Lee released a loud snort. "To whom?"

Inspector Conway's face flushed red as, with narrowed eyes, he put both hands on the desk and slowly rose to his feet. Leaning forward, he growled, "The Yard."

"Really?" Inspector Lee challenged. Mimicking Inspector Conway's stance, he closed the distance until their noses were almost touching. In a low, contemptuous voice, he enquired, "Are you certain it's not to the Bow Street Society?"

Inspector Conway clenched his jaw and dug his fingernails into the desk as he imagined punching the arrogant bastard whilst fighting the urge to do so.

"It must have come as quite a shock to the Mob Squad detectives to learn they've been working under the orders of a traitor."

Inspector Conway grabbed Inspector Lee's lapels and yanked him closer, prompting Inspector Pilker and the others to leap to their feet with a loud scraping of chairs. Yet, none of them moved away from their desks as, with a bright red face and flaring nostrils, Inspector Conway snarled into Inspector Lee's face, "You've not got the *first* idea about me."

"What the *devil* is going on here?!" Chief Inspector Jones demanded.

Inspector Conway immediately released Inspector Lee, and the two stepped back from one another.

"Conway, in my office—*now*," Chief Inspector Jones ordered. Despite being only thirty-three years old, his voice reverberated around the room.

"Yes, sir," Inspector Conway mumbled.

Chief Inspector Jones' hazel-brown eyes were hard as he glared at Inspector Conway's retreating form. The snow upon Chief Inspector Jones' brown bowler hat, burgundy scarf, and black, knee-length overcoat, showed he'd just arrived at the Yard. Like Inspector Lee, there was also dampness in his short, brown hair and moustache of the same colour. It wasn't clear whether the redness in his otherwise fair complexion was due to the cold weather or his anger, however.

"Why are you not at Chiswick High Road?" Chief Inspector Jones demanded from Inspector Lee once Inspector Conway had gone.

Inspector Pilker cleared his throat. "He's, erm, here to see me, sir."

"Why?" Chief Inspector Jones demanded.

"He has some information he believes may have some bearing upon one of my cases," Inspector Lee replied in a respectful tone.

"Then get it from him and return to your station," Chief Inspector Jones ordered.

"Yes, sir," Inspector Lee said quietly.

"I expect *better* from you all," Chief Inspector Jones warned. Slamming the door behind him as he left, he strode down the corridor and into his office. Slamming its door once he was inside, he tugged off his hat and plonked it onto one of the hooks of the nearby hat stand. Pulling off his coat and scarf next, he tossed these onto the adjacent hook before advancing upon Inspector Conway. "What in *Christ's* name do you think you're playing at, John?!"

Inspector Conway stepped back and bowed his head.

"You do realise you would've been *arrested* for *assault* if you'd punched him, don't you?!"

"Yeah."

"So, *why* take hold of him in the first place?!"

"I don't know."

Chief Inspector Jones glanced at the door and, moving in close, lowered his voice. "We have problems enough with Lee and Woolfe's ongoing investigation into the Society without *you* adding to our woes."

"I know. I'm sorry."

Chief Inspector Jones sighed and pinched the bridge of his nose. "I knew it was a bad idea leaving you in there after the board's verdict. It's been like a red rag to a bull. Perhaps we should move—"

"Nah." Inspector Conway vehemently shook his head. "It'll be like they've driven me out. I'll not have it."

Chief Inspector Jones narrowed his eyes. "It's not your decision."

Inspector Conway glared at him. "Nor's ending Weeks' commission with the Yard."

"*Don't* change the subject."

"Why not? It's the only bloody reason I'm still 'ere this mornin'."

Chief Inspector Jones sighed and pinched the bridge of his nose for a second time. "John." He met his gaze. "That wasn't my decision."

Inspector Conway stared at him. "You what?"

Chief Inspector Jones sat and, retrieving his pipe and tobacco from a drawer, tossed a box of matches onto his desk. "Have a cigarette and calm down first." Whilst he prepared and lit his pipe, Inspector Conway sat opposite and lit a cigarette from his pocket. They sat in silence for several minutes as they inhaled the smoke from both and waited for their anger to ease and finally disappear.

Two large windows behind and on either side of Chief Inspector Jones' desk overlooked a sparse yard and a tall red-brick wall beyond. The high ceiling and walls of the office were covered in plaster painted white. Gaslight hissed in the glass sconces of the chandelier suspended from the ornate rose and wall-mounted lamps. Chief Inspector Jones' dark-varnished oak desk dominated the space, with the remaining pieces of furniture comprising of the hat stand, a wooden filing cabinet, several bookcases, and a low-backed, brown leather Chesterfield sofa. A Turkish rug depicting leaves and flowers of varying shades of brown covered the majority of the dark-varnished oak floorboards. A second door in the far-left corner of the room led into Chief Inspector Jones' private lavatory.

Placing his pipe upon a wooden stand at his elbow, Chief Inspector Jones picked up the memo. "Assistant Commissioner Terrell thought it best to remove Dr Weeks' commission from the Yard given his insubordination at your discipline hearing."

"He was only defendin' me." Inspector Conway tapped the ash from his cigarette into the ashtray. "He don't deserve this."

"I agree, but 'this' isn't as dire as you think, John."

"He's gonna lose all his work."

"Not necessarily."

"But the Yard's work *is* all his work—"

"Dr Weeks, for all his drunken arrogance, is one of— if not *the*—best surgeons in London. I hardly think the inspectors and sergeants of the Metropolitan Police will risk the solving of their cases by summoning an inept surgeon instead of Dr Weeks, do you?"

"But the memo said—"

"I know what it said." Chief Inspector Jones replaced the memo with his pipe and took several puffs. "If I'm informed of anyone disobeying the order, I'll, naturally, have to act. If, on the other hand, I'm kept in the dark about it, there is precious little I can do." He smiled. "I wouldn't worry about Dr Weeks, John. His continued commission at the Yard is secured—albeit on an *unofficial* basis."

Inspector Conway stared at him, stunned. "I thought you'd gone mad."

Chief Inspector Jones chuckled. "Not quite." He checked his pocket watch. "Well, now. Time is marching on, and I have a great deal to do." He stood. "I suggest you go home and get some rest. You look as though you've been awake all night."

Inspector Conway gave a soft grunt as he got to his feet. "I have." He crushed out his cigarette in the ashtray. "Thank you, sir."

"Anytime," Chief Inspector Jones said with a smile that failed to soften the concern in his eyes.

Inspector Conway sensed Chief Inspector Jones' gaze on his back as he left but knew his friend was just worried about him. Nonetheless adamant about keeping his base of operations in the inspectors' room, he returned there with his head held high. Collecting his coat and hat, he put them on whilst standing at his desk. Glancing at its top as he turned to leave, he stopped. The report he'd read earlier was suddenly conspicuous by its absence. He looked to Inspector Pilker's desk but saw he and Inspector Lee were gone. Muttering a curse under his breath, he searched the piles of documents upon his own. Finally locating the report at the bottom of one of them, he opened the top drawer of his desk and put it inside. Adding the remaining documents to it, he closed and locked the drawer.

Although it was obvious his desk had been searched—and either Inspector Lee, Inspector Pilker, or both were responsible—he knew there was no hope of proving it. As he left the yard to begin his journey home to his bed, a part of him regretted not punching Inspector Lee when he had the chance.

THREE

To say Mr Christian Grosse liked to watch boxing would be the same as saying an artist liked to paint. It was more than a pastime; it was in every fibre of his being. The crunch of a bare knuckle against bone, or the thud of leather against flesh, always sent a shot of excitement into his heart. The stench of sweat and bodily odour was like a sweet perfume, and the crude profanities tossed out by the veteran members of the Fancy were like music to his ears. There was no other place he wanted to be than amongst the crowd in the cold, damp cellar of the *Key & Lion* public house on Nesbit Street, Hackney. Whilst it was true the 'ring' was nothing more than empty barrels and overturned tables with old, stained ropes between, it had hosted some of the most skilled and—dare he say it—*infamous* pugilists over the years.

Forty years old and approximately five feet ten inches tall with a slim build, Mr Grosse lacked the rough, disfigured knuckles sported by the pugilists he admired. His prominent nose had also retained its natural straightness, whilst his mouth had as many teeth as the next man. The neatness of his thick, dark-brown handlebar moustache mirrored that of his short hair and eyebrows of the same colour. His attire consisted of tan jacket and trousers, dark-green waistcoat and bow tie, off-white shirt, and scuffed, brown leather shoes. Finally, his dark-green Homburg hat was unique in the sea of bowlers, flat caps, and bare heads.

As he thought of the many set-tos he'd witnessed at the *Key & Lion,* a smile crept across his lips, and his eyes twinkled with delight. Pulled from his reverie by a shove from his neighbour, his face fell as he looked upon the fight unfolding before him. A great battle it was not.

Professional pug Joe Rake, known as the 'Raven' due to his impressive speed and agility, had accepted the challenge from amateur Marcus O'Shannon. At twenty, Joe had a four-year advantage over Marcus in both age and experience. The consensus amongst the crowd was Marcus would be dealt a fair knockout in the third or fourth round. So unanimous was it, no wagers had been placed on young Marcus—side bets or otherwise. It had come as something of a surprise, then, when he'd drawn first blood. The crowd had been stunned into silence the moment they'd caught sight of the claret. Yet, their jeers and insults had soon returned, with many intensifying their demands on the Raven to claim his 'easy' victory.

As with most amateurs who were facing their man for the first time, Marcus had thrown everything he had at his opponent in the opening round. By the end of the second, his speed had slowed, and his breathing was laboured. Testament, at least to Mr Grosse's mind, that youth didn't always guarantee stamina. Predictably, this had allowed Joe to deliver severe punishment to his opponent, and Marcus' eyes were now mere slits. Blood also poured from his temples, broken nose, and split lip.

A pug's mark—the spot where the ribs branch off the breastbone to either side—was the most vulnerable region below the neck and the spot where a strike could be the most devastating. Provided the London Prize Ring Rules were followed, of course. A strike to the mark was not only incredibly painful, but the subsequent winding gave the attacker ample opportunity to deal further punishment with little resistance. Unfortunately for Marcus, each of his attempts at Joe's mark were skilfully thwarted by a deftly executed side-step. The punches he threw at Joe's head didn't fare much better. Swift ducking coupled with a side-step, or an arching of his spine and a tossing back of his head, allowed Joe to remain elusive.

Consumed by fatigue, anger, and frustration, Marcus lunged his body forward, intent on putting his remaining strength into a final strike at Joe's mark. In doing so, though, he threw his head in front of Joe's body, thereby exposing it. Mr Grosse had seen many a seasoned pug adopt this ploy to "draw" their opponent into attempting an upper cut. At which point they'd duck to the right and deliver a hard left-handed blow to their opponent's body. If this was Marcus' intention, Mr Grosse seriously doubted he had either the stamina or the speed left in him to execute it. His suspicions were soon confirmed when Marcus failed to evade a devastating upper cut from Joe. Having dropped his left fist, Joe had drawn his arm back and swung it up between Marcus' clenched hands to drive his fist into Marcus' mouth, knocking out several teeth as he did so.

"Right in the sauce box!" Mr Grosse's neighbour shouted with glee.

Marcus' head and upper body were thrown violently back by the blow. This in turn sent him into a backward stumble with arms swinging like a windmill. Landing upon the ropes, he gripped the upper and regained his footing before lunging for Joe again. Once more, Joe deftly evaded punishment with a flawlessly executed side-step, followed by a knuckle-crunching blow to Marcus' left temple. The young amateur's head was forced sideways, and his torso twisted, before he crumpled to the floor.

"A knockout!" Mr Grosse's other neighbour shouted in wild delight.

In a heartbeat, Mr Duncan Sparrow, the referee and landlord of the *Key & Lion*, was in the ring along with Marcus' seconds. The latter dragged their principal back to his corner and, propping him against the barrel, poured water onto his face and down his throat. Meanwhile, Joe had returned to his own corner to wait, albeit with his gaze fixed upon Marcus.

A retired pugilist himself, Mr Sparrow had a crooked nose, misshapen cheekbones and jaw, and several missing teeth. The muscles in his shoulders, biceps, and thighs were still highly developed, though. No doubt hauling barrels from the cellar on a daily basis. He was approximately five feet six inches tall with chocolate-brown eyes and slicked-back dark-grey hair hidden under a tweed flat cap. His attire consisted of black trousers and waistcoat, poisoned-white shirt with sleeves rolled up to his elbows, and old, black leather boots. Retrieving a watch from the pocket of his waistcoat, he stood at the mark in the centre of the ring—the scratch—and announced in a broad West Midlands accent, "Time!"

Joe returned to the scratch at once, but Marcus remained propped against the barrel, his head bowed. One of his seconds gripped his hair and lifted his head whilst the other poured more water onto his face. Although Marcus spluttered at the sudden onslaught and attempted to shove his second away, he showed no sign of standing. After counting down eight seconds on his watch, Mr Sparrow gripped Joe's wrist and, raising his arm, declared, "I give you your *winner*—Joe 'The Raven' Rake!"

Cheers erupted from the crowd as several punched the air and hugged their neighbour in celebration of their winnings. A few also leaned into the ring to slap Marcus on the head and shoulders, laughing as they did so. This continued as the crowd filed past on their way to either the bookmakers or the narrow steps leading to the bar upstairs.

"Ge' ou' of it!" one of Marcus' seconds demanded as he shoved a spectator away from his principal.

Meanwhile, Joe was being congratulated and promised drinks on all sides. Approaching him with his hand extended, Mr Grosse said, "An excellent set-to, Joe." Although predominantly sounding from the East End of London, Mr Grosse's accent also had a Germanic twang to it.

"Ta, Mr Gross," Joe replied, his cockney accent muffled by his swollen lip.

Mr Grosse's German surname was pronounced 'Gross' as in 'cross,' rather than Joe's choice of something disgusting. Nevertheless, Mr Grosse was well-accustomed to the mispronunciation of his surname, so he barely noticed the faux pas. Giving Joe's swollen hand a firm squeeze and his shoulder a gentle slap, he said, "It'll lead to more, I'm sure."

"I hope so," Joe said.

Giving his shoulder another gentle slap, Mr Grosse stepped away to allow the stakeholder to give Joe his battle money. A share was also given to Marcus despite his loss.

"Another interesting set-to, Mr Sparrow," Mr Grosse remarked to his friend.

"Joe gave that nause a righ' lampin'," Mr Sparrow replied with a frown.

"Yeah; it was no Conway and Snyder."

"Can't you find me a couple or three of some good pugs?"

Mr Grosse put his arm around Mr Sparrow's shoulders as they headed upstairs. "I'll try, but you'll always get amateurs in these casual encounters."

"I don't fix fights," Mr Sparrow warned.

"No one's asking you to. It's just… a little planning can a great battle make."

Mr Sparrow pulled away from Mr Grosse as they emerged from the cellar and, going behind the bar, poured them both a pint of beer. "I've never fixed a fight, and I'm not startin' now."

"Your sporting nature will be the death of you," Mr Grosse remarked.

The main area of the *Key & Lion* was housed within a large, square room with a bar running along its back. Behind the bar were shelves containing barrels of ale and bottles of gin and other spirits. A door also led to the back hall and Mr Sparrow's private accommodation. To the right of the bar was a modest fireplace that was overdue a sweeping. To the left of the bar, beneath the large, plate-glass windows, was a row of square tables and benches. Between the bar and benches was the door to the cellar. The remainder of the space was occupied by low, round tables and stools, whilst the bare floorboards were strewn with old sawdust soiled with tobacco, ale, and vomit. Finally, Mr Sparrow had made a paltry attempt to mark the upcoming festivities by hanging a couple of paper chains from the rafters.

Mr Grosse took a tattered dark-blue notebook and pencil from the inside pocket of his jacket as he came to the bar. Licking the tip of the pencil's lead, he recorded Joe's victory and turned to a blank page. Writing a few notes about Marcus' dire performance, he closed the book and put it and the pencil away. Putting his hat on the bar, he smiled at his friend as he placed his drink in front of him.

"Oi oi, Grosse," Mr Oswald Baldwin said, clapping his hand upon Mr Grosse's shoulder as he came up behind him. Pulling it away again as he stood on his right, the *Gaslight Gazette* journalist pushed up the brim of his black bowler hat and leaned upon the bar with folded arms. In his mid-thirties, he had mousy-brown, unkempt hair, short sideburns, thick goatee beard and moustache. His attire consisted of dark-grey trousers with matching waistcoat, an off-white shirt complete with Eaton collar, and a dark-green silk cravat with a brown floral print. Worn atop all of this was an open knee-length black overcoat that had seen better days.

"Get another in, Duncan," Mr Grosse said with a smile. "An early Christmas gift for my friend here." He briefly put his arm around Mr Baldwin and squeezed his shoulder.

"That's very charitable of you, mate," Mr Baldwin said. "Just don't expect one back."

Mr Sparrow chuckled and, pouring Mr Baldwin a pint, set it down before him. Taking the monies for both drinks, he enquired, "'Ow's life been, Baldwin?"

"Can't complain." Mr Baldwin drank a large mouthful of beer. "Well, I can, but it won't do me any good." He grinned. "How'd the fight go?"

"Schrecklich," Mr Grosse replied, drinking his beer.

"As good as that, eh?" Mr Baldwin enquired with a smirk. Turning and leaning upon the bar with one elbow, he nodded to Inspector Conway eating alone at a table in the corner. "Maybe you can convince the Bulldog to come back out of retirement?"

"Off you go," Mr Sparrow replied with a playful twinkle in his eye.

"Not bloody likely!" Mr Baldwin straightened and faced the bar. "I've still got all my teeth, and I want to keep it that way."

Mr Sparrow and Mr Grosse chuckled.

The former shook his head and released a deep sigh. "Truth be told, though, pugs ain't what they were."

"*Boxing* is not what it was," Mr Grosse corrected. "When I was writing for *Bell's*, I saw some sights!" He drank more of his beer. "As soon as my book is published, everyone will see boxing for the true art form it is—even the toffs!"

Mr Sparrow chuckled. "You and that book."

"*Yes*, me and *that* book," Mr Grosse replied with indignation. "It shall be a masterpiece, a comprehensive history of the sport and its—"

"When you get 'round to finishin' it," Mr Baldwin sardonically interrupted.

"It *is* finished." Mr Grosse frowned. "Almost."

Mr Sparrow and Mr Baldwin chuckled.

"It is, I say," Mr Grosse insisted. "I just need to find a couple more pugs, write up their stories, and send it off to the printers."

"It's only taken you five years," Mr Sparrow teased.

"Who you lookin' for?" Mr Baldwin enquired. "Maybe I can help."

"Deon Erskine for one," Mr Grosse replied.

"Deon Erskine?" Mr Sparrow repeated. "Why do you want 'im for?"

"Why would I not?" Mr Grosse countered. "He's one of the greatest pugs in living memory." To Mr Baldwin, he said, "Thank you, but I've already got an address for him here in London."

Mr Baldwin glanced at Mr Sparrow who folded his arms.

"I thought Deon went off to New York City a few years back," Mr Baldwin said.

"'E did." Mr Sparrow coolly stated.

"New York City… in the United States of America?" Mr Grosse enquired, perturbed.

"Is there another?" Mr Baldwin enquired through a chuckle.

"I don't have the means to go there," Mr Grosse replied, disheartened.

"Best to forget 'bout Deon Erskine, then," Mr Sparrow said, lowering his arms.

As he moved down the bar to serve another customer, Mr Grosse hummed with a furrowed brow. Giving a half-shrug of his shoulder a moment later, he checked his pocket watch and drained his glass. "Time for me to be off." He tapped Mr Baldwin's arm as he put on his hat. "Sharp's the word—"

"And quick's the motion," Mr Baldwin finished with a grin. "Look after yourself, Grosse."

"The same to you, dear friend, the same to you." Mr Grosse patted Mr Baldwin's back and, bidding Mr Sparrow goodbye, headed out into the cold night air.

* * *

Inspector Lee's form was as rigid as his glare as he flicked through the pages of the Bow Street Society's Rules of Conduct and Membership. Sitting behind his desk in front of the window overlooking the dark, snow-covered rear yard of T Division's police station, he shook his head at a particularly riling passage. Recalling the few times he'd seen an arrogant and defiant Miss Trent, he realised her confidence was born from the soundness of her group's regulations. Granted, some contradicted others but so too did the Metropolitan Police's own Code of Conduct. Tightening his grip upon the book as Miss Trent's smirking face filled his mind's eye, he felt a shiver of joy as he imagined her being dragged away in handcuffs. The tension also receded from his face and limbs, thereby allowing him to settle back in his chair. Closing the book and reading its title, he replayed the fantasy of Miss Trent being arrested with a deep sigh of satisfaction.

"If I may be so bold, Inspector, you appeared to experience a whole host of emotions reading that," Dr Colbert observed from his seat opposite.

Inspector Lee put the book down upon his desk and, resting his elbows upon the arms of his chair, steepled his fingers. "It's an invocative read."

"It's also a blatant subversion of the law," Dr Colbert said with contempt.

"One cannot expect anything less from a group of glorified vigilantes," Inspector Lee remarked.

"It upsets me to know decent, respectable people have been coerced into debasing themselves to the level of common criminals in the name of Miss Trent's distorted form of 'justice,'" Dr Colbert admitted with a pained expression.

"We don't think she's the one behind it," Inspector Caleb Woolfe interjected.

The forty-nine-year-old policeman sat to the right of the door, opposite Inspector Lee's desk. His six-feet-four-inch, broad frame hid his chair from view while his knees obstructed the door. If they had been friends, Inspector Lee may have considered gifting Inspector Woolfe a comb for Christmas. Yet, a closer inspection of his colleague's matted, black hair told him it was already beyond hope. Given the hideous standard of Inspector Woolfe's personal hygiene at their past meetings, and Inspector Lee's desire to hold onto the contents of his stomach, the latter had taken the precaution of opening the window prior to the former's arrival. The moment Inspector Woolfe had stepped inside Inspector Lee was relieved he had. For Inspector Woolfe was still wearing that infernal fur coat of his with the same dark-grey suit and waistcoat, black tie, and white shirt beneath. The stench of damp mustiness tinged with sweat had worsened since their last encounter though and, along with the waft of rotten teeth whenever Inspector Woolfe spoke, Inspector Lee felt thoroughly revolted. How Dr Colbert could stand being in such close proximity to it was beyond him.

Dr Colbert turned and stared at Inspector Woolfe in disbelief. "I beg your pardon?"

"We think she may be working for someone else," Inspector Lee replied.

Dr Colbert moved his chair back and looked between them. "Who?"

"That's what we want to know," Inspector Woolfe replied.

Dr Colbert lowered his head as he considered this latest revelation. After a few moments, he looked to Inspector Lee, to Inspector Woolfe, and back again. "It would be logical for a man to be at the head of the Bow Street Society—"

"We don't know if it's a man or a woman," Inspector Woolfe interrupted.

"Irrespective of whether it is or it isn't," Dr Colbert continued in a condescending tone. "Miss Trent's guilt isn't lessened by the possible involvement of another. She is the one peddling this fiction after all."

"Now, look here—" Inspector Woolfe began with a narrowing of his eyes and a pointing of his finger as he leaned forward.

"We agree with you, Doctor," Inspector Lee interrupted, casting a look of disapproval at Inspector Woolfe. Waiting until he'd leaned back again and folded his arms, Inspector Lee continued, "But to kill the body, we must first remove its head."

"I suppose that follows," Dr Colbert conceded.

"And even vigilantes must fund their activities somehow," Inspector Lee went on. "The Bow Street Society will be no different."

Dr Colbert knitted his brow. "You wish me to uncover the source of their financing?"

"We know the Society relies on member donations and client commissions to operate," Inspector Lee replied. "We also know Miss Trent is paid a wage. All of which must be stored somewhere." Clasping his hands, he leaned forward and rested them upon his desk. "We want you to uncover the name and address of the bank where the Society's account is held."

Dr Colbert glanced at Inspector Woolfe and, upon seeing his nod, turned in his chair to face Inspector Lee. "I shall certainly do my utmost." He picked up the book and flicked through its pages with contempt. "I've been told to familiarise myself with this." He took the envelope from the back. "And this." Passing it to Inspector Lee, he tossed the book into the Gladstone bag at his feet.

Inspector Lee studied the envelope's red 'B.' "This is what was referred to in Inspector Fisher's file on Mrs Poppy Maxwell's murder."

Inspector Woolfe held out his hand. "Let me see."

Inspector Lee passed the envelope to him after studying its other side.

"Once I'm assigned to a case, I'll have ample reason to visit the Society's house," Dr Colbert said. "Otherwise, it will be difficult for me to search Miss Trent's office. Especially with Christmas coming up."

"That's to be expected," Inspector Lee said. "Please try to uncover the information in other ways before you attempt a search, however." He smiled. "We wouldn't want Miss Trent or the other members to become suspicious."

"It doesn't matter how long it takes, as long as you get it in the end," Inspector Woolfe returned the envelope to Dr Colbert.

"How do you intend to spend Christmas Day?" Inspector Lee enquired.

"With my wife and children," Dr Colbert warmly replied. "Yourself?"

"I've been invited to dine with friends," Inspector Lee replied.

"I'm going to be out of London on another case," Inspector Woolfe stated.

"Not on the blessed day of Christmas, surely?" Dr Colbert enquired.

"It wouldn't come as a surprise to me if it was," Inspector Lee remarked in all seriousness.

Inspector Woolfe cast a black look at him. "Nah. I'll be back long before then." He shifted his gaze back to Dr Colbert. "If anything happens with the Society when I'm gone, let Inspector Lee know by coming here or sending a note."

"Very well." Dr Colbert picked up his bag and dropped the envelope into it as he stood, prompting Inspectors Lee and Woolfe to do the same. "Thank you, gentlemen." He shook their hands. "Goodbye, Inspector Lee."

As Inspector Woolfe led Dr Colbert out, Inspector Lee took the kettle from a pot-bellied stove in the corner and used its hot water to prepare some tea. A silver teapot with matching cream jug and sugar bowl stood upon a tray on an oak sideboard to the left of Inspector Lee's desk. The remaining pieces of furniture consisted of a washstand, complete with jug, bowl, and towels, to the right of the window, and a hat and umbrella stand to the left of the door. Although his sergeants would soon be adorning the station with the traditional wreaths of holly, laurel, and ivy, he preferred to keep his office decoration free. Glancing at the clock on the wall above the sideboard as it chimed six, Inspector Lee added cream and sugar to two cups of tea before taking them over to his desk. Placing one on either side, he sat as the door opened.

"Is it snowing?" Inspector Lee enquired with a smirk as Inspector Woolfe brushed the fresh snow from his coat and head. At Inspector Woolfe's glare, he indicated the other cup. "I made you some tea."

Inspector Woolfe halted. With a wrinkling of his brow and a setting of his jaw, he kept a rigid gaze upon Inspector Lee as he sat in Dr Colbert's seat. "What are you after, Gideon?"

"Nothing," Inspector Lee replied in an innocent tone.

Inspector Woolfe picked up the cup and, studying his face for any hint of deceit, sniffed the mahogany-coloured liquid. Taking a tentative sip, he settled back in the chair with a loud creak. At Inspector Lee's questioning look, he stated, "Just checking it's not poisoned."

Inspector Lee's gaze cooled as his lips formed a hard line. Glaring at him with angry indignation, he said, "If I was going to murder you, Caleb, I wouldn't do it in a police station." He set his cup and saucer down with a clatter of china before dabbing at his mouth with his handkerchief. Returning his gaze to Inspector Woolfe, he waited for him to take another sip of tea before adding, "Unlike John Conway who thinks it's appropriate to threaten a fellow officer in the inspectors' room at Scotland Yard."

As Inspector Lee had hoped, Inspector Woolfe inhaled sharply at the news. Breathing in some of his tea at the same time, he was immediately gripped by a violent coughing fit. Putting the cup down with a thud as the coughing continued, his face soon turned bright red from the strain. Globules of brown saliva also flew from his mouth in all directions, prompting Inspector Lee to shield his own with his handkerchief. "Take another sip, man."

Inspector Woolfe duly did so and, after taking a second, much larger mouthful, cleared his throat and gave a final cough. "*Jesus Christ.*" Bowing his head, he wiped his face with one hand and gripped the arm of his chair with the other.

"That was unpleasant," Inspector Lee remarked in disgust, flicking a brown globule from his sleeve.

Inspector Woolfe lifted his eyes to glare at Inspector Lee. "Conway doesn't threaten other coppers. You must've said something to provoke him."

"I did nothing of the kind," Inspector Lee replied with mock indignation.

Inspector Woolfe wiped his nose with his sleeve as he settled back in his chair. "I don't believe you."

"Believe whatever you wish. The truth of the matter is John Conway is a loose cannon and a traitor—"

Inspector Woolfe narrowed his eyes. "I told you—"

"Yes, you told me: he's not a traitor." Inspector Lee gave a dismissive wave of his hand. "But his confession to the discipline board proves otherwise."

Inspector Woolfe shoved his chair aside as he stood. Turning away from Inspector Lee, he walked toward the hat stand.

"A confession he willingly gave," Inspector Lee continued.

Inspector Woolfe paced in front of the desk.

"And a threat he openly made," Inspector Lee added, watching Inspector Woolfe as he slowed to glare at him. "Speak to Inspector Pilker. He'll tell you what happened."

Inspector Woolfe shook his head.

"Then speak to Chief Inspector Jones," Inspector Lee added.

Inspector Woolfe stopped dead in his tracks and stared at him. "What's Jones got to do with it?"

"He witnessed the threat."

Inspector Woolfe lowered his gaze to Inspector Lee's desk as his mind whirled.

"And ordered Conway into his office where he undoubtedly gave him a thorough dressing down," Inspector Lee said, taking great delight in Inspector Woolfe's confusion for all his expression remained emotionless. It was made all the sweeter for the fact Inspector Woolfe knew nothing of the search he'd made of Inspector Conway's desk whilst he was with Chief Inspector Jones. Granted it had yielded no evidence of Inspector Conway's involvement with the Society, but only *he* knew that. Furthermore, any thought he may have had about enlightening Inspector Woolfe had been immediately silenced by Inspector Woolfe's blatant loyalty to the uncouth policeman. With mock concern, he said, "It's time to accept the facts, Caleb. John Conway has turned his back on the Metropolitan Police—on *us*—and joined the enemy's ranks."

"I don't have to listen to this," Inspector Woolfe muttered, heading for the door.

"You should."

Inspector Woolfe stopped, his hand on the doorknob and his back to the room.

"He'll only drag you down with him," Inspector Lee warned.

Inspector Woolfe scowled and, driving the door into the wall as he threw it open, stormed out.

Inspector Lee smiled.

FOUR

The sunshine warmed Mr Maxwell's back as a gentle breeze caressed his face. Lush green fields lined with hedgerows stretched out as far as the eye could see. Sitting atop a hill, surrounded by a wild meadow, he could smell the calming scents of lavender, daisies, and dandelions, amongst others. A brilliant blue sky adorned with fluffy white clouds provided the perfect backdrop to a perfect day. Feeling a dainty hand rest upon his own, he turned his head to see Miss Dexter sitting beside him. The look of contentment upon her face echoed that in his heart. Taking her hand, he gently drew her near and placed a delicate kiss upon her tender lips.

A thud from the neighbouring bedroom woke him with a jolt. Hearing another after realising he wasn't asleep anymore, he sat up and listened. A third thud caused him to look to his fireplace. Whoever it was seemed to be loading the adjoining hearth with coal. Pulling back his blankets, he hesitated at the thought of speaking to someone. Yet, the sound of a fourth thud piqued his curiosity enough to override his anxiety. Getting out of bed, he put a dressing gown on over his nightshirt, slid his feet into some slippers, and wandered next door.

There he found Miss Trent putting the last of the coal into the hearth and lighting its kindling with a match. In the middle of the room was a large tin bath filled with steaming water. A folded towel had been placed on the chair to its left whilst a washstand with cut-throat razor, brush, soap, and comb stood to its right. Finally, a table and chair stood on the far side of the fire. Hearing movement from the doorway, Miss Trent looked across and straightened with a smile when she saw him.

"You're just in time," she said, wiping the coal dust from her hands upon her apron.

Mr Maxwell looked from her, to the bath, and back again. "All-all this is for me?"

"Yes, and, to a lesser extent, me." She dipped her fingers into the water to gauge its temperature before joining him at the door. Offering a small smile that failed to reach her concerned eyes, she said, "You've hardly left your room, Joseph, and…" She gave him a quick sniff before gently teasing, "I can smell you from across the landing."

Mr Maxwell's face flushed a bright red. "Oh… erm, s-sorry." He looked down as he shifted his weight from one foot to the other. "I-I… I've really seen little point in-in …" He frowned deeply. "Anything, really." Feeling Miss Trent's hand upon his arm, he looked up to see her frowning back at him with deeply concerned eyes.

"I know," she said softly. "But…" She pulled her hand away and, taking a deep breath, exhaled as she glanced back at the bath. "We need to make sure you're prepared for whatever might happen at Oliver's trial. I've prepared you a hot bath and, when you're done, I have some nourishing stew simmering on the stove."

Mr Maxwell parted his lips to decline.

"I'm not going to take no for an answer this time," Miss Trent warned.

Mr Maxwell closed his mouth and gave a weak smile.

"I'm sorry if it sounds like I'm ordering you around, but it's only because I care—because *we* care."

The Miss Dexter of his dream filled his mind's eye, causing his longing for her, and the grief over losing her, to make his heart swell. Feeling it intensify the more he thought of her, he felt his throat constrict and his eyes sting. Swallowing hard as it overwhelmed him, he turned away and covered his mouth with his hand. "S-sorry," he said, his voice breaking under the strain. Clenching his hand into a fist and pressing it against his mouth, he tried his utmost but couldn't prevent the sob from escaping his lips. Feeling the dampness of his tears immediately after, he bowed and shook his head as he moved further into the room. "F-Forgive m-me, Miss Trent."

Miss Trent followed him and, placing a gentle hand upon his back, peered up into his face. "There is *nothing* for you to be forgiven for, Joseph." She rubbed his back as he broke down, sobbing. Watching him with intense concern in both her eyes and face, she allowed him the time to pour out his grief and regret.

She gave him her handkerchief when he wiped his eyes on the lapels of his dressing gown. "What happened to your wife and mother *wasn't* your fault. There was nothing you could've done to prevent Oliver from doing what he did." She rubbed his back in a circular motion as he sniffed hard and released a shallow, shuddering breath. "There is something you can do now, though. You can find the strength to ensure he faces justice. Not just for your wife and mother but for *yourself*."

Mr Maxwell nodded and gave a hard swallow. "Y-yes, I-I know. I-I will."

"The Society is behind you every step of the way." Miss Trent offered a reassuring smile. "Mr Elliott will be here in the morning to talk you through what to expect when you give evidence at the trial. He and I will also be there on the day to give our support." She held his arm and looked him in the eyes. "You can do this. I know you can."

Mr Maxwell gave a half-hearted laugh. "I-I'm glad one of us does."

Miss Trent's smile faltered as her eyes filled with concern once more. "Enjoy your bath." Returning to the door, she looked back at him and added, "If you call down to me once you're finished, I'll bring up the stew and a pot of tea."

Mr Maxwell gave her an appreciative smile. "I will. Th-thank you, Miss Trent."

Miss Trent smiled sadly in return and, closing the door, bowed her head as she left.

* * *

Grander than the *Key & Lion* in both style and size, the *Nimble Crow* public house on Cricketfield Road, Lower Clapton was also surrounded by the more pleasant residences of the "fairly comfortable" according to Booth's poverty map. Therefore, instead of the debtors and recurrent residents of the workhouse from the "very poor" Nesbit Street, the Crow's clientele included money lenders, clerks, and solicitors. The staggering contrast between the establishments fascinated Mr Grosse, especially since Lower Clapton was Hackney's neighbour. He brushed the snow from his shoulders and set his hat down upon the bar. "Good evening, Mr Farley. A pint of your finest, please."

"Good evening, Mr Grosse," Mr Kenrick Farley greeted in a forced upper-class accent. Approximately five-feet-six-inches tall, he had blue eyes and black hair that matched his handlebar moustache. His neck and chest were also thick and wide respectively. The snug fit of his stunning white shirt accentuated his broad shoulders and huge biceps, whilst his dark-grey waistcoat with pale-blue pinstripe highlighted the contours of his slender waist. Though hidden by the bar, his wide thighs seemed to push against the material of his dark-grey trousers as he moved. His silver pocket watch chain and cufflinks also caught the light from the electrified chandeliers hanging above the bar. Overall, his peak physical condition and fine attire meant he looked a decade younger than his actual forty-five years. Retrieving a glass from the shelf above his head, he poured some ale from a barrel on the counter behind him.

The oval-shaped bar dominated the middle of the room as it stood perpendicular to the pub's main doors. The space between was filled with standing customers, whilst others sat around low tables in small areas on either side. Partially enclosed by waist-high wooden panelling, these areas had the dual benefits of lower ceilings and large fireplaces. Additional seating sat to the left and right of the bar, followed by an identical set of dark-oak stairs on both sides. These led to a ballasted first-floor balcony. Overlooking the bar, its large floorspace had only a handful of tables, whilst four solid oak doors lined its walls—two at the rear and one at either end. Throughout the pub, plain wooden panelling lined the walls' lower halves whilst dark-green paper with swirling light-green leaves lined their upper. Intricate depictions of vines, leaves, roses, and shamrocks had been carved by hand into the panels of the enclosed seating areas and the outside of the bar. The panels also had additional adornments of fresh holly and ivy to create some festive cheer. The plaster ceiling roses were equally detailed and impressive, whilst the scantily clad women carved into the fireplaces' stone surrounds were often the target of filthy remarks. This was no doubt since, aside from Mrs Farley, no women were permitted on the premises.

Watching Mr Farley through the haze of expensive pipe and cigarette smoke, Mr Grosse enquired, "Is it worth going upstairs tonight?"

Mr Farley set the glass down before him and, taking payment, put it into the till. "There are a few pairings which might catch your eye."

"Glad to hear it. The club needs new blood." Mr Grosse drank some ale. "Have you sparred with any of them?"

"A few." Mr Farley smiled. "You know me."

"Indeed, I do. Your mittens never come out unless you're certain of six rounds."

"Any less, and it's not a fair fight." Mr Farley's smile faded. "I'd thought to see you earlier, Mr Grosse. Something I've missed?"

"Not at all." Mr Grosse drank some more ale. "I've been researching one or two promising amateurs—and trying to find the last few boxers for my book, of course."

"Who's that?" Mr Farley took a second glass from the shelf.

"Deon Erskine for one. Samuel Snyder for another."

Mr Farley stilled with the glass held under the barrel's tap. Staring at it as he poured the ale, he stated, "Erskine went to America."

Mr Grosse looked to his own drink as he turned it upon the bar. "Yes, so I've been told."

Mr Farley kept his gaze upon his glass as he turned to face him. "He wasn't much of a boxer." Drinking some of his ale, he swallowed it hard and mumbled, "or worth wasting ink over." Taking another mouthful of ale, he set his glass down upon the bar and met Mr Grosse's gaze. With a lifting of his features, he suggested in a lighter tone, "'The Hammer' Noah O'Hannigan is who you should be talking to."

Mr Grosse gave a weak chuckle into his glass. "Very amusing."

The tension returned to Mr Farley's face and voice. "It wasn't meant to be."

Mr Grosse pulled his glass away from his lips and stared at him. "Are you being serious?"

"Am I smiling?" Mr Farley replied in a sharp tone. His neck, shoulders, and arms had also become rigid, mimicking his hard gaze.

Mr Grosse's head jerked back as, with parted lips, he stared at Mr Farley in disbelief. "My dear Mr Farley…" He gave a weak smile. "Noah O'Hannigan is a drunkard, and an unpredictable one at that."

Mr Farley shook his head. "I've not seen that from him."

Mr Grosse looked at him sharply as he set down his glass. "He's a club member?"

Mr Farley folded his arms and lifted his chin. "Just joined."

Mr Grosse's fingers retracted against the bar top, becoming claw-like as he said in a malevolent tone born from the depths of his throat, "Noah O'Hannigan cares for nothing and no one but Noah O'Hannigan. If you put him in the ring, both you and the *Lower Clapton Boxing Club* will lose the fraternity's respect." He snatched up his drink. "Mark my words." He drained his glass. "He'll ruin you." He put the glass down with a thud.

Mr Farley leaned upon the bar with both hands as he watched Mr Grosse closely. Intrigued, he remarked, "I don't think I've ever heard you talk like this before."

"Which is all the more reason to listen to me." Mr Grosse slid his glass to him. "Another, please."

Mr Farley considered a moment and nodded. "That's true."

Mr Grosse withdrew his hands from the bar and straightened as the tension eased in his face and shoulders.

Refilling Mr Grosse's glass from the barrel, Mr Farley set it before him. "Who do you recommend I put in his place?"

"Well…" Mr Grosse gave Mr Farley the necessary coin and watched him deposit it into the till. "Joe Rake is a promising young amateur."

Mr Farley pursed his lips and shook his head as he returned to Mr Grosse. "Never heard of him."

Mr Grosse smiled. "We must correct that." He took a sip of ale. "I'll introduce you tomorrow afternoon." His smile grew as he looked to the rear of the balcony. "You can give him a tour of the club's gymnasium."

* * *

Inspector Conway took shallow breaths using the upper half of his chest as his lower throbbed in pain. The temperature had dropped further since he'd left the house and, despite his short visit to his local pub, the cold had managed to seep into his bones. Consequently, he'd been obliged to call upon another of the coffee stalls along the way. Demand for both its wares and warmth had been high, causing the procurement of his drink to take longer than he'd intended. It was almost eight o'clock when he entered the inspectors' room at the Yard.

Unlike earlier, none of the other desks were occupied. He knew his fellow policemen would be either making enquiries, bribing informants with a pint or two, or sitting by their hearth with their loved ones. The first two were the likeliest in his experience. In fact, his plans for tonight were almost identical to the one previous, albeit with a different set of informants and undercover Mob Squad detectives. He also expected to be called upon to verify his sergeant's identity once he and the rest of the gang were arrested during their robbery of the shop. Recalling his sergeant's smiling face, he hoped the arrogance of youth didn't put him in the path of a club or gun.

Pushing these thoughts from his mind as he took off his trilby and tossed it onto his desk, he did a double take upon realising his desk was bare. He cast his mind back to earlier. Twelve hours had passed since then. During which he'd slept, washed, changed into a clean dark-blue suit and waistcoat, and eaten. The continued throbbing in his chest did little to clear the fog in his mind. Nevertheless, he was fairly certain he'd only locked his files and documents away. His pen and inkwell, railway times, pocket map of London, and other odds and ends should've still been there.

"Good evening, sir."

Inspector Conway looked over his shoulder. Seeing a fresh-faced, smiling man in his early twenties with short, dark-brown hair and wide, round brown eyes standing in the doorway, he turned to face him. Casting his gaze over the newcomer's cheaply made brown cotton suit and tie and cream shirt, he found neither a crease nor a speck of dust anywhere. The manner in which he stood, with his shoulders squared and his hands clasped behind his back, also hinted at his rank. "Constable Caulfield."

His smile grew. "Actually, it's Sergeant Caulfield now, sir."

Inspector Conway closed the distance and extended his hand. "Well done, lad."

Sergeant Caulfield eagerly took his hand and gave it a firm, enthusiastic shake. "Thank you, sir. Coming from you, that means a lot."

A fleeting smile passed across Inspector Conway's lips. "What you doin' 'ere, Sergeant?"

Sergeant Caulfield clasped his hands behind his back and proudly lifted his chin. "Waiting for you, sir."

"You what?"

"Chief Inspector Jones told me to wait for you."

Inspector Conway glanced over Sergeant Caulfield's shoulder but knew Chief Inspector Jones would've left hours ago. Aside from the Mob Squad's cases, there was only one investigation Inspector Conway was officially assigned to. He doubted Chief Inspector Jones wanted a fledgling copper getting involved with the Bow Street Society. Men like Sergeant Caulfield were keen to make their mark anywhere, but there was something about being assigned to A Division that made them more vulnerable to recklessness.

Inspector Conway returned to his bare desk and sat behind it. Inserting the key into its top drawer, he began, "You can go home now—" He cut himself short as the drawer opened. Pulling it out to find it was empty, he checked the second and third drawers down. They, too, had been cleared. Cursing Inspector Lee under his breath, he leaned forward to peer into the back of each drawer in turn.

"I done that, sir."

Inspector Conway glared up at him and growled, "You'd better have a bloody good reason."

"Chief Inspector Jones' orders." Sergeant Caulfield looked from Inspector Conway, to the desk, and back again. "I put it in your new desk exactly how you had it here."

Inspector Conway sat bolt upright. "What new desk?"

Sergeant Caulfield swallowed his nerves under Inspector Conway's hard gaze. "The one in your new office, sir." He glanced out the window. "It has a great view of the Thames."

Inspector Conway slammed the top drawer of his desk and stood. Muttering a curse under his breath as he resolved to speak to Chief Inspector Jones first thing in the morning, he strode from the room. "Whereabouts is it?"

Sergeant Caulfield hurried after him. "I'll show you, sir."

FIVE

Mr Joe Rake leaned over the bar and, looking at his reflection in its polished top, touched his bruised cheek and cut temple. Neither did his crooked features any favours, but he was thankful he'd not woken with a pain in his head that morning. His knuckles were bruised and swollen, still, but that was to be expected. Feeling a hand pulling on his arm, he stepped back with a glance to Mr Grosse before tugging on his worn brown jacket.

Mr Grosse looked over him with a mixture of regret and disappointment. Regret that he had to endure a poverty-stricken existence, and disappointment that it was born out in his appearance. With a subtle nod to his unkempt blond hair, he said, "Tidy yourself up, boy."

Mr Rake quickly smoothed down his dirty hair with dirtier hands.

Mr Grosse turned and, seeing Mr Farley descend the stairs, released a soft, dejected sigh. He murmured, "You'll have to do." As the landlord neared, they walked around the bar to meet him. "Good afternoon, Mr Farley. I hope this day finds you well?"

"Well enough." Mr Farley cast an appraising glance over Mr Rake. "Is this him?"

"It is." Mr Grosse placed his hand upon the small of Mr Rake's back and guided him forward. "This is Mr Kenrick Farley, Mr Rake. Proprietor of the *Nimble Crow* and the *Lower Clapton Boxing Club*."

Mr Rake extended his hand after wiping it on his jacket. "It's good to meet you, sir."

Mr Farley's gaze dropped to the hand. Noting the deformed fingers and swollen knuckles, his enthusiasm for the lad cooled. Nevertheless, he gave his hand a firm shake, dwarfing it with his own in the process.

Oblivious to the change in Mr Farley, Mr Rake visibly relaxed. "I can't wait to tell my old mum *I* shook hands with Long-Armed Farley."

Mr Farley stilled at the flattering mention of his professional moniker. As his surprise at the lad's admiration sank in, Mr Farley realised he'd been too hasty in passing judgement over him. Deciding to give him the benefit of the doubt, he puffed out his chest and lifted his chin as his cheeks became lightly tinged with pink. "Your mum sounds like a fine woman."

Mr Rake smiled warmly as, with a tilt of his head, he rubbed the back of his neck. "She is, sir. She's done a lot for me and my brothers since our dad died."

Mr Farley gave Mr Rake's shoulder a firm squeeze. "Then you must make her proud."

Mr Rake nodded profusely. "Yes, sir. I want to, sir. I-I mean, I *will*, sir."

Mr Farley slapped the back of his shoulder. "Good lad." He gestured to his bruised face. "Who won?"

"Me," Mr Rake replied, his head held high.

Mr Farley's smile vanished. "But it wasn't a gloved fight."

Mr Grosse attempted to stand between them. "Time is getting on—"

Mr Farley grabbed Mr Rake's wrist and held up his hand, thereby pushing Mr Grosse aside. "These are the knuckles of a prize fighter." He released his hand. "Where did you fight?"

"I really don't think that matters—" Mr Grosse began.

"The *Key & Lion*, sir," Mr Rake replied, causing Mr Grosse to roll his eyes.

Mr Farley's eyes darkened as his countenance tightened. "*That* sorry excuse for a public house?" He glared at Mr Grosse. "You're either very brave or very foolish to bring me a fighter from that *cesspit*."

Mr Grosse's features tightened. "I meant it when I said Mr Rake has promise."

"Boxers who refuse the glove are excluded from our membership," Mr Farley said as he turned and headed back toward the staircase. "You know that, Mr Grosse."

"I do, but Mr Rake doesn't refuse the glove, do you, boy?" Mr Grosse said, hurrying after Mr Farley with Mr Rake following closely. All three stopped at the question, and Mr Grosse and Mr Farley looked to Mr Rake with expectant eyes.

"*No*, sir," Mr Rake insisted.

"Why not take it up before?" Mr Farley demanded.

"I've not had the chance, truth be told," Mr Rake replied. "Please, Mr Farley, sir. I want to do good and make my old mum proud. You're one of the best. Don't send me away."

Mr Farley shifted his gaze to Mr Grosse who enquired, "We don't want to disappoint her, do we?"

Mr Farley studied Mr Rake intently. Giving a small nod when he saw no hint of deception or insincerity in him, he turned and continued up the stairs. "Eligibility for club membership is strict for good reason. We box under the Queensberry Rules here. Sparring is encouraged, and matches are permitted as long as they contribute to a member's training. Otherwise, members are forbidden from participating in prize fights unless they are fought as part of a competition." He faced Mr Grosse and Mr Rake at the stairs' summit, preventing them from going any further. "Do you understand and accept these terms, boy?"

Mr Rake looked to Mr Grosse.

"Will you do what he says?" Mr Grosse clarified.

"Yes." Mr Rake looked back to Mr Farley. "Yes, I will, sir."

Mr Farley looked to Mr Grosse who gave a small nod. Folding his arms, Mr Farley pushed out his chest and lifted his chin to appear as tall as possible to the young Mr Rake. "As you come recommended by Mr Grosse, I will give you *one* chance. If you give me *any* reason to regret that decision, you will be removed from this club."

Mr Rake swallowed hard. "Yes, sir."

"Good." Mr Farley crossed the balcony and opened the left-hand door at its rear to reveal an immense room beyond. In its centre was a professional twenty-four-foot boxing ring raised off the floor by a frame with sets of wooden steps at its front and back. Four electrified chandeliers were suspended in a diamond formation from the exposed rafters of the roof directly above the ring. These, along with the large windows on either side of the roof, bathed the ring in brilliant light. This in turn made the cream of the canvas appear to glow.

Mr Rake's jaw fell open as he stared wide eyed at the sight.

Having entered the room ahead of him, Mr Farley stood to the left of the door and watched Mr Rake's astonishment with great satisfaction. This moment was one of his favourite parts of being the club's proprietor. Allowing Mr Rake a few moments to regain his senses, he led him and Mr Grosse around the room.

Varnished floorboards creaked under foot as they walked. The walls were exposed bricks painted a brilliant white, and the four windows at the rear of the room overlooked the yard and service alleyway. Three more windows on the left and right-hand walls provided additional light, giving the room an even larger feel. A second door behind them also led onto the balcony and, leaning against the wall between both, were stacks of folded wooden chairs.

A narrow wooden bench stood on either side of the ring, thereby allowing trainers and other boxers to observe the fight from behind the ropes. Three wooden tables lined the left-hand wall of the room. On the first were pairs of clubs ranging in weight from two to seven pounds. On the second were knotted skipping ropes. On the third were pairs of dumbbells weighing a pound each. On the right-hand side of the room, suspended from the rafters by strong rope, was a line of three bags weighing from ten to twenty pounds. Each bag was made from chamois skin stuffed with horsehair. In each corner of the room, large pendant-shaped inflated rubber bags—or "Flying Bags"— were suspended from triangular frames between the two walls. Finally, at the rear of the room, was a line of six oval-shaped bags approximately four times larger than a rugby ball. Each bag was suspended from the rafter and tethered to a metal ring embedded in the floor by long rubber bands.

Having pointed out and explained each item of equipment and apparatus in turn, Mr Farley stood with them in front of the ring. "As I said before: if you follow the proper rules—in *and* out of the ring—your club membership is assured."

"What do you say to *that*, young Rake?" Mr Grosse enquired with a broad smile as he slapped him on the back. "The *Lower Clapton Boxing Club* is renowned amongst the Fancy, and Mr Farley here is one of the best trainers in London. A *damn* sight better than the *Key & Lion*, hmm?"

Mr Rake nodded as he continued to look around him in a daze. "It's a world away, Mr Grosse."

Mr Farley exchanged amused glances with Mr Grosse before tapping Mr Rake's arm to get his attention. "Let me see the standard of your stamina, agility, and general physical condition. If you go back onto the balcony, you'll see a door to your left. That's the changing room. In there, you'll find a locker with a fresh pair of silk drawers, shoes, and gloves. Put them on and come back here."

"Yes, sir." Mr Rake practically bounced from the room.

"The blind enthusiasm of youth," Mr Farley gently derided.

"He can see what an excellent opportunity this is for him and his family," Mr Grosse pointed out. "Aside from his 'blind enthusiasm,' what do you think of him so far?"

"He's raw but easily put right."

Mr Grosse hummed. "And a far better choice than Noah O'Hannigan."

"Mr Ian Jeffers is downstairs, dear," Mrs Farley called from the doorway, prompting both men to turn toward her. In her late thirties, Mrs Rosa Farley was approximately five feet six inches tall with naturally curly brunette hair, a heart-shaped face, and enticing hazel eyes. Attired in a high-necked plum-coloured bustle dress, her already slender waist was rendered unnaturally narrow by her corset. In Mr Grosse's opinion, she was truly a beauty to behold. Yet, woe-betide anyone who dared to tell her so, or even look at her with lusty eyes. Her husband's jealousy had sent many a man to the physician in the past.

"The fellow from *Sporting Life*?" Mr Grosse enquired from Mr Farley.

"Yes," Mr Farley replied, heading for the door. "I shan't be long."

"Not to worry," Mr Grosse called after him. "We'll wait."

* * *

The Bow Street Society's meeting room, with its high ceiling and long table, felt cavernous to Mr Maxwell after spending so many days in his bed chamber. It wasn't until he'd taken a seat on a chair by the fire that he realised the last time he'd been in there was during the investigation into his wife's murder. A wave of nausea had swept through him in an instant, followed by a tingling sensation that left him feeling lightheaded. Bringing a shaking hand to his forehead, he'd pictured the sanctuary of his bed chamber and resolved to flee to it, despite the fact Mr Elliott was due to arrive at any moment. Yet, when he'd put his hands upon the table and attempted to stand, his legs were so weak, and his head so dizzy, he'd been obliged to sit again or risk fainting. After dropping onto his chair with a loud sigh, he'd pushed it back and hid his face between his folded arms upon the table.

Shortly thereafter, he'd heard Miss Trent greeting Mr Elliott at the front door, followed by their footsteps' echo as they approached the meeting room. Only when he heard its door opening did he lift his head and sit up straight. Coming to an abrupt halt upon seeing his bright red face, Miss Trent enquired, "Are you feeling unwell?"

Mr Maxwell pulled his knees together and, holding his elbows against his sides, rubbed his hands in his lap as he looked warily about the room. "It-it's just I… I haven't b-been in here since…" He momentarily bowed his head before leaning forward and meekly enquiring, "M-May I have some sw-sweet tea, please, Miss Trent?"

"Of course." Miss Trent looked to Mr Elliott standing beside her.

"Black, no sugar, please," Mr Elliott said.

Miss Trent turned concerned eyes back to Mr Maxwell. "Would you like to sit in the parlour instead?"

"N-no. Th-thank you." Mr Maxwell gave a weak smile. "I have to brave this room s-some time, don't I?"

Miss Trent frowned but nonetheless left the room to prepare the tea whilst Mr Elliott placed his satchel upon the table and sat opposite Mr Maxwell.

The cold air had turned his cheeks pink, thereby injecting vitality into his otherwise pale complexion. The strands of his dark-brown, wavy hair had also been pushed out of place by his pill-box hat, obliging him to smooth them down with a slender hand as he sat. Accustomed to Mr Elliott's habit of wearing clothes with a blue palette, Mr Maxwell was struck by the sombre choice of dark-grey frockcoat, cream shirt, and black trousers, cravat, and waistcoat. He also darted his green-brown eyes from his satchel, to Mr Maxwell, and back again, as he retrieved his notebook, pencil, and a large blue book. Placing the items upon the table, he set his satchel on the chair beside him and rearranged the pile several times before finally settling on a satisfactory combination.

Miss Trent returned with their tea which she set down before them. Giving both a warm smile as she left, she was careful to close the door behind her. Once alone, Mr Maxwell drained half of his cup, thankful for the soothing effect of the sugar upon his nerves. Meanwhile, Mr Elliott's back and shoulders were rigid as he took a sip of tea, swallowed, and took a second. Looking to Mr Maxwell through the steam, he made his mind up about something as he simultaneously put his cup down and said, "I owe you an apology."

Mr Maxwell's gaze snapped to Mr Elliott's face. Holding his cup close to his lips, still, he stared at him in confusion before lowering it. "You, Mr Elliott?"

"Yes." Mr Elliott broke eye contact as he moved his pencil from one side of his notebook to the other. "It wouldn't be appropriate for me to speak on behalf of my fellow Society members but they, and me, failed you."

Mr Maxwell frowned. "But… how?" His frown deepened. "You all helped to expose Oliver." Even now, the word 'father' left a bitter aftertaste.

Mr Elliott's stoicism weakened as he focused upon his teacup. "We did." He shifted his gaze to Mr Maxwell's hands and, finally, his eyes. "But none of us realised he'd been violent to you. We should've suspected it the moment Mr Verity reported seeing you with a blackened eye."

Mr Maxwell put down his cup. "But why would you, though? You hadn't met my father at that time. None of you had."

Mr Elliott's stoicism slid back into place despite the tinge of regret in his voice. "I'm a lawyer. I've seen the results of beatings and abuse countless times in the court rooms and police cells. Whilst it's true the others had no cause to suspect your father had been violent toward you, my experience and skills of observation meant I had no such excuse. I failed to recognise the signs and, in doing so, lost the opportunity to intervene and, possibly, save the lives of your wife and mother."

Mr Maxwell bowed his head as the mere mention of them caused his heart to swell with grief.

"I know saying it will never bring them back, or truly make amends for what happened, but I think it's still important I say it: I'm sorry, Mr Maxwell, for all the ways I wronged you."

Mr Maxwell sniffed and swallowed hard to ease the constriction of his throat. Feeling his eyes sting at the same time, he kept them downcast as he said quietly, "If you are guilty, so am I." He lifted his head as tears slid down his cheeks. "I-I keep going over and over in m-my mind what I could've done d-differently to change things—to *save* them. I was—I *am*—terrified of Oliver. Nightmares of-of what he's d-done wake me up at night and-and stop me from living the l-life Mother wanted f-for me." He took out his handkerchief and wiped his eyes and nose.

Crumpling it up in his hand, he pulled on the corner that stuck out from his fist as he stared at it. "But the truth is… Oliver would've f-found a way to g-get what he wanted." He wiped his eyes again, this time with his hand. "I *despise* him, Mr Elliott." He lifted his head and, looking him squarely in the eyes, said with unbridled determination, "As much as the thought of standing in front of him in court terrifies me, the thought of him walking away from the hangman angers me more." He sniffed hard and wiped the last of his tears away. "You haven't failed me, Mr Elliott, because you're going to help me make sure Mother and Poppy get the justice they deserve."

"Very well." Mr Elliott's voice and gaze softened. "Let's begin."

SIX

Having taken the 12:08 p.m. train from London—the only one that day—Inspector Woolfe had arrived at Tonbridge Junction railway station over an hour later. Emerging onto Station Approach, he was struck by how crowded the thoroughfare was. Noticing the curious looks of passers-by as they caught sight of his unusual height and appearance, he recalled the small group of children who had pestered him during his last visit. Glancing around, he was relieved to see no sign of the "little angels" anywhere. At the same time, he noticed the telegraph office on the opposite side of the road.

Prior to leaving London, he'd sent a telegram to the Rose and Crown hotel on the High Street at Tonbridge, notifying them he intended to rent a room for several days. Following his dire experience sleeping on an incredibly short bed at the pub during his last stay, Inspector Woolfe had purchased *Tonbridge for the Resident, the Holiday Maker and the Angler* by W. Stanley Martin and B. Prescott Row. In it, the Rose and Crown was recommended as "a fine specimen of a high-class family hotel" that had been "honoured by the attention of our Gracious Majesty herself." Although more expensive, he felt he'd be more likely to find a bed suitable for his height at the hotel than an inn. With such a good reputation, Inspector Woolfe was also adamant drink-fuelled disruptions of the peace were rare at the Rose and Crown. As a result, he would avoid the politically sensitive situation of intervening when he had no official jurisdiction to do so. Fortunately, his superintendent's great dislike for the Bow Street Society had made him agree to reimburse all expenses Inspector Woolfe expected to incur during his visit.

In addition to arranging his accommodation, he'd also confirmed with the London telegraph office that they had another in Tonbridge. He'd then sent a telegram to

Inspector Lee instructing him to send one there should anything significant happen with Dr Colbert and the Bow Street Society whilst he was away. He crossed the road and, calling into the telegraph office, gave instructions for his telegrams to be redirected to the hotel as soon as they arrived.

Afterward, he made the short walk to Pembury Road and the police station of Kent County Constabulary's Tonbridge Division. Standing at the bottom of the road, on the corner opposite St. Stephen's Church, the red-brick structure reminded Inspector Woolfe of a doll's house compared to the law courts and police station of Bow Street. Comprising of two two-storey houses linked by another two-storey building, it also had tiled roofs and sandstone cornices, quoins, ledges, and arches. Tall, narrow brick chimneys rose from the middle of the houses, whilst the central structure had a decorative, domed turret of white wood.

The ground's perimeter was lined by a low wall with brick pillars at regular intervals and iron railings between. A wide gateway on the far left led to a road that snaked around the building to, he presumed, a yard at the rear. A second narrower gateway at the front of the building led to a path that forked to the left and right. Three narrow windows overlooked the space between with wide, open shelters on either side. Finally, a narrow, wooden door stood on the far left and right, whilst large windows on the three buildings' ground and first floors overlooked the railings.

Passing through the gate, he walked down the path and went into the shelter on the right. Entering the building through a door on its left-hand side, he found himself in a lobby. Seeing another door in its far-left corner, he went through it into a large, high-ceilinged room with a balcony overlooking it on all sides. Recognising it as a magistrates' court—albeit not as impressive as the one at Bow Street— he saw two men standing in its centre.

The first was in his early forties with dark-brown hair, whiskers, and moustache. He was attired in a dark-blue tunic with matching trousers and black leather boots. The single line of silver buttons down the tunic's centre matched the buckle of his belt and crest on the coxcomb helmet tucked under his arm. The crest had the horse rampant of the Kent County Constabulary as its main feature, whilst the chevrons on his sleeves denoted him as a sergeant.

The second man was in his mid-thirties with dark-blond hair, short sideburns, and a small moustache. His pointed chin, defined cheekbones, and alert brown eyes gave him an authoritative air. Unlike his companion, he was attired in a dark-brown suit with matching waistcoat and tie with a starched Eaton collar, off-white shirt, and polished dark-brown leather shoes. Tucked under his arm was a brown bowler. Both men were approximately five feet seven inches tall with a broad build. As Inspector Woolfe walked toward them, the sound of his footsteps upon the hard floor alerted them to his presence.

"Good morning, sir," the sergeant greeted in a formal tone. "Detective Inspector Caleb Woolfe from the Metropolitan Police's E Division, I presume?"

"That's right," Inspector Woolfe replied.

"I'm Sergeant George Hunnicutt of the Kent County Constabulary's Tonbridge Division." He indicated the other man. "This is Detective Constable Thomas Begg from our newly formed detective branch over at Wrens Cross in Maidstone."

"It's good to meet you, both," Inspector Woolfe said, giving their hands a firm squeeze.

"And you, Inspector," Constable Begg said, his hand shooting out to take Inspector Woolfe's the moment it had released Sergeant Hunnicutt's. His eyes were also glossy and bright as they met Inspector Woolfe's emotionless gaze. "An absolute pleasure, in fact."

Inspector Woolfe had found the arranging of this visit less straightforward than his first. Back then, he was in

Tonbridge on an unofficial basis since he'd been forbidden from investigating the Bow Street Society by Chief Inspector Jones. Having had the conversation with Chief Inspector Jones several days ago, though, he now felt able to make this second visit official. He'd explained his intentions to his superintendent at Bow Street who'd contacted his counterpart at Wrens Cross to request the assistance of a detective officer for the duration of Inspector Woolfe's stay. Though certain the Tonbridge Division would be informed of Inspector Woolfe's imminent arrival by their senior officer, the superintendent at Bow Street had nonetheless sent a letter to that effect out of professional courtesy. It had come as no surprise to either Inspector Woolfe or his superintendent to discover the Bow Street Society's notoriety had already reached the ears of their Kent colleagues.

"We understand you're making enquiries into the background of Miss Rebecca Trent," Sergeant Hunnicutt began. "Is it in connection with her work as the clerk of the Bow Street Society?"

"Partly," Inspector Woolfe sneered with a hard, distinctive jaw line. "She's putting the lives of innocent people in danger, and I want to know why."

"Isn't the Bow Street Society some sort of private enquiry agency?" Constable Begg enquired with a furrowed brow.

Inspector Woolfe's eyes narrowed. "It is, but I want to know why *she* got involved with it in the first place. If it's because of criminal or amoral reasons, I want to put a stop to *it* and *her* before someone's killed."

"In that case, you have my wholehearted support," Constable Begg said with a firm nod.

"And ours," Sergeant Hunnicutt added.

"Thanks," Inspector Woolfe replied with genuine appreciation.

"Where would you like to begin, inspector?" Constable Begg enquired.

"Her baptism in the parish records," Inspector Woolfe replied. "Also, a visit to her aunt. Mrs Dorothea Trent." Recalling how his last attempt to speak to the woman had gone, he added, "You'd better come with us for that, sergeant."

"Very well," Sergeant Hunnicutt agreed.

* * *

It was late afternoon when Mr Baldwin entered Homerton High Street in Hackney. Since noon, rain had fallen in place of snow, turning the remnants of the latter into sludge. Contaminated further by manure and coal dust in the air, it wasn't a pleasant thing to get on one's shoes. Unfortunately, it was so widespread, there was little Mr Baldwin could do to avoid it. Shaking it loose from his feet, he muttered a curse at the potential expense of some new shoes. It was a bad end to a bad journey.

One of the poorer Hackney residents of College Street, Mr Baldwin's route to the *Gaslight Gazette*'s Fleet Street office began with a walk to Victoria Park Station on Riseholme Street. From there, he rode the North London Railway to Broad Street Station in the City of London. The last part of his journey depended on the coins in his pocket and the punctuality of the train. If he were late to Broad Street but had monies to spare, he'd hire a hansom cab. If he were on time to Broad Street but was as poor as a church mouse, he'd walk. The latter was more often the case, and today had been no exception. The return journey hadn't been much better, either.

Chilled to the bone as well as poor, Mr Baldwin had decided to beg a cup of tea from Mr Grosse whose business was conducted from an office above *Linton's Tobacconists.* Located on the corner of Homerton High Street and Church Road, opposite St. Barnabas' Church, *Linton's* was also where Mr Grosse bought his cigarettes. Hence, when Mr Baldwin approached, he first peered through its large plate-glass window to see if his friend was doing just that. Meeting the gaze of the proprietor's daughter as she stood behind the counter, Mr Baldwin flashed her a smile and tipped his hat. She smiled in return and lifted her hand in a discreet wave since her father was close by, speaking to a customer. Recognising them as a regular, but not his friend, Mr Baldwin walked a little further and entered the covered stone stairwell adjacent to the premises.

The moment he did so, he collided with a man emerging from it. The force of the impact was enough to send him into a backward stumble that almost drove him off his feet. Regaining his balance with flailing arms, he looked up in time to see a six-foot-tall man in his late forties walk past. Shocked, angered, and humiliated by the encounter in equal measure, Mr Baldwin immediately went after him. "*Oi!*"

His attacker stopped dead in his tracks, prompting Mr Baldwin to do the same.

"You almost had me clean off my feet!" Mr Baldwin shouted.

His attacker turned his head to reveal a fierce scowl and piercing green eyes glaring out from beneath the broad brim of a dark-brown Panama hat. His thick, dark-grey beard and moustache appeared almost blue in the fading daylight, reminding Mr Baldwin of a pirate he'd once heard about. The man's form was largely hidden by a knee-length, dark-brown coat, the only features visible being his narrow shoulders and clenched fists. In a broad New York City accent, he growled, "I'd shut my mouth, boy, before it was shut for me."

Mr Baldwin retreated at the threat and terrifying visage.

The man's lips formed a hard line as he turned his head and walked away.

"You just *had* to open your bloody mouth," Mr Baldwin muttered as he hurried back to *Linton's* with his heart pounding in his ears. Climbing the stairwell two steps at a time, he knocked once on the door at its summit and went inside.

* * *

Mrs Dorothea Trent pulled her grey woollen shawl tighter about herself as her pale blue eyes stared at Inspector Woolfe with a mixture of distrust and irritation. Sixty years old and approximately five feet four inches tall, she had blond hair so pale it appeared white. Dense wrinkles marred the corners of her eyes and mouth as her skin sagged from her cheekbones and chin. The tight bun atop her crown was in stark contrast to the loose fit of her high-necked, long-sleeved, dark-blue dress trimmed with cream lace at the cuffs and collar. Sitting by the open hearth in the kitchen of her cottage, its heat tinged her cheeks pink, whilst its dancing flames made the brass of her round spectacles sparkle.

"I told Rebecca of your visit," Mrs Trent informed him. "She was the one who said I ought to speak with you. I would've sent you back up that lane myself." She glanced at Sergeant Hunnicutt and Constable Begg. "All of you." Her gaze slid back to Inspector Woolfe. "Persecution. That's what this is. Just because she's a woman."

"I—" Inspector Woolfe began.

"*But* I said I'd speak to you," Mrs Trent interrupted, looking between them all. "So, what do you want to know?"

Inspector Woolfe glared at her.

Like before, she'd initially spoken to him from the upstairs window of her cottage—*without* a loaded revolver this time. Her response to his own introduction had been frosty but lacked the violent disbelief he'd encountered previously. The presence of the uniformed Sergeant Hunnicutt had also helped earn the old woman's trust, as Inspector Woolfe had hoped it would. The final introduction of Constable Begg had seemed to convince

Mrs Trent of their honesty since she'd invited them inside moments later. Now, the three sat shoulder to shoulder on an odd assortment of furniture opposite her: Sergeant Hunnicutt on a milking stool, Constable Begg on a kitchen chair, and Inspector Woolfe on a foot stool.

Drawing his knees together, Inspector Woolfe gripped the sides of the foot stool and tried in vain to get comfortable. Since she'd decided on who sat where, he was convinced she'd given him the shortest on purpose. Looking up at her, he fought to keep the anger from his voice as he said, "We couldn't find your niece's baptism in the parish records this morning. Was she born in Tonbridge?"

"Yes," Mrs Trent replied.

"When?" Inspector Woolfe enquired.

"The thirty-first of August, 1868," Mrs Trent replied.

Constable Begg recorded the date in his notebook.

"Who were her parents?" Inspector Woolfe enquired.

Mrs Trent released a deep sigh. "Hannah and Bennett Pottinger." She watched as Constable Begg recorded the information in his notebook. "May I ask the *relevance* of all this?"

"It's just routine," Sergeant Hunnicutt replied with a reassuring smile.

"I'm sure it is, but *why* are you asking it?" Mrs Trent glared at Inspector Woolfe. "It has no bearing on her work with the Bow Street Society. After all, that *is* the real reason for your visit, isn't it?"

Inspector Woolfe's eyes cooled, and his jaw tensed.

Mrs Trent, seeing she'd struck a nerve, smiled. "She and her friends' success have humiliated Scotland Yard. So, you are seeking a way to sully her good name."

Inspector Woolfe leaned forward to point at her.

Yet, the sudden movement of the immense man caused Mrs Trent to shrink back in her chair. "Get away from me, you *beast*!"

Sergeant Hunnicutt tried to pull Inspector Woolfe back, but the latter yanked his arm free and stood. Unable to reach his full height due to the low ceiling, Inspector Woolfe had to bend forward as he pointed at Mrs Trent once more. "Listen, you stupid old woman. Your niece is putting good people in danger, and I want to know *why*."

"I'll tell you why, you *brute*!" Mrs Trent cried, springing to her feet.

Taken aback by the elderly woman's agility, Inspector Woolfe straightened and grunted as he struck his head on a rafter. Bending down low again and holding his aching head, he glared at her. "I've a good mind to arrest you."

"*That* is why she does what she does," Mrs Trent said. "To protect good people from violent rogues like *you*."

"Let's all calm down," Sergeant Hunnicutt said, getting to his feet and standing between them. "Mrs Trent, please, sit down. Inspector Woolfe, may I ask you to do the same?"

Mrs Trent and Inspector Woolfe exchanged angry glances but returned to their respective seats. Giving a weak smile, Sergeant Hunnicutt thanked them and, sitting down, went on, "Mrs Trent, we're certain your niece's heart is in the right place. Sometimes, though, even the best of us can find ourselves mixed up in something greater than ourselves. We just want to make sure she isn't in any trouble. If she is, we only want to help her. Don't we, inspector?"

Mrs Trent turned expectant eyes to Inspector Woolfe.

"Yeah," Inspector Woolfe muttered, rubbing the bump that was already forming on his crown.

"Will you also help us?" Sergeant Hunnicutt enquired.

Mrs Trent straightened and, pulling the shawl tightly about herself, replied, "I'll do what I can."

"That's all we ask," Sergeant Hunnicutt said with a smile. "Inspector, was there anything else you wished to ask?"

Inspector Woolfe lowered his hand. "Why does your niece have your surname and not her parents'?"

In a subdued tone, Mrs Trent replied, "It was thought to be for the best."

Inspector Woolfe's voice softened with a hint of wonder. "You raised her?"

Mrs Trent's features turned downward as a deep sadness entered her eyes. "Yes. Hannah Pottinger was my late husband's sister. When she and Bennett died, Albert and I took little Rebecca in and looked after her the best we could."

The tension disappeared from Inspector Woolfe's face and shoulders as he imagined Miss Trent as a young child crying by her parents' graves. An ache formed in his breast as it brought back memories of his own parents' funerals. Pushing the painful recollections aside, he lowered his gaze as he enquired softly, "How old was your niece when they died?"

"Five," Mrs Trent replied. "I don't think she remembers anything of her father, and only a little of her mother." Mrs Trent took a handkerchief from her sleeve and held it in her lap. "Rebecca's love for the stage came from me, you know. I was an actress for a short time before I met and married my Albert."

Inspector Woolfe, suspecting Mrs Trent had changed the subject to divert attention away from the Pottinger's' deaths, parted his lips to enquire about them further when Constable Begg spoke first.

"Did Miss Rebecca have any suitors?" Constable Begg enquired.

"Only the one," Mrs Trent replied. "But she ended the engagement when she decided to pursue a life treading the boards in London." Mrs Trent turned her head away and placed her hand upon her cheek. "Now, *what* was his name…?" She frowned as she searched her memory. Lifting her hand, she turned her head back around to face them. "Graeme Winslow." She clutched the handkerchief in her lap. "He's since married another, of course."

Inspector Woolfe opened his mouth only to be prevented from speaking a second time.

"Has she told you of anyone in London?" Constable Begg enquired.

"No, and it's not my place to pry, either," Mrs Trent replied.

"Hasn't—" Constable Begg began.

"How did her parents die?" Inspector Woolfe interrupted, casting a warning look at the over-enthusiastic detective.

The colour drained from Mrs Trent's face. In a quiet voice, she said, "It was a tragedy. The rest is best left unsaid."

Inspector Woolfe tilted his head and leaned forward slowly. "Should I ask her?"

"No!" Mrs Trent cried, leaning forward sharply with wide eyes.

"Why not?" Inspector Woolfe enquired, keeping his voice calm.

Mrs Trent's features crumpled as she tightened her grip upon her handkerchief. "She doesn't know. We never told her." She gripped his arm. "She must *never* know. It would *destroy* her if she did."

Inspector Woolfe kept his eyes on hers. "Tell us what happened."

Mrs Trent furiously shook her head and, releasing his arm, stood. "No. No, I can't. I'm sorry, gentlemen. You're going to have to leave now." She shuffled swiftly across the floor and up the stairs, her handkerchief clutched tightly to her face.

SEVEN

Standing in the doorway of a shuttered shop, looking at a wall of torrential rain, Sergeant Ethan Gutman reconsidered his choice of employment for the umpteenth time that day. Bouncing his weight from one foot to the other, he blew into his clasped hands and rubbed them together. The memory of drinking tea behind the front desk of Chiswick police station taunted him as a harsh shiver exploded from his core. The cold then regained its grip upon his body, causing his muscles to ache from the tension.

In his late twenties, he was more accustomed to paperwork than legwork these days. Yet, when Inspector Lee had confided he couldn't trust anyone else to do this assignment, Sergeant Gutman had accepted it in a heartbeat. Hence why he'd been watching the comings and goings of the Bow Street Society's house for the past eight hours. *"Don't speak to anyone or allow them to see you,"* the inspector's voice echoed in his mind. *"Just note who visits and leaves."*

He'd encountered a handful of Society members a couple months' prior, at the conclusion of the Cosgrove case when he'd worn a robe and banged on the outside of a window. The ruse had proven effective in convincing the murderer to confess. The rain he'd been obliged to stand in had also proven effective in giving him a cold. There was also the time Miss Trent made an impromptu visit to Chiswick police station. It had led to an equally impromptu surveillance exercise in which he'd followed her back to Bow Street and watched the house for the remainder of the day. Unfortunately, there wasn't anything noteworthy to report.

"But what if someone recognises me, sir?" he'd enquired from the inspector that morning.

To which he'd rightfully responded, "If you're inconspicuous, you'll go unnoticed." He'd learnt from his last experience that standing in the same spot for hours at a time wasn't being inconspicuous. According to the inspector in their conversation afterward, at least. So, on this occasion, he'd alternated between the street, various shops, and the Royal Opera House's foyer throughout the day.

He'd also forgone his tunic and helmet in favour of a cheaply made dark-blue, knee-length overcoat and dark-brown bowler hat. The rest of his attire consisted of an off-white shirt, dark-grey waistcoat, pea soup-green tie, and black trousers. A dark-green woollen scarf and fingerless gloves—last year's Christmas presents from his mother—did little to keep out the cold, however. Finally, thin stubble covered his face and chin, whilst his sideburns and caterpillar-like eyebrows matched the dark brown of his short hair.

Careful to keep his head dry, he peered along Bow Street. The flames of the gas streetlamps were sent dancing by the wind blowing through their glass casings. The police station was as lively as ever, whilst carriages and hansom cabs regularly pulled up to the Royal Opera House. Glancing at the cobbled road, he saw the snow had been washed away by ever-expanding puddles and fast-flowing rivers in the gutters.

Hearing the approach of yet another vehicle, he looked up the street and saw a hansom cab passing the police station. Two large plate-glass windows, protected by wooden shutters, slanted inward toward the shop door behind him. He stood with his back against the one on the right to further conceal himself within the shadows. Watching as the cab slowed to a stop outside the Society's house, he failed to recognise the driver's face. Aside from their hands, the passenger was also completely hidden inside the cab's dark interior.

Sergeant Gutman checked his pocket watch and wrote down the time in his notebook: seven o'clock. Slipping the pencil behind his ear, he clutched his notebook to his chest as he watched the silhouetted passenger alight and disappear behind the cab to pay their fare. When the cab pulled away a few moments later to reveal the passenger standing beneath the streetlamp, Sergeant Gutman recognised them at once. Quickly retrieving his pencil, he wrote down Inspector John Conway's name against the time in his notebook.

Casting his gaze across Bow Street, Inspector Conway saw only darkened shops and passing cabs. The rain poured from the brim of his trilby hat and bounced off the pavement around him. Hearing only the clip-clopping of horses' hooves against the cobblestones beyond this, he satisfied himself that the thoroughfare was sufficiently deserted. Getting soaked by the freezing rain besides, he climbed the steps and knocked on the Society's door.

Aware of Inspector Conway's orders to maintain a close watch over the Bow Street Society, Sergeant Gutman was initially uninterested in his presence. Yet, a partial recollection of a conversation he'd had with Sergeant Miller caused him to rethink this. "He confessed to giving them evidence," Miller had said. *Was that about Conway, though?* Sergeant Gutman wondered. Lowering his head as he searched his memory, he remembered the excitable tone of Miller's face as he'd declared the verdict of Inspector Conway's recent discipline hearing. Returning his gaze to the Society's house, he saw Inspector Conway being let in by Miss Trent.

Once inside, Inspector Conway removed his hat as he glanced around and up the stairs.

"Mr Maxwell is dining with his brother tonight."

Inspector Conway's shoulders visibly relaxed. Taking off his coat, he hung it and his hat upon the stand in the corner. Fortunately, only the cuffs of his trousers were damp. Attempting to dry his face with an old handkerchief, he had a sombre edge to his voice as he enquired, "How is 'e?"

A pained look entered Miss Trent's eyes. Bowing her head, she wrapped her arms about herself and stared at his feet as she replied in a quiet voice, "Inconsolable." The memory of him sobbing played in her mind, causing a tremendous sadness to descend upon her. Feeling a heaviness in her chest and a tightening of her throat as a result, she forced the image from her mind. Clearing her throat as well, she lifted her head to reveal eyes glistening with unshed tears. "And…" She looked up and blinked several times. "Erm." She turned her head away as she held her folded arms and elbows tight against her body. "Guilty."

She turned her head back to him but immediately lowered it as she downcast her eyes. "He feels very guilty. And I…" She held the underside of her fingers against the tip of her nose and, in a voice strained with emotion, added, "I don't know how to make him feel better." Her fingers curled into a ball against her nose as she rested her elbow upon her arm. Staring at his feet for several moments, she took in a deep shuddering breath and, lifting her head to look heavenward, released it through puckered lips. "Forgive me, John." She dabbed at the corners of her eyes with her handkerchief. "It's just been very hard to see him like this, especially after everything that's happened."

Inspector Conway placed a hand upon her shoulder. In a gentle voice, he said, "You've got nowt to be sorry for."

"Don't I?" She snapped. "I should've questioned him further about his blackened eye as soon as Mr Verity drew my attention to it. Instead, I took it for granted that Mr Maxwell had simply been his usual clumsy self." She put her handkerchief away. "It was all happening under our noses, John, and *none* of us realised it—*I* didn't realise it."

Inspector Conway frowned deeply as he was reminded of the early morning conversation he'd had with his sergeant. "You can't be with 'em all the time."

Miss Trent momentarily looked back down at his feet as she sniffed hard. "I know." She swallowed. "You're right." She lifted her head to meet his gaze. "It can't be helped now." She looked away as she took in another shuddering breath and, slowly releasing it, felt the intense sadness ease a little. Pushing the remainder of it deep down inside, she adopted a formal tone as she continued, "He's due to give evidence at Oliver's trial tomorrow. Mr Elliott has prepared him the best he can, but it will all come down to how well Mr Maxwell can cope in open court."

Inspector Conway watched her with concern. "Are you gonna go with 'im?"

"Yes." Another pained look entered her eyes. "It's the least I can do."

Meanwhile, Sergeant Gutman was pondering whether he ought to get closer. The inspector's orders had been clear enough, but he hadn't mentioned Conway. Images of him giving Miss Trent Scotland Yard's open case files filled his mind's eye. If that was happening, he had a duty to gather as much evidence of it as possible. He fantasied about the inspector shaking his hand in front of his fellow officers and rewarding him with a promotion. *Then I could order Sergeant Miller to stand in the rain for hours on end*, he thought with a smile. Convinced of the potential merits afforded by his decision, he left the doorway and crossed the road further down the street. Hurrying along the pavement, he bent down low, crept up the steps, and crouched beneath the window to the right of the door. Peering over its ledge, he saw Inspector Conway and Miss Trent standing opposite one another at the foot of the stairs.

The former reached into his jacket and took something out. When he passed it to the latter, Sergeant Gutman saw it was an envelope. Rather than check its contents, though, Miss Trent carried it across the hallway with Inspector Conway at her side. Creeping across to the other window, Sergeant Gutman saw her disappear through the second door on the left. Inspector Conway stood in its doorway and reached inside a moment later. When his hand emerged, it was holding another envelope. It was a lighter brown compared to the first, however. Opening it, Inspector Conway leafed through its contents.

"Please, tell Richard that the Mrs Gove case is the only one we're currently investigating," Miss Trent said as she emerged from her office. "Hence why it's the only progress report I've given to you."

Inspector Conway nodded, slipping the envelope into his jacket.

"And thank him for his generosity." Miss Trent gestured to her desk where she'd locked away the other envelope. "The extra monies will help to keep coal on the fire come January." She gave a sad smile. "I don't have to tell you what that's like."

"It's the same for most people," Inspector Conway remarked.

Drawing her eyebrows together, she regarded him with concerned eyes. "It's been a few days since you went back to the Yard, hasn't it?"

"Yeah," Inspector Conway replied softly.

"How are things there now?"

Inspector Conway recalled the conversation he'd had with Chief Inspector Jones that morning about being moved to an office upstairs. His friend's explanation of wanting to shield him from the disparaging remarks and aggressive behaviour of his colleagues had made sense. Chief Inspector Jones' concern and willingness to act in his best interests were also appreciated. Nevertheless, it had felt like he was being exiled from the citadel. Disinclined to even consider telling Miss Trent about the complex political situation between him, Chief Inspector Jones and, to a lesser extent, Inspector Lee, though, he replied, "Fine."

Detecting the slight delay in his response, Miss Trent searched his face for any hints of the reason. When none were forthcoming, she shifted to the direct approach. "Really? It's just that, when we last spoke about it, you said—"

"Things change," Inspector Conway interrupted with a hard tone and even harder gaze.

Taken aback, Miss Trent parted her lips to respond, closed them again when she thought better of it, and instead enquired, "And Dr Weeks?"

"What about 'im?"

"Has anything been said about him walking out of your hearing?"

Inspector Conway suddenly headed back to the hat stand.

Stunned, Miss Trent stared a moment before hurrying after him. "What's going on, John? What's happened?"

"Nowt." Inspector Conway took his coat from the stand.

Miss Trent snatched it from his grasp and held it out of reach. "If it affects the Society or its members in any way, I have a right to know."

Inspector Conway glared at her but, upon seeing the look of determination on her face, knew she'd find out the truth one way or another. His glare shifted into a grave expression as his voice turned low. "Weeks has lost his commission to the Yard."

Miss Trent's face blanched, and she slowly lowered his coat. "What?" she enquired softly. "*When*?"

"This mornin'. I found a memo on my desk from Jones. It ordered all senior officers not to send for Dr Weeks for owt."

Miss Trent's eyes widened. "*Richard* ordered—?"

"'E said the order wasn't 'is but Assistant Commissioner Terrell's," Inspector Conway corrected in a strong voice.

Miss Trent pursed her lips together and furrowed her brow in concern.

"Because Weeks walked out of my hearin'," Inspector Conway softly added, averting his gaze to his coat. After a long pause, he said, "Jones doesn't think the order will be obeyed, though."

"He doesn't?" Miss Trent enquired with a sharp backward jerk of her head.

Inspector Conway shook his head.

"Not that I'm not relieved, but why?"

"Weeks is the best in London. Any policeman worth 'is salt's not gonna give up a chance to solve 'is case just because the surgeon's not favoured by the brass."

Miss Trent considered the point and slowly nodded. "That makes sense."

Sergeant Gutman strained to hear their voices over the din of the rain but, alas, his efforts were in vain. Seeing Miss Trent hand Inspector Conway his coat, Sergeant Gutman crept away from the window and back down the steps. Hearing the door open behind him a moment later, he ran across the road as fast as he could and ducked back into the doorway.

Having neither seen nor heard his retreat, Miss Trent gave Inspector Conway a warm smile as she bid him goodnight. In contrast, Inspector Conway had caught sight of Sergeant Gutman the moment he'd emerged from the house. Rather than draw the sergeant's attention to the fact, though, he calmly walked away.

Lee's goin' to get a shock come mornin', Inspector Conway thought with a smile.

* * *

"The standard of opponent is getting worse," Mr Grosse lamented as he and Mr Baldwin emerged from the *Key & Lion's* basement. Part of a much smaller crowd than before, it didn't take them long to reach the bar.

Mr Sparrow had already resumed his position behind it and, upon hearing the remark, said with a shake of his head, "It would of been a better set-to with the Raven."

"Yeah, I was expectin' to see him in the ring," Mr Baldwin said, leaning upon the bar with folded arms. "Where is he?"

Mr Sparrow gave a single-sided shoulder shrug. "The lad didn't come back."

Mr Grosse gave a weak smile. "Two pints of your finest."

"Cheers, mate," Mr Baldwin said, slapping him on the back.

Mr Sparrow poured their drinks and, placing them in front of them, took the necessary coin from Mr Grosse. "If things don't pick up soon—" He cut himself short as he saw Mr Farley enter the pub. Standing straight and squaring his shoulders, he glared at the newcomer. "Get out."

The din of conversation swiftly died away as Mr Farley approached the bar.

"Them mittens must've clogged up your ears," Mr Sparrow growled. "I said get out."

"I've a message from Joe Rake," Mr Farley announced.

Mr Sparrow darted his gaze to Mr Grosse and back again.

"He's decided to join a proper boxing club," Mr Farley said with a self-satisfied grin.

Mr Sparrow's arm shot out toward him, his fingers catching only air as Mr Farley deftly swivelled his waist and arched his back to avoid the attack. Taking several steps back to remove himself from arm's reach, he sneered, "You always did favour brute force over style, Duncan."

Mr Sparrow slammed both fists upon the bar and pointed at him, his face twisted in an ugly scowl. "Come 'ere, and I'll show you how 'brutal' I can be, Ken."

The corner of Mr Farley's mouth twitched. Looking Mr Sparrow fully in the eyes, he removed his coat and tie and tossed them onto a nearby table. With his back straight and his chin slightly lifted, he positioned his left foot in front and his right behind with an approximate distance between of fourteen inches. Forming loose fists with his hands, he bent and raised his right arm so his elbow was against his side, and his fist was in level with his left pectoral muscle. Next, he bent and lifted his left arm so that his elbow and fist were at a right angle to the ground. With a swift rocking motion as he shifted his weight from one foot to the other, he settled it firmly on his left foot whilst lifting the heel of his right.

Recognising Mr Farley's stance as the one boxers assumed when they toed the scratch, the pub's customers looked to Mr Sparrow for his answer to this blatant challenge.

Mr Grosse felt a rolling sensation in his stomach as he imagined the beating Mr Sparrow would surely receive at Mr Farley's hands. Urging Mr Sparrow to walk away in his mind, he felt his heart drop at the sight of him removing his apron. Leaning over the bar, he warned in a despairing voice, "*Don't* be *foolish*!"

Mr Sparrow removed his shirt and ordered his customers, "Clear a space."

Mr Grosse lay across the bar and gripped his arm as the sounds of many shuffling feet and moving furniture filled the pub. With eyes so wide, the white around his irises was visible, he cried, "*He'll knock you into the middle of next week*!"

Mr Sparrow looked at him sharply and, seemingly taken aback by the sheer level of desperation in his face, lost his scowl in an instant.

"You *mustn't* fight him," Mr Grosse pleaded with a firm shake of his arm.

"This is none of your concern," Mr Farley warned.

Mr Grosse slid off the bar onto his feet and, half-turning so he could see them both, said, "I refuse to stand by while you beat this man senseless, Mr Farley. It wouldn't be a fair fight and you know it."

"Oi, now, wait a minute—" Mr Sparrow began, his voice and face lacking conviction.

"And so do you," Mr Grosse interrupted firmly. "You've not boxed in *years*." He looked between them. "There *is* a way to settle this once and for all, though."

Mr Farley lowered his fists slightly as his gaze repeatedly darted between Mr Sparrow and Mr Grosse. "I'm listening."

"A prize fight between the most skilled boxers the *Key & Lion* and *Nimble Crow* have to offer," Mr Grosse announced.

The corner of Mr Farley's mouth twitched as he and Mr Sparrow exchanged glances.

"I'll not bring my boxers to this cesspit," Mr Farley sneered.

"I'll not make mine soft with the mittens, either," Mr Sparrow said.

"It wouldn't be a fair fight if it was held on a boxer's home ground," Mr Grosse pointed out. "No. *I* will find a suitable *neutral* location for the set-to." Catching sight of Mr Jeffers in the crowd, he added, "And it shall be reported on by *Sporting Life*'s finest, hm?"

Mr Farley and Mr Sparrow looked to the black bowler-hatted man standing to the far right of the bar. In his late thirties, he was approximately five feet eleven inches tall with a lean build and narrow face. His attire consisted of a threadbare, knee-length brown overcoat, dark-brown trousers, and scuffed black leather shoes. He darted his hazel eyes between Mr Grosse, Mr Sparrow, and Mr Farley as he rested his hand upon his neck beneath his Adam's apple. Though possessed of an upper-class accent, he attempted—and failed—to adopt a cockney twang as he replied, "Yeah. I do not see why I couldn't."

"Excellent." A broad smile lifted Mr Grosse's face. Looking between Mr Farley and Mr Sparrow, he enquired, "So, gentlemen, do we have an agreement?"

Mr Farley and Mr Sparrow eyed one another with suspicion as a heavy silence descended upon the room.

"We do," Mr Sparrow said, finally.

All eyes turned to Mr Farley.

"We do," Mr Farley said after another agonising pause. Putting his coat on, he slipped his tie into his pocket as he approached the bar. Extending his hand to Mr Sparrow, he said, "a gentleman shakes on it."

Mr Sparrow gave Mr Grosse a sideways glance. Upon seeing his subtle nod, he clenched his jaw and exhaled deeply through his nose as he gave Mr Farley's hand a brief yet firm shake. Releasing it with a shove, he growled, "Now get out."

"Gladly," Mr Farley said. As he walked to the door, he warned, "Prepare to enter the workhouse, Duncan." He opened the door and looked back at him. "Because you've just signed this pub's death warrant."

"You *bastard*," Mr Sparrow snarled, rushing around the bar. When he reached its end, though, he found his path blocked by Mr Grosse. "Get out of my way!"

Mr Grosse gripped his arms. "He's gone!"

Mr Sparrow looked to the door and, sure enough, Mr Farley had vanished.

"Don't worry," Mr Grosse reassured as he released him. "He'll pay for it in the ring."

"I hope you're right, Mr Grosse. For your sake," Mr Sparrow growled. Striding back along the bar, he went through another door that caused Mr Grosse and his fellow patrons to flinch when Mr Sparrow violently slammed it behind him.

EIGHT

Mrs Dorothea Trent's distressed reaction and swift retreat had played on Inspector Woolfe's mind all evening. When he'd retired to bed—which was again, too short for him—thoughts and ideas about the potential cause had kept sleep at bay. Consequently, there were dark rings under his eyes and a throbbing in his back as he trudged up Tonbridge High Street. He'd also gotten up with a dull ache in his chest that had worsened upon coming out into the cold air. At least he could take some comfort in his stomach being full, though. Thanks to the hearty breakfast the hotel's proprietors had bestowed upon him. Recalling the server's nervous look when enquiring if he'd like anything else to eat, Inspector Woolfe smiled in amusement before a brief coughing fit took hold.

"It's just up here." Constable Begg's voice penetrated his thoughts.

Casting a sideways glance at him as he regained his breath, Inspector Woolfe followed the direction of his finger to see some labourers digging up the frozen ground.

Overseeing their work was a stout man in his early fifties. He, like the others, was bundled up in a dark-brown coat, cap, scarf, and gloves. Their breaths, like Inspector Woolfe and Constable Begg's, formed clouds of steam as they hit the cold morning air. Although overcast, the sun was trying to burn through the clouds. Upon catching sight of Inspector Woolfe, the stout man smirked and said to the others, "I don't remember hearin' the freak show was in town."

The labourers stopped digging and, looking over their shoulders, huddled together when they saw the giant man approaching. Exchanging glances, they failed to share their associate's mirth.

"What was that?" Inspector Woolfe challenged as he towered over the stout man.

"N-Nothing, sir," the man replied. "Just a little joke, that's all. I meant no harm by it."

Inspector Woolfe presented his warrant card. "I'm Detective Inspector Woolfe of London's Metropolitan Police." He gestured to his companion. "This is Detective Constable Begg from the Kent police. We're looking for Mr Graeme Winslow. Is he here?"

"I'm him," a man in his late-thirties with the weathered appearance of someone much older replied as he raised his calloused hand. His sterling-grey eyes seemed to shine as they peered out from his muck-covered face, whilst his strong jaw and prominent nose gifted him with some good looks. Removing his cap to reveal a thick head of light ash-brown hair to match his unkempt moustache, he gave his shovel to his neighbour and approached the policemen. "What do you want?"

Inspector Woolfe glanced at the others. "Not here." He looked to the stout man. "He'll be back in a few minutes."

The stout man gave a jerky nod.

Leading Mr Winslow and Constable Begg down the High Street, Inspector Woolfe stopped by a pile of rubble once he was certain they were out of earshot. "Mrs Dorothea Trent told us you were once her niece's fiancé. Is that true?"

"Yeah," Mr Winslow replied. "But just for a month or two."

"Who ended the engagement?" Inspector Woolfe enquired.

"She did," Mr Winslow replied.

"Why?" Inspector Woolfe enquired.

"She wanted to go to London and be an actress. I would've gone with her, but…" He shrugged one shoulder. "Becky's not a home bird."

Inspector Woolfe furrowed his brow. "Why do you think she said, 'yes' in the first place?"

"She did love me," Mr Winslow rebutted. "But she wanted more than the life of a labourer's wife." He bowed his head and scratched its back. "Becky's the kind to wear lace, not wool." He lowered his hand. "Whereas my Lizzie's been just what I wanted."

"Your wife?" Constable Begg enquired.

"And mum to my son," Mr Winslow replied.

"Were you and Miss Trent happy?" Inspector Woolfe enquired.

A mischievous glint entered Mr Winslow's eyes as he grinned from ear-to-ear. "I'd say we were." He took a step closer, prompting Inspector Woolfe and Constable Begg to lean forward. Glancing over his shoulder, he leaned in close and said in a low voice, "She knew how to make a man happy." He tapped his nose and stepped back. "If you, er, get my meaning."

Inspector Woolfe's posture stiffened as a vision of the couple in bed sprang into his mind's eye. Feeling an unwelcome shift below his waistline, he straightened his back and fastened his coat. "We do." He forced the image from his mind and tried to focus on Mr Winslow's face instead. "Did she…" He cleared his throat, instigating another brief coughing fit. Turning his back to the cold breeze, he gave a final cough and enquired, "Did she ever talk to you about her parents?"

"Only to say they'd died when she was a child," Mr Winslow replied.

"Did she say how they'd died?" Constable Begg enquired.

Mr Winslow shook his head. "I didn't want to upset her, so I didn't ask."

Instinctively resting his hand upon his coat within the vicinity of his crotch, Inspector Woolfe enquired, "Were you born in Tonbridge?"

"No. Maidstone. I came here a few years after Becky's parents died," Mr Winslow replied. He tilted his head and knitted his brow. "But y'know, now that we're talking about all this, I remember asking a few people about her and her family when I first saw her in the High

Street. They said she lived with her aunt, and that was all I was told."

"Did you try to find out more?" Constable Begg enquired.

"I couldn't," Mr Winslow replied with a shrug of his shoulders. "All everyone said was 'the past is the past. Best to leave it there.'"

Inspector Woolfe and Constable Begg exchanged knowing glances.

* * *

"Come in," Chief Inspector Jones called in response to the knock on the door. Moving away from the window, he stood behind his desk as Inspector Lee entered.

"Good morning, sir." Inspector Lee removed his hat and, placing his gloves within it, tucked it under one arm whilst his other held his cane. "You wished to see me."

"Yes." Chief Inspector Jones' firm tone was given further gravitas by the tension in his face. "Inspector Conway has informed me that Sergeant Ethan Gutman was watching the Bow Street Society's house last night. Why?"

Inspector Lee's posture stiffened. Gripping the handle of his cane, he considered his options. "Did Miss Trent tell him that?"

"*Don't* try my patience, Gideon. Answer the question."

Inspector Lee put the tip of his cane upon the floor and hugged his hat tightly against his chest. Retaining an emotionless expression and a formal tone, he replied, "He was acting under my orders."

"That's as blatant as the nose on your face," Chief Inspector Jones scoffed. "I'm asking you '*why*.'"

"To keep a close eye on the Society's activities, sir."

"Inspector Conway is assigned to that duty."

Pulling his eyebrows together and down, Inspector Lee enquired in a vexed tone, "May I speak freely, sir?"

"You may."

Inspector Lee's grip upon his hat and cane eased as his face relaxed and, with a swift nod, he mumbled, "Thank you." He diverted his gaze to the empty chair before Chief Inspector Jones' desk. "I gave Sergeant Gutman the order to watch the Bow Street Society's house because I no longer trust Inspector Conway's integrity or loyalty to the Yard."

"That wasn't your judgement to make."

"Under the circumstances, sir, I felt it was my duty to protect the reputation and credibility of the Metropolitan Police." Inspector Lee met Chief Inspector Jones' gaze.

Chief Inspector Jones returned to the window and, clasping his hands behind his back, looked outside. "You refer to the board's verdict?"

"I do. And the confession Inspector Conway made at his hearing."

"The board's ruling was clear." Chief Inspector Jones turned to face him. "It deemed Inspector Conway acted under difficult and unusual circumstances. His service to the Yard before and in the days since has been impeccable."

"I wish I could agree with you, sir, but after hearing Gutman's account of what transpired last night, I have serious doubts."

Chief Inspector Jones' expression remained emotionless despite the knot forming in his stomach. "Go on."

"Not only did he witness Inspector Conway give an envelope to Miss Trent, but he also saw Miss Trent give him one in return." Inspector Lee paused a moment to allow the revelation to be digested. "It would appear as though the 'good' inspector is supplying the Bow Street Society with confidential information in exchange for money."

The knot tightened in Chief Inspector Jones' stomach as the heat of rage rose inside of him. Knowing that it was in fact Inspector Conway who'd given money to Miss Trent, he strongly suspected this was simply a ploy on

Inspector Lee's part to discredit Inspector Conway following their public confrontation the other day. Yet, he also knew he couldn't reveal the contents of either envelope without inviting awkward questions. He took in a slow, deep breath to calm his anger and decide upon a course of action as he returned to his desk and sat behind it. Casting a glance at its top drawer, he recalled locking Miss Trent's report on the Society's *Mrs Gove* case in it earlier. Reassured it was safely tucked away from Inspector Lee's prying eyes, he prepared his pipe with some fresh tobacco.

Meanwhile, having watched his senior officer closely, Inspector Lee was both surprised and frustrated by the absence of an angry outburst. When Chief Inspector Jones prepared his pipe, Inspector Lee had the distinct impression he was about to be dismissed from his office. This was *not* going how he had envisioned it would. Tucking his cane under his arm and squaring his shoulders, he loudly cleared his throat.

Chief Inspector Jones settled back in his chair and lit his pipe with a match, however.

"Excuse me, sir, but perhaps you didn't hear what I said—" Inspector Lee began.

"I heard." Chief Inspector Jones took a couple of puffs from his pipe and regarded him through the dissipating smoke. "If what you say is true, Sergeant Gutman only saw some envelopes."

Inspector Lee scowled.

"It's a tremendous leap to suggest they contained confidential information and a bribe," Chief Inspector Jones added.

"*If* it is true?" Inspector Lee enquired in an indignant tone.

"Your accusation has come on the heels of a confrontation between the two of you. It would be remiss of me to ignore the potential significance of its timing." Chief Inspector Jones took another puff of his pipe and watched as Inspector Lee's cheeks flushed pink. His hand also trembled as he tightened his grip upon his cane. Half-expecting him to spit bees at any moment, Chief Inspector Jones continued, "You failed to mention that Sergeant Gutman had seen the contents of the envelopes. Therefore, your accusation is nothing more than supposition born from a desire to have revenge on Inspector Conway for the public humiliation he dealt you."

Aware of Inspector Lee's involvement with Inspector Woolfe's investigation into the Society, Chief Inspector Jones also suspected it was an attempt to discredit Miss Trent as much as Inspector Conway. Yet, also aware that Inspector Lee thought him ignorant of his connection to Inspector Woolfe, Chief Inspector Jones, again, couldn't air these thoughts. Instead, he cut him off before he could speak, saying, "I shall overlook your contemptable behaviour on this occasion, Gideon, because I know your record is also unblemished until this point. Make any attempt to discredit your fellow officers with baseless accusations again, though, and I'll have no choice but to suspend you from duty and refer you to the discipline board myself. Do you understand?"

"*Yes.* Sir," Inspector Lee replied from behind clenched teeth.

"Good." Chief Inspector Jones rested his pipe upon its stand and opened a file upon his desk. "Return to your duties."

Inspector Lee turned sharply upon his heel and strode from the room. As he entered the corridor and closed the door, Sergeant Gutman hurried forward from where he'd been loitering by the window. Inspector Lee continued walking and, as Sergeant Gutman fell into step beside him, said in a low hiss, "Find me Inspector Conway's address at once."

Sergeant Gutman frowned deeply. "Yes, sir, but… why?"

Inspector Lee stopped at the corner and, glancing around, quietly replied, "We're going to find that envelope."

NINE

Miss Trent walked across the darkened first floor of the abandoned building, grateful for the moonlight pouring in through its windows. Finding a set of stairs in the far corner, she held their handrail and listened. Catching the low murmur of male voices over the sound of the Thames, she began her slow ascent.

Careful to keep any creaking to a minimum, she stopped halfway up to peer over the top. Spotting the men by the window on the far side of the room, she saw it was Chief Inspector Jones and Inspector Conway by their moonlit faces. She lifted her skirts to climb the remainder of the stairs, but the intensity in their voices piqued her curiosity. She lingered on the step to listen for a moment.

"I don't like bein' out of the way," Inspector Conway said in a low voice. "I want to be back downstairs."

"We discussed this," Chief Inspector Jones replied in a frustrated tone.

"Discussed what?" Miss Trent loudly enquired as she strode up the last few steps.

Both men looked at her like startled rabbits.

"Just some business at the Yard," Chief Inspector Jones replied with a contrived smile.

Miss Trent flattened her lips as she realised the significance of what she'd overheard. In a hard tone, she challenged, "Why have you moved Conway upstairs?"

Chief Inspector Jones' eyes momentarily bulged. "I-I beg your pardon?" He looked to Inspector Conway.

"I've said nowt," Inspector Conway insisted.

Miss Trent put her hands upon her hips. "I overheard what you said about wanting to be back downstairs, John. Why didn't you say something last night?"

"Because it wasn't important," Inspector Conway replied.

"I'd beg to differ," Miss Trent countered in disbelief. From Jones, she demanded, "Are you punishing him?"

"This has nothing to do with what happened with Inspector Lee," Chief Inspector Jones stated firmly.

Miss Trent's eyes widened. "What happened with Inspector Lee?"

Inspector Conway looked up and muttered through a sigh, "I wasn't gonna tell her."

Miss Trent folded her arms. "In the same way you weren't going to tell me about Dr Weeks losing his commission to the Yard?" From them both, she demanded, "Don't you trust me anymore?"

Chief Inspector Jones tilted his head and pinched the bridge of his nose. "Of course, we do. I was going to tell you about Dr Weeks, but John said he already had, so I didn't think there was any need to. As for Inspector Lee…" He glanced at Inspector Conway as he lowered his hand. "There was a minor… altercation between him and John."

"Did you hit him?" Miss Trent enquired hopefully.

"Nah. Wish I had, though."

"If you had, you would be in the cells now instead of your own office," Chief Inspector Jones pointed out firmly. "I moved John to protect him from his fellow inspectors. Many of whom seem determined to drive him from the service. Which leads me onto the purpose of this meeting." Chief Inspector Jones took a moment to calm his anger and refocus his thoughts. "Sergeant Gutman, acting under the orders of Inspector Lee, was watching the Society's house last night. He saw you and Inspector Conway through the window."

Miss Trent blinked. "But I've seen no one. If I had, I wouldn't have come here tonight *or* invited you to Bow Street, John."

"We know," Inspector Conway replied softly.

Miss Trent cast a hard look at them in turn. "Did you summon me here *knowing* I was being watched?"

"Certainly not," Chief Inspector Jones replied with a scowl. "I dealt with Inspector Lee and Sergeant Gutman this morning."

Miss Trent's lips flattened as she cast another glare between them. "If I was unaware of Sergeant Gutman watching me *then*, how did you expect me to ensure he wasn't watching me *now*?" She nodded toward the window. "How do you know he hasn't followed me here—to you?"

"He hasn't," Chief Inspector Jones replied.

"You can't know that for certain," Miss Trent said.

"Yes, I can," Chief Inspector Jones insisted.

"How?" Miss Trent demanded.

"Because I followed you 'ere," Inspector Conway interjected.

"*You*?" Miss Trent stared at him. "But I arrived after you."

"There's another door at the back," Inspector Conway said. "I come on ahead and got upstairs before you arrived. There was no one followin' you besides me."

The tension vanished from Miss Trent's face. "Good." She returned her attention to Chief Inspector Jones. "Did Sergeant Gutman see us exchange envelopes?"

"Yes, but he saw neither the money nor the report. Nevertheless…" Chief Inspector Jones' voice and expression turned grave. "During my meeting with Inspector Lee this morning, he accused John of accepting a bribe from the Bow Street Society in exchange for confidential information."

Miss Trent tensed.

"But as I said, it's been dealt with," Chief Inspector Jones swiftly added.

Miss Trent dropped a hand to her hip as, holding her forehead with the other, she turned away. With visions of the terrible fate this could bring down upon her friends, she said softly, "I can't believe this is happening."

"I'm sorry," Chief Inspector Jones said, matching her tone.

Miss Trent glared at him. "Is that *all* you have to say? First, I had to sit and watch as poor Mr Maxwell was torn to shreds by a vulture of a defence lawyer under the gaze of his murderous father. Now, you've told me Inspector Lee has accused John of corruption—a *criminal* act that he could be thrown into Newgate for—and all you can say is '*sorry?*'" She pursed her lips and repeatedly shook her head as she looked away again.

"'E's got no evidence, lass," Inspector Conway reassured.

"But he could still bring it to the attention of the discipline board, couldn't he?" Miss Trent pointed out. "You told me yourself, John, they would take into account the last set of charges you were found guilty of when considering any new accusations."

"Yeah, they would, but it's not gonna come to that," Inspector Conway said.

"I made it absolutely clear to Inspector Lee that I knew he was only bringing the accusation against John out of revenge for his humiliation," J Chief Inspector ones said. "He's not foolish enough to approach the board without either evidence or the support of his senior officer."

"I hope you're right," Miss Trent said, her voice, eyes, and expression laced with concern as she faced them once more.

"How's Mr Maxwell now?" Inspector Conway enquired, keen to change the subject.

"As well as can be expected. He's being looked after by Mr Snyder and Mr Elliott," Miss Trent replied. "I didn't want to risk leaving him and Miss Dexter alone in the house."

"Are they no longer on speaking terms?" Chief Inspector Jones enquired, surprised.

"It's complicated, as you know," Miss Trent replied through a sigh. "Will you at least send word if the situation with Inspector Lee changes?"

"I will," Chief Inspector Jones replied. "Don't worry. I'm certain everything will be fine."

"I hope so, Richard," Miss Trent said.

"Me, too," Inspector Conway added, softly.

* * *

Mr Baldwin whistled as he entered the *Key & Lion* carrying that evening's edition of the *Gaslight Gazette.* Tossing it onto the bar in front of Mr Grosse, he looked over his friend's shoulder to see him hurriedly closing his notebook. A fleeting idea he'd seen a telegram tucked amongst the pages was quickly dismissed as he clapped his hand upon Mr Grosse's other shoulder and said with a chuckle, "I wasn't trying to peek." He picked up the *Gazette* and held it in front of him. "Look who's on the front page."

"You wouldn't be the first to try," Mr Grosse replied with a weak smile.

"That notebook's more famous than you are," Mr Baldwin teased.

Mr Grosse chuckled as he slipped it into his jacket and, taking the newspaper, read aloud, "Son Faces Father in Court. The second day of the trial of Mr Oliver Maxwell for the brutal murder of his daughter-in-law saw his son, Mr Joseph Maxwell, take to the stand. A longstanding member of the Bow Street Society, it was that group which successfully brought Mr Oliver Maxwell to justice whilst the Metropolitan Police remained baffled. With obvious nerves, Mr Joseph Maxwell answered the prosecution's questions with little hesitation or deliberation. When the defence subjected him to a cross-examination, though, there were points when it was feared he might faint or sob. In all, the cross-examination lasted a full thirty minutes. After which, Mr Joseph Maxwell had to be led from the stand by the bailiff of the court." Mr Grosse chuckled. "And this fellow is a *journalist*?"

Mr Baldwin rolled his eyes. "Don't get me started." He took the newspaper back and tucked it under his arm. Glancing along the bar to see Mr Sparrow serving another customer, he leaned in close to Mr Grosse and enquired in a low voice, "Where's this set-to happenin' tonight?"

"I don't know what you mean." Mr Grosse sipped his pint.

Mr Baldwin gave a weak chuckle. "Come on, mate. You've gotta give me somethin'."

With his pint still held to his lips, he gave Mr Baldwin a sideways glance. "Mr Jeffers of *Sporting Life* has been given exclusive rights to the story." He looked ahead and took another sip. "I'm sorry, Oswald."

Mr Baldwin's face contorted into a scowl. "You can't do this to me, Christian. I've promised Mr Morse I'd—"

"There's nothing I can do." Mr Grosse turned to face him. "You saw what happened last night. An agreement was made, and a gentleman *never* goes back on his word." He drained his glass and put his hat on. "Look after yourself."

"Yeah, thanks," Mr Baldwin muttered, dejected, as he turned to the bar and tossed the newspaper down. Whilst Mr Grosse left, he leaned upon the bar with folded arms and bowed his head with a deep sigh.

"I can tell you where it's happenin'," a male voice said.

Mr Baldwin looked to the sixteen-year-old boy standing to his right. Barely five feet tall, the boy's lithe form was attired in a faded white shirt, scruffy-looking brown waistcoat, threadbare trousers, and heavy boots. A stained apron that was too long for him was also tied around his waist. Recognising him as Mr Sparrow's orphaned Pot Boy, Toby, he also knew he tended to exaggerate. "Yeah? How do *you* know that?"

"I've got ears, ain't I?" Toby scoffed. "Do you wanna know or not?"

Mr Baldwin glanced at Mr Sparrow, but he remained deep in conversation with another. Lowering his voice, Mr Baldwin enquired, "Where?"

Toby glanced around. "Not now. Later. Meet me in the yard, and I'll tell you."

"You don't know owt." Mr Baldwin stood up straight and collected his newspaper.

"I *do*, too!" Alarmed by the volume of his own voice, Toby shot a panicked glance to Mr Sparrow. Relaxing when he showed no sign of noticing, he inched closer to Mr Baldwin and quietly said, "It's a closed fight. We don't want it ruined by those who've got no place in bein' there."

Mr Baldwin considered. "The coppers, you mean?"

"*Yeah*." Toby grinned. "The coppers."

Mr Baldwin smiled. "Fine, boy. I'll meet you later."

Toby shook his trouser pocket. "With a little sumthin' for my trouble?"

Mr Baldwin gave him a gentle shove. "You'll get a shilling."

Toby grinned. "That'll do me right enough, sir." He walked behind him but stopped to lean back and whisper, "Pleasure doin' business with you, sir."

* * *

"But according to your statement, there was no one present other than you and your father. We only have your word that he attempted to smother you with a cushion."

"Y-Yes, but—"

"And isn't it true the members of the Bow Street Society who discovered the scene are friends of yours?"

"Y-Yes, but—"

"Joseph?"

"Who found you standing over the unconscious body of your father, correct?"

"Joseph?" Miss Dexter's gentle voice drowned out the intimidating one of Oliver Maxwell's defence lawyer echoing in Joseph's mind as he replayed his terrible ordeal. Feeling a hand upon his own at the same time, his focus shifted outward to see Miss Dexter's delicate features marred by sadness.

Pulling himself up in the armchair, he remembered he was in the Society's parlour, and an immense relief washed over him. Feeling a prickling sensation sweep across his body at the same time, he instinctively reached out to take her hand. "Georgina."

She slipped it free, however. Clasping it with her other in her lap, she bowed her head and straightened upon the sofa. "I wanted you to know how sorry I was to hear about what happened at the trial today."

Joseph held the arms of his chair and leaned toward her. "Thank you."

A pained expression descended upon Miss Dexter's face as she stared at her knees. Standing abruptly a moment later, she turned toward the door. "That was all."

"Georgina, wait—" Joseph tried to reach for her hand, but she slipped through his grasp once more and left.

TEN

"There's a great deal of building works happening in Tonbridge at the moment," Constable Begg said as he cut up his chop. "They're demolishing buildings on the west side of the High Street and moving them back to widen it." He ate a morsel of meat. "I also know they're demolishing some of those old cottages. I expect Mrs Trent's will end up being one of them."

"What's that got to do with anything?" Inspector Woolfe enquired, spitting out specks of meat as he did so.

Moving back to avoid them, Constable Begg grimaced as one landed on his plate. Scooping it up with his knife, he scraped it off on the plate's rim. "She'll be homeless, won't she? It might bring Miss Rebecca back here, and then your problem will be solved."

Luncheoning at the Rose and Crown Hotel, they sat by a window overlooking Tonbridge High Street. A handful of other guests were scattered around the dining room, but most, if not all, were in the town visiting their relatives ahead of the festive period. Wreaths of holly and ivy hung from the low beams, and mulled wine was routinely offered by those serving. The room's exposed floorboards were painted with a dark-brown varnish whilst the walls were adorned with a midnight-blue paper embossed with a light-blue flock design. A watercolour landscape depicting the town hung from the chimney breast above the stone hearth on the far side of the room.

Inspector Woolfe drank some of his pint, considered the possibility, and drank again. "Nah." He put down his glass with a sloshing of ale. "Someone is paying her to work for the Society and letting her live in its headquarters. She'd be mad to give all that up when she could bring her aunt to London to live with her instead."

Constable Begg's enthusiasm wilted with a drooping of his features.

"It was a nice idea, though," Inspector Woolfe added.

Constable Begg gave a feeble but appreciative smile. "Thank you, Inspector."

Inspector Woolfe grunted, instigating a coughing fit. Fighting to suppress it, he took a large mouthful of ale as his face turned bright red.

"Should I fetch a doctor?" Constable Begg enquired, concerned.

"Nah." Inspector Woolfe drained his glass and finished his meal. "What else have you found out?"

"Not much, I'm afraid." Concerned, still, Constable Begg watched him closely. "Everyone I spoke to either didn't know the Pottinger's or claimed to only know they were relatives of Mrs Dorothea Trent."

"Yeah, I got the same."

"Inspector, I hope you don't think I'm speaking out of turn, but… maybe the aunt was right? Why are the deaths of her niece's parents relevant to her work with the Society? Unless… do you think the aunt murdered them so she could raise her niece? She never had children of her own, as far as I've heard."

"She's not the type."

Although Constable Begg suspected most people were capable of murder given the right motivation and circumstances, he decided to keep his own counsel on this. "Why, then?"

"To satisfy a policeman's curiosity." Inspector Woolfe pushed his empty plate aside. "I want you to go through the parish records again. See if you can find Rebecca Pottinger's baptism and her parents' burial plots. She was born in 1868, and her parents died when she was five, so check 1873 and the years either side to be sure. I'm interested to know what's written on their gravestones."

Constable Begg wiped his mouth with his handkerchief. "Where will you be?"

"At the office of the *Tonbridge Free Press* on the High Street. If their archive has her parents' obituaries, I'll hopefully be able to find out how they died."

* * *

Despite the brilliant white daylight pouring through the adjacent windows, the far end of the corridor stayed in the shadows. Set back from the Yard's main stairwell, it was also deserted. A fact Sergeant Gutman was grateful for as he paced outside Inspector Conway's door. Repeatedly glancing at it and along the corridor, he tried to calm his pounding heart and restless mind. Hearing a drawer being closed within, he came to an abrupt halt and listened with bated breath.

"What are you doing here?"

Sergeant Gutman spun around.

A fellow officer was watching him from the mouth of the stairwell. In his early twenties, he was younger than Sergeant Gutman by a small margin. His cheap suit also made him appear well-dressed compared to Sergeant Gutman's shabby clothes. The officer walked toward him with an expression that was hard to read. "This floor is for police only."

"It's a good job I am the police, then, isn't it?" Sergeant Gutman held the lapels of his tattered coat as proudly as if it were velvet. "Sergeant Ethan Gutman."

The man glanced over him. "Sergeant Aiden Caulfield."

Sergeant Gutman held out his hand. "Pleased to meet you, Aiden."

"You, too." Sergeant Caulfield shook his hand. "Are you with the Mob Squad?"

Sergeant Gutman drew in a deep breath. "I'm not at liberty to say."

"You're an undercover detective, though, aren't you?"

"At times."

"But not currently?" Sergeant Caulfield probed. At Sergeant Gutman's enquiring look, he gestured to his unkempt appearance.

"Well, I'm obviously not undercover *here*, am I? If I were, I'd be a right wrong 'un." Sergeant Gutman laughed weakly.

"True. Excuse me." Sergeant Caulfield went past him to knock on the door.

"Are you with the Mob Squad?" Sergeant Gutman enquired, standing in front of him.

"No." Sergeant Caulfield tried to knock again.

Sergeant Gutman blocked him for a second time. "Maybe you can help me, then. I'm looking for Chief Inspector Jones."

"His office is on the ground floor. If you take a sharp right at the bottom of the stairs and follow the corridor all the way around, you'll see it on your left."

"My sense of direction is awful. Could you show me?"

"It's really not that difficult. *Excuse me.*"

Deciding to concede defeat, Sergeant Gutman moved out of the way and toward the stairs. Hearing him knock as he went, he looked back over his shoulder and saw him waiting patiently by the door. Realising Sergeant Caulfield was the kind to abide by etiquette, Sergeant Gutman stopped at the mouth of the stairwell and watched him. As he'd suspected, Sergeant Caulfield abandoned his task when his knock received no response. Giving him a small nod and quietly spoken "cheers" when he passed, Sergeant Gutman descended to the next landing. Following it around to the next set of stairs, he stopped and looked back at the upper floor. When he neither saw nor heard any sign of Sergeant Caulfield, he hurried back to Inspector Conway's door.

"It's me," he whispered.

The door opened, and Sergeant Gutman stepped inside.

"Found anything, sir?"

"No," Inspector Lee replied, his face contorted with displeasure.

"It was a worth a try, though, eh?" Sergeant Gutman feebly reassured. Truth be told, he'd doubted Inspector Conway would be so careless as to leave a Bow Street Society envelope filled with money lying around the Yard. His home was the likelier hiding place, but they'd drawn a blank there, too. "Where to now?"

"Chiswick," Inspector Lee replied. "I need some time to think."

* * *

With the passing of the snow, the usual liveliness had returned to Bow Street. Congested on both road and pavement, it held a peculiar fascination for Mr Stefan Voigt. Standing at the parlour window with his hands clasped loosely behind his back, he could've been mistaken for someone wiling away the afternoon. Yet, the unnatural stillness of his slack posture, inward gaze of his brown eyes, and grim twist to his mouth spoke to Miss Trent of a man carrying a terrible weight. She allowed him a few moments of solitude whilst she garnered all she could from his appearance.

In his mid-sixties, he had drooping skin around his eyes, cheeks, and chin. The top of his head was bald, but the back and sides were covered by thick white hair. Wiry whiskers also framed his face, whilst light-grey stubble covered the skin beneath his beak-like nose. Due to his stoop, it was difficult for Miss Trent to accurately gauge his height. Instead, she guessed it to be somewhere around five feet seven. The cut and quality of his black frockcoat and trousers, dark-green waistcoat, and white shirt were in line with a gentleman's wardrobe. The added adornments of a gold pocket watch and rings confirmed he was a man of considerable means.

"For them, life goes on," Mr Voigt observed in a voice devoid of emotion. His accent was also distinctly Germanic in nature. "They live, they love, they make their preparations for Christmas… My life shall be buried from this day forth." He turned to look upon the tree, his face remaining expressionless as his gaze shifted from branch to branch. "There is no joy for me now."

Miss Trent poured some tea and took it to him.

"You're most kind." Mr Voigt accepted the cup and looked to the tree once more.

The flames of almost one hundred slender, white candles illuminated the fir tree's dark-green foliage. They were fixed to shallow holders with a ball suspended beneath by wire. Both holder and ball were made from clay. Yet, whilst all the former were painted gold, several of the latter were also painted red or green. A string of small, brass bells was wrapped loosely around the tree from its tip to its base as a hand-carved wooden star painted gold, adorned its summit. A cluster of smaller candles were also positioned in the branches around the star's base, illuminating it. Beyond the tree, the parlour was decorated with wreaths and sprigs of ivy, holly, and mistletoe, a small Nativity scene on the mantel shelf, and a string of Christmas cards across the chimney breast.

Standing before her armchair, Miss Trent indicated the adjacent sofa. "Will you sit?"

"Yes, we should tend to the business at hand," Mr Voigt said with a grave expression. Carrying his untouched tea to the sofa, he put it down on the low table and slumped into the overstuffed cushions with his arms loose at his sides. His focus shifted inward as he chose his words carefully. "I came to England from Germany as a young man and was blessed with a successful life as a stockbroker in the city. I'd hoped my nephew would know the same blessing, but it was not to be."

Miss Trent wrote down the key points in her notebook.

"He took employment as a writer at *Bell's Sporting Life* after discovering a passion for 'boxing,'" Mr Voigt sneered.

"You didn't approve?"

"No." Mr Voigt momentarily met her gaze but gave a dismissive shake of his head as he looked away. "As a woman, you can't be expected to understand such things."

Miss Trent's lips flattened with a tightening of her features. She considered challenging his assumption but decided against it since she knew so-called 'polite' society frowned upon the 'fairer sex' attending boxing matches. If she were ever given the opportunity to, though, she wouldn't allow others' disapproval to stop her.

"It's brutality," Mr Voigt continued. "It isn't 'sport' or 'art' as some would have you believe."

"Did your nephew box?"

"He told me he'd tried it with the mittens once, but his appetite was strongest when he watched." Mr Voigt's eyes glazed over. "He left it all behind to become a private enquiry agent."

"Were you surprised by that?" Miss Trent scrutinised his reaction.

Mr Voigt blinked as he slid his gaze to her but looked to the fire a moment later. "It surprised, gladdened, and disappointed me." He downcast his eyes. "I was afraid such dangerous work would lead him to foul play." He closed his eyes. "Why didn't I *persuade* him to abandon that, too?"

"Hindsight can be both a blessing and a curse," Miss Trent observed.

Mr Voigt gave a jerky nod and bowed his head, thereby resting his chin upon his chest.

In a soft tone, Miss Trent enquired, "What happened to your nephew, Mr Voigt?"

"*Murdered*," Mr Voigt whispered. "He was murdered."

Miss Trent felt a chill course through her. "How did you find out?"

"The police. They told me a body had been found this morning in a warehouse at the docks." Mr Voigt took out his handkerchief and wiped it across his eyes. "He was to meet me for breakfast. I was worried when he didn't come.

I went to his place of business and found it a mess." He lifted his arm and pointed at the low table. "But his hat, shoes, pocket watch, cufflinks, handkerchief, and money were on his desk." He furrowed his brow. "What were they doing there? Where was he?" He lowered his arm. "No one knew. I went to New Scotland Yard. *They* knew."

Miss Trent watched him with sympathetic eyes as he wiped his once more.

"They took me to a dark room underground where a doctor with the foulest of tongues showed me my dear nephew's remains."

Miss Trent wrote Dr Weeks' name in her notebook with a degree of relief. *Richard's assumption that his order would be disobeyed was well-founded,* she thought.

"The police asked, 'Is this him?' and I told them it was," Mr Voigt continued. "They led me out. I wasn't permitted to say goodbye to him." He wiped his eyes more firmly this time. "The police are *swine*." He looked into the fire. "I thought 'Why should I help them if they will not help me?' Then I remembered this group, this Society. I took a cab straight here."

Miss Trent frowned. Once the police discovered Mr Voigt had hired the Bow Street Society, they'd undoubtedly blame it for his non-cooperation. "Do the police know what you found?"

"No. They will trample his belongings like bulls."

"We're obliged to inform the police of our involvement in this case, and of any new information we discover during our investigation," Miss Trent said, watching his reaction carefully. "With that in mind, do you still wish to hire us?"

Mr Voigt thought long and hard.

"Yes," he said finally. "The police will see him only as another dead foreigner and give his murder little attention. Your Society has no such prejudice."

Miss Trent knew of at least two policemen who didn't live up to Mr Voigt's assumption. Reluctant to enter into a heated debate, though, she decided to shift the conversation back to Mr Voigt's nephew. "I just have a few more questions. What is the address of your nephew's private enquiry agency?" She wrote it down as Mr Voigt recited it. "Was your nephew married?"

Mr Voigt adopted a hard tone. "It was his professional work that led to his death, *not* his domestic situation."

"We can't know that for certain unless—"

"Eunice is to be left alone," Mr Voigt commanded. "And that's all I'll say on it."

"Very well." Miss Trent wrote down the wife's name, nonetheless. "You mentioned your nephew's given name earlier, but I'll also need his surname and title to give to our members, please."

"I understand," Mr Voigt said with lingering anger. "It's Mr Christian Eckhart Grosse."

ELEVEN

Two days had passed since Dr Colbert was officially welcomed into the Bow Street Society, and he'd already accepted his first case. Miss Trent's letter had been delivered to the hospital when he'd been dealing with a patient. As a result, he hadn't read it until almost an hour later. By which point he was late for the proposed rendezvous at the group's house. A frantic search for a hansom cab and dash across London later, he'd arrived dishevelled and out of breath. Fortunately, she'd allowed him a few moments to gather himself before introducing him to Mr Callahan Skinner, the man who was to be his fellow detective in this ghoulish endeavour.

Dr Colbert was drawn to the thirty-eight-year-old the moment he saw him. Although shorter than him by seven inches, his broad shoulders, torso, and biceps exuded strength. This undeniable resilience was evidenced further by the iron contraption in place of his right hand and the burn scarring across his right cheek and jaw. In Dr Colbert's opinion, these, which others would insensitively refer to as 'disfigurements,' enhanced Mr Skinner's naturally handsome features. His well-shaped nose and moulded chin were also in keeping with physiognomy's defined characteristics of a man of good character and clean habits. When he was introduced as a former naval officer whose present employment was that of personal bodyguard, it didn't surprise Dr Colbert in the least.

According to Miss Trent's letter, Mr Stefan Voigt, a stockbroker in the City of London, had hired the Society to discover the identity of his nephew's murderer. The nephew being Mr Christian Grosse, a private enquiry agent. During their briefing, she had given him and Mr Skinner two addresses. The first being Mr Grosse's office and the second being the suspected location of his Earthly remains. Some other members—not present at the briefing—were investigating the former, whilst he and Mr

Skinner were to visit the latter. Therefore, following a second cab journey, he now stood in a dank underground morgue.

His first impression of the man supposedly responsible for the dissections conducted therein was unfavourable to say the least. Dr Percy Weeks, a twenty-nine-year-old Canadian whose reputation for surgical brilliance had reached even Bethlehem, had given them a less-than-warm welcome. There were also marked contrasts between him and Mr Skinner which had served to lower Dr Colbert's opinion further.

Instead of strength, Dr Weeks' narrow shoulders and thin arms exuded fragility. Instead of resilience, Dr Weeks' tired eyes, dry skin, and redness in his nose and cheeks exuded vulnerability born from alcohol dependence. Even without these indicators, Dr Colbert could've recognised him as a degenerate from the stench of stale beer that he wore like a prostitute's cheap perfume. Furthermore, if the principles of physiognomy were to be believed, the great wisdom and intelligence denoted by his highbrow were also being degraded by his vice. Such a tragic prospect distressed and incensed Dr Colbert in equal measure.

Dr Colbert watched Dr Weeks sweep his gaze over him and, a moment later, enquire from Mr Skinner with a lit cigarette in his mouth. "Who's this?"

Dr Colbert held out his hand. "Dr Neal Colbert from Bethlehem Hospital."

Dr Weeks looked at him sharply. "The asylum?" His movements were slow and hesitant as he took and squeezed Dr Colbert's hand. Casting a worried glance between the two, he enquired in a subdued voice, "Ya ain't 'ere to commit me, are ya?"

"Fortunately not," Dr Colbert replied. *Not yet*, he inwardly added.

"We're looking for Mr Christian Grosse," Mr Skinner said in a soft, Dublin accent.

Dr Weeks' eyes flashed with recognition. "'E ain't 'ere."

"Miss Trent thinks 'e is," Mr Skinner said.

"Miss Trent's wrong," Dr Weeks sneered. Turning away, he took a deep pull from his cigarette and strode over to his desk in the far corner. He pulled his chair up to the Empire typewriter set upon it and tossed his cigarette into a mug of mouldy coffee as he sat. "Ya'll know where the door is."

"I think you'd better search your memory, Doctor." Mr Skinner took a brown paper package from his coat and placed it in front of Dr Weeks.

Dr Colbert glanced at the package but looked again when he saw it was a bottle. A terrible inkling formed in his mind that caused his stomach to turn.

Meanwhile, Dr Weeks had straightened in his chair. Darting his gaze between the bottle and Mr Skinner, he reached for it but growled as the Irishman picked it up instead.

"Is Mr Grosse here?" Mr Skinner tore the paper with the tip of his iron finger to reveal a label printed with 'whiskey' and 'Dublin Distillers Company Ltd.'

Dr Colbert snatched it from him. "What do you think you are doing?"

Mr Skinner snatched it back. "Getting answers."

Dr Colbert opened his mouth to protest further, but the memory of his conversation with Inspectors Lee and Woolfe compelled him to reconsider. Folding his arms instead, he glared at Mr Skinner as he removed the bottle's cork with his iron finger and poured a measure into another mug.

"D'yall know the shit I'd be in if the coppers found out I were helpin' the Society?" Dr Weeks maintained a rigid stare upon the bottle, nonetheless.

"We can guess," Mr Skinner replied, recalling Miss Trent's warning that Mr Grosse might not be at Dr Weeks' dead room due to the surgeon losing his commission with the Yard. "Don't worry. They're not goin' to find out from us." He took a sip of whiskey. "You met Mr Grosse's uncle: Mr Stefan Voigt."

Dr Weeks wetted his lips, his gaze following the mug. "Maybe."

Dr Colbert clenched his hand into a fist beneath his arm at the spectacle. *This is cruel*, he thought. *Can't Mr Skinner see how unruly Dr Weeks' addiction is?* Drawing in a slow, deep breath, he resolved to speak to Miss Trent the moment they returned to Bow Street.

"He wants us to find his nephew's murderer," Mr Skinner said.

Dr Weeks sat back in his chair and tried to focus his attention on the Bow Streeters. Yet, he darted his gaze between the mug and bottle every few seconds. "So does Inspector Pilker."

"Is he the copper runnin' the investigation?" Mr Skinner enquired.

"Yeah," Dr Weeks replied. "And 'e ain't gonna stand for ya'll pokin' yer noses in."

"So, Mr Grosse *is* here," Dr Colbert said.

"I didn't say that," Dr Weeks retorted, narrowing his eyes.

"You didn't have to," Dr Colbert said drily. "How did he die?"

Dr Weeks held out his hand. "Gimmie the whiskey."

"Tell us everyt'ing you know first," Mr Skinner said.

Dr Weeks glared at him as he dropped his hand. Returning his gaze to the bottle, he nevertheless retrieved a file from under the mess. As he read its first page, he muttered, "Manipulatin' sonofabitch."

Mr Skinner grinned.

"Cause of death were fractures to 'is skull caused by blows to the top of 'is head," Dr Weeks said, glancing up at the mug. "Examination of the skull showed a fracture at its base. I reckon that were caused by the force of the first blow. That blow also bent the outer table of 'is skull causin' fractures to form 'round the wound like the legs of a spider. It also sent a bone fragment into 'is head. The

117

second blow were hard enough to shatter both the inner and outer tables of 'is skull."

Dr Weeks turned the page and, repeatedly darting his gaze from it to the bottle and back again, continued, "There were some bruisin' on 'is face, jaw, cheeks, and temple. 'E had a couple of fractured ribs, some bruisin' to 'is liver and kidneys, and bruisin' on 'is stomach, back, and between 'is ribs and breastbone. I reckon them injuries were dealt by fists between an hour to two hours before the second attack. 'Is body were icy cold to the touch when I examined 'im, but it were as cold where they found 'im, so that ain't somethin' that can be relied on in 'is case. Only a few of 'is muscles contracted into a state of rigor mortis, though, so I reckon 'e were beaten between midnight and two o'clock this mornin' but died between five and six."

"The poor man," Dr Colbert remarked, saddened. "He would've been unconscious during that time?"

"Yeah," Dr Weeks replied, rubbing the back of his neck.

"The bastard left him to die," Mr Skinner observed in a bitter tone.

"What do you think was used to beat him with?" Dr Colbert enquired.

"The second blow caused further damage to the skull, so it ain't easy to say for certain," Dr Weeks replied.

"But if you were to guess, where would your suspicions lie?" Dr Colbert probed.

Dr Weeks leaned back in his chair and wetted his lips as he stared at the bottle. "A life preserver."

Dr Colbert furrowed his brow. "One of those rings which are tossed into the water when someone falls overboard?"

Dr Weeks and Mr Skinner stared at him.

Dr Colbert felt uncomfortable under their gaze. "Unless there is another sort?"

"The kind I'm talkin' 'bout is a wooden cane with a large ball of lead tied to it by catgut," Dr Weeks said. "A well-made one'll easily crack a man's skull."

"It's hardly a preserver of life, then, is it?" Dr Colbert countered.

"It is when yer bein' robbed," Dr Weeks replied.

"Where was he found?" Mr Skinner enquired.

"In a warehouse at the West India Docks' Import Dock by an officer of their private police force," Dr Weeks replied. "'E reported it to a patrollin' K Division constable."

"Aren't those docks full of steamers these days?" Mr Skinner enquired.

"How the hell should I know?" Dr Weeks rebuffed. "I jus' get directed to the meat."

"At what time?" Dr Colbert enquired, resisting the urge to roll his eyes at Dr Weeks' turn of phrase.

"Eight o'clock," Dr Weeks replied, resting his arms either side of the file and leaning toward the bottle.

"Was he wearin' a hat and shoes?" Mr Skinner enquired.

"Nah. A search were made, but nothin' were found." Dr Weeks looked at him sharply. "How d'ya know 'e weren't?"

"I didn't." Mr Skinner offered the bottle. "Thanks."

Dr Weeks snatched it and, admiring its label for a moment, took a large swig. Slowly slouching in his chair, he closed his eyes and groaned softly in pleasure as the whiskey slid down his gullet.

Dr Colbert frowned at the sight.

"We'll see you at Bow Street some time," Mr Skinner said as he headed for the door.

Dr Colbert stared at his retreating form. *Dr Weeks? A member of the Bow Street Society?* he thought, stunned. Returning his attention to the Canadian, he thought better of asking the question when he saw him take a second swig. Considering whether it was wise to leave him alone, he recalled how violent his patients could be when they were denied their vice of choice. Deciding that caution was the better part of valour on this occasion, he uttered a quiet "good day" and left. Albeit with a bitter taste in his mouth.

TWELVE

Miss Agnes Webster stepped onto the square landing and stood to the left of the door. Most of her slender form was hidden by a shin-length, dark-brown woollen coat, with only the lower pleats of her burgundy cotton skirts visible. Holding an immense umbrella at her side as if it were a walking cane, she turned her head toward the light of the lantern hanging from the ceiling. Although only twenty, the plainness of her features and dryness of her fair complexion gave her the appearance of someone older. Her wiry, chocolate-brown hair was wrapped into a bun nestled in the nape of her neck. Its lack of adornment mirrored the simplicity of the narrow brown hat pinned to the front-right side of her head.

Casting a cursory glance over the door, she noticed a holly wreath with red ribbon hanging from its centre, a wooden plaque to its right, and some splintering to its frame. The plaque had the words *C.E. Grosse. Private Enquiry Agent* written in white paint, whilst the splintering appeared to begin at the lock. Leaning her umbrella against the wall, she reached for the knob but accidentally pushed the door open with her fingertips instead.

She listened.

Hearing nothing but the carts and carriages trundling along Homerton High Street in the distance, she eased the door wide and glanced over the office's interior. It was a rectangular room with a low ceiling, small open fireplace on the far right, and a sash window opposite the door. The lower pane of which was smashed, leaving only a jagged piece of glass behind. To the right of the window was a shabby-looking desk, whilst a hat stand stood to the left of the door, and a trio of cupboards stood to its right. The walls were covered in faded mustard wallpaper with a dark-brown stripe, whilst the floor was made of dilapidated, sun-bleached boards which bent and creaked under Miss Webster's feet.

Crossing to the desk, she found some personal effects arranged in a neat row upon its top. Namely, a peculiar-shaped hat, scuffed brown-leather shoes, handkerchief, cufflinks, pocket watch, and a handful of coins. Examining the handkerchief first, she found it was made of cotton and had its corner embroidered with the initials *C.E.G.* Moving onto the shoes, her inspection of their soles revealed much wear and tear. The cufflinks and pocket watch were polished gold, and the money was six shillings' worth. Picking up the hat, she looked over her shoulder as she heard someone climbing the stairs.

"Only me," Mr Snyder called, coming into view when he stepped onto the landing. Noticing the splintered wood on the frame, he stood perpendicular to it and ran his hands over its outer and inner sides. "Someone's used a jemmy on this."

"Yet Mr Grosse's belongings are here," Miss Webster said in her usual monotone as she indicated the items on the desk. "Including his peculiar-looking hat."

"'E was known for that." Mr Snyder crossed the room to join her.

"You knew him?" Miss Webster passed him the hat.

"Nah." Mr Snyder examined it. "But 'e's mates with the Fancy."

"The what?"

"The Fancy. You know, the people who follow boxin' like it's a religion."

"I've never heard of it." Miss Webster dismissed the fact as irrelevant. "What have they said about Mr Grosse?"

"That 'e's the bloke to go to if you want a good man."

"For…?"

"A fight. If someone wanted a good man to fight, Grosse would find 'im for 'em. If they had a man in mind, 'e'd find out 'bout 'im, see if 'e had owt in 'is life that made 'im a bad choice for the ring." Mr Snyder put the hat down and, going behind the desk, pointed to the window as he passed. "That's broke, too."

"Yes, I saw." Miss Webster went over to it and peered into the yard below. "The glass is only on the outside, though." She stood to the left of the window and peered along the outer wall. "I can see a drainpipe. Whoever forced their way in left via the window and used the drainpipe to reach the yard." She stepped back from the window and, bending forward, peered at the remaining piece of jagged glass. "This may be blood smeared here, too."

"The Locke's would know, if they were 'ere."

"But they aren't," Miss Webster stated, her voice and expression devoid of emotion. "So, we must do what we can." Expecting the window to be locked, she was caught off guard when it easily slid upward within its frame. Momentarily losing her balance as a result, she put her other foot down to steady herself. "Our house-breaker must have been startled into leaving," she mused aloud. "Otherwise, they would've taken their time and discovered the window was unlocked."

Meanwhile, Mr Snyder was looking through the rest of the desk's contents. Aside from Mr Grosse's belongings, its top contained scraps of paper, ink blotters, half-empty bottles of ink, and well-thumbed copies of *Bell's Sporting Life*, *Fistiana – or The Oracle of the Ring*, *Bradshaw's Railway Times*, and *Art of Boxing* by Daniel Medoza. Several pages of *Bell's Sporting Life* had their top corner downturned. Upon going to them, Mr Snyder found they contained blow-by-blow accounts of boxing matches annotated with handwritten notes. In *Bradshaw's Railway Times*, the earliest departure times of rural routes were circled and annotated with pairs of handwritten initials. Remembering her work in the recent Maxwell case, Mr Snyder held out the open *Bradshaw's* to Miss Webster. "Can you tell if this is Mr Grosse's writin'?"

Miss Webster took the guide and glanced over the page. "Perhaps, if I have a sample confirmed to be his. I'll ask Miss Trent to request one from Mr Voigt." She returned the guide. "Why are there initials beside the times?"

Mr Snyder closed the guide and set it aside. "The old way of boxin'—the no mittens kind—was done in fields, out of sight of coppers and beaks. Word would ge' 'bout the Fancy of when and where a set-to was gonna 'appen, and we'd all go down there on the train."

"Are they still held now?"

"Sometimes." Mr Snyder pushed back the chair and searched the desk's bottom drawer. Pulling out piles of pamphlets advertising gloved matches in clubs across London, he tossed them onto the desk for Miss Webster to examine further. "Most are like this nowadays. The *Key & Lion* pub's the only place you can see a good old no-mittened set-to in London now."

"Watching men beat each other senseless is hardly appealing," Miss Webster sneered.

"Fair dos." Mr Snyder gave a single-sided shoulder shrug. Finding nothing of interest in the middle drawer, he moved onto the top. Inside was a pile of letters from Mr Voigt, pencils with chewed ends, and a paper file. Taking out the last, Mr Snyder opened it upon the desk. A photograph of a bare-chested boxer adopting the 'toeing the scratch' stance was the first of the documents held therein. In his early forties with neatly combed dark hair, highly developed bicep muscles, and dark eyes, the boxer seemed vaguely familiar to Mr Snyder. Turning the photograph over, he smiled as he recognised the name written there: *Deon Erskine*.

"What have you found?" Miss Webster peered over his shoulder.

"A photograph of Deon Erskine. 'E was a good 'un." Mr Snyder set the photograph aside and picked up the next document in the file. This time it was a telegram with the previous day's date. The receiver was Christian Grosse, and the sender was the *Amateur Athletic Union of the United States of America.* It stated:

SINCE 1888 OUR RECORDS SHOW
DEON ERSKINE HAS NOT
PARTICIPATED IN ANY OF OUR
CONTESTS STOP

"Mr Grosse was lookin' into 'im." Mr Snyder gave her the telegram and read the next page in the file. "This 'ere's 'is fight record and where 'e was born and the like."

Miss Webster read the couple of lines. "Do you think someone hired Mr Grosse to investigate him?"

"Maybe." Mr Snyder rubbed his bearded chin. "There's a rumour goin' 'round 'bout Mr Grosse writin' a book 'bout the history of boxin' in London." Mr Snyder stood and went with Miss Webster to the cupboards. Upon searching the first and second respectively, they found countless files filled with notes on the lives and fights of numerous boxers.

"John 'The Bulldog' Conway," Miss Webster read aloud from one. "He fought his first boxing match in 1869 at the age of sixteen, losing to the Ox of Whitechapel, Samuel Snyder, after fifteen gruelling rounds." She peered over the file at him. "I didn't know you were a boxer."

Mr Snyder chuckled. "Not anymore, lass."

"How old were you when you fought the inspector—I assume it *is* the inspector Mr Grosse writes of?"

"Yeah." Mr Snyder looked up at the ceiling as he worked out the dates. "I must of been 'bout twenty-one."

"John Conway retired from the ring soon after and joined the Metropolitan Police in 1870 at the age of seventeen." She added in a sardonic tone, "That's certainly up for debate."

"'E had no choice," Mr Snyder pointed out firmly. "'E needed the money."

"He was *paid* to hit him?"

"'E would of got a share of the stakes, yeah."

Miss Webster furrowed her brow. "Excuse me, but I think we may be talking at cross-purposes. I was speaking of Mr Elliott's allegation that Inspector Conway struck Mr Thaddeus Dorsey. What were you speaking of?"

Mr Snyder looked away and closed the cupboard. "Nowt."

Struck by his sudden change in demeanour, Miss Webster watched him closely. "Would he have been paid for fighting you?"

"Yeah." Mr Snyder gathered up the pamphlets from the desk.

Miss Webster replayed their earlier conversation and tilted her head. "But you became defensive *after* I commented that it was up for debate whether the inspector had truly retired from boxing." She stood behind him. "Is he still fighting, Mr Snyder?"

"Nah." Mr Snyder added the copies of *Bradshaw's Railway Times* and *Bell's Sporting Life* to the pile.

Miss Webster wasn't entirely convinced but nevertheless decided to let the matter lie. "If he was writing a book, he would've had a partial draft at the very least. We should try to find it."

Mr Snyder glanced over the desk. "And 'is little blue notebook 'e always had with 'im. 'E never let anyone see what was in it, but them of the Fancy think it has the names of all the boxers 'e'd ever seen fight, their managers' names, too. The no gloves kind of boxin', the kind me and the inspector done, is sumthin' you'd be arrested for these days—even if you was just watchin' it. If Mr Grosse put 'is notes into 'is book, it could get a lot of people in trouble. Maybe not with a beak, but jus' bein' known for that kind of boxin' is enough to get you barred from what the gents call the 'respectable' boxin' clubs."

"It could also ruin a gentleman's reputation within polite society," Miss Webster observed as she considered the ramifications such a scandal would have on his family, too. The thought immediately led to her recalling something Miss Trent had said during their earlier meeting with her. "Wasn't Mr Grosse married? He may have given the notebook and manuscript to his wife for safekeeping."

"I don't think he would of done."

"Because she's a woman?" Miss Webster challenged.

"Nah, 'cause 'e never let the notebook out of 'is sight," Mr Snyder retorted.

"Oh." Miss Webster downcast her eyes. "I apologise for assuming the worst of you."

"There's nowt to apologise for, lass." Mr Snyder had a warm twinkle in his eye as she met his gaze. "'E might of given her the manuscript, though, so no harm in askin."

* * *

"That was all Dr Weeks told us," Mr Skinner said. Standing in the hallway of the Society's house, he rested his iron hand in the pocket of his dark-grey overcoat. His other hung loosely at his side with a walking cane tucked under his arm. The sound of the grandfather clock chiming the hour distracted his gaze and, upon seeing it was three o'clock, he enquired, "Is there anyt'ing else you want me to do, Miss Trent? As the captain and Her Ladyship will be expectin' me back by four."

Miss Trent's face lifted with a smile whose warmth filled her eyes. "That's it for now, thank you. Will you be able to attend the meeting tonight?"

"I think so," Mr Skinner replied. Tucking the cane under his other arm, he offered his hand to Dr Colbert who stood beside him. "It was good workin' with you, Doctor."

"Thank you." Dr Colbert gave his hand a firm squeeze.

"Good afternoon to you both," Mr Skinner said, taking the cane from under his arm as he left.

"Should I also expect you at the meeting, Doctor?" Miss Trent enquired.

"I wouldn't miss it for the world," Dr Colbert replied in a flat tone. "I have my rounds at the hospital first, however."

Miss Trent's smile shrank into a polite one. "In that case, I mustn't keep you."

"No, but I must."

"Oh? And why is that?"

Dr Colbert glanced at the parlour and kitchen doors. "May we speak in your office?"

"Of course." Miss Trent led him there and, upon entering, indicated the vacant chair before her desk. "Please, sit." Taking the one behind, she rested her clasped hands upon the desk and leaned forward. "What's troubling you, Doctor?"

Having frowned at the sight of the wretched piece of furniture, Dr Colbert nonetheless sat upon it and proceeded to repeatedly shift his weight in a futile attempt to get comfortable. "The things Mr Skinner said Dr Weeks had told us were completely true. Mr Skinner failed to mention that he bribed Dr Weeks with a bottle of Irish whiskey to gain the information, however. So, regrettably, it falls to me to not only inform you of the fact but enquire what you intend to do about it—if anything."

Miss Trent parted her lips.

"May I also add that, given Dr Weeks' blatant addiction to alcohol, it was a highly irresponsible act on Mr Skinner's part."

"I agree."

"You do?" Dr Colbert searched her face.

"Yes." Miss Trent kept a rigid gaze upon him. "And I shall discipline Mr Skinner accordingly."

Dr Colbert looked from her, to the door, and back again as he reeled from the absoluteness of her reply and the definitiveness of her tone. "Good." He took a moment to reconsider his response and, finding he was indeed pleased with the outcome, gave a firm nod. "*Good.*" He stood.

"Did you try to stop Mr Skinner?"

"I did."

"How did he react?"

Dr Colbert frowned. "He snatched the bottle from me and said he was trying to get the answers we needed."

"Was there a reason why you didn't pursue the matter?"

Dr Colbert pictured Inspectors Lee and Woolfe. "I thought it futile given the circumstances and Mr Skinner's apparent determination to give Dr Weeks the bottle regardless of my feelings."

Miss Trent recalled several occasions when Dr Weeks had stubbornly continued to drink, particularly during Society meetings. It wasn't beyond the realm of possibility to think he would've found a way to get possession of the bottle even if Dr Colbert had confiscated it. Conceding the validity of his argument, she stood. "I understand."

"I'm glad you do," Dr Colbert retorted. Yet his thoughts soon returned to the surgeon swigging the whiskey as if it were water. "I fear he may be in a drunken stupor as we speak."

"Alas, there is no 'maybe' about it," Miss Trent said sadly. Recalling an instance during the recent Maxwell case when Dr Weeks failed to attend a meeting following a visit from Mr Skinner and Miss Webster, Miss Trent wondered if this was the first time the bribe had been given. Feeling her anger rise at the thought, she strode around the desk and held the door open. "Thank you for bringing it to my attention."

"My duty as a doctor gave me little choice." Dr Colbert joined her at the door. "Thank you for dealing with it so swiftly and judiciously. It's most pleasing to hear." As he uttered these final words, he was surprised to find he meant them.

THIRTEEN

Upon nearing *Linton's Tobacconists*, Miss Dexter was reminded of her father's warning never to smoke a cigarette. According to him, women who did have, in his words, "low morals." Having only seen men enjoying the activity—fellow Bow Street Society members, in fact— she pondered if this meant they, too, were amoral. Dr Weeks certainly was, but Mr Locke was a gentleman and so was above such things, wasn't he? Perplexed by her father's logic, and gripped by curiosity, she followed Mr Elliott into the otherwise forbidden establishment.

Shaped like a box, the already tiny shop was made smaller, still, by the wide counter dominating its right side. Its gas-lit, smoke-filled interior further increased the sense of confinement, resulting in an oppressive and unnerving atmosphere. Looking over her shoulder as they ventured further in, Miss Dexter was surprised by some empty chairs in the corner. Grateful they were unoccupied, she nonetheless wondered if they were used by customers smoking their purchases. Especially since shelves to their left and right were filled with a bewildering array of cigar, cigarette, and match boxes.

Returning her gaze forward, she followed Mr Elliott to the counter. Made from mahogany, it had a polished top and panelled sides. The former held two display cases of silver and brass snuff boxes, whilst the latter was adorned with colourful posters advertising Redford's and Nosegay tobaccos.

Faux marble pillars lined the top of a wide shelving unit behind the counter. Between each was a glass-fronted display cabinet containing colourful tins of tobacco. The unit held rows of earthenware jars whose shape reminded Miss Dexter of the vases used in urn burials. Though labelled and painted in strong yet singular colours, they struck her as rather plain compared to the other goods. Miss Dexter assumed the absence of festive adornments within the shop was to avoid them being accidentally ignited by customers.

"Good afternoon, sir. I'm Mr Elliott, a lawyer and member of the Bow Street Society. This is my fellow member, Miss Dexter, who is also an artist."

Miss Dexter smiled politely at the man behind the counter.

In his late-forties, he had dark-brown hair greying at the tips, alert hazel eyes, and a long, narrow nose. Though attired in white shirt and black trousers, waistcoat, and tie, much of his form was hidden by a cream apron tucked beneath his arms and tied in the middle of his back.

"Are you the proprietor?" Mr Elliott enquired.

"I am. Mr Anthony Linton."

The two men firmly shook hands.

A door at the rear of the shop opened, and a woman in her early twenties entered. Her nose and eyes held a familial resemblance to Mr Linton's, whilst her rich dark-brown hair was tied into a messy bun at the back of her head. The delicate curve of her face was mirrored by the collar of her shapeless sapphire-blue dress whose skirts were covered by an off-white apron tied around her waist.

"This is my daughter Tabitha," Mr Linton introduced. "Mr Elliott and Miss Dexter are from the Bow Street Society, love."

Tabitha's hazel eyes became bright with interest. Moving down the counter to join them, she ran her gaze over Mr Elliott several times as she rested an arm upon the countertop and lifted her bust with a squaring of her shoulders. In an unnaturally sounding middle-class accent, she greeted, "Good afternoon, sir."

"Good afternoon," Mr Elliott said, his voice and expression devoid of emotion. Turning to Mr Linton, he continued, "We've been informed a Mr Christian Grosse leases a room from you. Is that correct?"

"It is," Mr Linton replied. "'E does his private enquiry business from it, but I've not seen 'im today."

"His uncle was up there this mornin', though," Tabitha interjected with a coy smile.

"We know," Mr Elliott stated. "It's his commission that has brought us here."

Mr Linton and his daughter straightened in unison as concern filled their faces.

"Has somethin' befallen Mr Grosse?" Mr Linton enquired.

"I'm afraid it has," Mr Elliott replied. "He was found deceased this morning."

Tabitha gasped.

"An accident?" Mr Linton enquired, putting his arm around his daughter.

"Murder," Mr Elliott replied.

Tabitha softly cried out as she buried her face in her father's shoulder.

"This is not for your ears, love," Mr Linton said. "Go in the back."

"I must insist she stay," Mr Elliott said, prompting the pair to look at him with a mixture of anger and dismay. "Mr Voigt has commissioned the Bow Street Society to expose his nephew's murderer. It could be your daughter who holds the key to their identity."

Mr Linton and Tabitha exchanged concerned glances. Putting his arm around her again, Mr Linton said, "We understand." He gently rubbed her shoulder as sadness entered his voice and eyes. "Mr Voigt does right by gettin' the Society's help. The police can't even solve a simple housebreaking."

"Whose house was broken into?" Mr Elliott enquired.

"No one's, but someone was in Mr Grosse's office last night," Mr Linton replied. "I heard them movin' around in there, so I shouted a constable was bein' fetched, and they scarpered so quick, they broke a window that weren't even bolted."

"How awful," Miss Dexter said, shocked.

"Did you see their face?" Mr Elliott enquired.

"That I did not, sir." Mr Linton's face creased with regret. "From my window, I saw but a shadow go down the drainpipe and clamber over the wall."

Taking his notebook and pencil from his satchel, Mr Elliott wrote a brief record of the account.

"I expect you'll be wantin' to see Mr Grosse's office, sir?" Mr Linton ventured.

"Our fellow Society members, Mr Snyder and Miss Webster, are doing so as we speak," Mr Elliott replied.

Mr Linton and Tabitha simultaneously looked up.

"Did Mr Grosse often have visitors?" Mr Elliott enquired.

"Tabitha serves the customers most days," Mr Linton said, looking at her.

Wiping the underside of her nose with her knuckles, she gave a gentle sniff and returned her head to her father's shoulder. "He did, sir."

"Did he have any regular visitors?" Mr Elliott probed.

"Jus' the one, sir," Tabitha replied. "A friend of 'is."

"Do you know his name?" Mr Elliott probed further.

Tabitha's eyes looked down and to the left as she searched her memory. After a moment, she met Mr Elliott's gaze. "Spaldin'. Mr Osborne Spaldin'."

Mr Elliott wrote down the name. "Did Mr Grosse argue or disagree with any of his visitors?"

Tabitha lifted her head from her father's shoulder and nodded. "He had a right barney with an American gent the other day."

"Did you hear what was said?" Mr Elliott enquired.

"I did not, sir," Tabitha replied. "I could of if I'd lurked by the stairs, but I'm not that kind."

"How do you know he was American?" Miss Dexter enquired.

"He come in 'ere askin' where Mr Grosse was," Tabitha replied.

"How long did the argument last?" Mr Elliott enquired.

"Jus' a little while," Tabitha replied. "Then the American gent come down them stairs like a bull. 'E nearly knocked poor Osborne clear off 'is feet."

Miss Dexter retrieved her sketchbook and pencil from her satchel. "I'd like to draw Mr Spalding and the American gentleman's likenesses if I may? I need you to describe what they look like to me, though."

Mr Linton and Tabitha exchanged wary glances.

"They shan't know the information came from you," Mr Elliott reassured.

Mr Linton frowned. "I don't know, sir. I run a quiet and respectable business here."

"Will it 'elp find poor Mr Grosse's murderer?" Tabitha enquired.

"It might," Miss Dexter replied.

Tabitha looked to her father.

"Go ahead, love," Mr Linton said with a gentle smile.

Tabitha looked between Miss Dexter and Mr Elliott. Easing herself away from her father, she rested her hands upon the counter and calmed her nerves and grief by recalling the many happy hours she'd spent talking to Mr Grosse. Finally swallowing the last of her doubt, she said, "I'll tell you."

* * *

The sound of Christmas hymns drifted from St. Stephen's church as Inspector Woolfe stood before a grave in its well-tended yard. Dense clouds darkened the afternoon and threatened more snow, whilst the icy air chilled him despite his fur coat. Placing a cigarette between his lips and lighting it with a match, he coughed as its smoke filled his lungs. All the while, his gaze remained fixed upon the headstone. "Hannah Pottinger," he read aloud. "Twelfth of March 1850 to the twenty-third of October 1873." He took a second pull from his cigarette, prompting another cough. Wiping his mouth with his dirty sleeve afterward, he mused, "She was only twenty-three when she died." He glanced at the bare stone beneath the dates. "It's not much to show for a life, is it?"

"No," Constable Begg agreed, his hat in his hands. "But it's still more than what Mr Pottinger got."

"Where's he buried?"

Constable Begg looked beyond the far wall. "In the non-consecrated ground with the other suicides."

"Is that what the parish record said?"

"I couldn't find him in the records. Mr Reynolds, the old church warden, told me where he was."

"You shouldn't make a judgement on no evidence." Inspector Woolfe headed for the gate.

"But why else would Mr Pottinger be put over there?" Constable Begg hurried after him.

"Murder."

Constable Begg came to an abrupt halt. "*Murder*?"

FOURTEEN

Miss Webster checked the house number against the address given by Mr Linton. *17 Glyn Road, Homerton, Borough of Hackney,* she read. "This is it," she announced, slipping the note into her pocket.

Part of a terraced row, Mr Grosse's house was in a fairly good state of repair. Spotless rectangular bay windows on the ground and first floors were framed by smooth, wide stonework and pillars. Thick curtains barred one's view of the interior, but even from where she stood, Miss Webster could see they were made from heavy, plum damask. Though marred by the damp weather and unavoidable soot in the air, the house's brickwork had also retained its distinguished appearance. As she led Miss Dexter into the small front garden, surrounded by a waist-high brick wall, she noted its bare, yet well-tended flowerbeds and pots. The path and front step, adorned in a brown and cream geometric mosaic, were also worthy of approval. Her expectations were high when she used her umbrella's handle to tap thrice upon the front door.

Several moments passed.

"Maybe she isn't home?" Miss Dexter suggested when no one came to the door. "I can imagine the news of her husband's death was terribly upsetting. Maybe she's decided to stay with friends?"

"The lamps are lit," Miss Webster replied.

Peering through the door's stained-glass window, past the black wreath that hung there, Miss Dexter saw the yellow glow of wall-mounted gas lamps in the hall beyond.

Miss Webster tapped thrice a second time.

Several more moments passed and again, no one answered.

"We should—" Miss Dexter began.

"*Shush*," Miss Webster interrupted with a lifting of her hand.

Miss Dexter clamped her mouth shut.

"I can hear someone crying," Miss Webster whispered as she put her ear to the door.

Miss Dexter crept forward and, turning her head, leaned in close to the stained-glass window. She whispered, "Mrs Grosse?"

"There is only one way to find out." Miss Webster turned the knob and pushed the door ajar.

Miss Dexter put her hand upon Miss Webster's arm as she moved to enter. She whispered, "I don't think we should go in."

"We need to know if she has her husband's notebook or manuscript," Miss Webster whispered back. Their remaining search of his office had only uncovered some banknotes hidden beneath a floorboard. "Besides, if she's distraught, she may need someone to comfort her."

Miss Dexter frowned but nonetheless released Miss Webster's arm. Nibbling her lower lip as she followed her inside, she closed the door and listened. The sound was coming from upstairs but now they could hear it clearly, they realised it was something else entirely.

"She's laughing…" Miss Dexter whispered, deeply perturbed, as all manner of thoughts whirled through her mind. Feeling a tightening in her stomach as the pounding of her heart filled her ears, she retreated to the door. "We must leave."

Miss Webster looked toward the stairs.

"*At once*," Miss Dexter urged.

Yet, Miss Webster crept forward.

"*Agnes*!" Miss Dexter cried, struggling to keep her voice to a whisper.

Miss Webster held the handrail and slowly climbed the stairs until she could peer through the balustrades onto the landing. Several items of clothing, including a dress and some trousers, were strewn across the floor. The trail led through an open doorway to a large, brass-framed bed. With its head against the wall, Miss Webster had a direct view of its occupant.

A woman in her thirties was lying upon her back, her naturally frizzy strawberry-blond hair sprawled across the pillows. Her otherwise fair complexion was flushed a bright pink as her brown eyes darted left and right, drinking in the sight of another hidden by the half-open door. Reaching out, she put her arms around them and pulled them closer as she arched her back to press her naked breasts against their body.

When her bedfellow came into view, Miss Webster saw it was a man in his mid-thirties with unkempt chocolate-brown hair, a bushy moustache, and green eyes. His biceps were unusually large as he put his arms around the woman and, lifting her from the bed, held her against him as he kissed her with a demanding passion.

Returning it in equal measure, the woman moaned softly and ran her fingers through his hair and over his back. The man shifted, and she released a sharp cry of pleasure, prompting Miss Webster to look away. The rapid creaking of the bed that followed convinced her it was time to leave, and she hurried down the stairs as quietly as she could. Grabbing hold of Miss Dexter as she passed, she led her outside and back to Mr Snyder's cab, pausing only to close the door as they went.

* * *

An explosion of pain in his head greeted Dr Weeks as he emerged from unconsciousness. Feeling a dull ache in his limbs at the same time, he forced his eyes open only to close them at the sight of the gas light. He groaned and slowly rolled onto his side, his body feeling like a lead weight. The sudden coldness against his cheek was a reminder that he'd passed out on a marble slab in his Dead Room. Rubbing his face, he contemplated getting up or drinking some more. He felt around the slab and, finding the bottle, sighed as he saw it was empty. "*Shit.*"

"You're finally awake, I see," a voice sardonically remarked.

Dr Weeks sat bolt upright, knocking the bottle onto the floor

Inspector Lee was sitting behind the desk, watching him with a cool expression.

"Ya nearly gave me a heart attack," Dr Weeks growled.

"You're certainly in the right place to die from one." Inspector Lee stood.

Dr Weeks glared at him. "What do ya want?"

"All in good time." Inspector Lee reached into his coat as he approached. "First, there's this." He pulled out a sheet of paper and dropped it into Dr Weeks' lap.

"What is it?" Dr Weeks picked it up.

The moment he read it, he felt the hair on the back of his neck and arms lift. A shiver swept through his body at the same time, leaving a lightheaded, trembling sensation in its wake. He read the first line again, unable to process what he was seeing as a sense of impending doom grew within his chest. "Where did ya get this?"

"The Toronto police kindly procured it for me after I discovered the identity of the Society's client in the Cosgrove case." Inspector Lee plucked the paper from Dr Weeks' grasp and, strolling around the slab, read aloud, "Percival Michael Weeks. Born: Twelfth of December 1867 in Toronto in the Ontario province of Canada. Mother: Evangelina Breckenridge."

As Inspector Lee approached him from the other side, Dr Weeks slid back and drew his knees up to his chest. Gripping the edge of the slab with one hand, he felt his body turn cold as the blood drained from his face.

"Father: Lord Michael Weeks."

Inspector Lee turned the page of the parish record around and shoved it into Dr Weeks' face, forcing him to lean backward. "You're a bastard child of the aristocracy."

"Don't say that!" Dr Weeks snarled, failing miserably to push him away.

Inspector Lee stepped back and, folding the document, slipped it into his jacket. Retrieving a second from the other side, he turned it around for Dr Weeks to read. "The Toronto police were also kind enough to find the midwife who delivered you. This is her sworn statement." He smirked. "In case there is any doubt over the parish record's validity. I would've preferred a certificate, but births weren't formally registered in Ontario province until 1869." Folding the statement, he put it with the record. "Nevertheless, your parentage certainly explains much of your behaviour."

Dr Weeks bowed and turned his head away.

"The drunkenness. The rudeness," Inspector Lee continued. As he closed the distance between them, Dr Weeks swung his legs over the side of the slab and turned his back upon him. Yet, Inspector Lee rested his hands upon the slab and, leaning forward, enquired softly into his ear, "How does it feel, carrying the burden of your mother's shame?"

Dr Weeks dropped his chin to his chest as pain filled his eyes.

"Knowing your father never wanted you?" Inspector Lee added.

Dr Weeks turned his head away with a grimace as his eyes became wet with tears.

Inspector Lee straightened, prompting Dr Weeks to turn his head forward and rub at his eyes with the heel of his trembling hand. In a voice strained with emotion, he feebly retorted, "Ya don't know shit."

"I know you don't want your shame exposed to the world," Inspector Lee replied, firmly. "And you certainly don't want the world to know that you were conceived as a result of a scandalous liaison between an errant actress and married aristocrat."

"What do ya want from me, ya heartless sonofabitch?"

Inspector Lee smiled. "Just a small errand, that is all."

Dr Weeks lifted his head. "What kinda errand?"

"I want you to procure a Bow Street Society envelope from Miss Trent's office and deliver it to me."

"I ain't a damn member."

"You were seen leaving the Society house during the Maxwell murder case."

"That don't mean I'm a member."

"True, but it could be the final nail in the coffin for your commission with the Yard."

Dr Weeks' eyes narrowed. "What do ya want a Society envelope for anyway?"

"To keep it for my own reference. Since they are involved in so many of our cases, I think it would be wise for us to be able to identify their correspondence," Inspector Lee replied in an innocent tone that matched his unobtrusive expression. Naturally, he'd considered putting a request to Dr Colbert for his envelope. Yet, if his plan were to go awry, Inspector Lee didn't want to risk Dr Colbert naming him as the envelope's secondary recipient to Miss Trent, Inspector Woolfe, or anyone else.

Dr Weeks glanced at Inspector Lee's jacket. "And ya'll give me the record and statement if I get it?"

"You have my word."

Dr Weeks bowed his head and wiped his eyes as he considered the offer. After several moments had passed, he said, "Fine." He held out his hand, "Ya got yerself a deal."

"Excellent." Inspector Lee gave his hand a firm squeeze. "I knew you'd see reason in the end."

FIFTEEN

Hearing the hall clock chime the quarter hour, Miss Trent checked her pocket watch: seven forty-five. She glanced over the meeting room and counted the chairs. Satisfied there would be enough, she left the room and headed for the kitchen to prepare the tea and coffee pots. As soon as she went inside, though, a knock on the front door pulled her back. Wiping her hands upon her apron, she strode past the stairs and unlocked the door.

"You made it," she remarked upon opening it.

"Yeah." Dr Weeks stepped inside. "Why wouldn't I?"

Miss Trent put her hands upon her hips and lofted a brow.

"Okay, yeah," Dr Weeks conceded, as he recalled at least one occasion when the drink had kept him away. "Jus' gimmie some coffee, and I'll be fine."

Miss Trent smirked. "I was about to serve it."

She returned her gaze to the door as a woman in her late-twenties entered. Her loosely curled, blond hair was pinned into a mass upon her crown with red flower-tipped pins. The cold night air had tinged her cheeks and nose pink, accentuating their delicateness. She flashed Miss Trent a smile that warmed her eyes. In an East-End-of-London accent, she greeted, "Hello, Becky."

"Polly." Miss Trent closed the door. "Make yourselves comfortable." She indicated the meeting room's open doorway. "The others should be here soon."

Miss Polly Hicks removed her ankle-length brown coat and passed it to Dr Weeks to hang on the hat stand with his own. The remainder of her attire consisted of a dark-red silk bustle dress with a low, square neckline and intricate beaded decoration. The severe curve of her waist and lift of her compacted bust hinted at the corset beneath, whilst her heeled boots gave an additional inch to her five feet seven inches in height.

Standing behind her, Dr Weeks ran his hands slowly up and down her sides.

"I'll fetch your coffee," Miss Trent said in a flat tone.

Dr Weeks kissed Polly's neck as he watched the clerk go into the kitchen. "Ya should help her with that."

Polly turned and wrapped her arms about his neck. Pressing her body against his, she grinned. "I'm not goin' anywhere, love."

Releasing a soft grunt as he felt a certain part of his anatomy stir, he took her hands and gently lowered them. "Ya heard her; we ain't gonna be alone fer much longer."

Miss Hicks pouted. "You're a bloody tease, Perce."

"Don't worry…" He lifted her chin. "I'll make up fer it later." He kissed her.

Closing her eyes as she gripped the lapel of his jacket, Miss Hicks savoured every moment before reluctantly allowing him to pull away. "I'll hold you to that, love."

"I hope ya do." Dr Weeks turned her around and gave her behind a playful smack. "Now, go help yer friend."

Miss Hicks put her hands upon her hips and cast a playful glare across her shoulder at him. "You'll be the death of me."

Dr Weeks winked at her.

Rolling her eyes but smiling nonetheless, she went into the kitchen.

As soon as she was out of sight, Dr Weeks moved quickly into Miss Trent's office and searched it for an envelope with the Society's distinctive 'B' in the corner. Hearing a sudden knock on the front door, he lunged to close the one to the office. He held his breath as he listened. Skirts rustled past and, a moment later, Miss Hicks' voice greeted the newcomer.

"Oh, good evening," Dr Colbert's voice greeted in return. "Is Miss Trent at home? She has invited me to attend the Bow Street Society's meeting."

"That she is, sir," Miss Hicks replied in the most upper-class voice she could muster.

Dr Weeks covered his mouth to muffle his chuckle.

"I'm Dr Neal Colbert of Bethlehem Hospital. I've recently joined the Society. Are you also a member, Miss…?"

"Polly Hicks, sir. I am. I'm also an old mate of Miss Trent's."

"Where might I find her?"

"In the kitchen. She's just finishing off the tea and coffee, but if you'd like to go into the meeting room over there, she'll be with you shortly."

"Thank you, Miss Hicks."

"You're most welcome, sir."

Dr Weeks heard the rustling of skirts as she returned to the kitchen.

Creeping over to the desk, Dr Weeks tried to open its top drawer but found it wouldn't budge. Releasing a soft sigh, he gave it several tugs but, still, it remained in place. Attempting to open the remaining two drawers, he cursed under his breath upon discovering they were also locked. "Damn piece of *shit*," he muttered, violently shaking the middle drawer.

"What the devil are you doing, man?"

Dr Weeks simultaneously released the desk, straightened, and looked sharply toward the door with wide eyes. He took several steps back under Dr Colbert's disapproving gaze. "Nothin'."

"It looked to me like you were mistreating Miss Trent's property."

"I were lookin' for somethin', actually."

"In Miss Trent's desk?" Dr Colbert probed with sceptical eyes.

"Yeah." Dr Weeks moved around the desk to join him. "An envelope. I, uh, got a letter to send to my mom in Canada."

Dr Colbert considered the answer and concluded it wasn't beyond reason. Especially since Dr Weeks had undoubtedly boasted of his Bow Street Society work to his family. "Couldn't you have asked Miss Trent for one?"

"Nah. She don't like givin' anythin' away."

Dr Colbert hummed. "Indeed." He took the code book from his jacket and pulled the envelope from between its pages. "Here. Have mine."

Dr Weeks blinked but then smiled broadly as he took it. "Thanks." He momentarily held it up. "This'll impress my mom." He leaned in close as he tucked it into his jacket. "I'd appreciate it if ya didn't say anythin' 'bout this to Miss Trent."

Dr Colbert considered the request but, upon balance, thought it harmless enough. "Very well. My lips are sealed."

SIXTEEN

The scent of fresh ivy filled Dr Colbert's nose as he looked down the table at his fellow Bow Street Society members. The mantel shelf behind him had been adorned with a garland of the plant as a subtle reminder that Christmas Day was fast approaching. Other than this, the meeting room was as formal as any other.

Beside him were Mr Skinner and Dr Weeks on his left and right respectively. A momentary reconsideration of the Irishman's character in light of the whiskey incident failed to convince him he was a wolf in sheep's clothing. If anything, he believed it had been a case of the right intention being deployed through the wrong method. He was confident Mr Skinner wouldn't repeat his mistake once Miss Trent had brought his attention to it. Alas, Dr Weeks remained a source of great sorrow to him. A stay in the asylum could help win the battle with his addiction, but Dr Colbert doubted Dr Weeks would permit such a thing.

Cabmen had a reputation for being roughly spoken, difficult, and confrontational at times. Their vehicle's design also meant they could watch their passengers without drawing attention to themselves. Young women were particularly vulnerable to a cabman's wandering eye, or so Dr Colbert had heard. Yet, the warmth Mr Snyder had shown him upon their meeting had taken him off-guard. Although his voice was rough, Mr Snyder's words had been good-natured, and his demeanour placid. With regards to his physical characteristics, the only ones Dr Colbert could consider sub-par were the leather-like appearance of his skin and wiry follicles of his beard and sideburns. The former, he concluded, was likely a result of his working conditions, whilst the latter hinted at a poor diet. Neither gave him cause to believe Mr Snyder was anything other than what he seemed to be: a gentle soul.

Miss Dexter, Miss Webster, and Miss Hicks' presence wasn't entirely welcome. Given the violent nature of Mr

Grosse's death, Dr Colbert thought it hardly appropriate to allow the women to hear the grisly details. Several of his patients at the asylum were female and, as such, were more susceptible to disturbances of the mind. Whether they be caused by shock, hysteria, or an emotional imbalance. Miss Hicks had undoubtedly witnessed violence whilst serving in pubs, but he was adamant the same couldn't be said for Miss Webster, a secretary, and Miss Dexter, an artist.

He looked to Miss Trent at the head of the table, reminding himself of the responsibility she'd been given. He had to concede, then, that she must be in possession of an uncommonly strong fortitude for her sex. *A strength she had seen in Miss Dexter, Miss Webster, and Miss Hicks, perhaps?* He pushed his lower lip against his upper as he gave an unconscious nod. *It's certainly a possibility.*

They, and all thoughts of them, vanished the moment his gaze shifted to Mr Elliott, however. He'd only seen such a flawless complexion in the paintings of the great masters. Indeed, Mr Elliott was a Renaissance Era prince made flesh. There were no hints of villainy in his physical characteristics, only beauty. *An honest man to a fault, perhaps*, Dr Colbert mused. Rubbing his arm beneath the table as he continued to drink in Mr Elliott's visage, he recalled their introduction. He'd been rendered speechless when he'd looked upon him. A reaction that Mr Elliott had met with little show of emotion. Even his voice had lacked vigour. The revelation of Dr Colbert's position at the asylum had also garnered an equally unenthused response. Afterward, Miss Trent had reassured him it was simply Mr Elliott's nature. Yet, he couldn't believe it. No man with breath in his body was devoid of emotion. Mr Elliott just kept his buried, for whatever reason, and he was determined to find out why.

Suddenly realising that he was leaning toward a favourable assessment of the Society and its members, Dr Colbert felt astonished and perturbed in equal measure. Although the members' behaviour and characteristics made them appear harmless, the truth was they *were* harmful. Not because of what they said or did but because the Society itself existed. Furthermore, their disarming friendliness was precisely what made them so dangerous. One never recognised the Devil when he was thrust before one for that very reason. He resolved to strengthen his guard in future and inwardly renewed his vow to rid London of the Society's menace.

"Before we begin, I'd like to thank you for your discretion today," Miss Trent said. "Mr Maxwell has been confronted with enough horror during his father's trial, he doesn't need to worry about Mr Grosse's murder, too."

"How is he?" Miss Dexter softly enquired as she leaned forward.

"He's coping," Miss Trent reassured. "And with our support, he'll get through this."

"I hope that sonofabitch Da of 'is gets strung up," Dr Weeks remarked.

"As do we all," Miss Webster said.

"Does he know about the meeting?" Mr Elliott enquired.

"No," Miss Trent replied. "He's currently dining at his brother's home. So far, I've managed to keep him in the dark about the Grosse case."

"I think that's wise," Mr Elliott said.

"I agree," Dr Colbert interjected.

"Why?" Mr Elliott challenged. "You hardly know the man." He glanced around the table. "Unlike the rest of us."

"That's true," Dr Colbert said, calmly. "But I've seen the damage such horrific events can do to a man's mind. Mr Maxwell needs time and space to heal from the murder of his wife and suicide of his mother before he can be safely exposed to more violence."

"My thoughts exactly," Mr Elliott stated in a cool tone.

Dr Colbert couldn't help but smile.

"But do not mistake Mr Maxwell for one of your patients," Mr Elliott warned.

Dr Colbert's smile vanished.

"He's a dear friend of ours and a good man besides," Mr Elliott added.

"I shall treat him with the utmost respect," Dr Colbert said. "You have my word."

"Thank you," Mr Elliott said, his monotone momentarily softening.

"May I remind you Dr Colbert is a part of this Society like everyone else in this room," Miss Trent said. "His brief membership doesn't make him any less capable."

"You're right," Mr Elliott said. "I apologise if I offended you, Doctor."

"You didn't." Again, Dr Colbert couldn't help but smile.

Miss Trent opened her notebook and said in an authoritative tone, "Mr Christian Eckhart Grosse, to give him his full name, was found at eight o'clock this morning in a disused warehouse at the Import Dock of the West India Docks by an officer of their private police force. The discovery was subsequently reported to a patrolling constable of the Metropolitan Police's Stepney Division."

"It would be helpful to see the place for ourselves," Mr Elliott said. "I should think the police have completed their scrutiny of the area by now, and the responsibility of the docks' security returned to the private force. I recommend Dr Weeks accompany Miss Dexter to the exact spot where Mr Grosse was found so she may capture some photographs of it."

"I shall do my best," Miss Dexter said with a small smile.

Dr Weeks glared at Mr Elliott.

"I agree," Miss Trent said, prompting Dr Weeks to shift his glare to her. "Mr Skinner, Mr Snyder, I'd like you to go with them."

"Fine by me, lass," Mr Snyder said.

"Sure t'ing," Mr Skinner said. "I want to talk to the fella who found Mr Grosse, too. Them private police forces make it easier to get into Buckingham Palace than

149

the docks. If the fella let Mr Grosse in, he would've been paid for his trouble."

"Dr Weeks?" Miss Trent looked at him with expectant eyes.

Dr Weeks' glare eased as he considered the potential risk to his already tenuous commission with the Yard. Concluding Mr Elliott was right—much to his annoyance—he straightened and momentarily lifted his hand as he leaned back in his chair. "Yeah, okay."

"Thank you," Miss Trent said. "Detective Inspector George Pilker of Scotland Yard has been assigned to investigate. Aside from Dr Weeks, have any of you met him?"

"No," Mr Skinner replied as the others murmured the same or shook their heads.

"Should we expect the usual unfriendliness from him?" Miss Webster enquired with distaste.

"'E ain't gonna like ya'll pokin' yer noses into 'is case, if that's what ya mean," Dr Weeks replied.

"The intolerance of the police is becoming tiresome," Miss Webster said. "Surely by now we have proven our intentions are honourable?"

"With all due respect, regardless of the Society's intentions, it remains a group of civilians taking an interest in matters which, legally, they have no right to interfere with," Dr Colbert said. "The police are simply doing their job."

"If that were true, there would be no need for the Society," Miss Webster said.

"One could argue there is no need for the Society even now," Dr Colbert said.

"Enough," Miss Trent ordered, drawing everyone's attention to her. "We are here to investigate the murder of Mr Grosse, *not* debate the Society's role in law and order. Dr Colbert, Miss Webster, whilst I respect your views on the police's continued hostility toward us, they hold no relevance to our current discussion. Please, keep them to yourselves."

"As you wish," Miss Webster muttered through a semi-clenched jaw as she turned her head away.

"Of course," Dr Colbert said softly. "Forgive me."

"Forgiveness isn't required," Miss Trent said. "Focus is."

Miss Webster's facial muscles were rigid as she sipped her tea.

"I shall make Detective Inspector Pilker aware of our involvement in his case by the usual means," Miss Trent said.

Dr Colbert parted his lips to enquire what these "means" were but thought better of it.

"Please give us your findings, Dr Weeks," Miss Trent invited.

Drinking the remainder of his coffee, the Canadian put the cup down with a thud as he opened the file in front of him. "Grosse died 'cause of fractures to 'is skull caused by blows to the top of 'is head inflicted by what I reckon were a life preserver, but the weapon ain't been found, so I can't say for sure."

"Pardon me, Doctor, but what is a 'life preserver?'" Miss Dexter enquired.

"It's similar to a club," Mr Elliott replied.

"But made by tying a large ball of lead to a cane with catgut," Dr Colbert added.

Miss Dexter tried to envision it. "That sounds awful."

"Nevertheless, it's an easily concealed defensive weapon," Mr Elliott said. "As a consequence, it's favoured amongst plain-clothed police officers."

"Perfect for sneakin' into a warehouse full of people," Mr Skinner mused aloud.

"As I were sayin'," Dr Weeks continued in a hard tone. "'Is skull had a fracture at its base that I reckon were caused by the force of the first blow. This also bent the outer table of 'is skull, causin' fractures to form 'round the wound like the legs of a spider. It also sent a bone fragment into 'is head. The second blow were hard enough to shatter both the inner and outer tables of 'is skull." Dr

Weeks cast his gaze around the table. "This weren't an attack done in anger. If it were, I would've expected to see more blows by the life preserver and 'is skull lookin' like a smashed eggshell."

"A delightful image," Dr Colbert mumbled in an ironic tone before sipping his tea.

"His attacker could have been disturbed," Mr Elliott said.

"But even then, ya would've seen more than two blows," Dr Weeks said. "If yer angry, ya go in hard and fast." He repeatedly struck the table to illustrate his point. "Ya don't hit 'im once, stop, and hit 'im again."

"And that is what you suspect happened?" Mr Elliott enquired.

"Yeah," Dr Weeks replied. "Someone wanted 'im dead, but they weren't willin' to go beyond that."

"Given your expertise in matters of the mind, what is your opinion, Dr Colbert?" Mr Elliott enquired.

"Oh." Dr Colbert gave a weak smile and felt the back of his neck warm under Mr Elliott's gaze. "Well, I would agree with Dr Weeks. The two blows certainly seem to hint at a measured, calculating mind, rather than a violent madman."

"Perhaps," Mr Elliott said. "I shall reserve my judgement."

"Mr Grosse died between five and six this mornin'." Dr Weeks cast a glare at Mr Elliott. "But there were a lot of leakage from 'is skull, so I reckon that were done between midnight and two. There were bruisin' on 'is jaw, cheeks, temple, stomach, back, and between 'is ribs and breastbone. Some of 'is ribs were fractured, and 'e had bruisin' to 'is liver and kidneys. All this suggests 'e were in a fight that I reckon happened a coupla hours *maximum* before 'e were hit by the life preserver."

He closed the file and tossed it onto the table before taking a cigarette from his pocket and placing it in the corner of his mouth. "Ain't no way of knowin' from 'is corpse if 'e were in the fight at the warehouse." He lit the cigarette with a match. "But I reckon that's where 'e died." Shaking out the match, he tossed it into his cup as he took a deep pull.

"Do the police know why Mr Grosse was at the warehouse?" Mr Elliott enquired.

"If they do, they ain't told me," Dr Weeks replied, exhaling the smoke toward the fire.

"He could of been meetin' someone," Mr Snyder suggested.

"Maybe the docks' private police officer," Mr Skinner added.

"It's possible," Mr Elliott said. "Especially if we discover Mr Grosse was investigating thefts at the docks."

"He wasn't that sort of private enquiry agent," Mr Snyder said.

"What 'sort' was he?" Mr Elliott enquired.

Mr Snyder leaned forward and rested his folded arms upon the table. "Mr Grosse was well-known by the Fancy for 'is hat. 'E was also the bloke you went to if you wanted a good man to face in the ring. 'E'd get owt worth knowin' 'bout anyone; 'is life, 'is work, and 'is fights."

"And he would be paid for it?" Dr Colbert enquired.

"That's what I've been told," Mr Snyder replied.

"A broker of information," Mr Elliott said.

Mr Snyder scratched his cheek. "You could say that."

"The cupboards in his office were filled with files on the lives and fight records of numerous boxers, both past and present," Miss Webster said as she retrieved two such files from her satchel and placed them upon the table. "Including this one about the brief career of one John 'The Bulldog' Conway."

"That name seems familiar somehow," Dr Colbert remarked, furrowing his brow.

"It regularly appears in the newspapers," Mr Elliott said.

Miss Trent pursed her lips as she watched him pick up the file and examine its contents. Although she'd read them for herself prior to the meeting, she knew Mr

Elliott's long-standing dislike of her friend could prove problematic. She exchanged concerned glances with Mr Snyder. They'd discussed withholding the file but had decided it would be pointless since Miss Webster had already seen it.

"Is he a criminal?" Dr Colbert enquired.

"Some would certainly think so," Mr Elliott coolly stated, thinking of Mr Dorsey.

"Not me," Dr Weeks said, glaring at him.

"I said 'some,'" Mr Elliott pointed out.

"He's a detective inspector at Scotland Yard," Miss Trent clarified.

"A *damn* good one," Dr Weeks interjected.

"Who's engaged in illegal boxing?" Dr Colbert enquired, stunned.

Miss Trent and Mr Snyder exchanged another glance.

"Not anymore," the latter replied.

"Allegedly," Miss Webster said.

"What do you mean?" Mr Elliott enquired.

"I suggest you ask Mr Snyder," Miss Webster replied, looking to the cabman.

"Conway ain't boxin' anymore," Mr Snyder said.

"But he was and recently," Miss Webster said. "Was it during his suspension?"

"Does it matter?" Dr Weeks challenged.

"What makes you think it was recent?" Mr Elliott enquired.

"Mr Snyder practically told me in Mr Grosse's office," Miss Webster replied.

Mr Elliott looked to the cabman with expectant eyes.

"Conway ain't boxin' anymore," Mr Snyder repeated in a firm tone.

Mr Elliott and Miss Webster exchanged displeased glances.

"To answer your question, Dr Colbert," Miss Trent began, drawing their attention to her. "Detective Inspector Conway has worked closely with the Society in the past and is assigned the task of keeping an eye on us for the

Metropolitan Police. He'll also give Detective Inspector Pilker the list of members who I've assigned to investigate Mr Grosse's murder."

"Does he share his colleagues' attitude toward the Society?" Dr Colbert enquired.

"He tolerates us," Mr Elliott replied. "And we tolerate him."

"Don't presume to speak for the rest of us," Miss Webster warned.

"Yeah," Dr Weeks added.

"The man beats his prisoners," Mr Elliott said, anger breaking through his monotone.

"*One*," Dr Weeks countered,

"That we know of," Mr Elliott said.

"The word of a madman ain't proof," Dr Weeks said, narrowing his eyes.

"I would beg to differ," Dr Colbert interjected. "In some cases, at least."

"Inspector Conway has shown me nothing but kindness," Miss Dexter said.

"You've never been his prisoner," Mr Elliott countered.

"And nor have you," Miss Trent stated, catching Mr Elliott off-guard. "Dr Colbert, as you've heard, Inspector Conway is something of a controversial figure within our group. You'll have to form your own opinion."

Dr Colbert gave a weak smile. "I intend to."

"Good," Miss Trent said. "Let's move on."

"There is *one* piece of noteworthy information in the inspector's file," Mr Elliott said.

"I'm aware of it," Miss Trent said.

"What is it?" Dr Colbert enquired.

"That I won a prize fight against Conway in 1869," Mr Snyder said. "'E wasn't a copper back then, though."

"I thought you were a peaceful man, Mr Snyder," Mr Elliott remarked.

"Me, too," Miss Dexter interjected as she stared at the cabman, stunned.

"I am," Mr Snyder said. "I love the art, not the violence, of boxin'."

"And, like Inspector Conway, he is retired from the ring," Miss Trent pointed out.

Relief washed over Miss Dexter's face. "I'm sorry I doubted you, Sam."

"It's forgotten, lass," Mr Snyder reassured.

"Is the other file yours?" Dr Colbert enquired.

"No, I've not got one." Mr Snyder opened the file as he stood and put it in the middle of the table. "This is Deon Erskine's." He tapped the photograph. "That's 'im."

The others also stood and, whilst his fellow Bow Streeters studied the photograph and fight record, Mr Elliott picked up the telegram. "Sent by the *Amateur Athletic Union of the United States of America*, it reads: 'Since 1888, our records show Deon Erskine has not participated in any of our contests. Stop.'" Mr Elliott passed the telegram to Dr Colbert. "Why was this file of greater interest than the others?"

"It was in 'is desk," Mr Snyder replied.

"There was no other reason?" Mr Elliott enquired.

Mr Snyder gave a one-sided shoulder shrug. "Not that I saw."

"But you suspect Mr Erskine may have been the reason for Mr Grosse's visit to the warehouse?" Mr Elliott enquired.

"Him or another fighter," Mr Snyder replied. "Boxin's got sumthin' to do with it somewhere."

"The private police officer could've givin' him information about someone he'd worked with," Mr Skinner said. "Someone new to the ring."

"It's possible," Mr Elliott said.

"What else did you discover at Mr Grosse's office?" Dr Colbert enquired.

"His shoes, hat, handkerchief, cufflinks, pocket watch, and money had been arranged upon his desk," Miss Webster replied.

"Where Mr Voigt said he'd found them earlier," Miss Trent interjected.

"The bottom pane of the sash window was also partially broken," Miss Webster said. "I found some glass on the outside ledge and in the yard. What I assumed to be blood was smeared upon the edge of the glass that remained."

"Someone had also used a jemmy on the door and knackered the frame," Mr Snyder added.

"Mr Linton told us he'd heard someone moving around in Mr Grosse's office last night," Mr Elliott said. "He shouted through the wall that a constable had been fetched, and the trespasser broke a window and escaped down the drainpipe. Although he didn't see their face, Mr Linton saw their silhouette climbing down. Yet, Mr Grosse's belongings remained on the desk. A thief usually takes something for his trouble, even when disturbed."

"The window was unbolted, but he still smashed it," Miss Webster said. "That suggests he was too frightened to think clearly."

"It does, but humans are creatures of habit," Dr Colbert said. "Even if his fear prevented him from having the presence of mind to steal the pocket watch and cufflinks, the money would've held a value so obvious, he would've taken it out of instinct if nothing else."

"So, what ya'll sayin'? Someone broke into 'is office to put 'is things inside?" Dr Weeks enquired.

"Well now." Dr Colbert folded his arms and strummed his chin as he considered the question. "That *is* an intriguing hypothesis."

"It don't make any damn sense to me." Dr Weeks crushed out his cigarette in his cup.

"It does if one considers the possibility that it was a friend of his," Mr Elliott said.

"Or that they wasn't lookin' for money," Mr Snyder suggested.

All eyes turned to him as the others returned to their seats.

"But what of the money we found under the floorboard?" Miss Webster enquired.

"They would of found that before they'd scarpered," Mr Snyder replied.

"Not if Mr Linton had disturbed them first," Miss Webster said.

"We found it easy enough," Mr Snyder said in a casual tone.

"What do you think they were looking for?" Mr Elliott enquired.

"There's been a rumour goin' 'round for years that Grosse was writin' a book 'bout the history of boxin' in London. That's what I think all 'is files was for. Erskine's, too," Mr Snyder replied. "But…" He lowered his voice and leaned further forward, prompting the others to do the same. "What 'e was proper known for in the Fancy was 'is notebook. He never let a soul see it, but most think it's got every fight 'e's ever been a party to, bareknuckle *and* the mitten kind. Dates of fights, names of the boxers and their backers, the results, places where the set-to's happened, monies that was won, the fights that was fixed by 'im and others—*everythin'*. That's what I think they was looking for."

"Those who engage in so-called 'bareknuckle' boxing are guilty of assault in English law," Mr Elliott said. "Those who encourage such activities are aiding and abetting a criminal act. Those who spectate may find themselves put before a magistrate under a charge of illegal assembly. In short, prize fighting is illegal and has been, in one form or another, since the first part of this century."

"Yeah, but it still got the crowds in," Mr Snyder said. "Back in my day, you had the sharps and the flats puttin' the sport to shame, but there was still some who wanted to make it respectable. Now, it's just all 'bout the coin and soft fightin' with the mittens."

"It doesn't change the illegality of it all," Mr Elliott said.

"Where's this notebook now?" Dr Weeks enquired. "'Cause it weren't on 'is body."

"We don't know," Miss Webster replied. "It wasn't in his office, either. Nor was the manuscript for his book."

"Between the two, the notebook has the most potential as a damning piece of evidence in the prosecution of fighters and their backers who are, or have been, involved with illegal bareknuckle boxing. Whilst the numbers may be few and far between these days, those involved would want to avoid their names coming to the attention of the police and magistrates. Especially if a great deal of money is involved as you suggest, Mr Snyder, and the backers are otherwise respectable members of high society.

"With regards to the book, given Mr Grosse's rumoured intention for it, I'm going to assume it was written as an historical account with all references to illegal activities removed."

"Nevertheless, we should find it, still," Miss Webster stated.

"I agree." Mr Elliott said.

"Keepin' their name from a beak's ears is a good reason for wantin' the poor fella dead," Mr Skinner said.

"It is," Mr Elliott agreed. "And with that in mind, Inspector Conway should also be considered a suspect. If not for Mr Grosse's murder, then certainly for his beating."

"*Bullshit*," Dr Weeks growled.

"Not when one considers his brief participation in the sport," Mr Elliott stated.

"By that logic, one must also consider Mr Snyder a suspect," Dr Colbert pointed out.

"Mr Snyder's employment isn't threatened by his past boxing career," Mr Elliott said. "Whereas Inspector Conway, who was recently suspended from the police—"

"For helpin' ya'll out," Dr Weeks interrupted.

Mr Elliott looked at him with hard eyes as he continued, "Wouldn't want to repeat the experience or lose

159

his employment by his brief participation in the sport being made known to his senior officers."

Dr Weeks leaned forward, scowling at him. "Conway *ain't* involved."

"We can't know that for certain," Mr Elliott said. "Can we, Miss Trent?"

The clerk was deeply disturbed by the thought of Inspector Conway as a murderer. So much so, she could barely stomach it. The thought of him beating Mr Grosse to protect himself made her feel worse, since it seemed the likelier of the possibilities. "No." She swallowed hard to repress her revulsion. "But the case against him is circumstantial." She met Mr Elliott's gaze. "Only on that basis may we include him on our list of suspects."

"That—" Dr Weeks began.

"Is my final answer on the subject," Miss Trent interrupted.

Dr Weeks narrowed his eyes.

"Understood?" Miss Trent enquired.

Dr Weeks continued to glare at her.

"Do you understand, Doctor—?" Miss Trent began.

"*Yeah*, I *understand*," Dr Weeks replied, sitting back in his chair, before muttering under his breath, "I understand ya'll a bunch of traitors."

"What was that?" Miss Trent challenged.

"Ya don't want me repeatin' it," Dr Weeks warned.

Miss Trent's lips flattened, and her features tightened at the snub. Nonetheless, she understood—and shared—Dr Weeks' anger and frustration. "So be it."

SEVENTEEN

Releasing a soft sigh, Miss Trent decided to let the matter be. She enquired, "Miss Webster, did you find anything else of significance in Mr Grosse's office?"

"There were old editions of *Bell's Sporting Life* and copies of *Fistiana —or The Oracle of the Ring* and *Bradshaw's Railway Times* on his desk," Miss Webster replied. "We brought them back with us."

"*Bell's* was marked where the stories 'bout the fights was, and someone had wrote notes on 'em," Mr Snyder said.

"If you could acquire a known sample of Mr Grosse's handwriting from his uncle, Miss Trent, I can confirm if the notes are his," Miss Webster said. "All the better if he has the manuscript for Mr Grosse's book."

"Very well," Miss Trent said. "I'll contact him in the morning."

"The first trains goin' to the countryside was also marked in the Bradshaw's, with written initials beside 'em," Mr Snyder said.

"Why those trains?" Miss Dexter enquired.

"Bareknuckle boxin' was done in fields, out of sight of coppers and beaks," Mr Snyder replied. "Word would ge' 'bout the Fancy of when and where a set-to was gonna 'appen, and they'd all go down there on the train."

"I thought the Regulations of Railways Act of 1868 put a stop to people travelling out of London for prize fights," Mr Elliott said.

"Yeah, it did," Mr Snyder said. "Don't mean it don't still happen from time to time."

"Mr Voigt told me his nephew wrote for *Bell's Sporting Life* prior to becoming a private enquiry agent," Miss Trent said.

"That makes sense," Mr Snyder said.

"He must have utilised his connections within the 'respectable' and illegal boxing worlds to establish himself as an information broker under the guise of a private enquiry agent," Mr Elliott said.

"I agree," Dr Colbert said.

"We also found a pile of pamphlets for mittened boxing matches held at various clubs across London." Miss Webster placed these and the other publications upon the table.

"They're members of the *Amateur Boxin' Association* that was made by clubs back in '80. It dishes out the rules for competitions and prizes," Mr Snyder pointed out. "I ain't visited any, but I heard they want to make the sport 'respectable.'"

"You don't agree it should be?" Dr Colbert enquired, picking up on his sardonic tone.

"It already is," Mr Snyder replied. "It don't need mittens and toffs, just the Fancy gettin' rid of the fixed set-tos."

Mr Elliott picked up a pamphlet announcing an *Amateur Boxing Association* fight at the *Lower Clapton Boxing Club* based at the *Nimble Crow* public house. "Given the illegality of bareknuckle boxing and the debateable respectability of the mittened kind, would I be correct in assuming the Fancy are suspicious of strangers taking an interest in their activities, Mr Snyder?"

"You would," the cabman replied as he sat back in his chair and rested his hands upon his thighs.

"I propose you should call upon these public houses and boxing clubs in the first instance." Mr Elliott held the pamphlet over the pile to illustrate his point. "The landlords of the public houses will know you, which should protect you when you ask questions. It may also loosen their tongues."

"I can do that," Mr Snyder said.

"Shouldn't we report the illegal boxing to the police?" Dr Colbert enquired.

"In theory," Mr Elliott replied.

"If you peach, no one's gonna say owt," Mr Snyder warned.

"But according to the Bow Street Society's Rules of Conduct and Membership, we are obliged to cooperate with the police at all times," Dr Colbert argued. "You agree with me, don't you, Mr Elliott?"

"In principle, yes," Mr Elliott replied. "If we risk losing the cooperation of the Fancy by reporting the illegal fighting to the police, though, our obligation to Mr Voigt has to outweigh our obligation to the law."

"The police have been aware of the illegal fights for some time," Miss Trent said.

"Or at least one has," Mr Elliott remarked, glancing at Inspector Conway's file.

"An intentional failure to thwart them," Dr Colbert observed with a frown.

"We have other suspects beyond the world of boxing," Miss Webster pointed out. "Dr Weeks, was Mr Grosse wearing his wedding ring?"

"Nah," Dr Weeks replied.

"It wasn't at 'is office, either," Mr Snyder said.

"It must have been stolen," Mr Elliott said.

"Or removed by Mr Grosse," Miss Webster said.

"It would've been with his other t'ings," Mr Skinner said.

"Assuming it was he who put them there," Mr Elliott said.

"Mr Grosse could've removed his ring long before that," Miss Webster said. "In fact, I believe that's *precisely* what happened, considering the behaviour I witnessed at his house."

"What kind of behaviour?" Mr Elliott enquired.

"The adulterous kind," Miss Webster replied in disgust.

Miss Trent's eyes widened. "I beg your pardon?" She looked to Miss Dexter for an answer, but she bowed her head and downcast her eyes. With her mind still awash with questions, she demanded from Miss Webster, "Explain yourself. Immediately."

Miss Webster stilled at the vehemence of the clerk's response. Suddenly becoming acutely aware of the silence around her, she looked to the others. "I-I don't know what there is to explain—"

"How did you come to witness Mrs Eunice Grosse committing adultery?" Miss Trent demanded. "I presume it was without her knowledge?"

"Yes, but it wasn't intentional on my part either," Miss Webster replied. "And, quite honestly, you have no right to speak to me like this."

Miss Trent placed her pencil into the fold of her notebook and, clasping her hands, rested them upon the table. In a low, yet firm voice, she said, "Miss Webster, when the actions of a member threaten the reputation of this Society, I have every right to defend it in any way I deem reasonable. You have admitted to witnessing Mrs Eunice Grosse committing adultery. I want to know how you came to witness it without her knowledge. That, in my opinion, is a reasonable request."

Miss Webster squared her jaw and darted her gaze from Miss Trent to Miss Dexter and back again. Realising she couldn't argue with the clerk's logic, she briefly closed her eyes as her facial muscles slackened. "I agree." She dropped her gaze to her notebook and, toying with the edge of its page, continued in a subdued voice, "We knocked on the front door but failed to get an answer. We were about to leave when we heard what we thought was a woman crying. Isn't that correct, Miss Dexter?"

"Yes," Miss Dexter meekly replied.

"We were concerned," Miss Webster told Miss Trent, her usual monotone replaced by a quiet, worried voice. "I tried the door handle, and it was unlocked, so we went inside."

"You could've been arrested for unlawful entry if you were caught," Mr Elliott said.

Miss Webster frowned. "But I was only going by what the members' code states. That we may break the rules if there is a sufficiently justifiable reason for us to do so. We thought Mrs Grosse was in distress because of her husband's murder. We wanted to comfort her."

"Go on," Miss Trent said.

Miss Webster picked up her pencil and held its ends as she rotated it. "As we moved further inside, we realised the sound wasn't sobbing but laughter. Given the time of our arrival, I presumed Mrs Grosse must've had a visit by the police earlier in the day. Also, that she must've been told of her husband's murder. I was, understandably, surprised, intrigued, and, yes, angered to hear her laughing."

"Where was the laughter coming from?" Mr Elliott enquired.

Miss Webster exchanged uneasy glances with Miss Dexter. "Upstairs."

"*Damn*." Dr Weeks chuckled. "She didn't wait 'round, did she?"

"What happened next?" Miss Trent enquired, casting a warning look at the surgeon.

"Miss Dexter stayed in the hallway whilst I… crept upstairs," Miss Webster replied, her voice becoming quiet at the last. "If I'd thought for one moment she had company, I wouldn't have, I promise you."

Miss Trent frowned, but the sincerity was clear to hear in Miss Webster's voice.

"Where were they?" Dr Weeks enquired, leaning forward with a grin.

Miss Webster glanced away as she quietly replied, "In the bedroom."

Dr Weeks' grin grew into a smile. "Bet ya fainted at the sight of all that flesh, eh?"

Miss Webster tutted and rolled her eyes. "Hardly."

Dr Weeks chuckled. Sitting up, he cupped the air in front of his chest. "How were she?"

"*Oi*, less of that, love." Miss Hicks swatted his arm. Dr Weeks laughed.

"I didn't look," Miss Webster snapped. "As soon as I realised what was happening, I hurried back downstairs, and we returned to Mr Snyder's cab." She squared her shoulders and took a moment to calm her anger. "We decided to wait in case they left the house. Fortunately, fate was on our side as they emerged around thirty minutes' later."

"He lasted longer than Perce," Miss Hicks remarked in a dry tone.

"*Hey*," Dr Weeks scolded.

"It ain't nice, is it, love?" Miss Hicks sneered.

Miss Dexter took a sketch from her satchel and placed it in the middle of the table. "I sketched her lover's likeness when they kissed under the streetlamp."

"And Mr Snyder recognised him," Miss Webster added.

"Noah O'Hanigan's 'is name," Mr Snyder said. "'E's known as 'The Hammer' amongst the Fancy."

"Which kind of boxing is he involved in?" Mr Elliott enquired.

"Bareknuckle," Mr Snyder replied.

"At least some good came of your antics, Miss Webster," Miss Trent remarked, leaning her elbow upon the table as she rubbed her temple. "Clearly, the adultery is a motive for murdering Mr Grosse." She lowered her hand and straightened. "*If* the woman you saw was indeed Mrs Eunice Grosse."

"Could a woman have dealt such a blow, though?" Dr Colbert enquired.

"Yeah," Dr Weeks replied. "Ya know what they say, Doc: Hell hath no fury like a woman."

"Scorned," Miss Webster curtly added.

"What?" Dr Weeks looked at her, confused.

"The final word should be 'scorned,'" Miss Webster replied. "What you said is an idiom derived from a line in *The Mourning Bride* by William Congreve. In full, it's 'heaven has no rage like love to hatred turned, nor hell a fury like a woman scorned.'" She lifted her chin. "Mrs Grosse was hardly rejected by her lovers, however."

"My point were women can hit hard, too, if angered," Dr Weeks said.

"I'm aware of that," Miss Webster replied. "But you should at least try to be accurate when drawing upon literary examples to support your arguments."

Dr Weeks narrowed his eyes.

"Mrs Grosse couldn't of done it," Mr Snyder said. "Women ain't allowed by 'proper' boxing rings."

"She could of disguised herself," Miss Hicks pointed out.

"I agree," Mr Elliott said. "If she and Mr O'Hanigan were there together, he could've dealt the fatal blows."

"Thereby making him guilty of murder and her guilty of being his accomplice," Dr Colbert mused aloud.

"Not necessarily," Mr Elliott said. At Dr Colbert's questioning look, he continued, "In 1846, Lord Chief Baron Pollock heard the case of Regina *v.* John Swindall and James Osbourne. Both men were eventually found guilty of the manslaughter of an elderly pedestrian who one of them had driven down with his cart during an impromptu race. Since there were no other witnesses to the deed, it was impossible to determine who had been responsible. It was concluded both men were guilty as they had incited one another into driving at a dangerous and furious rate. As a result of this verdict, the precedent of common purpose, or joint enterprise, entered English case law."

"And how does that apply to Mrs Grosse and Mr O'Hangian?" Dr Colbert enquired.

"Should they be brought to trial, they would stand equally accused of Mr Grosse's murder," Mr Elliott clarified.

"Because no one witnessed the crime?" Dr Colbert probed.

"Yes, and because each would've assumed the intention to murder Mr Grosse when they became aware of the other possessing the murder weapon," Mr Elliott replied.

"*Fascinating*," Dr Colbert said with genuine interest.

"In the meantime," Miss Trent began, addressing Miss Webster. "You may speak to the suspected Mrs Grosse in the morning. Miss Hicks, please accompany her." At the barmaid's assent, the clerk added, "Obviously, if there is no answer to your knocks, please *don't* go inside."

"I shan't. Thank you, Miss Trent," Miss Webster agreed.

"If you can do so tactfully, try to garner some more information about Mr O'Hanigan, as he may have another connection with Mr Grosse through his boxing," Miss Trent said. "Also, see if Mr Grosse gave her his notebook or manuscript."

"Don't worry, Becky," Miss Hicks reassured. "I'll make sure it's done proper this time."

Miss Webster pursed her lips at the insinuation but knew Miss Hicks was right.

"Thank you," Miss Trent said, maintaining a formal tone. "Miss Dexter, I'd like you to draw some copies of your sketch."

Miss Dexter lifted her head, her eyes illuminated by her smile. "Yes, of course."

"I'll ask around the pubs and clubs about him," Mr Snyder said. "See if he was seen with Mr Grosse."

"Good." Miss Trent consulted her agenda. "Other persons whom we know had a connection with Mr Grosse are his uncle, Mr Voight, and Mr Linton and his daughter Tabitha. Miss Dexter, could you give the findings from your discussion with the Lintons?"

Miss Dexter's eyes were soft and filled with an inner glow as she continued to smile. Retrieving two further sketches from her satchel, she placed them beside the first upon the table. "Mr and Miss Linton were most upset when Mr Elliott told them of what had befallen poor Mr Grosse." Her gaze repeatedly darted between the sketches and Mr Elliott. "They seemed quite fond of him."

"They also confirmed Mr Voigt had visited their shop and Mr Grosse's office this morning," Mr Elliott said.

"Given the apparent level of affection you say Mr Voight had for his nephew, Miss Trent, it's surprising he failed to mention his concern for him to the Lintons. One would've expected him to enquire with them about his whereabouts, especially after the unnerving discovery of Mr Grosse's possessions on the desk. Either he knew what had happened to his nephew and was giving himself an alibi by calling upon the office, or he was in such a heightened state of anxiety he became blinkered to everything apart from reporting his nephew's disappearance to the police."

"His grief over his nephew's death appeared genuine," Miss Trent said. "As did his determination for us not to disturb Mrs Grosse."

"If the woman I saw *was* her, Mr Voigt would undoubtedly want to keep her adultery a secret to prevent a scandal," Miss Webster said.

"I agree," Mr Elliott said. "As with the inspector, I think we should consider Mr Voigt a suspect until we find evidence to the contrary."

"Yeah," Mr Snyder said.

"Very well," Miss Trent noted the decision. "Please continue, Miss Dexter."

"Miss Linton said Mr Grosse's friend, Mr Osbourne Spalding, visited him often." Miss Dexter held up the second sketch. "She described him to me, and I sketched this likeness of him." She slowly rotated her torso so the others could study the drawing before doing the same with the third. "This is an American gentleman who came into the shop asking for Mr Grosse. When Miss Linton had told him where he was, he went upstairs to the office. He argued with Mr Grosse, but she couldn't hear what was said." She put the sketches on the chalkboard and clasped her hands against her skirts as she faced the others. "When the American gentleman left, he walked into Mr Spalding and almost knocked him over."

"Mr Spalding may be able to shed some light on the argument as he called upon Mr Grosse immediately afterward," Mr Elliott stated.

"I shall make copies of his likeness as well," Miss Dexter said as she returned to her seat. "And the American gentleman."

"Do you recognise either, Mr Snyder?" Mr Elliott enquired.

"I do Mr Spaldin' a bit, but I couldn't tell you where from," Mr Snyder replied. "Nowt comes to mind about the American gent. I'll ask about 'em at the pubs and clubs, too."

"Thank you," Miss Trent said. "Miss Dexter, Mr Elliott, please show the sketch of Mr O'Hanigan to the Lintons in case he called upon Mr Grosse at his office. Miss Webster, Miss Hicks, please show the sketches of the American gentleman and Mr Spalding to Mrs Grosse. Hopefully, someone will recognise the American and know Mr Spalding's current whereabouts." At their agreement, she enquired, "Dr Colbert, what is your opinion of these men based upon your knowledge of physiognomy?"

Dr Colbert squinted at the sketches. Standing, he clasped his hands behind his back as he approached before leaning forward to study their faces more closely. "None of them have the physical characteristics said to be associated with someone in possession of an honest nature and clean habits." He straightened. "The shape and tilt of the eyes of Mr Spalding and the American are quite rat-like. Yet, the high brow of both suggests a marked intelligence."

He paused as a thought occurred to him. "The telegram in Mr Erskine's file was from America. I wonder…" He retrieved the photograph and, comparing it to the sketch of the American, frowned. "Hmm. Not at all similar." He replaced the photograph and studied the third sketch. "Mr O'Hanigan certainly bears the marks of violence in his misshapen nose, ears, and cheeks, whilst the low positioning of his brow suggests subnormal intelligence." He straightened and faced the others. "Physiognomy is, arguably, more akin to a guessing game than a science, however. I urge you to take my conclusions with a degree of scepticism."

"Thank you, Doctor," Miss Trent said, allowing Dr Colbert to sit. "Do you have anything more to add, Mr Elliott?"

"I do." Mr Elliott consulted his notes. "Firstly, Mr Linton and his daughter were initially reluctant to describe the American and Mr Spalding. Mr Linton cited a concern for his business' reputation as the reason. I'm inclined to believe him. Secondly, I'd like to enquire after Mr Grosse's notebook and manuscript with the Lintons. There's a small chance he may have given either document to them for safekeeping."

Miss Trent nodded as she made a note of this. "Dr Colbert, you may go with Mr Elliott and Miss Dexter, if you wish."

Dr Colbert sat bolt upright. "Yes. Yes, of course." He looked at Mr Elliott. "I'd be delighted."

"Good." Miss Trent checked the time upon her pocket watch. "If there is nothing further to discuss, I'd like to end the meeting." She stood and gathered her things, prompting the others to do the same. "Mr Skinner, may I have a word with you in my office?"

"Sure t'ing," Mr Skinner replied and followed her from the room.

"Don't forget your promise, love," Miss Hicks said, her lips close to Dr Weeks' ear.

"Ain't no chance of that, darlin'," Dr Weeks said. Pulling her into his lap, he held her close as they kissed.

Tutting loudly at the sight, Miss Webster strode from the room. "Disgusting."

Meanwhile, Miss Dexter's face flushed bright red as her eyes looked everywhere but at Dr Weeks and Miss Hicks. Hurriedly retrieving her satchel, she couldn't help but glance at them as she left the room. This caused her face to redden further. Bowing her head to hide her embarrassment, she called, "Goodnight, everyone."

Knowing that the success of his task to eliminate the Society relied upon his ability to befriend its members, Dr Colbert decided to attempt to disarm them by portraying himself as insecure. It was with a sheepish smile, then, that he approached Mr Elliott whilst ignoring the unruly behaviour of the surgeon and barmaid. "I hope I wasn't too forthright tonight. I sometimes speak before I think."

"We are all entitled to our opinions," Mr Elliott said, picking up his satchel.

"True, but I wanted to make a good impression." Dr Colbert followed him from the room.

"You did," Mr Elliott stated, oblivious to Dr Colbert's 'concern.

As they put on their coats, Dr Colbert found himself trying to think of an excuse to stay in his company. "Do you live in London?"

"Yes," Mr Elliott replied, fastening his coat.

Dr Colbert noticed the absence of a wedding ring.

"Are you sure Her Ladyship doesn't mind me coming to dinner?" Miss Dexter enquired as she and Miss Webster put on their things nearby.

"Quite sure," Miss Webster replied. "She's looking forward to it." Hearing the approach of a carriage, she went to the window and peered outside. "The carriage is here."

"Mine?" Dr Colbert called.

"No, ours," Miss Webster replied, unbolting and opening the door.

"Goodnight, sirs," Miss Dexter said, giving Dr Colbert and Mr Elliott a brief curtsey as she joined her friend.

"Goodnight," Dr Colbert said, watching them leave.

"I'll drive you back," Mr Snyder said as he emerged from the meeting room with Dr Weeks and Miss Hicks.

"Nah, we'll get our own cab," Dr Weeks said, leading Miss Hicks by the hand to the hatstand. "'Sides, Mr Skinner lives farther."

"I'd forgotten about that," Mr Snyder said.

"My carriage should be here soon," Dr Colbert offered.

Dr Weeks helped Miss Hicks into her coat and put on his own. "We ain't waitin'." He put his arm around Miss Hicks' waist and, kissing her again, led her from the house.

"I'd like to accept if I may?" Mr Elliott enquired.

"Of course." Dr Colbert smiled with genuine warmth. "I'd be delighted to have your company."

"Good." Mr Elliott's expression remained emotionless as he put on his hat.

EIGHTEEN

Mr Skinner stared at Miss Trent in disbelief. "It wasn't a bribe. It was—"

"You demanded Dr Weeks give you information about Mr Grosse's death in return for a bottle of whiskey," Miss Trent interrupted. "That alone defines what you did as bribery. I do *not* tolerate corruption of any kind within this Society. Do I make myself clear?"

"He was goin' to tell me what I wanted to know anyway; the whiskey just sweetened the deal."

Miss Trent put her hands upon her hips as she maintained a cold expression. "Dr Weeks is in a precarious position with Scotland Yard as it is. He doesn't need them accusing him of corruption as well."

Mr Skinner sighed and looked away. "I told you—"

"*Don't* give him anymore," Miss Trent demanded, talking over him.

Mr Skinner glared at her. After a moment's consideration, though, his features softened, and he gave a small nod. "All right," he said softly. "I can see your point." He frowned. "I don't want the captain thinkin' I'm corruptin' Dr Weeks either." He offered a weak smile. "I'll keep my gifts to myself in future."

Miss Trent lowered her arms. "Thank you." She glanced at the door. "Mr Snyder will drive you home."

Mr Skinner's smile grew. "Best to tell him how far it is first. He might not want to."

Miss Trent allowed herself to relax as she gave a weak smile of her own. "I'm sure that won't be a problem."

* * *

"How *ghastly*!" Lady Katheryne Owston exclaimed with her hand upon her chest. In her late-forties, she had tightly curled, warm, chestnut-brown hair that complemented the burgundy of her high-necked bustle dress and silk gloves. A gold locket hung around her neck, catching the firelight as she moved, whilst gold and ruby earrings framed her face. "And so close to the blessed day of *Christmas*, too."

Miss Webster hummed. Standing beside her guardian and employer, she had her back to the fire despite the guard blocking the frightening flames from view.

The small lounge was adorned with boughs of holly, ivy, and laurel, their lush greenery and red berries adding a much-needed warmth to the cream of the wood-panelled walls. Bows of red ribbon were also tied to the furniture, whilst a magnificent pine tree stood proudly in the corner. Candles lit up its sprigs as chains of golden bells weaved their way through its branches, and tin ornaments added bursts of colour to its dark-green canvas. Located on St George's Street in the borough of the City of Westminster, Lady Owston's three-storey townhouse was festooned in Christmas decorations from its basement to its attic.

"According to Miss Trent, his uncle is grief stricken," Miss Webster said.

"As is to be expected," Lady Owston said with regret.

"Unlike his *wife*," Miss Webster said, disgusted.

"Now, Agnes, you don't know she *was* his wife," Lady Owston reminded her. "Not yet." Carrying her small glass of mulled wine to the sofa, she perched upon its edge and took a sip. "But let us forget this *horrid* business for tonight and discuss *Paris* instead." Smiling broadly, she looked to Miss Dexter sitting beside her.

Although she also held a small glass of mulled wine, it was untouched. Furthermore, her glazed eyes were staring at the fireguard. Lady Owston's smile faded into concern. "Miss Dexter?" When no response was forthcoming, she placed a gentle hand upon her knee and leaned closer. "Georgina?"

Miss Dexter blinked as she suddenly came back to herself. Looking at Lady Owston and Miss Webster, she blushed upon realising she'd been lost in thought She offered an apologetic smile. "Forgive me."

"Is the Society's case weighing upon your mind?" Lady Owston enquired.

"A little." Miss Dexter looked at her wine. "And Joseph—I mean, Mr Maxwell."

"Joseph has been on all of our minds," Lady Owston said gently.

"I know." Miss Dexter met her gaze. "But it isn't right for him to be on mine."

"But he's as much of a dear friend to you as he is to us, child," Lady Owston said.

"And, from what Miss Trent said, the trial has been quite harrowing for him," Miss Webster added as she sat on Miss Dexter's other side.

"My feelings run deeper than that of a friend, though." Miss Dexter bowed her head. "I love him."

Lady Owston placed her hand upon Miss Dexter's. "We know, child."

"We barely know one another, and he withdrew his proposal of marriage to me—that was made in a most unconventional way—to marry Poppy who was brutally murdered by his father. In no way would our coming together now be appropriate or even respectable," Miss Dexter said, her voice trembling with emotion. "And yet…" She pursed her lips as her eyes glistened with unshed tears. In a voice barely above a whisper, she added, "My heart yearns for him."

"Love is rarely rational," Lady Owston said in a soothing voice. "Have you spoken to him since his father was arrested?"

"A little." Miss Dexter wiped her eyes with her handkerchief.

"Perhaps you should stay in England—" Lady Owston began.

"*No*." Miss Dexter shook her head. "I must accept that Joseph and I can never be and going to Paris will help me to do that. Besides…" She gave a feeble smile. "It's always been my dream to visit."

"We can have more than one dream, child," Lady Owston said.

"But not all can come true," Miss Dexter countered sadly.

Lady Owston frowned.

"Are you sure you want to leave him behind?" Miss Webster enquired. "We'll be in France for an entire month. There is also the time it will take us to travel to and from Paris."

"I'm grateful for your concern. *Truly*, I am, but visiting Paris is something I must do," Miss Dexter said.

Lady Owston gently squeezed her hand. "Very well, child, but you have until the boat leaves Dover to change your mind. We shan't be offended in the least if you do. Will we, Agnes?"

"Not at all," Miss Webster replied.

"Thank you." Miss Dexter smiled softly. "But I don't think I will."

NINETEEN

Dr Weeks blew between his clasped hands and rubbed them together as the severe cold of the night turned his breath to steam and numbed his fingers. The rocking of the hansom cab also caused the coffee and gin he'd drunk earlier to slosh against the sides of his otherwise empty stomach, thereby making him nauseous. Taking a lump of bread from his pocket, he ate it in two bites and washed it down with some brandy from his hip flask. A warm sensation passed over his face and hands a moment later, keeping the shivering at bay.

Yet, knowing it wouldn't last for long, he wrapped his fraying scarf around his head, covering his jaw and nose. He also pulled his knee-length coat tighter around his body and folded his arms to hold the exposed fingers of his gloved hands in his armpits. The sides of the cab sheltered him from the wind for the most part. Nevertheless, he slouched against the seat and pressed his chin against his chest to further contain his body heat.

The lighting of the kerosene lamp, and the dressing in old clothes that followed, had failed to awaken Polly in his bed. He'd been summoned to the ass-end-of-nowhere so many times during the night, though, he doubted his imminent departure would've earnt him anything more than a "Take care" from his lover. The hiring of the cab had proven more problematic, on account of the late hour and frigid weather. Fortunately, he was well-versed in the locations of the nearest ranks and shelters.

As the cab veered to the right and slowed to a stop, Dr Weeks unlatched its doors and alighted onto the pavement. Taking some coins from his pocket, he held them under the light of the cab's Davey lamp until the driver reached for them. At which point, he withdrew his hand. "Ya'll get more if yer still 'ere when I get back."

"I'll be 'ere," the driver gruffly agreed.

Dr Weeks held out the coins again, allowing him to take them.

"If you're not in there all night," the driver added.

"I ain't plannin' on stayin'," Dr Weeks said, thinking of Polly.

Entering the red-brick building of the Metropolitan Police Service's T (or Kensington) Division, he approached the high oak-panelled counter adorned with fresh laurel and ivy. Sitting behind it was the dark-grey-haired Sergeant Patrick Miller who, lifting his head, smiled upon seeing the Canadian. "Good evenin', Doctor. It's been a while since we've seen you here."

Dr Weeks passed him a sovereign. "Ya ain't seen me now."

"Not a soul." Sergeant Miller slipped the coin into his boot.

Going into the corridor to the left of the counter, Dr Weeks headed toward Inspector Lee's office with his hand inside his coat. As soon as Inspector Lee's door came into view, he took out Dr Colbert's envelope and planned in his mind what he would do: g*o in, hand over the envelope, take the record and statement.* "Then burn the damn things," he muttered under his breath.

He reached for the doorknob but stopped as his mind suddenly recalled Miss Trent's earlier words: *With our support, he'll get through this.* She'd been talking about Mr Maxwell, but Dr Weeks knew she could've just as easily been talking about him. He looked down at the envelope, certain she'd offer to help if she knew. *She's a good one*, he thought. *They all are… But not me.*

He grimaced as Inspector Lee's voice echoed through his mind. *How does it feel, carrying the burden of your mother's shame? Knowing your father never wanted you?* Dr Weeks hung his head as a tremendous ache gripped his heart and tightened his chest. *I know you don't want your shame exposed to the world,* Inspector Lee had said, and it was true. Knowing he'd come into this world on the wrong side of the blanket, the product of an adulterous affair, made him feel dirty to his core. He'd carried the fear others would see the guilt in him since he was a child, since he'd realised his home was different from everyone else's. Whenever the truth had come out… A pained expression formed upon his face, and he pushed the memories away. *I ain't gonna let that happen*, he vowed. *Not this time.*

He opened the door and went inside.

"You're early," Inspector Lee remarked from behind his desk. "Miracles do happen after all."

Dr Weeks narrowed his eyes and closed the door. "Let's jus' get this over with." He crossed over to the desk and tossed the envelope onto it.

"Did you encounter any problems getting it?" Inspector Lee picked it up and studied it.

"Nah." Dr Weeks swept his gaze over the desk. "Where's my papers?"

"Don't worry. They're safely locked away."

"I want 'em. Now."

"Unfortunately, we can't all get what we want in this life," Inspector Lee rebuffed.

Dr Weeks' blood ran cold. Staring at him as he suddenly felt like his whole body was in a vice, he quietly enquired, "What… what did ya jus' say?"

"You heard me well enough."

"We had a *deal*. The record and statement for the envelope."

Inspector Lee put down the envelope and, resting his elbows upon the arms of his chair, steepled his fingers. "I don't recall agreeing to such a thing."

The rhythm of Dr Weeks' pounding heart filled his ears as wild imaginings of what Inspector Lee might have planned filled his mind's eye. "Ya treacherous *sonofabitch.*" His features twisted into a murderous glare. "Ya gave me yer word!"

Inspector Lee stood. "You should never trust the word of a policeman." He walked around the desk, careful to give Dr Weeks a wide berth. "Especially one who is blackmailing you." He poured some tea from the pot into a china cup. "You've proven yourself on this occasion, but your membership—and loyalty—to the Bow Street Society give me cause to question how much I can truly trust you." He faced him. "So, I've decided to keep the documents until I'm convinced you shan't betray me to Miss Trent and her motley group of amateur sleuths."

"I did what ya asked, Gideon," Dr Weeks growled. "Gimmie my *damn* papers."

"No."

"Ya can't do this to me," Dr Weeks insisted, desperation creeping into his voice.

"I can, I have, and there is nothing you can do about it, except do as I ask. Otherwise, I will ensure every man, woman, and child has heard of the bastard child, Dr Percy Weeks, before the week is out." Inspector Lee picked up his cup of tea. "If you'll excuse me, I have some forms to complete."

Dr Weeks watched him in stunned disbelief as he returned to his desk and sat.

"Goodnight, doctor." Inspector Lee switched his cup for his pen.

Dr Weeks swallowed hard, his eyes darting from Inspector Lee, to the envelope, and back again. Realising snatching it wouldn't get him the record and statement, though, he headed for the door.

Waiting until he'd heard it close behind him, Inspector Lee put down his pen and picked up the envelope. Retrieving a telegram from underneath a folder upon his desk at the same time, he read it over for the second time that evening. Sent by Inspector Woolfe, it stated:

RETURNING TO LONDON
NOON TOMORROW STOP

Locking it away in his desk, Inspector Lee slipped the envelope into the inside pocket of his suit jacket as he went out into the corridor. "Sergeant!"

Miller appeared from around the corner.

"Send for my driver," Inspector Lee instructed.

"Yes, sir."

* * *

Miss Trent wrinkled her nose at the overpowering smell of vinegar as Inspector Conway drenched his chipped potatoes in it. Falling into step beside him as they walked away from the window of the small fried fish shop, she watched him shovel several of the soggy things into his mouth. Having met a stone's throw from Spitalfields Market on Princes Street in London's East End, the late hour didn't seem to matter to the many food vendors selling their wares from window and stall alike. Though they might not have been as crowded as during daylight hours, the little dark streets and alleyways around Spitalfields were nonetheless occupied by those seeking cheap sustenance.

"Want some?" Inspector Conway held out the paper-wrapped pile.

"No," Miss Trent replied. "Thank you."

Inspector Conway continued eating as they turned left onto Wood Street. Walking toward Church Street, with its imposing structure of Christ Church, he remarked between swallows, "Word's got 'round of old Grosse bein' done in."

"Did you know him?"

"I've seen 'im at the *Key & Lion* once or twice. Never talked to 'im."

"Sam said he was well known by the Fancy."

"He was." Inspector Conway ate some more.

"Did you ever see him with a Mr Spalding or a Noah O'Hanigan?"

Inspector Conway's chewing slowed as he searched his memory. "I know of O'Hanigan but I never seen 'im with Grosse. I don't know of any Mr Spalding." He ate some more. "You got the report for Jones?"

"I do." Miss Trent stepped into the darkened doorway of a closed shop. "And the one for the Mrs Gove case investigated by Lady Owston. We were able to successfully extract the compromising letter from her would-be blackmailer."

"Good." Inspector Conway ate the remaining chips and screwed the paper into a ball, causing him to flinch in pain. Releasing a slow, deep breath, he stuffed the ball into his pocket.

"I wish you'd have those ribs looked at," Miss Trent said, concerned, as she looked upon his blackened eye and bruised face. It had only been a matter of days since she'd watched him box in the *Key & Lion*'s cellar.

"There's nowt they could do but bind 'em."

Miss Trent cast a worried glance over him but knew he couldn't be convinced. She decided to return to the matter at hand by folding back the skirt of her coat and unbuttoning a large pocket concealed within its lining. Taking three files from it, she put her coat back in place and explained each in turn as she handed them over. "The final report on the Mrs Gove case. The first report on the Christian Grosse case, with a list of the members currently assigned. I believe Detective Inspector George Pilker of Scotland Yard is the investigating officer?"

"He is. I'll let 'im know."

"And…" She kept hold of the third file as he took it, thereby compelling him to meet her gaze. "The file on you from Mr Grosse's office."

"You what?"

Miss Trent allowed him to take it. "It records where and when you were born, the names of your parents and siblings, and your brief prize-fighting career."

Inspector Conway's frown deepened with each line he read.

"We think he compiled it with the intention of including it in his book about the history of boxing in London. We've been unable to find the manuscript, however." A pained look entered her eyes as a sorrowful expression formed upon her face. "John, I have to ask. I don't want to, but I must."

Inspector Conway looked her squarely in the eyes. "I didn't kill 'im."

"Did you beat him?"

Inspector Conway closed the distance between them and, in a gentle voice, said, "I know what's been said of me… by Elliott, mostly. I know what this says." He lifted the file. "And I know what I've done at the scratch, but I done *nowt* to Grosse."

The tension eased in Miss Trent's face. "I didn't believe you had, but we had to consider all possibilities."

"Yeah, it's just sumin' that's gotta be done." Inspector Conway held out the file. "You'd best keep hold of this until Grosse's murderer is found out. Let me know if you find that book of 'is, too."

Miss Trent took the file. "I will."

TWENTY

From his vantage point on the first-floor landing, Mr Maxwell watched Miss Dexter check her satchel's contents in the Society's hallway below. As she rummaged, her gaze darted toward the rear of the house and her things before she walked out of sight. The sound of a door opening reached Mr Maxwell's ears a moment later, followed by the sound of her footsteps as she entered the room, walked around it, and returned. When she came back into view, he felt his heartrate increase. The delicate pink of her cheeks reminded him of last night when she'd sketched by candlelight in her studio. She'd been unaware of him watching her then, too.

Taking a deep, pained breath, he closed his eyes and inwardly scolded himself for his improper behaviour. Feeling his eyes sting as he imagined her wounded expression at discovering his voyeurism, he tugged at his cravat and swallowed hard. The sight of her tears the other night had further fractured his already broken heart. He couldn't bear to witness them again and so vowed not to watch her from a distance any longer. With his heart racing, he squared his shoulders, wiped his sweaty palms upon his frockcoat, and descended the stairs.

Miss Dexter turned toward the kitchen as soon as she saw him.

"*Wait*!" Mr Maxwell cried, reaching out as he ran down. "Please." He halted after a few paces. "Don't go."

Miss Dexter stared at his feet. "I must get ready to leave."

"I-I just want to-to talk… for a while." Mr Maxwell swallowed to ease the tightening of his throat. "Y-you were working l-late last night."

Miss Dexter looked up.

"I-I heard you from m-my room," Mr Maxwell hastily added.

"Oh." Miss Dexter's cheeks turned bright pink as she downcast her eyes. "I thought… never mind."

"I-I did."

Miss Dexter stared at him in utter horror. "Joseph—"

"B-But only for a few moments," Mr Maxwell half-whimpered. Wringing his hands, he timidly approached her. "I-I couldn't help it. Y-Your door was open, and I… I glanced and-and there you were." His voice became quiet. "As beautiful as an angel."

Miss Dexter turned away. "Don't. Please."

Mr Maxwell moved closer, still. "Whilst I-I'm in hell." His voice shook. "For this is hell f-for me, Georgina. B-Being so close and yet n-not."

Miss Dexter looked over her shoulder at him. "We cannot—"

"Mr Snyder and Mr Skinner will be here soon," Miss Trent said from the kitchen door.

Startled by the sudden interruption, the pair turned, wide eyed.

Miss Trent put herself between them as she held out some sketches to Miss Dexter. "These were in the kitchen."

Miss Dexter took them with a weak yet appreciative smile. "Thank you."

Miss Trent folded her arms and looked between them. "How did you sleep, Mr Maxwell?"

"W-Well, thank you," Mr Maxwell mumbled. Feeling his face warm under Miss Trent's gaze, he looked to the sketches. "How d-delightful. I-I've never seen Mr Baldwin l-looking so handsome."

"You mean Mr Spalding," Miss Trent said.

"D-Do I?" Mr Maxwell looked over the sketch a second time. "No… that is mm-most definitely Mr Baldwin."

"What is his first name?" Miss Trent enquired.

"Oh, erm." Mr Maxwell rubbed the back of his neck. "Oswald, I-I think. Why?"

"Osbourne Spalding. Oswald Baldwin," Miss Dexter said. "They sound remarkably similar."

"Yes," Miss Trent agreed. "Miss Linton must've misheard."

"Who?" Mr Maxwell enquired.

Several knocks sounded from the front door, prompting Miss Dexter to put the sketches into her satchel whilst Miss Trent went to answer it. Furrowing his brow, Mr Maxwell parted his lips to ask his question again. The sight of Mr Skinner on the porch, and Miss Dexter hurrying toward him as she pulled on her coat, made him reconsider, though. Instead, he turned away and, smoothing down his frockcoat, went into the kitchen in search of some mince pies.

* * *

"Didn't expect you back so soon, truth be told," Mr Zechariah Ellis said, his powerful voice cutting through the din of the West India Import Dock. In his mid-forties, he had a squat frame with broad shoulders and thinning mutton chops that matched the dark blond of his short hair. The skirt of his dark-brown, knee-length overcoat fluttered in the wind behind him as he kept his fists firmly in its pockets. A battered, dark-green cloth top hat sat at an angle upon his head, whilst his light-brown trousers and waistcoat were as ill-fitting as his heavy black leather boots. A wooden club hung from a loop on his belt and swung in time with his long strides.

The quayside was a hive of activity. Steamships were moored beside wooden jetties as an army of workers used ropes and pulleys to unload netfuls of crates and barrels. Voices filled the air, the odd word breaking through the otherwise indistinguishable cacophony punctuated by ships' horns and seagulls' calls. The scents of rum, coffee, spices, animal hides, bodily odour, musty clothes, and smoke also formed a perfume that constantly shifted between pleasant and putrid.

Already suffering from a pounding headache, Dr Weeks grimaced at the noise as he shielded his bloodshot eyes from the low sun. Having been rudely awoken by Polly pouring cold water on his face, he wasn't in the best of moods. After leaving Chiswick, he'd returned home and drank himself into a stupor on the sofa. Yet, despite the blissful oblivion, his thoughts had immediately returned to Inspector Lee's possible next move when he'd awoken and stayed there.

Walking behind Mr Ellis, but ahead of Mr Snyder, Miss Dexter, and Mr Skinner, he muttered, "Me, too" as he retrieved his hip flask. Taking a large swig from it, he grimaced at the wave of nausea that immediately came over him, turning his face ashen grey. Weaving toward the quay's edge to lean upon a mooring bollard until it passed, he caught a whiff of animal hides. The overpowering stench increased his nausea tenfold, thereby forcing him to lunge for the bollard, only to fall onto his knees beside it and empty the contents of his stomach into the Thames.

"Dr Weeks!" Miss Dexter cried as she rushed to his side.

"Leave 'im be, lass," Mr Snyder called. "It's the drink."

"You *poor* man." Miss Dexter offered Dr Weeks her handkerchief.

Dr Weeks looked from it, to her face, and back again before pushing it away and wiping his mouth with his sleeve. "I'm fine." Getting to his feet and walking past her, he muttered, "No need to get so damn excited."

"I only wanted to help," Miss Dexter said meekly as she followed.

"Well, I didn't ask fer it, and I sure as hell don't need it," Dr Weeks said.

"I'm sorry," Miss Dexter said, her voice and expression etched with regret.

"Good night, were it?" Mr Skinner jibed as they neared.

"Somethin' like that," Dr Weeks muttered upon passing him.

"Full of festive cheer, ain't 'e?" Mr Skinner enquired from the others.

"Sam is right, we should leave him be," Miss Dexter replied sadly.

Dr Weeks felt a pang of guilt at that and how he'd behaved toward her. Dismissing the idea of apologising as a futile exercise now the moment had passed, he instead took several more swigs from his flask. *"Your parentage certainly explains much of your behaviour… The drunkenness. The rudeness."* Inspector Lee's voice echoed around his head, increasing his guilt. Taking another swig from his flask to dull the feeling, he muttered a curse under his breath as his guilt was replaced by self-loathing.

"This 'ere's the one," Mr Ellis announced as they came to the last warehouse lining the quayside. Removing its large padlock, he slid back its heavy doors to allow an ever-increasing shaft of light to illuminate a mountainous landscape moulded entirely from wooden crates. It stretched out into the warehouse's dark corners, with only a few pools of white daylight here and there courtesy of the roof's windows. The smell of caffeine had struck the group the moment Mr Ellis had opened the doors. Yet, as they followed him inside, it became overpowering.

Mr Ellis stood to the left, holding his club at his side. "You can take a look 'round," he pointed the club at them, "but *no* touchin'. This 'ere's company property."

"Did you say the same t'ing to Mr Grosse?" Mr Skinner enquired.

"Who?" Mr Ellis squinted at him.

"The fella beaten to death in your warehouse," Mr Skinner replied.

"I never met 'im before," Mr Ellis said.

"Ya found 'im back there." Dr Weeks nodded to the far-right corner of the warehouse. "How d'ya suppose 'e got in if it weren't ya?"

Mr Ellis' mouth twitched as he cast an uneasy glance between them. "You can't put that on me. I had nowt to do with 'im bein' done in."

"Never said you did," Mr Skinner said. "But maybe you left the doors unlocked in exchange for a few coins?"

Mr Ellis picked at a splinter on the end of his club. "Maybe."

"But you wouldn't of done that and not known what Mr Grosse wanted it for," Mr Snyder pointed out. "It's your job to guard the place, ain't it?"

"Yeah." Mr Ellis cast another uneasy glance between them as he considered his options. "Okay. *Maybe* I did let 'im in and *maybe* I knew what for, but that don't mean I was 'ere when 'e was done in."

"Nah, but I reckon ya were 'ere before that," Dr Weeks said.

"To keep an eye on t'ings," Mr Skinner added.

"Why don't you show us, lad?" Mr Snyder gently encouraged.

Mr Ellis' lips formed a hard line as he darted his worried eyes from the others, to the doors, and back again. Striding toward the middle of the warehouse, though, he tightened his grip upon his club and breathed heavily through his nose.

The piles of crates formed a veritable maze with paths varying in size from a few inches to a few feet. Their height meant it was impossible to see over them, and the Bow Streeters found themselves in shadow most of the time. Leading them along a path so narrow they had to side-step their way along it, Mr Ellis took them around a corner where a large area of bare floor suddenly opened before them.

Although surrounded by piles of crates, Mr Snyder noticed they'd been arranged in tiers. The lowest of these was noticeably higher than the barrels lining the space, suggesting a makeshift accommodation for spectators. Venturing further inside, Mr Snyder noticed some fresh holes in the floor. Counting eight in total, he saw they formed a square of four and twenty feet. Finally, he found a shallow gash in the square's centre. Pointing to the holes, he said, "Someone put up a ring."

Dr Weeks entered the hole formation and, walking around it, crouched on its left side. He pointed to a spattering of dark-red dots on the floor. "There's some blood 'ere."

"Who was fightin' in the set-to?" Mr Snyder enquired.

"A *fight*? *'Ere*?" Mr Ellis gave a nervous chuckle. "You're *mad*."

Dr Weeks stood. "The blood tells a different story."

"And Mr Grosse was known for findin' fighters," Mr Skinner said. "No reason he couldn't have found this place, too."

"And you said you took money off 'im," Mr Snyder said.

"We ain't interested in reportin' ya to the coppers." Dr Weeks lit a cigarette. "We jus' wanna know if a fight were held 'ere."

Mr Ellis frowned deeply as he eyed Dr Weeks, Mr Snyder, and Mr Skinner with suspicion. After a long pause, he admitted, "It did."

A soft click sounded from Miss Dexter's box camera as she took a photograph of the blood spatter. Fortunately, it was directly underneath a window, so there was ample light. She doubted whether the same could be said about the spot where Mr Grosse's body was found.

"I let 'em all in, locked the doors, and watched the set-to," Mr Ellis said. "When they left, I locked up. Mr Grosse was *livin'* when I last laid my eyes on 'im."

"What about this mornin'?" Mr Snyder enquired.

"I come back to make sure nowt was damaged, didn't I?" Mr Ellis enquired in a defensive tone. "As I was wanderin' over there, I found 'im, 'is head lookin' like cracked china." He loosened his shoulders. "So, I went off and found a Bobby."

"Why didn't you make sure nowt was damaged before leaving?" Mr Snyder enquired.

Mr Ellis averted his gaze. "I wanted to get 'em all off the docks before someone saw."

"'E were over 'ere." Dr Weeks led them through the maze of crates.

The spot was so far away from the windows, it was practically in darkness. Several walls of crates also hid it from view, thereby concealing Mr Grosse's body from the spectators.

"I'm afraid I shan't be able to capture any useful photographs here," Miss Dexter said, a little forlorn. She swapped her camera for her sketchbook. "I'll draw it instead."

Dr Weeks leaned against the wall, smoking. The dim light was helping his headache and nausea—much to his relief. Taking a small swig from his flask, he watched Miss Dexter start her sketch.

"Can only get 'ere through the crates," Mr Snyder observed. "Who was watchin' the set-to?"

"I wasn't gonna take their names, was I?" Mr Ellis sardonically replied.

"Stackin' the crates in tiers wouldn't of been done in a few hours," Mr Snyder mused aloud. "Some of the blokes workin' the ware'ouse would of had to do it, and was maybe allowed to watch the set-to as payment."

"What did Inspector Pilker make of it?" Mr Skinner enquired.

"'E ain't told me," Dr Weeks replied. "'E were fussin' 'bout over there whilst I were back 'ere with the meat."

"He's not goin' to tell us either," Mr Skinner said. "How was Mr Grosse lyin'?"

"On 'is back," Dr Weeks replied. "Suggestin' 'e were facin' 'is murderer when 'e were hit the first time."

"Someone 'e was talkin' to?" Mr Skinner enquired.

"Could be," Dr Weeks replied with a one-sided shoulder shrug.

"You never told us who was in the set-to," Mr Snyder said.

"Don't be daft!" Mr Ellis cried. "They'd do *me* in if I peached." He brandished his club as he walked away. "Now, get what you need and scarper, the *lot* of you!"

TWENTY-ONE

Standing with his left elbow resting upon his folded right arm, Dr Colbert rubbed at his upper lip to disguise the fact he was shielding his mouth from the smoky air. Feeling the back of his throat become irritated, he clamped his mouth shut. The irritation only increased, however, and a cough burst forth from his lips a moment later. Managing to mutter an apology before another cough escaped, he moved over to the draughty window behind Mr Baldwin's desk. Taking in a few deep breaths, he felt the chilly air from Fleet Street calm his angry throat.

Looking back at Mr Baldwin, he compared his face to his memory of Miss Dexter's sketch and realised the likeness she'd captured was incredibly accurate. The only difference was temporary. Namely, the small bruise marring the right side of his lightly stubbled jaw. Studying his face further, he saw the edges of his eyes were red and sore, whilst the skin beneath was dark and puffy.

He shifted his gaze to Mr Baldwin's typing hands and noted the right had a length of torn, black cloth tied tightly around its palm. Reading his article next, he felt his stomach turn at the lurid description of where and how Mr Grosse was found. "May I ask how you cut your hand, Mr Baldwin?"

The journalist paused in his typing to glance over his shoulder at him. "The razor slipped when I was shavin'."

"And the bruise?" Mr Elliott enquired. "How did you come by that?"

"I fell over," Mr Baldwin snapped.

Dr Colbert returned to Mr Elliott's side. "Were you and Mr Grosse close?"

The journalist continued typing. "No."

"You'll hold no guilt over your article then," Dr Colbert remarked.

Mr Baldwin struck the keys harder. "Someone's got to write it."

"We were told you were the only regular visitor to Mr Grosse's office," Mr Elliott said.

The speed of Mr Baldwin's typing increased as he stared, unblinkingly, at the page.

"That in itself suggests you were a good friend of his," Mr Elliott said. "Or enemy."

Mr Baldwin slammed both hands upon the typewriter's keys, thereby causing their many arms to become jammed against the paper. With wide, anger-filled eyes, he demanded, "What do you want from me?!"

The din of many typewriters ceased in an instant as the other *Gaslight Gazette* journalists occupying the large, open office were distracted by the commotion. Ignoring their curious and concerned looks, Mr Baldwin waited for an answer.

"The truth," Mr Elliott stated.

"It *is* the bloody *truth*," Mr Baldwin said. "I live in Hackney. I sometimes passed the time of day with Grosse over a cuppa or a pint, but *that* was it." He eased the arms of the typewriter's keys from the paper before removing it from the machine and inserting a clean sheet.

Mr Elliott showed him the sketch of the American. "Do you remember colliding with this gentleman on your way to 'passing the time of day' with Mr Grosse two days ago?"

Mr Baldwin stilled as he looked upon the face. The anger also receded from his eyes and expression. "Yeah. He almost had me clean off my feet. Threatened me, too, when I said sumin' about it."

"Had you seen him before?" Mr Elliott enquired.

"No," Mr Baldwin replied.

"Have you seen him since?" Dr Colbert enquired.

Mr Baldwin hesitated. "No."

"Do you know who he is?" Mr Elliott enquired.

"*No*," Mr Baldwin snapped. "Why you askin' me all these questions for?"

"The not-so-small matter of Mr Grosse's murder," Mr Elliott replied. "What did you and he talk about that day?"

"I don't remember." Mr Baldwin put a hand-rolled cigarette between his lips and, lighting it with a match, took several deep pulls before continuing his typing.

"Mr Grosse didn't mention his previous visitor at all?" Mr Elliott probed.

Once again, the speed of Mr Baldwin's typing increased. "He might of."

"Did he, or didn't he?" Dr Colbert challenged.

Mr Baldwin momentarily ceased his typing to glare at him. "I *don't* remember."

"Mr Grosse was assaulted before his death," Mr Elliott said.

Again, Mr Baldwin's typing momentarily ceased. This time it was accompanied by a downturned mouth and mournful eyes as he stared at the page, however.

"His office was also broken into on the same night," Mr Elliott went on.

Mr Baldwin stopped typing altogether and, curling his fingers, appeared to read what he'd written.

"Whoever it was smashed a window and cut their hand upon the glass as they escaped," Mr Elliott said, his gaze dropping to Mr Baldwin's injured appendage.

"Christian was a good bloke," Mr Baldwin said in a dejected voice. He looked Mr Elliott in the eye. "I never would've done owt to hurt 'im."

"Do you know of anyone who would?" Mr Elliott enquired.

Mr Baldwin lowered his gaze. "No."

"No one within the Fancy?" Mr Elliott probed.

Mr Baldwin hesitated. "No."

"You were aware his private enquiry agency specialised in discovering the lives and careers of boxers?" Dr Colbert enquired.

"Everyone was," Mr Baldwin replied. "It was the worst-kept secret in London."

"He was known for recording his findings in a notebook. Did you ever see him with it?" Mr Elliott enquired.

Mr Baldwin leaned back in his chair and crushed out his cigarette in a nearby ashtray. "A few times."

"Do you know where he kept it?" Mr Elliott enquired.

Mr Baldwin shook his head. "Wish I did."

"Don't you have it?" Dr Colbert enquired.

Mr Baldwin gave a feeble chuckle and replied in a contrite tone, "Chance would be a fine thing." Shifting his gaze to the unfinished article in his typewriter, his eyes glazed over as he seemed to stare through the paper at something hidden beneath. "He never let anyone read it. Not even me."

"When was the last time you saw him?" Mr Elliott enquired.

A haunted look entered Mr Baldwin's eyes as he turned his head toward the window. "The night 'e was done in. At the *Key & Lion*."

"Did he have his notebook with him?" Dr Colbert enquired.

"Yeah," Mr Baldwin replied. "'E put it away as soon as I come along, though."

"Did you happen to catch sight of its contents?" Dr Colbert probed.

Mr Baldwin averted his gaze. "Not what was written in it, 'e was too quick for me, but…" He paused as he pictured the scene in his mind. "There might of been a telegram."

Mr Elliott and Dr Colbert exchanged glances. The former enquired, "Concerning Deon Erskine?"

Mr Baldwin gave a weak chuckle with a small shake of his head. "That bloody book of his." He looked out the window. "It could have been, I don't know. I didn't see what was written on it." He returned his gaze to the Bow Streeters. "Grosse was askin' about Erskine at the *Key & Lion* a few days ago, though. 'E wanted to put him in his new book, him and your Mr Snyder."

"What did he discover?" Mr Elliott enquired.

"Not much," Mr Baldwin replied. "Only that Erskine had gone off to America. No." He averted his gaze to his typewriter. "There was somethin' else." He looked out the window and fell silent for several moments as he searched his memory. "No." He shook his head and met their gaze. "Can't remember."

"What did Mr Grosse's notebook look like?" Mr Elliott enquired upon realising Mr Snyder hadn't furnished them with a description.

"Tattered, dark blue," Mr Baldwin replied. "Narrow, too."

"Did he ever show you the manuscript for his book or mention where he kept it?" Mr Elliott enquired.

Mr Baldwin gave a curt shake of his head. "He never said, and I never asked."

"Did Mr Grosse say where he was going after the pub when you saw him last?" Dr Colbert enquired.

Mr Baldwin bowed his head and, clenching his eyelids together, rubbed his temples between his thumb and index finger. "No. I asked, but 'e wouldn't tell me." He dropped his hand into his lap as he lifted tired eyes to the Bow Streeters. "Is that it, now?"

"Do you recognise this man?" Mr Elliott showed him the sketch of Mr O'Hanigan.

The haunted look returned to Mr Baldwin's eyes. "I've seen 'im at the *Key & Lion* a few times, but I don't know 'is name."

"Thank you." Mr Elliott put both sketches into his satchel. "You've been most helpful."

As the Bow Streeters returned downstairs, they felt Mr Baldwin's eyes boring into their backs. Emerging into Fleet Street a few moments later, they each took in a lungful of air.

"He was lying," Dr Colbert remarked.

"Without a doubt," Mr Elliott agreed. "The question is: why?"

* * *

Mrs Eunice Grosse twisted a strand of her strawberry-blond hair around her finger as she stood at her parlour window overlooking Glyn Street. Attired in a scarlet-and-cream-striped cotton bustle dress, her naturally slender torso was sculpted into a harsh hour-glass shape by a tight corset. As a result, her hips and bust were wide, whilst her waist was extremely narrow. The corset also pushed her breasts up and together, thereby granting her with a bare, heaving cleavage framed by the lace of her dress' low, square neckline. Nevertheless, it rose and fell as she took in several shallow breaths.

Meanwhile, Miss Hicks sat on the overstuffed dark-green sofa opposite the fire, whilst Miss Webster had chosen the armchair to its right. Facing Mrs Grosse, the ornate wooden fireplace and three-panelled guard obscured the latter's view of the hearth. Although she'd learnt to keep fires from her line of sight whenever calling upon friends or witnesses, etc., Miss Webster's fear could still be triggered by their snapping and popping. Therefore, for all she couldn't see, Mrs Grosse's fire, the sounds it generated, were enough to cause her to rub the middle finger of one hand with the thumb and index finger of her other. Feeling a small degree of comfort from the motion, she refocused her attention on the widow.

Failing to notice her fellow Bow Streeter's distress, Miss Hick's attention was instead upon her opulent surroundings. Well, they were opulent to *her*. Even Dr Weeks' rooms weren't as finely furnished. Its walls were adorned in a paper depicting brightly coloured birds and flowers amongst swirling green leaves and vines on a dark background. Its floor was a plush dark-green carpet, whilst the remainder of the furniture consisted of a ladies' bureau in the corner, a display cabinet filled with china ornaments and trinkets, and several side tables. One of which had a music box that struck the complex, notched patterns of large, brass discs to generate the sound. Even if she saved her wages from now until she was a hundred, Miss Hicks doubted she could afford such a home.

"I can't believe this has happened," Mrs Grosse said with a forlorn expression.

"You have our condolences," Miss Webster said for propriety's sake. When Mrs Grosse had confirmed her identity upon answering the door to them, Miss Webster had felt both relief and anger. Relief because she'd been vindicated in her disgust at the woman's behaviour, and anger because Mrs Grosse hadn't followed the appropriate mourning etiquette and worn black. Adopting her usual monotone, she added, "It must be heart-breaking to lose your husband in such a horrific manner."

Mrs Grosse dismissed her words with a wave of her hand, however. "Oh, that." She came away from the window and, standing beside the fire, toyed with the pendant on her gold necklace. "Mr Voigt told me last night, when he *demanded* I leave this house by the end of the week!" She clutched the pendant as a pained look fell upon her face. "I ask you: how could he be so *heartless*?" She slowly walked back and forth in front of the fire. "And how could Christian be so *cruel* as to not leave a *will*?"

The corner of Miss Webster's mouth lifted as delight swept through her. Knowing it wouldn't be either ladylike or wise to gloat at the adulteress' misfortune, though, she softly cleared her throat and assumed an emotionless mask. "Mr Voight has taken ownership of the house?"

"He has!" Mrs Grosse stopped and, placing one hand upon her hip, rubbed her eyebrow with the other. "I don't know what I'm to do, or where I'm to go."

"Will Mr O'Hanigan not take you in?" Miss Webster enquired, thinking of Mr Maxwell's ordeal to ensure she sounded appropriately concerned.

Mrs Grosse stilled. Slowly swivelling her head toward Miss Hicks and back to Miss Webster immediately afterward, she stared at her with a flat gaze. "I… I don't understand. What… How did…" She closed her eyes and turned away sharply. "No." She wrapped an arm around her stomach as she leaned against the wall with one hand.

"He couldn't." She suddenly cast a fierce glare at Miss Webster. "How did you know of him?"

Miss Webster stood and slowly walked toward her. "We saw you leaving together. Our driver recognised Mr O'Hanigan and provided us with his name. We also saw you kissing by the light of the lamppost." She adopted a challenging tone. "Less than *twenty-four* hours after your husband was *murdered*."

"How *dare* you come into *my* home and *judge* me." Mrs Grosse spun around and glared at her. "You have *no* right."

"Perhaps not," Miss Webster conceded for all she didn't agree. "But as members of the Bow Street Society assigned to investigate your husband's murder, we have a right to know where you were that night."

Mrs Grosse gave a defiant lift of her chin. "I was here. With Mr O'Hanigan. In bed."

Miss Webster swallowed her disgust. "All night?"

Mrs Grosse smirked. "Yes."

"And neither of you paid a late-night visit to the docks?" Miss Webster pressed.

Mrs Grosse's smile vanished as she firmly replied, "No."

"Wasn't you worried when your old man didn't come 'ome?" Miss Hicks enquired.

"Christian often stayed away," Mrs Grosse replied. "He never asked questions of me, and I never asked questions of him."

"A convenient arrangement for you and Mr O'Hanigan," Miss Webster sneered.

"*Most* convenient, yes," Mrs Grosse replied. "Christian wanted a wife to make his friends jealous with. I wanted a husband who could satisfy me. Unfortunately, neither of us got what we wanted."

Miss Webster turned her head away as she released a sound of disgust.

"Aside from our mutual wish to avoid a scandal, of course," Mrs Grosse added.

"Did you know what he done for money?" Miss Hicks enquired, watching Miss Webster as she moved toward the window to calm herself.

"Consultancy work of some kind," Mrs Grosse remarked with a circular motion of her hand. "I had no inclination to find out as long as it kept him from the house."

Miss Hicks showed her the sketch of the American. "Do you know 'im?"

Mrs Grosse glanced at the sketch. "He's a friend of Noah's. His name escapes me."

Miss Webster turned upon her heel. "*One* final question, *Mrs* Grosse. Did your *husband* give you a notebook or manuscript?"

Mrs Grosse fixed her with hard eyes. "No. He did *not.*"

"We are finished here. Miss Hicks?" Miss Webster strode to the parlour door and, as she waited for her fellow Bow Streeter to join her, said, "I hope you find somewhere to spend Christmas."

"Thank you," Mrs Grosse said, taken aback.

"I hear there are plenty of openings in the bawdy houses," Miss Webster said coldly.

Mrs Grosse's face flushed a bright pink as she advanced upon the Bow Streeters. "Get out!"

"Gladly." Miss Webster closed the parlour door in Mrs Grosse's face.

* * *

"Rest assured, Miss Trent, I shall *personally* see to it that *none* of the people connected with Mr Christian Grosse, directly or otherwise, so much as *breathes* in the direction of," Inspector Pilker read aloud from the list in his hand, "Dr Colbert, Mr Elliott, Mr Snyder, Mr Skinner, Miss Webster, Miss Hicks, *or* Miss Dexter."

"We've been commissioned to investigate Mr Grosse's murder by his uncle—"

"I don't care if you've been commissioned by Her Majesty the Queen, the Society is *not* to interfere with *my* investigation in any shape or form," Inspector Pilker interrupted.

Miss Trent put her hands upon her hips. "We wouldn't be interfering if you cooperated with us."

Standing in the Society's hallway, Inspector Pilker had his back to the open front door whilst Miss Trent had hers to the stairs. If she was possessed of a shallower character, she might have been offended by his failure to remove his hat upon entering. As it was, she was drawing upon every last ounce of strength to not unleash the full weight of her wrath upon him.

"We're not all like John Conway," Inspector Pilker said with distaste. "And the Society *aren't* police, so *stay* away."

Miss Trent followed him as far as the door. As she watched him go down the steps to the street, though, the sight of another's approach caused her heart to sink. Gripping the door's edge tightly, she put her other hand upon her hip and waited until they'd reached the steps' summit before speaking. "Inspector Woolfe. To what do I owe the 'pleasure?'"

"Can I come in?"

"If you've come to give me another lecture about how the Society shouldn't interfere with police investigations, save your breath. Detective Inspector Pilker has just given me one."

"It's not about that," Inspector Woolfe said with a sombre tone and expression.

Intrigued and taken aback in equal measure, Miss Trent stepped aside. "Very well."

TWENTY-TWO

Miss Trent stirred the sugar into the tea before passing the cup and saucer to Inspector Woolfe. His immense hand dwarfed them, making her think she should've given him a mug instead. She watched him drink half the cup's contents in one swallow and place it upon the low table with more delicacy than she'd expected. Leaving her own tea untouched, she rested her hands within her lap as she flicked her gaze back to his face.

The first drops of rain struck the parlour window as the day grew dark, causing the room to become enshrouded in gloom. Since it was mid-afternoon, the only light came from a fire in the hearth. It fully illuminated Inspector Woolfe as he sat on the sofa opposite. His face was haggard, suggesting he was sleep deprived, whilst his clothes were dishevelled. She doubted they'd been changed in the past few days. Fortunately, he'd left his foul-smelling fur coat on the stand in the hallway.

"You have my full attention, Inspector. What is this about?"

Inspector Woolfe turned serious eyes to her. "I've been to Tonbridge."

Miss Trent adopted a challenging tone. "Were you disturbing my aunt again?"

Inspector Woolfe's eyes narrowed. "I *spoke* to her, and your old fiancé, Mr Winslow."

Miss Trent's features tightened. She hadn't been aware of Inspector Woolfe's intentions regarding the latter and, knowing Graeme as well as she did, she strongly suspected he wouldn't have held his tongue. "My years spent in Tonbridge are irrelevant to the Bow Street Society. You speaking to my friends and family is a gross intrusion of my privacy."

"You surrendered any right to that when you became the Society's clerk."

For that rude comment alone, she hoped Graeme had shocked Inspector Woolfe with his revelations about their brief, yet intimate engagement. "You said this wouldn't be another lecture."

"It's not."

"So, why are you here?" Miss Trent demanded.

Inspector Woolfe's expression turned grave. "I found out something in Tonbridge that I thought you should know."

Miss Trent felt a knot form in her stomach. "What is it?"

"It's your parents," Inspector Woolfe replied in a heavy, sombre tone.

"If you're going to tell me they're dead, I already know."

"Do you know how?"

Miss Trent felt the knot in her stomach tighten and her heart rate increase. "No."

Inspector Woolfe hesitated. "They were murdered."

Miss Trent felt her heart clench, followed by a coldness that erupted from her core to send a prickling sensation across her entire body. Time seemed to stop as she stared at him, unable to form any words or thoughts. It was like she was frozen.

The breath she'd been holding suddenly burst forth from her lips as the true, horrific meaning behind Inspector Woolfe's words jolted her back to reality. Tears immediately welled up in her eyes, and her lips twisted with despair. A heaviness also built rapidly within her chest. Clapping her hand over her mouth, she stood and went over to the window.

"I'm sorry," Inspector Woolfe said with genuine regret.

Her breathing came in short, sharp bursts as, with tears rolling steadily down her face, she stared outside.

Inspector Woolfe cautiously approached. When he tried to place a gentle hand upon her back, though, she moved away sharply.

"*Don't* touch me." She turned fierce, damp eyes upon him.

Inspector Woolfe lifted his hands and took a step back. "I was just—"

"I know what you were trying to do, *Inspector*. You're the *last* person I want comfort from." Quaking all over, she crossed to the fireplace and retrieved a cigarette and match from a silver box. Placing the cigarette between her lips and lighting it, she took a long, deep pull. She gripped the mantel shelf's edge with one hand as she lowered her head and exhaled the smoke. After a second-long, deep pull, she tossed the cigarette into the fire and returned to her armchair.

Inspector Woolfe lingered by the window. "Do you want me to leave?"

"What I *want* is *answers*."

A pained look flashed through his eyes. "I've not come here to hurt you."

Turning her back upon him, she roughly wiped her face and eyes with a handkerchief.

Inspector Woolfe gave her a wide berth as he walked back to the sofa.

Swallowing her grief, Miss Trent stared at the clock on the mantel shelf and realised Mr Maxwell wouldn't be back for another hour. Although he was inept at offering comfort, just having him in the house would've eased her intense feeling of isolation. She couldn't even telephone Sam since he was out on Society business.

"Here." Inspector Woolfe's voice broke through her thoughts.

Parting her lips to decline whatever 'comfort' he was offering, she was instead taken aback by the fresh cup of tea in his hand. Meeting his eyes, she was further surprised by the genuine concern they held. Rendered speechless by this unusually kind gesture, she stared at him before remembering he was waiting for her to take the drink. "Oh." She returned to her senses with a curt shake of her head and brief closing of her eyes. "Sorry." She took the drink and cradled it in her lap. "Thank you."

"There was no easy way to say it, but I still could've done a better job of it," Inspector Woolfe said with regret.

"Regardless of how you sugar coat it, it's still a bitter pill to swallow." Miss Trent lowered her gaze. "I'm sorry for being so rude. You were only trying to help."

"You get accustomed to it," Inspector Woolfe said, his voice retaining a hint of regret despite the flippant nature of his remark.

Miss Trent took a mouthful of tea, grateful for the extra sugar he'd added.

"Do you remember them at all?" Inspector Woolfe enquired, watching her intently.

"My mother mostly. I was only five years old when they died."

As silence naturally fell between them, Inspector Woolfe finished his tea and placed the empty cup and saucer upon the low table. "Do you still want those answers?"

Miss Trent took another mouthful of tea to ease her crippling sadness and rising anxiety at the prospect of hearing what had happened to her parents. Taking a deep, shuddering breath to fortify herself further, she lifted her head to look him squarely in the eyes. "I do," she replied in a resolute tone. "I need to know the truth." Her voice faltered. "No matter how painful it may be."

"If you want me to stop at any time, say so."

"I will." She took in a slow, deep breath as she squared her shoulders and lifted her chin. "Tell me everything you know."

Inspector Woolfe moved closer and lowered his voice. Although it retained its deep gruffness, Miss Trent was strangely comforted by the sound. "I found a story about your parents' murder in the archive of the *Tonbridge Free Press*. Detective Constable Thomas Begg, who I borrowed from the Kent County Constabulary's detective branch in Wrens Cross, Maidstone, found their graves but only the burial record of your mother, Hannah Pottinger. Mr Reynolds, the old church warden at St. Stephen's church Church in Tonbridge, told Begg where your father, Bennett Pottinger, was buried."

Miss Trent downcast her eyes.

"Was you taken to their graves?" Inspector Woolfe enquired.

"No. I was too young at the time to understand." Miss Trent frowned. "That's what my aunt has since told me, at least."

"I've left instruction with Sergeant George Hunnicutt at the Pembury Road police station to show you where they are if you wish to pay your respects."

"I do, thank you." Miss Trent offered another feeble smile. "Was Sergeant Hunnicutt the one who investigated my parents' murders?"

Inspector Woolfe shook his head. "He found his predecessor's report on it in the records, though. It confirmed what I'd read in the newspaper."

Miss Trent took a large mouthful of tea as she felt her anxiety rising again. In a quiet voice, she enquired, "What did you read?"

"That your father was a casual poacher who got himself caught up in the murder of a groundskeeper."

Miss Trent paled. "Was he... the one responsible?"

"I don't think so, and neither did Hunnicutt's predecessor."

Miss Trent released a deep breath through partially closed lips as she looked down at his knees. "Thank goodness."

"But half of Tonbridge does."

Miss Trent looked up sharply with wide eyes. "I beg your pardon?"

Inspector Woolfe leaned forward and said in as gentle a voice as he could muster, "Begg couldn't find your father's burial record because his grave is in the non-consecrated ground beside the churchyard."

Miss Trent stared at him. "I… I don't understand. If he wasn't guilty, why…?" Her mouth slackened as a terrible thought occurred to her. "Did my father… did he murder… *himself*?"

"No."

Miss Trent closed her eyes and sighed, "Thank *God*."

"He was buried there because no one could prove his innocence over the groundskeeper's murder," Inspector Woolfe said. "After he was shot, the groundskeeper was left at the servants' door of the big house he worked for. Hunnicutt's predecessor suspected it was your father who'd carried him there. He also suspected it was your father's mate and lodger, a labourer called Mitchell Goodman, who'd accidentally shot the groundskeeper in the first place. Both men were seen scarpering from the scene—Goodman from the direction of the woods, your father from the direction of the house. The groundskeeper died less than a day later. He never woke up, so he couldn't say who'd done what."

Miss Trent frowned deeply and rubbed her temple. "I don't understand. Were my father and Goodman hung for the crime?"

Inspector Woolfe's expression turned grave. "Mitchell was hung for shooting your parents."

Miss Trent stared at him. Feeling the sting of tears, she turned her head and tried to blink the sensation away. "Why?"

"Hunnicutt's predecessor suspected Goodman had overheard your parents talking about going to the police."

Miss Trent felt a wave of nausea.

Concerned, Inspector Woolfe studied her face. "Do you want me to go on?"

Miss Trent gave a curt nod and released a soft sound of disgust. "Yes."

"Goodman scarpered, and your parents' bodies were found by your uncle the next morning. When the police searched the house, they found a bloodied shirt stuffed up the stove's chimney. Your uncle identified it as your father's."

"The groundskeeper's blood from when he'd carried him?"

"That's what Hunnicutt's predecessor thought."

"Where was I when… my parents died?"

"At your aunt's house, luckily. By the sounds of him, I don't think Goodman would've stopped at murdering you, too, if it meant saving his own neck."

Miss Trent drank the remainder of her tea as she tried to process everything she'd heard. "If Goodman murdered the groundskeeper, and my parents to keep them quiet, why was my father's innocence in doubt?"

"Because no one but Goodman and your father knew who'd shot the groundskeeper. There were no other eyewitnesses."

"But Hunnicutt's predecessor—"

"A copper's suspicions don't hold water without evidence."

Miss Trent downcast her eyes as she bowed her head. "No… I suppose not." She set down her empty cup and saucer upon the table. Mr Elliott's explanation about the law of common purpose sprang into her mind at the same time, clarifying the reality Sergeant Hunnicutt's predecessor had been faced with. Yet, the fact her father had been considering going to the police despite the precarious legal position he was in spoke volumes to her. Only an innocent man would readily throw himself upon the mercy of the court.

Wiping her eyes with her handkerchief, she took a deep, shuddering breath and lifted her head to offer him a weak, yet appreciative smile. "Thank you for telling me. I knew my parents were dead but was never told the circumstances or reason. Truth be told, it's a question that's haunted me since childhood." She furrowed her brow, "With all due respect, Inspector, why isn't my aunt here instead of you?"

"She didn't want to break her heart by breaking yours," Inspector Woolfe replied with genuine concern. "She never wanted to lie to you. At the time, she and your uncle thought it was best to keep the horror of your parents' death from you. She'd tried telling you over the years but couldn't find the words." He lowered his gaze. "I also know what it feels like to lose your parents."

Miss Trent frowned deeply. "I'm sorry."

Inspector Woolfe lifted his gaze and, upon seeing the genuine sympathy in hers, stood and went over to the fireplace. "But this isn't about me." He glanced over the mantel shelf without registering its contents as he suppressed the thoughts and emotions associated with his own loss. Once successful, he turned toward the clerk. "I think you should visit her."

"I will." Miss Trent gave a sad sigh as she stood. "When the Maxwell trial is over."

"How is Mr Maxwell?"

Miss Trent looked at him, surprised. "Coping. Thank you for asking."

"I'm not the monster you think I am."

Miss Trent offered a small smile. "No. You're not."

Inspector Woolfe moved closer. "And you're not as formidable as I thought you were."

Miss Trent's smile grew as she gently teased, "Don't get carried away, Inspector."

Inspector Woolfe gave a soft grunt and ran admiring eyes over her form. "There's one thing I still don't understand."

Miss Trent folded her arms and lifted her chin. "What's that?"

"If your parents' deaths have been on your mind all these years, why didn't you get the Society to investigate them?"

"Because the Society isn't for my personal use."

"Was that your employer's decision?"

"It was *my* decision."

Inspector Woolfe smirked. "You don't deny you're employed by someone, then. Who is he?"

"Whom?" Miss Trent retorted with a defiant look in her eyes.

Inspector Woolfe released a weak chuckle. "Didn't think that would work." He closed the distance between them and lowered his voice. "If you ever need something else investigating…" He ran his eyes over her form once more. "I'd be happy to help."

"Thank you." Miss Trent gave a weak smile to hide her disgust as she stepped around him. "But I doubt that situation will ever arise."

Inspector Woolfe narrowed his eyes as he watched her walk away before turning toward him with her hands upon her hips.

"By the way, will you be informing Inspector Lee of your discovery about my parents?" She enquired.

"It's got nothing to do with Inspector Lee."

"But you are working together, aren't you?"

"What makes you think that?"

Miss Trent glanced at the window. "Sergeant Gutman has been loitering around outside again. He's one of Inspector Lee's men, isn't he?"

"Yeah, but that doesn't mean we're working together."

"No, but it would make sense. After all, you both want the Society destroyed."

"I just want to protect people," Inspector Woolfe growled. "As for Inspector Lee, what I found out in Tonbridge is none of his business. This is where my investigation into your life there ends."

"Is that so?" Miss Trent carefully considered the credibility of his statement. His compassion appeared genuine, but she had trouble believing it was coming from him. Eventually, she decided to give him the benefit of the doubt and lowered her hands from her hips to rest at her sides. "Very well," she conceded. "Thank you."

"I don't have to tell you to keep this between us," Inspector Woolfe said.

"I shan't tell a soul." She glanced over his tired face. "And you should get some rest."

"I can't." Inspector Woolfe headed for the door. "Not until I've told Inspector Lee what I've *not* found out in Tonbridge." He looked back at her. "Remember, Sergeant George Hunnicutt will take you to your parents' graves. If I were you, I'd do the decent thing and petition for your father to be moved to consecrated ground."

Miss Trent offered a small, yet appreciative smile. "I will. Thank you, again, Caleb, and Merry Christmas."

"Merry Christmas." He opened the door and softly added before leaving, "Rebecca."

TWENTY-THREE

Descending the stairs into the basement of the *Key & Lion*, Mr Snyder was disappointed by the few spectators gathered around the makeshift ring. Recalling how crowded it had been the night Inspector Conway had fought, he conceded the poor attendance could be due to the fact it was early afternoon. That was his hope, at least, as he approached the ropes and watched the last few minutes of the set-to unfold.

A sixteen-year-old boy, who bore the bruises and wounds from another fight on top of the ones sustained in this, was against a bruiser at least forty years his senior. Although the latter had the benefit of experience, his pace was slow, and his movements were sloppy. Meanwhile, the former had the benefit of a swift pace but lacked the strength and skill to deliver devastating blows.

"I've seen my old lady fight better than this," Mr Snyder's neighbour remarked.

"Who are they?" the cabman enquired.

"The lad's Marcus O'Shannon. The old bruiser's Conor Fylan."

A spectator on the other side of the ring released a cry of encouragement as Marcus avoided Conor's punch by ducking to the right, thereby causing it to pass over his shoulder. Marcus immediately followed this with a strike to Conor's nose. Yet, the short distance Marcus had drawn back his arm meant the blow lacked any real power. Consequently, Conor was only dazed and able to retaliate within seconds.

Advancing upon him at greater speed than the young amateur thought possible, Conor penned him in the corner. With his body bent and his chin close to his chest, he repeatedly struck out with alternate left and right bows to Marcus' stomach, chest, and ribs. Due to the limited space around him, Marcus could do nothing but keep his fists up, his arms together, and his elbows against his stomach.

From his vantage point, Mr Snyder could see how loose Marcus' defence was, though. Therefore, it came as no surprise when Conor brought the bout to an abrupt end by pulling and lifting his right arm all the way back and driving his fist into Marcus' temple. Mr Snyder flinched as he heard the tell-tale crunch, knowing the tremendous strength put behind the blow allowed its force to feel as hard as a steam train.

Marcus was sent staggering sideways with arms flailing. Immediately pushed back into the ring by the spectator, he stumbled and fell onto his stomach. Having thrown his hands down to break his fall, Marcus felt a crunch in his left wrist, followed by an explosion of pain up his arm. Rolling onto his back, he drew his knees up and clutched his wrist against his chest as, with a face contorted by agony, he moaned through gritted teeth.

Spurred into action by the sight, Mr Sparrow and Marcus' seconds immediately climbed into the ring. As the latter dragged their principal back to his corner and examined his wrist, Conor strolled back to his own corner to wait. Meanwhile, Mr Sparrow took out his pocket watch and counted down the permitted timeout. After which he called, "Time!"

Conor returned to the scratch, but Marcus shook his head despite his seconds' attempts to coerce him into continuing. Counting down eight seconds, Mr Sparrow gripped Conor's wrist and declared him the winner when Marcus failed to join them at the scratch. A few murmurs arose from those watching, but most simply headed for the stairs, mumbling their disappointment. In contrast, Mr Snyder felt concern for both men. Marcus because the broken wrist had undoubtedly ended his boxing career early, and Conor because the meagre crowd meant a meagre purse.

"Mr Sparrow," Mr Snyder greeted with his hand outstretched.

Gripping it firmly with his own, Mr Sparrow's face was lit up by his smile. "The Whitechapel Ox as I live and breathe."

As Mr Sparrow withdrew his hand, Mr Snyder pointed at the dark-grey piece of cloth binding it. "Was you on the card, too?"

Mr Sparrow released a soft chuckle as he momentarily lifted his hand and glanced at it. "I ain't been up to the scratch in years. I done this being cack-handed with a barrel." There was a twinkle in his eye as he added, "But I can put you on the next card if you're wanting a return to the ring." He cast a cursory glance around them before leaning in close. "The Bulldog done some recent set-tos. I could get him in another if it was the Whitechapel Ox he was facing." He rubbed his nose with a knowing look in his eyes. "Would be a fair purse in it for you, too." He withdrew with a few nods.

Mr Snyder chuckled.

"You wouldn't be knocked into a cocked hat like young O'Shannon," Mr Sparrow added.

"I'll think about it," Mr Snyder said, a part of him curious how such a set-to would go.

Mr Sparrow's face lit up with another smile. "You'd be doing me a good turn. My customers have been aggin' about the quality of the pugs and legging it to the mittened fights since I lost Joe Rake. A proper good old set-to between the Whitechapel Ox and Bulldog would have them back here in a heartbeat."

"I said I'll think about it." Mr Snyder chuckled. "Nowt sayin' the Bulldog would want in either."

"You ended his boxing days, the first time around. He'll want in."

Mr Snyder smiled but still had his doubts. "What about Joe Rake? Can't you get 'im back for a fair purse?"

Mr Sparrow's expression cooled. "He's gone soft and taken up the mittens."

Mr Snyder inwardly mused if that was partly the reason for the *Key & Lion*'s customers abandoning the bareknuckle fights. Nevertheless, he decided to shift the focus of their chat to the reason for his visit. "Did you hear of old Grosse bein' done in? Poor bloke."

Mr Sparrow's smile faded. Turning his back upon him, he went to the nearest stake and untied the uppermost rope from it. "Ar."

After the docks, Mr Snyder, Mr Skinner, and Miss Dexter had returned to Bow Street where they'd met Mr Elliott and Dr Colbert. Recalling their conversation in which they'd related Mr Baldwin's responses to their questions, Mr Snyder enquired, "Do you remember 'im bein' 'ere that night?"

Mr Sparrow loosely coiled the rope around his arm as he went to the next stake and untied it from there, too. With his head down, he replied, "Ar, he was talking to Baldwin who was having a benny over Grosse's notebook."

"Why was that?" Mr Snyder followed Mr Sparrow to the third stake as he continued to coil up the rope. Removal of the ring after a fight, especially an illegal one, was common. Given what Mr Sparrow had said about losing customers to the gloved fighting, though, he wondered if the ring would be put back up anytime soon.

"Baldwin wanted a look, and Grosse wouldn't let him."

"I'd want a look, too, wouldn't you?"

"Most would, but Grosse never let anyone see inside it."

"Makes sense, if what's said was in it was in it."

Mr Sparrow nodded.

Mr Snyder considered his next words carefully. "I heard there was a set-to in the warehouse on the docks where Grosse was found. Do you know owt about that?"

Mr Sparrow lifted his head sharply to glare at him. "Why do you want to know for?"

"I just wondered who was in it," Mr Snyder replied. "Maybe a pug who'd fight 'ere."

Mr Sparrow straightened, his unblinking gaze fixed upon Mr Snyder as he tightly gripped the coiled rope. "I'd stop wondering."

"Fair dos." Mr Snyder went over to the fourth stake and untied the rope from it. "It's a shame old Grosse was done in. He could of found another pug for you."

The tension eased in Mr Sparrow's face as he joined Mr Snyder, coiling the rope as he did so. With downcast eyes, he remarked sadly, "Ar. Grosse was a good man for that."

"Was none who come close to 'is knowledge of boxin'."

Mr Sparrow hummed, taking the rope from Mr Snyder once he'd untied it.

"'E was writin' a book, wasn't 'e?"

Mr Sparrow smiled sadly. "Him and that book of his." He gave a weak shake of his head as he lamented, "Poor beggar's not going to finish it now." He glanced at Mr Snyder. "He wanted to put you in it."

"A book on boxin's not been done right if it don't have the Whitechapel Ox in it," Mr Snyder joked.

Mr Sparrow gave a feeble chuckle.

Mr Snyder scratched his cheek as they went to the fifth stake. "Wasn't Deon Erskine the other one he wanted in it?"

Mr Sparrow stilled. "Was he?" He hurriedly untied the rope and strode to the sixth stake, haphazardly wrapping the rope around his arm as he did so. "I don't know."

"What happened to old Erskine?" Mr Snyder watched him closely.

"Legged it to New York City a few years back." Mr Sparrow hurriedly untied the rope from the stake and strode across to the seventh.

"To fight with the mittens?"

"I don't know." Mr Sparrow tossed the rope over his arm once he'd untied it and went to the eighth stake.

"The *Amateur Athletic Union* know nowt 'bout 'im," Mr Snyder said.

Mr Sparrow stared at him. "The what?"

"The *Amateur Athletic Union of the United States of America*," Mr Snyder clarified. "Grosse had a telegram from 'em."

Mr Sparrow frowned deeply as he looked to the stake. "He did…"

"It was in 'is notebook, or so I heard." Mr Snyder untied the rope from the stake and passed it to him. "He never said he was sendin' it?"

"Hm?" Mr Sparrow looked up sharply. Realising what he'd asked, he replied, "No." He walked back to the first stake and untied the rope from it. Once done, he set the rope down on a nearby barrel. "Want a pint? On the house."

"That's very kind of you." Mr Snyder smiled.

"No kindness. I want you back in that ring." Mr Sparrow chuckled.

"I'll think about it," Mr Snyder said, walking with him to the bar upstairs. "You don't know where Grosse's notebook and book are, do you?"

Mr Sparrow put his arm around Mr Snyder and gave his shoulder a hard squeeze. Leaning in close, he said in a low, firm voice, "Don't myther on about Grosse." A contrite smile lifted his features as he released him and, in an upbeat tone, said, "I'll get you that pint."

* * *

Miss Dexter could only imagine what her Pa-Pa would say if he knew she'd visited *Linton's Tobacconists* for a second time. She'd chosen not to inform him of the first simply because she knew he'd worry about her respectability and safety. Which confused her since she'd not taken to smoking since she and Mr Elliott were last in the shop. Her Ma-Ma had remarked upon the scent of tobacco on her coat, though, but only to express her disapproval at the sorts of places the Society was sending her daughter to.

Mr Linton studied the sketch of Noah O'Hanigan intently.

"May I purchase some cigarettes whilst I'm here, please?" Dr Colbert enquired from Tabitha as he reached into his coat.

"Certainly, sir." Tabitha flashed him a smile.

"I wouldn't have placed you as a man who smoked," Mr Elliott remarked.

"It's a minor vice I indulge in after dealing with particularly trying patients," Dr Colbert said and pointed out his preferred brand upon the shelf. "Edwina abhors the smell."

"Your wife?" Mr Elliott enquired.

"Yes, of ten years," Dr Colbert replied, paying the necessary coin as he slipped the box of cigarettes into his coat.

"She sounds lovely, Doctor," Miss Dexter interjected.

"Thank you." Dr Colbert smiled warmly.

"He isn't familiar to me, sirs," Mr Linton said. "Is he to you, love?"

Tabitha studied the sketch. "No."

"His name is Noah O'Hanigan," Mr Elliott said. "Have you heard it before?"

"Never, sir," Tabitha replied.

"Neither have I," Mr Linton added.

Miss Dexter returned the sketch to her satchel.

"Did Mr Grosse place into your possession a tattered, dark-blue notebook?" Mr Elliott enquired.

"The one he always had with him?" Tabitha queried.

"Yes," Mr Elliott replied. "We believe it may hold some significance."

"He wouldn't part with it, even to fuel his fire in the depths of winter, sir," Tabitha said, amused. "He wouldn't have given it to us."

Mr Elliott's lips formed a hard line as he reflected humour had no place in a conversation as serious as this.

In much the same way it was unwelcome within the court room. Taking a moment to calm his disquiet at the young woman's poor choice of words, he enquired, "Did he place his manuscript on the history of boxing in London into your possession instead?"

"No, sir," Mr Linton replied as Tabitha shook her head.

Mr Elliott parted his lips to thank the Lintons and bid them farewell when the sound of another entering the shop distracted him.

Turning in unison with his fellow Bow Streeters, his gaze met the hazel eyes of a slim man in his mid-forties with a long face and protruding ears. His hair, narrow sideburns, and thin moustache were blond in colour, whilst the cheeks of his otherwise fair complexion were bright red from the cold. Removing a black bowler hat as he'd entered, he reached into his knee-length, dark-brown coat as he approached the counter. From it, he produced a warrant card that he presented to the Lintons. "Detective Inspector George Pilker of Scotland Yard. Am I talking to Mr Anthony and Miss Tabitha Linton?"

"You are," Mr Linton replied. "These are—"

"I know who they are," Inspector Pilker said, casting a black look at the others. "Dr Neal Colbert, Mr Gregory Elliott, and Miss Georgina Dexter from the Bow Street Society, right?"

"That is correct," Mr Elliott replied. "We were just leaving."

"Good." Inspector Pilker returned his attention to the Lintons. "I understand a Mr Christian Grosse rented a room from you. I'd like to see it."

"Good day to you," Dr Colbert said, addressing the trio before following Miss Dexter and Mr Elliott outside. Watching Inspector Pilker commence his questioning of the Lintons through the glass, he frowned upon seeing Tabitha point at them. This prompted the inspector to look their way, followed by him striding out the shop with a fierce glare.

"Halt!" Inspector Pilker demanded upon emerging.

"Yes?" Mr Elliott enquired in his usual monotone.

"Give it to me." Inspector Pilker held out his hand.

"What are we meant to have?" Mr Elliott enquired.

"Evidence. Give it to me, and you can go on your way," Inspector Pilker replied.

The Bow Streeters exchanged glances.

"I know you have it. Miss Linton has just told me you do. Give it to me. Now." Inspector Pilker demanded.

Dr Colbert frowned. "You're still going to have to clarify what it is we're supposed to have, Inspector."

"You took some documents from Mr Grosse's office," Inspector Pilker said, glaring at him. "Documents which could prove to be vital evidence in the identification of Mr Grosse's murderer. They are the property of the Metropolitan Police as long as our investigation is ongoing, so give them to me."

"We don't have them," Mr Elliott stated.

"I'm not above arresting you lot!" Inspector Pilker warned.

"We don't have them because they are with Miss Trent at Bow Street," Mr Elliott clarified. "We are returning there now. I will personally see to it that any and all pieces of evidence we hold are delivered to you at New Scotland Yard."

Inspector Pilker jerked his head back, parted his lips, closed them again, and furrowed his brow. "*Very well.*" He cast a glare amongst them. "I'll be there later this afternoon. Deliver them to me then."

"I shall make it my utmost priority," Mr Elliott said in all seriousness.

Taken aback by his cooperation, Inspector Pilker gave a firm nod, muttered "Good," and strode back inside.

"Will you also deliver Inspector Conway's file?" Dr Colbert enquired, dryly.

"That is my intention, yes," Mr Elliott replied in a heartbeat.

Miss Dexter gave a sad shake of her head.

* * *

"What about Noah O'Hanigan?" Mr Snyder mused aloud, setting down his pint.

"What about him?" Mr Sparrow enquired as he wiped down the bar top.

"Won't 'e go in your ring?" Mr Snyder enquired.

Mr Sparrow shook his head and continued his work. "He's a drunk."

In addition to Mr Elliott and Dr Colbert, Mr Snyder had also met Misses Webster and Hicks upon returning to Bow Street. Recalling their conversation in which they'd related Mrs Grosse's responses to their questions, he enquired, "Who's that American gent O'Hanigan's been goin' 'round with?"

Mr Sparrow momentarily paused in his work to search his memory. "I don't know."

Mr Snyder took a mouthful of ale as he considered asking the landlord if he knew where either man was. Given Mr Sparrow's less-than-subtle warning about Grosse, though, he decided against it. A glance at the clock above the bar also told him he needed to get a move on if he wanted to visit the other pubs before supper. Finishing his pint in a matter of minutes, he pushed the empty glass away. "Thanks." As he turned to leave, though, a short, lean man in a blue bowler hat stepped into his personal space.

"Are you Mr Samuel Snyder perchance?" the man enquired in a nasal voice. His attire consisted of a faded, grey overcoat that had lost its buttons, a dishevelled dark-blue suit with curled, tobacco-stained lapels, and a twisted black tie. His gaunt face, tired brown eyes, and lacklustre moustache and whiskers hinted at the hard times he'd fallen upon. Fixing the cabman with his gaze, he stood with rounded shoulders and a natural stoop as he dry-washed his hands. "A word? Please? If I may? It will only take a moment."

Mr Snyder looked to the bar and, upon seeing Mr Sparrow was now serving a customer at its far end, lowered his voice to reply to the stranger. "I'm 'im. What do you want to talk 'bout?"

"You are a Bow Street Society member, are you not?"

"I am. Who are you?"

"E.P. Westcott, a bookmaker by trade, a pauper by circumstance." He tilted his head as he kept a close eye on Mr Sparrow. "I have some information the Society will be very interested in. Valuable information."

"How valuable?" Mr Snyder enquired with a hint of scepticism.

"The name of the man who murdered Mr Christian Grosse."

Mr Snyder's brows lifted.

"Yes, I thought that might convince you." Mr Westcott gave a smug smile.

TWENTY-FOUR

"What's 'is name?" Mr Snyder enquired, casting a glance in Mr Sparrow's direction. Fortunately, he remained deep in conversation with his customer.

"First thing's first," Mr Westcott replied and held out his open hand.

Mr Snyder rummaged around in his pockets and, finding a few shillings, dropped them into his palm. "What's 'is name?"

Mr Westcott counted the money and looked at him sideways. "You have nothing more?"

Mr Snyder gripped the lapel of Mr Westcott's overcoat. "Just one thing."

Mr Westcott lifted both hands and gave a worried smile. "This will do nicely."

Mr Snyder released him.

Mr Westcott slipped the money into his pocket. "Oswald Baldwin."

"Mr Grosse's mate?" Mr Snyder narrowed his eyes. "Why should I believe owt you say?"

Mr Westcott glanced over at Mr Sparrow before nodding to a table in a deserted corner of the pub. "Over there." Leading Mr Snyder to it, he sat with his back to the wall to have an unimpeded view of the bar. Once Mr Snyder sat opposite him, he leaned forward with his elbow upon the table and used his bowler hat to both muffle his words and hide his lips. "I saw him with the body."

Mr Snyder leaned upon the table with folded arms and studied Mr Westcott. "When?"

"After he'd done him in."

"At the warehouse?"

"Yes." Mr Westcott sighed. "I saw Mr Baldwin searching Mr Grosse's body."

"What for?"

"Isn't it obvious?" Mr Westcott briefly peered over his hat to ensure no one was close by. "The *notebook*." Mr

Westcott lowered his voice to barely above a whisper. "But he didn't find it, so he settled for the less valuable of his things. His hat, watch, money, shoes, handkerchief, and cufflinks." Mr Westcott turned his head a little and quietly lamented, "I wanted those."

Mr Snyder cupped his chin and rubbed his right cheek as he mused aloud, "You never *saw* Mr Baldwin do Grosse in, then?"

"I didn't have to, did I? He never told a soul Grosse was there, and there was plenty of them to tell."

"Like who?"

Mr Westcott frowned. "Warehousemen, mostly."

"Who was in the set-to?"

Mr Westcott lowered his hat as he sat bolt upright. "I don't know anythin' about a set-to." He stood and, giving a brief bow, hurried away. "Be seein' you, Mr Snyder."

Mr Snyder pursed his lips and, releasing a deep sigh through his lips, wondered if he'd ever get the fighters' names.

* * *

Mr Voigt's jaw was clenched as he regarded Miss Trent with cold eyes. His arms were also rigid at his sides, whilst a vein in his temple visibly twitched. He lifted the hand holding the sample of his nephew's handwriting but kept his elbow against his side. With a distinct tautness to his voice, he said, "You requested this."

"Thank you." Miss Trent took the sample and glanced over it. It was a letter he'd written to his uncle a few weeks' prior asking for money.

"And his manuscript…" Mr Voigt held a folder out to her. "Incomplete forevermore."

Miss Trent took it and, casting a cursory glance over its contents, saw it was filled with numerous handwritten pages, most of which were dog eared. She could also see where he'd run out of paper as his writing had grown steadily smaller as he'd neared the bottom of the page.

"Thank you. Our member, Miss Agnes Webster, will use the letter to identify the handwriting in the manuscript and publications we found as his."

"How could it not be?" Mr Voigt curtly enquired.

"Your nephew would've undoubtedly had frequent visitors to his office. Any of them could've given him the publications. Furthermore, given the potentially illegal subject matter of his manuscript, it's wise to make certain it's his original work and not another's."

"Perhaps." Mr Voigt's lips flattened, and his nostrils flared as he breathed deeply through his nose. "There is something else." A pinkness also crept up his face from the base of his neck. Lifting his chin, he stated, "Your members spoke to Mrs Grosse when I expressly forbade it. Does the Society disrespect all its clients, or have my wishes been ignored because I'm a foreigner?"

"Your wishes were ignored because, as your nephew's wife, Mrs Grosse is a natural suspect in his murder," Miss Trent replied in a hard tone. "The Bow Street Society isn't prejudiced against anyone, Mr Voigt. As you yourself pointed out during our first meeting."

"I came here because I thought the Society was different from the police. I was wrong."

Miss Trent folded her arms. "In other words, you thought we would follow your orders. Thereby ensuring your daughter-in-law's adultery would go undiscovered."

Mr Voigt's face flushed bright red. "This is *contemptable*!"

"Not only was Mrs Grosse's public display of adultery witnessed by our members, but she has admitted it to them this morning," Miss Trent said, maintaining her calm composure despite his wrath. "Do not think to sully the good name of this Society, to preserve the ill-deserved 'respectability' of your daughter-in-law."

Mr Voigt clamped his mouth shut and visibly clenched his jaw as his hands did the same at his sides. Glaring at her as he loudly breathed through his nose, he forced his breathing to slow and took several long, deep breaths. At the same time, the tension eased in his face as the anger faded from his eyes. Regret soon took its place, however. In a subdued voice, he enquired, "What is your intention?"

"For the information?"

"Yes."

"We don't have one."

"You don't have one?"

"Aside from keeping it under consideration whilst we investigate your nephew's murder," Miss Trent clarified.

"Will it be told to the police?"

"We're obliged to inform them of it, yes." Miss Trent adopted a gentler tone. "It gives your daughter-in-law and lover a substantial motive for murdering your nephew."

Mr Voigt turned and walked across the hallway as his face turned ashen. "I know."

"How long have you been aware of her adultery?"

Mr Voigt's features drooped as anguish filled his eyes. "A month, maybe less. Christian told me in a letter. It cut deep into his heart."

"How did he become aware of it?"

Mr Voigt's voice trembled. "He found them together. They *laughed* at him." He pursed his lips together and drew in a slow, deep breath through his nose as he lifted his chin and clenched his hands at his sides. "They *shan't* be *laughing* now."

Assuming he referred to his imminent eviction of Mrs Grosse from his nephew's house, Miss Trent allowed the statement to hang in the air. Although she couldn't condone Mrs Grosse's behaviour, she also couldn't condone his decision to abandon her to a fate worse than death on the streets. Nevertheless, she decided he was in no state to argue. Going to him, she adopted a gentle tone as she enquired, "Would you like some tea?"

He flashed a sad, yet appreciative smile. "Yes. Thank you, Miss Trent."

* * *

"I did warn you." Inspector Lee looked down his nose at Inspector Woolfe sitting before his desk. Standing behind it with a cup of tea, Inspector Lee had a sip and replaced it upon its saucer. "The key to the identity of Miss Trent's employer is in London, not Tonbridge."

"Her past had to be looked into," Inspector Woolfe countered.

"And it proved to be an absolute waste of both your time and the Kent Constabulary's." Inspector Lee turned aside and lifted the cup to his lips. "My efforts, on the other hand, have borne considerable fruit." He had a sip and took his time replacing it upon the saucer.

Inspector Woolfe leaned forward. "Like what?"

Inspector Lee carried his drink to the sideboard and, setting it down, dabbed at the corners of his mouth with his handkerchief. "Proof of Conway's corruption."

Inspector Woolfe leapt to his feet and advanced upon him. "I told you—"

"He was seen accepting a Bow Street Society envelope from Miss Trent by Sergeant Gutman," Inspector Lee interrupted, speaking over him. "A bribe, Caleb."

Inspector Woolfe stepped back sharply, shaking his head. "Nah." He turned away. "Conway wouldn't."

"He would and has." Inspector Lee went over to him and, breathing through his mouth to avoid catching a whiff of the foul odours emanating from him, moved in close as he lowered his voice. "I know it's difficult for you to accept because he is your friend, but—"

"That's got *nowt* to do with it!" Inspector Woolfe snarled, brown globules of salvia flying from his mouth.

Feeling one land upon his cheek, Inspector Lee closed his eyes in disgust and swallowed the bile that had risen to his throat.

"Conway's a good copper and a good bloke. He'd *never* take a bribe from *anyone*! Especially not from *them*!" Inspector Woolfe yelled in his face.

"Fine." Inspector Lee wiped his cheek with his handkerchief as he returned to his desk. "I can't expect you to believe me. Inspector Conway and I have never seen eye to eye after all." He fixed Inspector Woolfe firmly with his gaze. "Search his house. If you find nothing, I shan't say another word on the matter."

Inspector Woolfe narrowed his eyes. "I ain't searchin' his house."

Inspector Lee released a faux sigh of regret. "You leave me no choice." He reached for the telephone. "I wanted to avoid getting Chief Inspector Jones involved for your sake."

Inspector Woolfe snatched the receiver from him and slammed it down upon its cradle. "I won't let you ruin him, Gideon."

"Prove me wrong." Inspector Lee looked up at him with hard eyes. "Search his house and find exactly what you expect to: nothing."

Inspector Woolfe glared at him. "I will." He pointed at him. "Then I'll report *you* to Jones."

Inspector Lee remained silent as he kept an emotionless expression.

Inspector Woolfe straightened. "You'd better start packing away your desk." Shoving his chair aside as he strode out of the office, he caused the entire wall to shake as he slammed the door behind him.

A self-satisfied smile crept across Inspector Lee's lips as he imagined himself in his new role as head of the Mob Squad. "Oh, I will, Caleb. As soon as possible."

TWENTY-FIVE

It was dark by the time Mr Snyder entered the *Nimble Crow* public house. Having garnered no further information from the establishments he'd called upon since leaving the *Key & Lion*, he intended to end his search after this visit. The remaining boxing clubs on the list were dotted across London, meaning a whole day's travel was required to visit them all.

Unlike the *Key & Lion*, the *Nimble Crow* was filled with customers. The din of conversation was almost deafening, whilst the thick haze of cigarette smoke made it difficult to see. Removing his hat, Mr Snyder manoeuvred his way through the densely packed crowd toward the bar. A few disapproving looks were cast toward his cheap and tired-looking apparel, but no deriding remarks were made. Putting his hat on the bar upon reaching it, he looked left and right in search of the landlord or server.

A well-built man with broad shoulders and large biceps straining against the material of his pale-blue shirt stood at the far end on the right. His caterpillar-like black eyebrows were pushed down and together as his body leaned sideways toward his left hand on the bar. At the same time, he scrutinised a note held in his right. Also attired in tailor-made light-grey waistcoat and trousers, the man was the Kenrick Farley who owned the pub, or so Mr Snyder was told.

Mr Snyder glanced at his immediate neighbours, but no one sought to be served. Resigning himself to a long wait, he formed a plan in his mind for when he'd finished his business. What he'd been told at the *Key & Lion* would have to be reported back to Miss Trent at Bow Street. His wife and daughters were also preparing supper at home. Being without his cab meant his return journey would be difficult, but there wasn't any way he could've left it unattended outside the pubs and clubs.

"May I help you?" a man's voice enquired, drawing Mr Snyder from his thoughts.

"Pint of ale, please," Mr Snyder replied upon seeing it was the man with the note.

"The *White Swan* is around the corner," the man said in a forced upper-class accent. "I think you'd find it more suited to your purse."

"Are you Mr Kenrick Farley?" Mr Snyder enquired, choosing to ignore the dismissal.

"Depends on who's asking," the man replied.

Mr Snyder offered his hand. "Mr Samuel Snyder. They call me the—"

"The Whitechapel Ox. I've heard of you. Yes, I'm Farley." The man gave his hand a brief squeeze. "Are you interested in becoming a member?"

Mr Snyder smiled. "My boxin' days are long gone. A pint of ale wouldn't go amiss, though."

Mr Farley cast a disapproving glance over Mr Snyder's appearance but nevertheless reached for a glass. "One won't do any harm, I suppose." Allowing himself to relax, his natural East End of London accent filtered through as he added, "It's not every day you get a legend of the ring in your pub."

Mr Snyder chuckled. "There was better pugs than me."

"But none more sporting." Mr Farley set the glass before him. "On the house."

Mr Snyder gave a warm smile. "Thanks, that's very kind." He took a sip, needing to pace himself after the numerous pints he'd drunk at the other public houses. "Joe Rake and Noah O'Hanigan are the new talent these days, aren't they?"

Mr Farley held his arms wide as he rested his hands upon the bar and leaned his weight upon them. "Rake is. O'Hanigan's a drunk."

"I heard that." Mr Snyder had another sip. "And that Rake's taken up the mittens. Is 'e a member 'ere?"

Mr Farley's expression became emotionless as his eyes cooled. "You've not come here for Rake, but to hear about Mr Grosse." He straightened and took the note from his pocket. "Mr Sparrow warned me about you. That you were asking questions over at the *Key & Lion* about Mr Grosse and his murder."

"Why didn't you say owt before?" Mr Snyder enquired with intrigue rather than concern.

"Because the *Nimble Crow* prides itself on its respectability. I'm not about to ruin it by causing a public disturbance." Mr Farley glanced at his nearby customers, but they remained engrossed in their respective conversations. "I heard you're a member of the Bow Street Society these days. Did they send you?"

"Yeah. We've been asked by Mr Grosse's uncle to find 'is murderer."

"It's not me, or anyone here, or anyone I know."

Mr Snyder showed him the sketch of the American gent. "Could it be 'im?"

Mr Farley studied the sketch. "Could be."

"Do you know 'im?"

"He's Amias Winfield. Noah O'Hanigan's manager and trainer."

Mr Snyder felt relief wash over him. "Do you know where I can find 'im?"

Mr Farley shook his head. "Why?"

Mr Snyder put the sketch away. "'E was heard havin' an argument with Mr Grosse in his office two days ago. You don't know what that might of been about, do you?"

"Not for sure, but it might've been over my decision to cancel O'Hanigan's membership here." Mr Farley retrieved another glass from the shelf and poured himself some ale from the barrel. "When I told Mr Grosse I'd accepted O'Hanigan's membership application, he was angrier than I'd ever seen him." He took a mouthful. "He said putting O'Hanigan in the ring would ruin the club's reputation. I trusted Mr Grosse's judgement, so I told Mr Winfield his man was out. He must've gone from here straight to Mr Grosse's office, if the argument was two days ago, like you said."

"O'Hanigan wasn't in the set-to at the warehouse where Mr Grosse was done in?"

"No." Mr Farley set down his glass with a thud.

"Who was?" Mr Snyder enquired, lifting his own to his lips.

Mr Farley held his arms wide and rested his hands upon the bar as he turned his head away. "I don't know. I wasn't there." He met Mr Snyder's gaze. "None of us were." He straightened and plucked up his drink. "I've got customers to serve."

"Mr Grosse was writin' a book," Mr Snyder said as Mr Farley turned to move further down the bar. "Did 'e talk to you about who 'e was putting in it? Pugs like Deon Erskine, or the Bulldog?"

Mr Farley put his drink down with another thud. Gripping the glass tightly, though, he put his other hand upon the bar and leaned toward him. In a low voice, he said, "I don't know anything about the book, Erskine, the Bulldog, or Mr Grosse's murder. I've got customers to serve, so I suggest you finish your pint and leave." He straightened. "It was nice meeting you." He took another mouthful of ale and strode down the bar.

Deciding it was wise to heed his advice, Mr Snyder drank the rest of his pint, put on his hat, and left with more questions than he'd come with.

* * *

"Come in," Chief Inspector Jones called in response to the knock upon his door. In mid-preparation of leaving, he stood by the hat stand in his overcoat and scarf when a constable entered. Following closely behind was Mr Gregory Elliott. Taken aback, Chief Inspector Jones momentarily stilled. Immediately regaining his composure, though, he assumed a cool tone as he enquired from the constable, "What is the meaning of this?"

"I've an appointment with Detective Inspector Pilker," Mr Elliott stated.

"Given Mr Elliott's membership of the Bow Street Society, I thought you might want to oversee the meeting, Chief Inspector," the constable explained.

"Thank you." Chief Inspector Jones removed his overcoat and scarf. "Please, fetch Inspector Pilker and return to your duties." He hung up his things as the constable left and, moving behind his desk, indicated the vacant chair in front. "Please, sit, Mr Elliott."

Casting a cursory glance over his surroundings, Mr Elliott duly accepted the invitation. Resting his satchel upon his lap, he watched Chief Inspector Jones settle into his chair. "It would appear the Metropolitan Police's mistrust of the Bow Street Society goes beyond even my estimation. I assure you this isn't an exercise in espionage."

"Whilst I appreciate your openness, Mr Elliott, I must also remind you of your group's reputation and the integral part it played in the suspension of one of my officers. You can hardly disapprove of our caution over your unannounced visit."

A knock sounded upon the door.

"Come in," Chief Inspector Jones called.

Inspector Pilker entered, stilled when he saw Mr Elliott, and closed the door.

"Mr Elliott alleges he's here for an appointment with you," Chief Inspector Jones said.

"Yes, sir," Inspector Pilker cautiously approached. "Earlier today, I was informed by a witness that the Bow Street Society had removed potentially significant evidence from a key location of interest. I arranged for Mr Elliott to deliver the evidence to me here."

Chief Inspector Jones slid his gaze to the Bow Streeter. "Have you brought it?"

"I have." Mr Elliott stood and retrieved Mr Grosse's copies of *Bell's Sporting Life*, *Fistiana*, and *Bradshaw's Railway Times* from his satchel. Putting them on Chief

Inspector Jones' desk, he next retrieved Mr Grosse's manuscript and files from his satchel and added them to the pile. Picking up the topmost file, he held it out to Chief Inspector Jones. "I'd like to draw your attention to this in particular, Chief Inspector."

Glancing at the cover, Chief Inspector Jones saw it was blank. Taking it from the Bow Streeter, he stilled the moment he laid eyes upon John Conway's name on the file's first page. Glancing at Mr Elliott, who's expression remained emotionless, he stood and took the file over to the window as he studied the rest of its contents. Eventually, he enquired in a hard tone, "Where did the Society get this?"

"The office of Mr Christian Grosse," Mr Elliott replied. "The man whose murder the Society has been commissioned to investigate."

Chief Inspector Jones closed the file and met Mr Elliott's gaze. "Thank you for bringing this to my attention. You may leave now."

"May I enquire whether you intend to act upon this information?" Mr Elliott enquired.

"I'm afraid I'm unable to discuss such matters with you," Chief Inspector Jones replied. "Goodnight."

Mr Elliott's features tightened at the dismissal. "Goodnight, Chief Inspector." He headed for the door. "Inspector."

"Ensure he's escorted off the premises," Chief Inspector Jones ordered once Mr Elliott had left.

"Yes, sir," Inspector Pilker replied, hurrying after the Bow Streeter.

Opening the file again, Chief Inspector Jones frowned as he read Inspector Conway's boxing career. A moment later, he reached a decision and tucked the file under his arm as he left his office. Going to the first floor via the cramped elevator, he didn't wait to knock on Inspector Conway's door before striding inside. He found his friend standing by his desk, albeit preparing to leave with his hat in his hand. Slamming the door and tossing the file in front of him, Chief Inspector Jones ordered, "Read it."

Inspector Conway set down his hat and picked up the file. He recognised it at once. "I don't have to. I know what it says."

Chief Inspector Jones' eyes narrowed. "Did Miss Trent tell you of its existence?"

"Yeah." Inspector Conway put the file down. "How come you've got it?"

"*Mr Elliott* has just delivered it, *in person*," Chief Inspector Jones replied through semi-clenched teeth. "Why the *hell* did neither of you inform me of this?"

"It's in the past," Inspector Conway replied. "It's got nowt to do with Grosse's murder."

"That is *irrelevant*. I should've been informed. How am I supposed to protect you if you're hiding things from me?"

Inspector Conway's eyes cooled. "I don't need protectin'. *Sir.*"

"Now is not the time for stubborn pride, John." Chief Inspector Jones picked up the file. "I should be able to dissuade Inspector Pilker from taking this any further on the basis it only mentions your boxing exploits up to the point of your enlistment into the police." The tension eased from his face and voice. "You're fortunate this Mr Grosse didn't include your recent 'activity' in the ring."

"I could of got Miss Trent to burn that, but I didn't," Inspector Conway said, firmly. "Not 'cause I thought no one would see it, but 'cause givin' it to Pilker was the right thing to do."

"The right thing isn't always the soundest course to take," Chief Inspector Jones lamented.

"It is for me." Inspector Conway put on his hat. "Sir."

Chief Inspector Jones sighed softly. "Just make sure it's not the death of you or the rest of us."

* * *

Rocking from side to side with the motion of the cab, Inspector Woolfe found himself wishing the driver would spur the horse into a gallop. Plagued by the dull ache in his chest, still, he also felt like a weight had been placed upon his ribs, preventing him from expanding his lungs. This, coupled with a difficulty swallowing, compelled him to stretch out his body as far as the small interior would allow. Bending his neck and curling his shoulders forward immediately after, he strummed his fingers upon his knees. Due to the slant of the bench and his abnormal height, they were raised as high as his shoulders and pressed tightly against the wooden doors. Yet, he knew his discomfort wasn't entirely caused by the cramped conditions.

As the cab turned onto Ballance Road, Hackney, Inspector Woolfe felt the same dropping sensation in his stomach he had whenever he visited the dentist. This was swiftly followed by a ferocious conflict between an urge to retreat and a need to eliminate his problem. Each differed in the amount of pain he'd be obliged to face, but he knew enduring the worst of it was the only way to move forward. Finding little comfort in this realisation, he alighted from the cab and paid its driver.

The house was in darkness, thereby confirming his suspicion its sole resident had begun his night's work. Nevertheless, Inspector Woolfe hesitated in opening its door as he gave some final consideration to retreating. Beyond, the sparse hallway and steeps stairs may as well have been a gigantic cave, given the spike of adrenaline he felt upon seeing them. Feeling his mouth go dry and his heartrate increase as he stepped inside, he stood stock still and listened.

Nothing.

A part of him was annoyed at the silence. If he'd heard snoring coming from upstairs, he would've had no choice but to abandon his task. As it was, the absence of life meant he had no choice but to see it through. He hoped not to a bitter end. Closing the door and putting himself in darkness, he allowed his eyes to adjust before venturing further.

A cursory glance over the parlour's interior told him it was little used and devoid of festive cheer. Dust covered all the surfaces except the sideboard beside the door. On its top was that morning's edition of the *Gaslight Gazette*, a few coins, and some vinegar-saturated paper screwed into a ball. Opening the sideboard's drawers and cupboards, Inspector Woolfe rummaged through each but came out empty handed.

He returned to the hallway and looked at the top of the stairs through the ballasts. Seeing only wall, he moved around to the foot of the stairs and looked up and to his left. He could just about make out the top of a doorframe in the corner of the landing. *If that's a bedroom at the rear of the house, what's at the front?* Gripping the handrail tight, he flinched as the first stair creaked under his weight.

He listened.

Nothing.

He climbed the remaining stairs, careful to keep the noise to a minimum. Although Conway was out, Inspector Woolfe knew the walls of these terraced houses were paper thin. If a neighbour overheard his movement, they might mistake him for a housebreaker and fetch a constable. Searching a fellow officer's house without permission would go down as well as Conway sharing evidence with the Bow Street Society. Inspector Woolfe felt his stomach turn upon realising he believed his friend's alleged transgression was true.

Stepping onto the landing, he saw a door into a second bedroom at its far end. He conducted a brief search of both rooms but again found nothing. The thought that his lack of success was due to his lack of enthusiasm to uncover anything entered his mind but was quickly dismissed. Regardless of his feelings toward Inspectors Conway and Lee, it was still his sworn duty as a policeman to investigate the accusation of corruption as thoroughly as possible.

He went downstairs and continued his search in the kitchen. Aside from the privy in the yard, it was the last place Conway could've hidden the money. *Or someone else*, he thought. Meticulous examinations of the cupboards, drawers, pantry, and stove revealed no sign of the money or envelope. Turning his attention to any boxes, bottles, or jars large enough to conceal them, he steadily made his way through the contents of every shelf and cupboard.

Nothing.

For the first time since he arrived, Inspector Woolfe felt the weight upon his chest lessen. Taking a few deep breaths, followed by a few coughs, he lowered and shook his head at the ridiculousness of Inspector Lee's accusation. Casting another glance around the room to be sure, he muttered, "There's nowt here." Feeling his heart swell with relief and then anger, he turned sharply toward the door, intent on returning to Chiswick High Road to confront their so-called 'colleague.'

That's when he saw it.

A lone flour jar stood upon a narrow shelf above the door.

The weight returned to Inspector Woolfe's chest, and his heartrate increased.

Swallowing hard against the ache that had also formed in the back of his throat, he approached the shelf as tentatively as if he expected it to fall. Thoughts of finding nothing and something competed for space in his mind's eye, with the worst-case scenario causing his stomach to roll.

Taking the jar down, he tightly gripped the spherical handle of its lid as he braced himself, before tugging it loose and pulling it free.

All at once, his stomach plummeted, his chest tightened, and his eyes widened as he gazed upon the envelope with a distinctive red 'B' tucked inside. Through

its open flap, he saw what he'd hoped he wouldn't: a pile
of crisp, white banknotes.

TWENTY-SIX

It had been a long night. With sleep being a prospect not worth considering, Inspector Woolfe had occupied a darkened corner of a public house before returning to his modest rooms. The flour pot he'd taken from Conway's kitchen had tormented him throughout. Incessant thoughts of how it had come to be there and what he should do with it kept leading him back to Inspector Lee and Sergeant Gutman.

He'd dismissed the possibility of it belonging to Conway moments after he'd found it. Setting their friendship aside, there were too many questions preventing the notion of Conway as a corrupt copper from being credible. Such as, why had he returned to bareknuckle boxing if he was receiving money from the Society? Who else knew he never locked the door to his house? Most importantly of all, who benefited from Conway being out of the way?

Inspector Woolfe had his suspicions. Yet, he needed evidence before he could act upon them. In this vein, he'd sent a message to Dr Colbert at first light, announcing his intention to call upon him at home that morning. Although he wasn't hungry, Inspector Woolfe had eaten breakfast at the behest of his landlady before making his way to 6, Sussex Mews.

The house's impeccable appearance was symbolic of the middle-class status of its resident. Located a stone's throw from Hyde Park, it was also well-situated for a medical man keen to maintain the health of his body and mind. Smoothing down his wild hair and straightening his days-old attire, Inspector Woolfe climbed the few steps and pulled the doorbell. A claxon sounded beyond, shortly followed by footsteps.

"Good morning, Inspector," Dr Colbert greeted. "Come in."

Inspector Woolfe wiped his feet on the mat and glanced around the hallway. Realising it was longer than his rooms put together, he fought the urge to scowl at the perceived injustice of it all. He'd had to fight for everything he had. Whereas someone like Dr Colbert seemed to have been given everything he wanted just because he'd been born to the right parents.

"I hope it's to your liking." Dr Colbert's voice penetrated his thoughts.

"What is?" Returning his gaze to him, Inspector Woolfe saw the file in his hand. "Thanks." Flipping through its pages, he caught the words "Grosse" and "murder." Too distracted by his own thoughts, though, he paid little heed to the rest.

"I'm to attend another meeting this evening," Dr Colbert said.

"Let me know what happens and *only* me."

"Is Inspector Lee still unavailable?"

"What do you mean?"

"Well, he's refused all my requests to see him whist you've been away."

"Yeah, he's still unavailable." Inspector Woolfe thought, *the arrogant bastard.*

Dr Colbert stared at him with sceptical eyes before conceding, "The less people involved, the better, I suppose." He thought of the number of Society members involved in the investigation of Mr Grosse's murder. "Whereas Miss Trent prefers a crowd."

"Do any of them suspect you?"

Dr Colbert gave a small smile. "I've given them no reason to."

"Good."

"In fact, I rather think my enthusiasm has disarmed them," Dr Colbert added.

Inspector Woolfe narrowed his eyes. "Don't tell me you're one of them now."

"Dear me, *no*." Dr Colbert gave a weak chuckle. "Several of them fascinate me, however. One in particular concerns me greatly."

"Who's that?"

"Dr Weeks. His dependence upon alcohol is crippling, and yet none of them seem to see it." Dr Colbert's eyes glanced sideways before he lowered his voice. "If given the right circumstances, I could arrange for his treatment at the asylum." Sadness entered his eyes as he lamented, "It pains me to see such a brilliant mind being destroyed by vice."

"Two thirds of the Metropolitan Police would be up in arms if you put him in Bedlam," Inspector Woolfe said in all seriousness. "Not to mention the bloody Society."

"You can understand my argument, though?"

"Yeah, but Weeks is never going to change. Anyway, I've not got time to waste on that lush." Inspector Woolfe straightened and squared his shoulders. "Will you get the envelope Miss Trent gave you? I want to take it with me."

"I'm afraid that's impossible."

Inspector Woolfe felt a heat form in his core as, anticipating Dr Colbert's answer, he enquired, "Why's that?"

"Because it will be halfway to Canada by now."

Inspector Woolfe simultaneously jerked his head back and lifted his brows. "*Canada*?" He stared at him in disbelief. "Didn't you give it to Inspector Lee?"

"No. Dr Weeks."

"*Weeks*?" Inspector Woolfe turned away and, rubbing his mouth and jaw, reeled from the revelation. *Would Weeks have given the envelope to Inspector Lee? If so, how did Inspector Lee get him to betray Conway like that?* Inspector Woolfe remembered hearing of Dr Weeks walking out of Inspector Conway's discipline hearing after defending him to the board. *It doesn't make sense,* he thought. *Unless… Inspector Lee's got something on him.* Inspector Woolfe felt the heat rising from his core, along with his anger, as he determined this was the likeliest possibility. *The scheming sonofawhore*, he thought, remembering Inspector Lee's smugness the last time they'd spoken.

"Are you feeling okay, Inspector?" Dr Colbert enquired, concerned.

"What did Weeks say he wanted it for?" Inspector Woolfe enquired as he faced him.

"Oh, erm…" Dr Colbert searched his memory. "He said he was writing a letter to his mother and wanted to impress her by sending it in a Bow Street Society envelope. Miss Trent was otherwise engaged, so I offered him mine."

Inspector Woolfe's eyebrows lifted. "You were at the Society's house?"

"Yes. It was before the meeting. I came upon Dr Weeks trying to open the desk in Miss Trent's office."

Inspector Woolfe scowled. This latest revelation strengthened his suspicion that Inspector Lee must have something on Weeks. For all the surgeon's bluster, he was a coward at heart. Inspector Woolfe knew he wouldn't have risked provoking Miss Trent's wrath without good reason. A reason that possibly frightened him more than the formidable clerk. Resolving to expose the truth one way or another, Inspector Woolfe strode from the house. "Thanks."

"You're welcome?" Dr Colbert replied, confused, as the door closed behind him.

* * *

Mr Baldwin cupped his hands against his lips and blew between his palms. Rubbing them together, he held them under his arms as he hunched his shoulders and scurried along Fleet Street. With his body shivering against the fiercely cold December morning, he pressed his chin against his chest and kept his eyes upon the ground. He avoided his fellow pedestrians by catching sight of their hurrying feet from the corner of his eye. Yet, when he attempted to enter the door of the *Gaslight Gazette* office, he collided with a wholly unexpected and unmovable obstruction.

Stumbling backward, his head snapped up with a glare. "*Oi*! What you doing—?!" His words were cut off by the swift restriction of his throat at the sight of Mr Snyder, however. The hard expression upon the cabman's face filled Mr Baldwin with dread, prompting him to take a step back.

"We'd like a word with you," Mr Snyder said.

Mr Baldwin glanced up the street. Hearing the scrape of a shoe, he looked sharply over his shoulder and saw Mr Skinner directly behind him. "What about?"

"Mr Grosse," Mr Snyder replied.

"I told Mr Elliott all I know." Mr Baldwin pressed his elbows to his sides as he tightly held his coat's lapels together and repeatedly glanced between the Bow Streeters.

"That's not true, is it, lad?" Mr Snyder softly enquired.

Mr Baldwin removed himself from between them. "Yeah, it is."

"We know you searched his body," Mr Skinner said.

Mr Baldwin stared wide eyed at him as his face turned ashen.

Suddenly, he shoved Mr Skinner aside and ran.

The Irishman stumbled but, regaining his footing, went after him in an instant.

Panting hard, Mr Baldwin felt a burning in his chest and a pain in his side as he weaved his way along the crowded pavement. Hearing rapid footfalls behind him, he glanced over his shoulder and felt his stomach clench at the sight of Mr Skinner hot on his heels. Darting his gaze in all directions, he desperately sought a way to elude him.

Seeing the dense traffic, he sharply veered to the right and increased his speed to dash in front of, and past, an on-coming cab. The driver immediately yanked upon his reins, causing his horse to rear up on its hind legs to avoid running the journalist down. Mr Baldwin didn't slow, however. Instead, he ran behind an omnibus coming in the opposite direction and then in front of a cart on its way from a brewery.

Meanwhile, Mr Skinner had stopped whilst the cab's horse reared up. Once its hooves were back on the ground, he'd jogged past it and stood in the middle of the road, searching for any sign of Mr Baldwin. Spotting him in front of the cart, he burst into another run to try to catch him up. Narrowly missing being struck by a cab in the process, he spun around to avoid it. When he'd regained his bearings and made it safely to the pavement, though, Mr Baldwin was gone.

* * *

Dr Weeks groaned as he awoke to an ache in his shoulders, neck, and lower back. Squinting his eyes open, he saw piles of documents and mugs of old coffee. Noticing his typewriter beyond, he closed his eyes and released another groan, this time of relief. All the slabs in the Dead Room were currently occupied. Since it was his habit to pass out on one, the likelihood of him sharing it with a corpse was high. Easing his arms off the desk, from where they'd laid either side of his head, he felt the ache subside. He tried to remember the night before but, as expected, it was an utter blank. Abandoning the endeavour, he lifted his head and peeled the piece of paper from his cheek. Seeing a damp patch in the middle from his drool, he discarded it into the bin and leaned back in his chair as he rubbed his face and eyes.

"You look how I feel," Inspector Woolfe remarked.

Dr Weeks dropped his hands and, squinting through the gloom, saw the immense policeman standing by the doors. Unable to stomach the prospect of being taken to some God forsaken place to examine a body, he turned away and rummaged around on his desk for a cigarette and match. "Find another damned surgeon. This one ain't for hire."

Inspector Woolfe approached him like a predator advancing upon its prey. "I'm not here for that."

"Then get the hell out." Dr Weeks slipped the cigarette between his lips and lit it.

Inspector Woolfe instantly plucked the cigarette from his mouth and dropped it into a mug.

"Hey! What d'ya think yer doin'?!"

Inspector Woolfe gripped him by the scruff of his shirt and pulled him to his feet. "Where is it?"

Dr Weeks turned his head away in disgust at the stench of rotten teeth. "Jesus *Christ*, Woolfe! When were the last time ya went to a dentist?!"

Inspector Woolfe tightened his grip and held him against him. "*Where* is it, Weeks?!"

"Where's what?! I don't know what yer talkin' 'bout!"

"The Bow Street Society envelope!"

Dr Weeks' face blanched, his lips parted, and his complexion became clammy as he stared at him. Trying to speak, he found he couldn't. The tightness in his throat and chest prevented the words from coming out.

Inspector Woolfe narrowed his eyes at the reaction. Not only did it confirm Dr Colbert's story, it spoke volumes about Dr Weeks' state of mind. He was undoubtedly afraid, but did that fear come from guilt over what he'd done, or from a suspicion that Inspector Woolfe knew what Inspector Lee held over the Canadian? Speaking in a voice made even more intimidating by its softness, he said, "You have until the count of five to tell me where it is. 1… 2… 3."

"I-I don't…"

"4."

Dr Weeks closed his eyes as he cowered and cried, "I don't have it!"

Inspector Woolfe brought him closer so their noses were touching. "What did you do with it?!"

Dr Weeks trembled. "I can't."

"Tell me what you did with it, *Doctor*, or I'll break your bloody arms!"

"I can't, damnit!" Dr Weeks looked him in the eyes. "So ya may as well break 'em."

The tension in Inspector Woolfe's face eased as he studied the surgeon's face. Loosening his grip on his shirt and moving him back a little, he nonetheless kept hold of him. "I think I can guess."

Dr Weeks bowed his head.

"But do you know money was put in it, and that money was put in Conway's house?"

Dr Weeks' head shot up, and he stared at him, stunned. "*Conway?*" He gave several curt shakes of his head. "Nah. Nah, I didn't. I *swear.*"

Inspector Woolfe released him and smoothed down his shirt. Although he was being gentle, he could tell Dr Weeks remained terrified of him. "That's all I wanted to know. For now." Their eyes met. "You're going to have to tell me everything eventually. If you want to help me protect Conway."

Dr Weeks gave a curt nod. "I-I do." He averted his gaze. "Jus'… give me some time, yeah?"

Inspector Woolfe moved away from him. "You have it." He headed for the door. "But don't take too long."

Dr Weeks felt sick to his stomach as he watched him leave. As soon as he was gone, he collapsed into his chair and held his head in his hands.

TWENTY-SEVEN

Mr Baldwin burst into the *Key & Lion* public house and, briefly cupping the back of his neck, repeatedly turned his head as he scanned the room and approached the bar. Taking a sharp step back at the last moment upon seeing Mr Sparrow at its far end, he immediately headed over to him. He put his elbows down and, leaning forward until his chest was brushing the bar top, fixed him with a desperate, unblinking gaze. In a low voice, he enquired, "How much for a room?"

Mr Sparrow, having initially smiled at the journalist, adopted a grave expression when he saw his flustered state. He'd seen the same in youths entering the ring for the first time. It rarely ended well. "Too much for you."

"Just a couple of nights, that's all I need it for."

"Try the workhouse."

Mr Baldwin gripped Mr Sparrow's arm as he turned. "I thought we was mates!"

Mr Sparrow shrugged his arm loose and cast him a warning look. "I can't help you."

Mr Baldwin's face and neck flushed as, in a low voice fraught with fear, he pleaded, "Duncan… please."

"Whatever trouble you're in, it's nothin' to do with me."

"Duncan!" Mr Baldwin cried helplessly as the landlord walked away.

* * *

Westminster Abbey was a place Miss Trent had wanted to visit since arriving in London. Yet, like many others, she'd allowed her permanent residence in the capital to fool her into thinking she would have ample opportunity to do so "another time." This time never came and, as the weeks turned into months, the desire to admire the treasures on her doorstep ebbed and flowed with the peaks and troughs of daily life. So, it was with a sense of great satisfaction, she passed through its doorway and strolled down its aisle.

Tilting her head back to admire its impressive ceiling and colourful stained-glass windows, she lingered in the aisle to savour the Abbey's grandeur. The quiet atmosphere was also welcome after the chaos of London's streets. Walking along a row of pews adorned with red velvet bows, she sat on the third one in and ran her gaze over the intricate stone masonry and soothing candlelight.

The echo of footsteps reached her ears a moment later. Quiet at first, it grew in volume as the person neared her position. They then changed direction, moving toward her right, before she felt a coat brush against her back. Hearing the creak of wood immediately after, she faced forward and waited.

"Most people visit Poets Corner," a male voice remarked close to her shoulder. The subtle warmth of his breath upon the back of her neck suggested he was leaning forward, with clasped hands between his knees as if in prayer.

"I'm not 'most people,' Richard."

"That is true." Chief Inspector Jones lowered his voice further, acutely aware of how easily it travelled. "I had a rather unexpected visitor today."

"I know. He told me when he returned to Bow Street."

"Did he also tell you he'd pointed out John's file to me and enquired what I intended to do with the information?"

"No." Miss Trent pursed her lips as she deeply exhaled through her nose. "But it doesn't surprise me."

"It surprised me." Chief Inspector Jones' voice was firm as he added, "You should've told me about Mr Grosse's file on John—both of you should have. As it was, I had to hear it from Mr Elliott—a member of the Bow Street Society. Do you know how foolish it made us look? Especially since Detective Inspector Pilker was present. If I hadn't known better, I would've thought Mr Elliott was gloating."

"Mr Grosse had files on numerous boxers—"

"That isn't the point."

"No, the point is, John's file covered his early boxing career. *Not* his recent return. Therefore, in the spirit of maintaining transparency with the police and trust of the Society members, I thought it wise to pass it onto Inspector Pilker. Besides, Miss Webster was the one who'd discovered it, so I had little choice but to acknowledge its existence."

Chief Inspector Jones' voice turned grave. "I'll have to notify Assistant Commissioner Terrell."

Miss Trent bowed her head. "I feared you might."

"I'll try to use the small degree of influence I have with him. He might be persuaded that, as it was in the past, it's not worth admitting it as evidence in the Christian Grosse murder case."

Miss Trent turned toward him. "We've found nothing to suggest John and Mr Grosse ever met, let alone had a disagreement. The fact John once dabbled in bareknuckle boxing *prior* to becoming a policeman shouldn't have any bearing on his current position at the Yard."

"No, but the powers that be loathe a scandal and, given John's recent misdemeanours, the assistant commissioner might decide to dismiss him to prevent even the suggestion of one."

"If he does, I shall lodge a formal complaint."

Chief Inspector Jones gave a weak smile.

"I'm serious, Richard."

"I know you are. I can just imagine what the assistant commissioner's expression would be should you march into his office, demanding John's reinstatement."

The corner of Miss Trent's mouth lifted. "Now who's not being serious?"

"One must take one's amusements where one can." Chief Inspector Jones smiled softly.

"Provided it's not at a friend's expense."

"Agreed." Chief Inspector Jones' smile faded. "I think you're right. The lack of evidence that John had a connection to Mr Grosse beyond being one of the many former boxers he was interested in should go in his favour. I'll forego speaking to Tyrell for the time being, but I think you and John should refrain from communicating with one another. Even under the guise of an official meeting."

"Very well." Miss Trent placed a gentle hand upon Chief Inspector Jones' shoulder. "I appreciate what you are doing for him, for all of us."

Chief Inspector Jones gave a weak smile. "Who knew being a Chief Inspector would be this difficult? I sometimes wonder if I would've been better off staying as a constable."

"You wouldn't have." Miss Trent pulled her hand away. "Your conscience wouldn't have let you."

"No. I suppose it wouldn't."

* * *

Dr Weeks paced the floor as he rubbed his face and neck with one hand and combed through his hair with the other. He darted his gaze repeatedly darted from the floor to the door and back again at the same time. When no sounds were forthcoming from the hallway, he wrung his hands, momentarily slipped them into his coat pockets, and wrung them again. Coming to an abrupt halt, he took out a cigarette with trembling hands and slipped it between his lips. A search of his coat revealed no trace of a match, however. "*Shit.*"

"Please, don't smoke in here," Dr Locke said from the doorway.

Dr Weeks looked up sharply and stared in shock at her drab appearance.

Entering the office of her private medical practise, she closed the door but remained within its vicinity. She folded her arms. "How may I help you, Doctor?"

"Damn, darlin'…" Dr Weeks remarked, his eyes suddenly consumed with concern as he took in her brown dress and drawn face. Taking the cigarette from his lips and returning it to his coat, he added, "Ya look like death warmed up."

"How may I help you, Doctor?" Dr Locke repeated, firmly. "Are you ill?"

"Nah, I… I were hopin' to speak to yer husband. Is 'e 'ome?"

A pained look entered Dr Locke's eyes as her features tightened. In a voice tense with emotion, she replied, "He's not receiving visitors at the moment. Is there a message I should give him?" She doubted he could comprehend it, but it was polite to ask, nonetheless.

Dr Weeks averted his gaze and, turning away, paced some more. "When will 'e be receivin' 'em?" He stopped and looked at her. "It's kinda urgent."

Dr Locke moved closer but stopped with a fair distance between them, still. "It's hard to say." She ran her gaze over his dishevelled clothes, noted his bloodshot eyes, and realised his voice lacked its usual vigour. Fearing the worse, she swiftly closed the distance. "Has something happened to Miss Trent? Or someone at the Society?"

"Nah, nothin' like that."

Dr Locke lowered her head as she briefly closed her eyes and breathed a small sigh of relief.

"It's… personal business."

Dr Locke met his worried eyes with curious ones of her own. "Oh?"

Dr Weeks frowned as he considered whether to take her into his confidence. Remembering their conversation at the Walmsley Hotel, in which she'd reassured him she had no interest in exposing him as a member of the Bow Street Society, he wondered if that protection would extend to his parentage. Nothing he'd ever seen or heard from her suggested it wouldn't. In fact, both she and her husband seemed unusually liberal in their thoughts and attitudes. Swallowing hard, he felt his heartrate increase as he cautiously replied, "I need 'im to take somethin' back for me. Somethin' that were stolen."

"My husband isn't in the business of finding treacherous resurrectionists."

Dr Weeks moved closer to her. "It ain't like that." He looked into her eyes but, realising he couldn't stomach telling her whilst he could see her face, he turned and walked toward the window. Feeling a wave of nausea come over him, he bent forward and, gripping the window ledge, took several deep breaths. Once the worst of it had passed, he retained his position and peered through the window at the darkening street. "It's a statement by the midwife who were at my birth… and the parish record sayin' who my parents were."

Dr Locke kept her distance, but her voice was gentle as she enquired, "Who were your parents?"

Dr Weeks grimaced as he glanced under his arm at her. Turning to perch upon the window ledge, he wrapped his arms about himself, curled in his shoulders, and bowed his head. "My mother's Evangelina Breckenridge." He covered his eyes with his hand as he clenched them shut. "My father's… Weeks. Lord… Michael Weeks."

A heavy silence descended upon the room.

Eventually, Dr Locke observed in a flat tone, "You're the illegitimate child of a married aristocrat."

Dr Weeks' face contorted with pain, compelling him to press his chin against his chest and lean forward to hide it. A deep, shuddering breath sounded from him a moment later, followed by a strangled sob. As his eyes dampened, he tightened his arms' grip upon his body and clutched the loose sides of his coat. When the tears inevitably slid down his face, he rocked back and forth upon the ledge but still couldn't bring himself to look at her. "No one were supposed to know…" His face crumpled into another grimace, "… 'bout my shame."

"But someone does?" Dr Locke's voice remained flat despite her concern.

"Yeah." Dr Weeks stood and, crossing over to the fireplace, put his back to her as he retrieved a hip flask from his coat and unscrewed it with shaking hands.

Dr Locke's mouth formed a hard line. "That shan't solve your problems. It will only add to them."

"I need it," Dr Weeks mumbled, taking a large swig of whiskey.

Dr Locke joined him at the fireplace. When he tried to take a second swig, she snatched the flask from him. "You're as bad as Percy." Striding over to her desk, she put the flask down with a dull thud. "Why can't you face your problems, instead of smothering them with heroin and whiskey?"

Dr Weeks followed but halted abruptly at her question. He suddenly realised the significance of all those telephone calls she'd made from his Dead Room to her butler at home. "Yer husband's a heroin addict?"

"He is." The pained look once again formed in Dr Locke's eyes. "And you're an alcoholic, but that isn't why we are here. You want my husband to steal the midwife's statement and the parish record from whomever has it. Unfortunately, he is in no fit state to string a sentence together, let alone break into someone's home. Miss Trent and the Bow Street Society could—"

"*No*!" Dr Weeks cried, rushing forward. "They ain't to know 'bout this, d'ya hear?!"

Dr Locke glared at him. "Then we have nothing more to say to one another." She picked up the flask and shoved it against his chest. "Wallow in self-pity. It seems to be what you both do best." Turning sharply, she headed for the door. "Good day, *Doctor*."

Dr Weeks narrowed his eyes and went after her. As soon as he entered the hallway, though, she'd gone. He looked at the flask in his hand and, for the briefest of moments, considered leaving it on her desk. Alas, an intense feeling of guilt and self-loathing compelled him to take another swig instead.

Having a second upon leaving the house, he put the flask away and mumbled, "I ain't a damned addict." Yet, he failed to believe it.

TWENTY-EIGHT

The spoon clinked against the cup as Miss Trent stirred her tea long after the sugar had dissolved. She watched Mr Elliott with a hard look in her eyes despite the contrived smiles she gave to whomever glanced her way. The lawyer was recounting his visit to New Scotland Yard to his fellow Society members, but Miss Trent was failing to hear his words. Instead, she studied the minute movements of his features and expressive hands. Whilst she agreed with Chief Inspector Jones that Mr Elliott wasn't gloating, the passionate conviction belied by his demeanour led her to suspect Mr Elliott thought he'd achieved a kind of victory over Inspector Conway.

"How are we to continue our investigation if Detective Inspector Pilker now possesses the only evidence we had?" Dr Colbert enquired. Although he'd made a concerted effort to hide it, his worry was nonetheless intimated by his tone. Additionally, thoughts of abandoning the case before it was solved—thereby losing his only excuse to enjoy Mr Elliott's company—were also increasing his anxiety.

"I've compiled a detailed itemised list." Miss Trent set down her spoon and passed copies of the document to those around the table. Aside from Mr Elliott and Dr Colbert, Mr Snyder, Mr Skinner, Miss Dexter, Miss Hicks, and Miss Webster attended the meeting. Dr Weeks was conspicuous by his absence.

Miss Webster read the lines accompanying the entries for Mr Grosse's manuscript, the *Bradshaw's Railway* Times, and the copies of *Bell's Sporting Life*. She gave a subtle nod of satisfaction upon seeing her findings about the handwriting found in each. After comparing it to the known sample of the letter provided by Mr Voigt, she'd concluded it was Mr Grosse's. A small, but important, piece of information.

"I see Mr Grosse censored his manuscript," Dr Colbert remarked. Meeting the lawyer's gaze, he added with a smile, "as you suspected he would, Mr Elliott." He consulted the list. "I don't see the notebook here, though. Mr Voigt and Mrs Grosse didn't have it?"

"No," Miss Webster replied. "It's worth noting Mr Grosse's manuscript was also unfinished."

"Why is that significant?" Dr Colbert enquired.

"It suggests he hadn't uncovered the whereabouts of Mr Deon Erskine," Miss Webster replied.

"He hadn't talked to me, either," Mr Snyder said. "Mr Sparrow said Mr Grosse wanted to put me in his book, too." He took a mouthful of tea. "But I think he got close to finding Erskine before he died."

Miss Webster consulted the list. "The telegram from the United States of America said they had no record of him."

"Yeah, but what if Mr Grosse found out he'd never gone?" Mr Snyder enquired.

Mr Elliott lifted his chin and mused aloud, "Mr Baldwin said there was something else Mr Grosse had discovered about Erskine, but Mr Baldwin couldn't remember what it was. It's possible it could've been his address."

"So, he did," Dr Colbert said, amazed. "Your memory is astounding, Mr Elliott."

"I made a note of it," Mr Elliott said in a flat tone.

Dr Colbert's lips parted before he gave a weak chuckle. "Yes, of course you did, how silly of me." He returned his gaze to Mr Snyder even as he felt the back of his neck warm. "Wouldn't it have been easier for Mr Grosse to locate you first?"

"Yeah, but that's what makes me think he was close to finding Erskine," Mr Snyder replied. "He might of thought to talk to him and then to me."

Dr Colbert hummed as he looked past Mr Snyder's shoulder, considering his argument. "It's possible, I suppose."

"Getting too close to finding Erskine could've been why he was murdered," Mr Skinner said.

"There is currently no evidence to support your supposition, however," Mr Elliott countered. "Given his flight, and the fact he was seen searching Mr Grosse's body, it's a likelier possibility Mr Baldwin murdered Mr Grosse for his notebook. When he failed to locate it, he instead took his hat, shoes, handkerchief, money, and pocket watch. His remark about Mr Grosse uncovering something further about Mr Erskine could've been an attempt to divert our suspicions elsewhere."

"But Mr Grosse's possessions were returned to his office," Miss Webster pointed out. "Furthermore, Mr Grosse was never seen without his notebook. If Mr Baldwin had murdered him, why couldn't he find it?"

"Someone else could of thieved 'em," Miss Hicks replied.

"There wouldn't have been the opportunity to as, one presumes, Mr Baldwin would've searched Mr Grosse as soon as he was unconscious," Mr Elliott said with a frown.

"Just because Mr Westcott didn't see Mr Baldwin take the notebook, doesn't mean he didn't," Mr Skinner said. "Mr Grosse could've also left his notebook in his office on this occasion. Mr Baldwin could've put down his t'ings on the desk when he was looking for it and forgotten about them when he did."

"Mr Grosse wouldn't of gone to the set-to without his notebook," Mr Snyder said.

"Mr Baldwin's decision to run away suggests he knows more than he's told us," Mr Elliott said. "Locating him should allow us to answer these questions, too."

"We got his address from Mr Morse at the newspaper," Mr Skinner said. "I've been there since this mornin' and seen no sign of him."

"I know we agreed not to involve Mr Maxwell in this case—" Mr Elliott began.

"An agreement that still stands," Miss Trent interrupted.

"But he has been Mr Baldwin's colleague for some time," Mr Elliott continued in a cool tone. "He may know where he might've gone to hide; the homes of friends, relatives, or even lovers."

"No," Miss Trent said in a resolute tone.

"He wouldn't need to know why," Miss Webster pointed out.

"I said 'no,' and I expect my decision to be respected," Miss Trent warned.

Miss Dexter bowed her head as she sipped her tea. Her lack of contribution to the meeting thus far was largely due to being distracted by thoughts of Mr Maxwell and the recent encounters she'd had with him. She was also conflicted about whether she should inform him of her imminent visit to Paris. Whilst she knew it would be cruel to conceal it from him, she also knew she couldn't face an emotional goodbye. He'd undoubtedly try to persuade her to stay and, although her heart was set on Paris, she feared he might succeed.

"I'll go back to his house after the meeting in case he's there," Mr Skinner said.

"Thank you," Miss Trent said, glancing up from her notebook.

"And if he isn't?" Miss Webster subtly challenged.

"We'll cross that bridge if we come to it," Miss Trent firmly replied.

"Couldn't Mr Westcott have murdered Mr Grosse, stolen the notebook, and accused Mr Baldwin after seeing him take Mr Grosse's possessions?" Dr Colbert enquired, keen to ease the tension.

"Westcott's on hard times," Mr Snyder replied. "If he had the notebook, he would of gone off to get monies from the folks who was in it, not spent time on me for a few shillin's."

"Yes." Dr Colbert furrowed his brow. "I see your point."

"Please, give us your findings from the public houses and boxing clubs, Sam," Miss Trent invited.

"All the clubs knew of Mr Grosse, but only the *Lower Clapton Boxing Club* at the *Nimble Crow* had done dealings with 'im," Mr Snyder said. "Mr Kenrick Farley, the pub's landlord and club's owner, didn't let Noah O'Hanigan join because Mr Grosse had said he was a drunk who would do in the club's reputation if he put him in the ring."

"'E's probably right. My Perce couldn't do owt in a fight," Miss Hicks said.

Dr Colbert's mouth formed a hard line as he was reminded of his alarm upon finding Dr Weeks wasn't amongst his fellow Society members. Their lack of concern—particularly Miss Hicks'—both angered and dismayed him. Clearly, Dr Weeks' addiction to alcohol was so in-grained, his associates had ceased attempting to help him. That was Dr Colbert's hope, at least.

Mr Snyder picked up the sketch of the American gent from the table. "Farley also said this bloke's name is Amias Winfield, and that he's O'Hanigan's manager. Farley told Winfield he wasn't going to let O'Hanigan join his club on the same day Winfield almost knocked down Mr Baldwin."

"The basis for Mr Winfield's argument with Mr Grosse," Mr Elliott remarked.

"Farley thought so," Mr Snyder said. "He also said Grosse was the angriest he'd ever seen him when he told him not to let O'Hanigan join."

"Mr Grosse must've known he was the one his wife was committing adultery with," Miss Webster stated.

"Farley never said, and I never asked," Mr Snyder said.

"Mr Voigt has confirmed he did," Miss Trent said. "But we shall discuss Mrs Grosse further in a moment. What did you discover at the public houses, Sam?"

"Nowt at any of them but the *Key & Lion*," Mr Snyder replied. "Mr Sparrow, its landlord, said he knew nowt about the set-to at the warehouse and told me to stop wondering about it. When me and him come up to the bar, he also told me to stop mythering on about Mr Grosse."

"What was Mr Farley's reply to your question about the fight?" Mr Elliott enquired.

"The same as Sparrow's; he knew nowt about it," Mr Snyder replied. "He also told me to get out when I asked him about Grosse's book." Mr Snyder took a mouthful of tea. "There was sumin' else. Sparrow told Farley I was asking questions at the *Key & Lion*, so Farley was expecting me when I got to the *Nimble Crow*." He folded his arms and, resting them upon the table, leaned forward. "Sparrow and Farley ain't mates. For them, boxin's not a sport, it's a way of life. For as long as I can remember, Sparrow's been for the old way, and Farley's been for the softer, mittened kind. Farley's also about making his club 'respectable.' They hate each other's bones."

"If that's the case, Mr Sparrow must've had a strong reason for warning Mr Farley about you," Miss Webster said. "A reason that could be one, or both, of them is responsible for Mr Grosse's murder."

"There is no evidence for your supposition, however," Mr Elliott said.

"We could find some," Mr Skinner said. "Or prove to ourselves they're innocent."

"There's no motive," Mr Elliott pointed out.

"Mr Sparrow is still holding bareknuckle boxing matches. That's motive enough, surely?" Dr Colbert enquired.

"That would make everyone who watches them a suspect, too," Mr Snyder countered.

"What did Mr Sparrow and Mr Farley say about Mr Erskine?" Mr Skinner enquired.

"Farley said he knew nowt. Sparrow said he'd gone to America," Mr Snyder replied.

"Could you elaborate on your suggestion to find the evidence, Mr Skinner?" Miss Trent enquired.

Mr Skinner looked between Miss Trent, Mr Elliott, and Mr Snyder. "I thought I could join the *Lower Clapton Boxing Club* to keep an eye on Mr Farley."

Miss Trent stared at him in astonishment. "Are you being serious?"

"Completely," Mr Skinner asserted.

"With all due respect, I doubt he'd accept your application," Mr Elliott said.

Mr Skinner narrowed his eyes and lifted his false hand. "*This* will guarantee it."

"I beg to differ," Mr Elliott said.

"Don't you think I can fight?" Mr Skinner challenged.

Mr Elliott's expression and tone were cold as he replied, "With weapons? Yes. With mittens? No."

Mr Skinner leapt to his feet and, leaning over the table, shoved his false hand into Mr Elliott's face. "I'd use *this* for defence. It doesn't need a bloody mitten." He straightened and looked to Miss Trent. "People love a sideshow. I won't have any trouble getting them to talk to me. Farley included."

"Some peepers ought to be put on Mr Sparrow, too," Miss Hicks said. "I could do that if I was workin' behind his bar."

"These men are experienced boxers," Mr Elliott said. "And, as such, could pose a considerable danger should they discover you're Bow Street Society members."

"I agree," Dr Colbert interjected, deeply perturbed by the proposals.

"I've looked after meself 'til now," Miss Hicks said. "A barmaid's life ain't pretty."

"And I'm not a cabin boy on his first voyage," Mr Skinner said. "I've been a bodyguard to Captain and Lady Mirrell for years. I know how to fight."

"Are Mr Sparrow and Mr Farley likely to confide in you, Sam?" Miss Trent enquired.

Mr Snyder considered his answer long and hard. After several moments had passed, in which the expectant and worried eyes of his fellow members remained fixed upon him, he shook his head. "They wasn't happy when I was asking about things."

Miss Trent hummed and rotated her pencil between both hands as she stared at it, deep in thought. Inspector Woolfe's lecture about putting innocent people's lives in danger unnecessarily sprang into her mind. It was accompanied by the recollection of sending Miss Webster into the *Queshire Department Store* to uncover its secrets. A shiver ran through her at the thought of how that case had ended.

Prior to assigning Miss Webster the task, she hadn't known the full extent of what they were dealing with. What Mr Skinner and Miss Hicks had proposed was different, however. They all had strong suspicions over the risk. Whilst she admired their tenacity and courage, she couldn't knowingly send them into danger. Squaring her shoulders as she released a slow, deep breath, she placed her pencil in the fold of her notebook and rested her clasped hands upon its pages. "I admire, respect, and appreciate your dedication to finding Mr Grosse's murderer, Mr Skinner, Miss Hicks. I can't agree to what you propose, however."

Dr Colbert visibly relaxed as he briefly closed his eyes and exhaled with relief.

"Don't be daft, Becky," Miss Hicks said. "It's just work."

"No. It isn't." Miss Trent said, meeting her confused eyes with hard ones of her own. "It is you putting yourself in harm's way in the hopes of overhearing or seeing something that *might* assist our investigation." She shifted her gaze to the Irishman. "The same applies to you, Mr Skinner." She looked between them. "As clerk of this Society, it's my responsibility to keep you safe. That must be the priority above everything else. Including finding the truth."

Dr Colbert beamed from ear to ear as he felt his heart swell with deep admiration.

"You've let Mr Locke put himself in front of a gun before," Mr Skinner pointed out.

"That was different," Miss Trent said.

"Because he's not a cripple?" Mr Skinner challenged.

"Because we didn't know it was loaded," Miss Trent rebuked. "Furthermore, please do *not* use that word. It's neither flattering nor relevant to anyone in this room."

"So say you." Mr Skinner pulled his chair closer to the table with a loud scraping of wood and sat. "My point is: he was allowed to take the risk. Why aren't we?"

"Unlike that occasion, and others like it, we can be more certain about the dangers you'd be facing at the *Nimble Crow* and *Key & Lion*," Miss Trent replied. "As Inspector Woolfe keeps reminding me: I shouldn't put any of your lives in danger unnecessarily."

"But it *is* necessary," Mr Skinner countered. "Mr Sparrow and Mr Farley aren't going to talk otherwise."

"I ain't gonna be alone, Becky," Miss Hicks said. "My Perce'll go wherever there's drink."

"That doesn't reassure me," Miss Trent sardonically replied.

"Farley's pub's full of toffs," Mr Snyder said. "Mr Elliott could keep an eye on Mr Skinner."

"I don't know if being described as a 'toff' is flattering or offensive," Mr Elliott said.

"It's full of gents," Mr Snyder corrected.

"Thank you," Mr Elliott said.

"You *agree* with the plan, Sam?" Miss Trent enquired, taken aback.

"I've known Sparrow and Farley for years. Never known either to hit a woman," Mr Snyder replied. "The pubs are goin' to be full of customers when Mr Skinner and Miss Hicks are there, too. They're not goin' to do owt when they're about."

"That would depend on how loyal the Fancy is to them," Mr Elliott said.

"They're loyal but not *that* loyal," Mr Snyder said.

"Come on, love," Miss Hicks urged, addressing Miss Trent.

"Don't try to pressurise me into agreeing," the clerk warned. "I'll give the matter some more thought and inform you all of my decision in the morning."

"If I may say something?" Dr Colbert enquired, raising his hand.

"Of course," Miss Trent replied in a tense voice as her features became rigid.

"I agree with you, Miss Trent, that placing Mr Skinner and Miss Hicks in such a situation alone would be dangerous and highly irresponsible of the Society," Dr Colbert said. "Coupling them with another would reduce but not eliminate the risk. I'd like to propose we advise the police of the situation and allow them to uncover whatever it is Mr Sparrow and Mr Farley may be hiding."

Only the crackling of the fire and the muffled sounds of carts and carriages trundling along Bow Street could be heard as the others stared at him in disbelief.

"The *police*?" Miss Webster enquired in disgust.

"Yes," Dr Colbert replied. "I think they would be best suited to face such dangers."

"Mr Voigt wouldn't have hired us if he trusted the police to do their job," Mr Skinner said in a hard tone. "We'd be betraying his faith in us if we got them involved now."

"The police prefer to work against us rather than with us," Mr Elliott stated.

"Enough." Miss Trent said, firmly. "I said I'd give the matter some more thought and I will."

Dr Colbert's mouth formed a hard line as he clenched his hand into a fist beneath the table. He considered going to speak to Inspector Woolfe once the meeting was over but decided against it. He couldn't risk them seeing him with the policeman, after all.

"In the meantime," Miss Trent went on. "Miss Hicks, Miss Webster, please give your findings from your conversation with Mrs Grosse."

"She was angered by her late-husband's failure to write a will," Miss Webster said. "Which suggests she expected to inherit the house. Although *how* she thought such a thing is beyond me. She freely admitted she kept her husband away from the house at any opportunity for the sole purpose of meeting her lover." She turned her head away, "It's disgusting."

"Mr Voigt would agree with you," Miss Trent said. "Aside from being angered by our disobedience of his order to not disturb Mrs Grosse, he revealed his nephew had written to him about the adultery. According to Mr Voigt, his nephew had said his wife and Mr O'Hanigan had laughed at him when he'd walked in on them in bed together."

"If Mrs Grosse expected to inherit the house, and Mr Grosse knew of her adultery, she could've persuaded Mr O'Hanigan to murder her husband to avoid a divorce," Mr Elliott said. "As I once told Mr Maxwell, the only grounds a husband needs for a divorce is evidence of his wife's adultery."

"We have no evidence to support your supposition, however," Miss Webster said, purposefully repeating the lawyer's words back to him. As his eyes and expression cooled, she allowed the corner of her mouth to lift in amusement.

"Mrs Grosse could be in danger, still," Miss Dexter said, deeply concerned.

"I don't understand," Dr Colbert said.

Miss Trent's voice and expression was grave as she explained, "Although we have no evidence to suggest Mrs Grosse persuaded Mr O'Hanigan to murder her husband, we've been told by Mr Snyder and Mr Farley that Mr O'Hanigan is a boxer and a drunk. If one puts anger into the mix, it could prove a dangerous cocktail."

Dr Colbert leapt to his feet. "We must help her at once."

"She's not going to listen to owt we say," Miss Hicks warned. "Not after what Miss Webster said to her."

Miss Webster averted her gaze.

"But it's our duty as Bow Street Society members to protect her, isn't it?" Dr Colbert enquired, alarmed.

"I thought you said that was the job of the police?" Mr Skinner countered in a sardonic tone.

Dr Colbert blinked. "Yes, it is, but…" He gave a dismissive shake of his head. "That's *not* the point. Mrs Grosse is in danger! We have to do *something*!"

"And we will," Miss Trent replied. "Mr Elliott, please speak to Inspector Woolfe at Bow Street police station after the meeting. He should be able to contact the nearest division to Mrs Grosse and arrange for a constable to call in on her." To Dr Colbert, she added, "Unless we're certain Mrs Grosse is in imminent danger, that's all we can do for now."

Dr Colbert's face blanched. "Mr Elliott is going to speak to Inspector Woolfe?"

"Yes," Mr Elliott replied.

"Do you object?" Miss Trent enquired.

"No." Dr Colbert sat. "Not at all."

"Good." Miss Trent nonetheless watched him as he bowed his head and sipped his tea. "Does anyone have anything else to report?"

The others shook their heads and murmured that they didn't.

"In that case, this meeting is over." Miss Trent closed her notebook. "Mr Snyder, could you drive me to Mr Maxwell's house on Duncan Terrace, please? We're to attend court again tomorrow, and he'd like to wear the cravat from his mother."

"Of course, lass," Mr Snyder replied.

"I'll gather my things," Mr Elliott said, taking his satchel with him as he left the room.

TWENTY-NINE

Inspector Woolfe held rigid eyes upon Dr Weeks as the latter repeatedly shifted his weight from one side of his chair to the other. Briefly folding his arms, Dr Weeks rested his elbow upon the chair's arm, leaned sideways, and rubbed his face with a bowed head before conducting a hurried search of his coat for a match and cigarette. Throughout the spectacle, Inspector Woolfe had observed Dr Weeks' trembling hands, the way his gaze darted everywhere but him, and the perpetual grimace etched upon his features.

Sitting on opposite sides of his desk at Bow Street, their meeting had been a spontaneous but not wholly unexpected, one. When Dr Weeks eventually found his smoking paraphernalia, Inspector Woolfe re-read the last few lines of the statement in his hand. None of its claims were credible when viewed through the lens of Dr Weeks' friendship with Inspector Conway. Returning his attention to Dr Weeks, he saw his cigarette had already been smoked halfway down. In a cold tone, he enquired, "Did you honestly think I'd believe this drivel?"

"Ya should." Dr Weeks crushed out his cigarette in the ashtray. "It's the truth."

"You wouldn't betray Conway for money." Inspector Woolfe discarded the statement.

"It's there in black and white, ain't it? Written and signed by me." Dr Weeks folded his arms and held them tight against his chest as he slouched in his chair.

Inspector Woolfe narrowed his eyes. "What's Inspector Lee got on you?"

Dr Weeks turned his head away. "Nothin'." A pained expression formed as he quietly added, "I put the envelope and money in Conway's house 'cause 'e nearly cost me my commission with the Yard." He bowed his head with a harsh grimace. "That's all there is to it."

Inspector Woolfe stood and advanced upon him. "No one made you walk out of that hearing. You did it to defend your mate." He gripped his shoulder and pulled him back to look at him. "You can't lie to me, Weeks, so there's no point in trying. *What's* Lee got on you?"

Dr Weeks suddenly leapt to his feet, forcing Inspector Woolfe to step back. "*Nothin'*, d'ya hear?!" He snatched up the statement from the desk and waved it in Inspector Woolfe's face. "*This* 'ere's the damned truth! If ya don't believe it, that's yer problem, but I'm stickin' by it!" He shoved it against Inspector Woolfe's chest, obliging him to take it. "Give it to the Yard and clear Conway's name."

Inspector Woolfe's expression turned grave. "You could be arrested for this, you know."

Dr Weeks held out his wrists. "Then arrest me. I don't give a damn anymore."

Inspector Woolfe glanced over his pale, tired face and bloodshot eyes. Releasing a sigh, he pushed Dr Weeks' hands aside and turned away. "Get out of my sight."

A knock sounded on the door.

"What the bloody hell is it?!" Inspector Woolfe boomed.

The door opened and a nervous-looking constable peered around its side. "Mr Elliott from the Bow Street Society is downstairs, sir. He has asked to speak to you."

Inspector Woolfe and Dr Weeks exchanged glances.

"What about?" The former enquired.

"A Mrs Grosse, sir," the constable replied.

Inspector Woolfe looked to Dr Weeks who clarified, "The widow of the private enquiry agent found dead at the docks."

Inspector Woolfe grunted his acknowledgement and headed for the door. "I'll talk to him." He stopped in the corridor and looked at Dr Weeks' dishevelled state. "Show the doctor out by the back door."

"Yes, sir," the constable said.

"Thanks," Dr Weeks mumbled.

Inspector Woolfe gave another grunt and strode away.

* * *

Mr Maxwell listened to the murmur of voices coming from downstairs. Sitting by the fire in his room, he'd been on the same page in his book for the past thirty minutes. Its plot had done little to distract him from his wild imaginings of what tomorrow might bring. Although the trial was nowhere near complete, he nonetheless held a crippling fear the jury would believe Oliver's lies and acquit him. If that happened, he knew it would only be a matter of time before Oliver put him six feet under. He shuddered.

"Good evening."

"Miss Webster." Mr Maxwell set his book aside and stood.

"Am I intruding?" Miss Webster enquired from the doorway.

"N-No." Mr Maxwell smiled weakly as he joined her. "It's good to see you."

"Her Ladyship and me were distressed to hear of your experience in court the other day. We're sorry you had to endure such awful and insensitive questioning."

"The lawyer w-was only doing his duty." Mr Maxwell stepped out onto the landing with her and closed his door. "But thank you." He crossed over to the handrail and peered down into the hallway. Disheartened when he neither saw nor heard any sign of Miss Dexter, he turned to Miss Webster. "I-I'll be relieved when it's over."

"As will we all." Joining him, Miss Webster felt bolstered when she saw the hallway was unoccupied. "Forgive my boldness, but I feel it's necessary for me to raise the matter of your infatuation with Miss Dexter."

Mr Maxwell blinked. "My…?" He frowned. "I love her. It's n-not an infatuation."

"Whether it is or it isn't is irrelevant," Miss Webster said in a cold tone. "The fact remains no good will come of your relentless pursuit of her."

Mr Maxwell rested his thumb and forefinger on either side of his Adam's Apple as his other hand clutched the lapel of his frockcoat. Staring at her at the same time, he felt a churning sensation in his stomach as his heart pounded in his ears. "I—" His voice was strangled by the constriction in his throat. Swallowing hard, clearing it, and swallowing again, he went on, "I-I'm not *pursuing* her. Y-You speak as if I-I were a p-predator."

"Aren't you?" Miss Webster countered.

"*No!*" Mr Maxwell cried. "I *love* her!"

"You're also the widow to a murdered wife."

Mr Maxwell held his throat. "I-I know."

"Miss Dexter is a sophisticated young woman with the ambition and talent to become a great artist. Your selfishness could ruin her entire life."

Mr Maxwell felt nauseous as he imagined a destitute Miss Dexter in the workhouse. In a feeble voice, he said, "That is the *last* thing I want f-for her."

"I'm glad to hear it."

"I-I want her to be happy and successful," Mr Maxwell insisted.

"You'll have no qualms about staying away from her, then."

"S-Staying away from her?" Mr Maxwell felt a weight form in his chest as his nausea increased. "F-for how long?"

"Forever. If necessary."

Mr Maxwell's face turned ashen as a chill swept through his body. "F-F-Forever?" He pictured an easel without an owner in a gloomy, bare room at Duncan Terrace. The house he would've shared with Miss Dexter if he'd been brave enough to defy Oliver. The image faded away in his mind's eye as a tremendous sorrow descended upon him. Feeling as though he was on the verge of crumbling completely, he rushed back into his room, mumbling that he needed to be alone.

His grief-stricken state provoked a pang of guilt in Miss Webster that she hadn't expected. Immediately regretting her actions, she then realised they were justified by the fact she'd acted in Miss Dexter's best interests. Feeling her regret and guilt vanish at once, she lifted her chin and returned downstairs to prepare for the arrival of Lady Owston's carriage.

* * *

"Are you sure you don't want me to come in with you, lass?" Mr Snyder enquired from the driver's seat of the Society's cab. "Red-shirt should be okay for a bit."

"I'm sure." Miss Trent alighted onto the pavement. "I'll only be a few minutes."

Pulling her fur coat tighter about herself to ward against the cold, night air, she climbed the few steps and used Mr Maxwell's latch key to let herself in. As was to be expected, the hallway beyond was in pitch blackness. Its furniture was also covered in dust sheets, and its clock had wound down. Consequently, the silence was eerie as Miss Trent went to a nearby side table where she'd left a candle in a candlestick during her previous visit.

Since leaving the house, Mr Maxwell had requested the retrieval of several items. She didn't mind getting them for him, since his reluctance to return to the scene of his wife's murder was more than understandable. Retrieving a box of matches from her coat pocket, she successfully lit one after a few attempts. Igniting the candle's wick, she shook out the match and returned it to the box. As she picked up the candlestick and turned toward the stairs, though, she flinched as she came face to face with Mr Oswald Baldwin. Her features tightened. "What are you doing—?"

Yet, the glint of his knife cut through her words, stopping her short.

THIRTY

"Do what I say, and no one gets hurt." Beads of sweat were scattered across Mr Baldwin's face as he stared at her with unblinking eyes. In the candlelight, Miss Trent could see his knuckles had turned white from holding the knife. He made a jerky movement with it toward the door behind her. "In there."

"I'm not alone. Mr Snyder's outside."

Mr Baldwin darted his gaze to the front door and back again.

Miss Trent decided against trying to snatch the knife from him. Even in the dim light, she could see it was sharp. In a gentle voice, she enquired, "Why are you here, Oswald?"

"I said 'in there.'" His temple twitched wildly.

She gripped the trunk of the candlestick to allow for a better swing should she be obliged to defend herself. Holding it at arm's length, she turned slowly to avoid alarming him further. Yet, she stilled the moment she saw the door to which he referred. Feeling a prickling sensation as a chill coursed through her, she said, "Not in there. Please." She looked over her shoulder at him. "That's where Joseph's wife was strangled." She looked to the hallway's opposite side. "The Breakfast Room is only across the hall." She looked back over her shoulder at him, hoping to appeal to his humanity. "I'd prefer to go into that room instead."

Mr Baldwin held the knife close to her cheek. "It don't make any difference to me."

"So, we'll go into the Breakfast Room?"

Mr Baldwin furrowed his brow and darted his gaze between the two doors. "Fine." He held the knife's tip in front of her left eye. "But don't try owt."

"I shan't. Thank you, Oswald."

Momentarily taken aback by the sound of his name, he lowered the knife, only to raise it again a heartbeat later. Gesturing toward the Breakfast Room with it, he lightly pressed its tip against the middle of her back as he followed her down the hallway. When they entered the room, Miss Trent was distressed to find its curtains were drawn. The hope she'd held of Mr Snyder seeing the candlelight through the window was dashed in an instant. Realising she had no choice but to wait for him to become concerned on his own, she felt a weight form in the pit of her stomach. Her hands also began to sweat, making it difficult to keep a firm grip upon the candlestick. She slowly moved toward the table. "I'm going to put this down."

The dull thuds of Mr Baldwin walking across the rug swept past her and, when she caught a glimpse of his form in the sphere of candlelight a moment later, she braced for another encounter with the knife. Yet, to her relief, he was moving away from her, toward the window. She put the candlestick down upon the table and watched him push the curtain aside and peer outside.

"You'll be safe as long as you don't harm me," she said.

Startled by the sudden break in the silence, he spun around with the knife held aloft. When he realised it had only been Miss Trent speaking, he lowered the knife but kept it at arm's length. "What did you say?"

"You'll be safe as long as you don't harm me." She put her hand upon a nearby chair. "But I don't think you will." She glanced at the chair. "I'm going to sit. Will you join me?"

Mr Baldwin blinked rapidly as he darted his gaze between her and the chair.

Miss Trent sat and rested clasped hands upon her lap. With her back flush against the chair's rest, she held a calm expression despite the tension she felt. "I want to help you."

"No, you don't." He scowled. "You want me at the end of a rope."

"We're not in the business of sending innocent men to the gallows."

"You…" He momentarily lowered the knife. "You think I'm innocent?"

"We know you are."

Mr Baldwin's scowl returned, and he shook his head. "No. You're only saying that 'cause I've got this."

"I'm saying it because it's the truth."

Mr Baldwin's scowl intensified. "Why should I believe owt you say?"

"Because you haven't any other choice."

Mr Baldwin advanced upon her. "I've got this." He held the tip of the knife close to her face. "And this gives me all the choice I want."

"Use it, and you're choosing to end your days on the gallows."

Mr Baldwin's hand shot back as if burnt. Even in the dim candlelight, she could see the colour drain from his face as the horror of what she suggested struck him like a lightning bolt. He took a sharp backward step. "Murder?" He gave a feverish shake of his head. "I can't…" Feeling the weight of the knife in his hand, he suddenly tossed it aside, causing it to tumble across the rug as it landed. "What am I doing?"

Revulsed and wracked by guilt, he went over to the window whilst slowly crossing his forearms upon his crown and gripping the hair on the back of his head. Upon reaching his destination, he crouched before it and rested his forehead against the curtain-covered glass. "I'm no better than the bastard who done in Christian," he mumbled, sliding his fingers through his hair and bowing his head. With tightly clenched eyes and trembling shoulders, his grief finally overwhelmed him, and he openly sobbed against his knees with a brief, yet harrowing moan of anguish.

"What happened?" Mr Snyder's voice broke through the darkness.

Miss Trent's tension and fear vanished at the sound. Briefly closing her eyes to compose herself, she looked to her would-be murderer with a mixture of sympathy and trepidation. In a quiet voice, she replied, "Nothing."

Although his concern was far from eased, Mr Snyder decided against pressing her further when he saw her put gentle hands upon Mr Baldwin's shoulders and speak softly into his ear. She said, "It's time to go, Oswald."

Mr Baldwin lifted his head to reveal a reddened, tear-soaked face, trembling lips, and snotty nose. "What?"

"We have to leave now," Miss Trent replied in a gentle tone.

Mr Snyder moved forward, causing the floorboard to creak.

Mr Baldwin's gaze shot over to him. Recognising him at once, he gripped Miss Trent tightly and stared up at her with wide, unblinking eyes. "Don't take me to the coppers. *Please*. I never done it. I *swear*."

"There's no need to be afraid, Oswald." Miss Trent held his arms in return and allowed him to lean upon her as she guided him to his feet. "We're taking you back to the Society's house on Bow Street where you can eat, rest, and tell us everything you know about Christian's murder. You want to help us find out who killed him, don't you?"

Mr Baldwin gave a jerky nod.

Miss Trent smiled. "Good." Slipping her arm around his, she led him from the room. As they passed Mr Snyder, she said, "Fetch the knife, Sam. It fell onto the rug by the window."

The revelation made Mr Snyder feel sick.

Collecting the offensive item nevertheless, he extinguished the candle, locked the front door with his latch key, and joined the shaken pair at his cab.

THIRTY-ONE

"Goodnight, dear." Mrs Clara Jones put her hand upon her husband's shoulder.

"Hm?" Chief Inspector Jones looked up. Seeing her in her dressing gown, he realised what she'd said. With a warm smile, he gave her hand a gentle squeeze, prompting her to rest her other upon his cheek and kiss him softly.

"It's late," she cautioned.

"I shan't be much longer."

Mrs Jones looked to the open file in his lap and left the room.

Once alone, he returned to reading about Inspector Conway's early boxing career. Overall, it had been an admirable one, albeit short-lived. Until his recent return, that is. His lips formed a hard line as he considered how best to keep it from Inspector Pilker. He knew no one who'd seen Inspector Conway fight would dare go against him. There was also a loyalty peculiar to those of that ilk. Nevertheless, Mr Grosse's file on Inspector Conway could serve as a reminder to Inspector Pilker to delve deeper. Especially since the opinion of Inspector Conway at the Yard was unfavourable.

Chief Inspector Jones lifted his gaze to the fire as he pondered his options, ethical or otherwise.

His thoughts soon turned to the discipline hearing. Inspector Conway could've exposed him as the Bow Street Society founder to strengthen his defence. Yet, despite facing dishonourable dismissal by not speaking up, he'd kept his secret, thereby protecting both his and the Society's future.

Chief Inspector Jones reached his decision in an instant.

He tossed the file onto the fire and watched it burn.

* * *

"He could of done you in," Inspector Conway grimly observed.

"Mr Baldwin's a reprobate but not a murderer," Miss Trent reassured.

Standing on the central pier of Blackfriars Bridge, they had its frost-covered granite walls at their backs as they faced one another. Although it was late, they'd seen a fair number of vehicles cross the bridge but only a scattering of pedestrians. Beyond the opposite side of the bridge was the slanted roof of the train station and St. Paul's Cathedral on the horizon. Set against a dramatic backdrop of large, grey clouds drifting across an otherwise black night sky, the silhouette of its immense dome was clear to see despite the moon's absence.

"The bloke had a knife to your throat," Inspector Conway reminded her.

"And I emerged unscathed," Miss Trent countered.

Turning toward the river, Inspector Conway winced as a sharp pain shot through his chest.

"Unlike you." Concerned, Miss Trent cast an appraising glance over him.

Careful to use the top of his lungs, Inspector Conway slowly exhaled. Taking a larger breath immediately after, he felt the tension ease from his chest muscles at the same time. With a shallow cough, he said, "I'll live."

She crossed the pier and stood beside him. As he gazed out at the river and the industrialised urban sprawl that surrounded it, she studied his weathered face. Her focus soon shifted to his eyes, however. Cold, they held a hint of melancholia as they stared past the horizon. Knowing of the solitary existence he led, she questioned whether she'd assumed him to be lonely and attributed an air of sadness where there was none. Faced with the possibility of questioning him about it, she decided to raise her true motive for meeting him, instead.

"I'd like your advice, John," she began. "I'd usually consult Richard on Society matters but, given the breadth of your experience as both a policeman and head of the

Mob Squad, I'd thought you'd be the better person in this instance."

He looked along the wall at her. "I'll do my best."

"Sam encountered some hostility from Mr Sparrow and Mr Farley when he asked them about Mr Grosse. These reactions, coupled with Mr Sparrow warning Mr Farley of Sam's visit despite the fact he hates him, has led Sam to suspect they're hiding something about the murder. To discover what that could be, Mr Skinner has proposed becoming a member of the *Lower Clapton Boxing Club* to keep an eye on Mr Farley, whilst Miss Hicks has proposed becoming a barmaid at the *Key & Lion* to keep an eye on Mr Sparrow. My question is this: how can we infiltrate Mr Farley and Mr Sparrow's inner circle without resorting to such a dangerous method?"

"You can't."

"We must."

"But you can't."

"Why not?"

"Because Sparrow and Farley are veterans of the Fancy. They're not goin' to let anyone near who they don't trust."

"We thought they trusted Sam," Miss Trent said through a frustrated sigh.

"Sam's known for bein' part of the Society these days. They was never goin' to tell him owt worth knowin'."

"You're not helping, John."

"You wanted my advice; I'm givin' it you. If you want to get Sparrow and Farley on side, you're goin' to have to get amongst them."

"I can't put Mr Skinner and Miss Hicks in harm's way like that."

"Why not? You've done it before."

"That was different. I was unaware of the danger Mr Queshire posed."

Inspector Conway fell silent as he gave the problem further consideration.

"The things worth havin' ain't always easy to get," he said after some time had passed. "But that don't mean they're not worth fightin' for." He turned his head away as his eyes resumed the same distant gaze as before. This time, though, the melancholia was unmistakeable. "I've put young lads in harm's way. Lads with wives, children. Some of them have come back hurt."

A pained look swept across his features. "Some of them ain't come back at all." He downcast his eyes. "I keep on doin' it because I have to. The lads know, accept, and face the risks 'cause they want to keep the good ones safe. The only way to do that is by gettin' rid of the criminals who'd cut their throat with one hand and thieve their silver with the other." He met her gaze. "Mr Skinner and Miss Hicks want to keep the good ones safe, too. Richard set up the Society to protect and help the people who can't, or won't, take the protection and help from us coppers. If you stop it from doin' that, you might as well close it."

"But what if they don't come back, John?" Miss Trent enquired in a voice hushed by fear. "How could I live with myself?" She frowned deeply. "How do you live with yourself?"

The pained expression returned to his features as he looked back across the river. "I have to." He momentarily lowered his head whilst he composed himself. Seeming to make a decision, though, he turned toward her and said in a resolute tone, "I'll get some of my lads to watch 'em."

Miss Trent stared at him, taken aback. "Mob Squad detectives? But what if someone at the Yard finds out? We've already caused enough trouble for you as it is—"

"No one's gonna find out 'cause no one's gonna know who they are but me."

Miss Trent frowned. "Not even Mr Skinner and Miss Hicks?"

"It's safer for everyone that way."

"But how will they know whose help to seek if things go wrong?"

"I'll give my lads full descriptions of Mr Skinner and Miss Hicks, so they'll know who to keep eye on. Don't worry, they'll look after them like they was one of their own."

Miss Trent's frown deepened. "Are you sure of that? The Bow Street Society aren't exactly popular with the police at the moment."

"As sure as I am that the sun will come up tomorrow."

"Why?"

"Because it'll be me who's askin'."

* * *

Chief Inspector Jones pushed the remaining file fragments into the flames with a brass poker, keen to ensure no distinguishable writing was left intact. The question of how he would explain the file's absence to Inspector Pilker sprang into his mind, only to be swiftly dismissed with a simple answer: it was misfiled.

A sudden knock on the front door caused him to stand bolt upright.

He listened.

A second, swifter knock came.

Chief Inspector Jones checked the time on the mantel clock: half past eleven.

A third, more frantic knock followed.

Chief Inspector Jones tilted his head and rubbed the tip of his eyebrow as he released a deep sigh. Aware of his obligation to speak to whomever it was in case it was Yard business, he nonetheless cursed the intrusion and delay to his bedtime as he went to the front door.

"One moment," he called, sliding back its bolts and turning the key.

A sharp, clenching sensation gripped his core when he saw his visitor's face. This was immediately followed by a bombardment of wild imaginings, each more fantastic than the last. He threw the door wide. "What is it, Caleb?"

"I'm sorry for disturbing you at home, sir—"

"Do you have any idea what time it is?" Chief Inspector Jones demanded as his initial alarm subsided.

"This can't wait, sir."

The heaviness in Inspector Woolfe's voice, coupled with the serious look in his eyes, was enough to convince Chief Inspector Jones of the urgency of the situation. He moved back to allow his subordinate to enter before securing the door once more.

"My wife is asleep so be quiet," Chief Inspector Jones ordered in a hushed voice as he led him down the hallway and into the parlour.

"Yes, sir," Inspector Woolfe mumbled.

Once safely inside with the door closed, Chief Inspector Jones demanded in a hard tone, "What is the emergency?"

"I don't know how to put it in words, sir." Inspector Woolfe went over to the fireplace, thereby putting some distance between them. Turning to him, his gaze looked everywhere but Chief Inspector Jones' face before settling on his chest as he quickly added, "Inspector Lee's trying to entrap Conway."

Chief Inspector Jones' features visibly tightened. "That is a very serious allegation, Caleb."

Inspector Woolfe adopted a grave tone. "I know, sir."

"Do you have evidence to support it?"

"No, sir."

Chief Inspector Jones studied his face intently. "But you do have something, otherwise you wouldn't have come to me like this. Tell me."

Inspector Woolfe looked him squarely in the eyes. "When I came back from Tonbridge, I visited Inspector Lee at Chiswick." He averted his gaze, and his voice quietened. "He's been working with me on the investigation into the Bow Street Society."

Chief Inspector Jones felt vindicated when Inspector Woolfe confirmed his long-held suspicions. He also held his tongue in anticipation of what Inspector Woolfe was certainly about to tell him.

"He told me Sergeant Gutman had seen Inspector Conway and Miss Trent exchange envelopes." Inspector Woolfe's lips curled into a snarl. "He accused Inspector Conway of giving the meddlers evidence in return for money."

"He put the same allegation to me."

Inspector Woolfe's head and eyebrows simultaneously lifted. "He did?"

"Yes." Chief Inspector Jones joined him at the fireplace before continuing in a hushed voice, "There was an altercation between Inspectors Conway and Lee a few days ago in which John took hold of Gideon. I'm almost certain he would've assaulted him if I'd not put a stop to it."

Inspector Woolfe lowered his head and turned away with a deep frown.

"I believe Inspector Lee made the allegation of corruption against Conway as revenge for the humiliation he'd suffered at his hands."

Inspector Woolfe faced the fireplace and stared at its mantel shelf as his focus turned inward.

Chief Inspector Jones tilted his head and peered up into Inspector Woolfe's face. "There's something else you're not telling me."

"I didn't believe what Inspector Lee had said about Inspector Conway. He told me to search his house and prove him wrong."

Chief Inspector Jones straightened as his posture stiffened and his features visibly tensed. Watching Inspector Woolfe with hard eyes, he enquired, "And did you?"

Inspector Woolfe mumbled, "Yes, sir."

Chief Inspector Jones' face contorted into a scowl. Feeling his anger rise, he clenched his jaw as he fought to keep it under control. The memory of forbidding Inspector Lee from doing as Inspector Woolfe had done both intensified and dulled his fury. Intensified because Inspector Lee had clearly disobeyed his order by coercing

Inspector Woolfe into doing it for him, and dulled because that coercion was circumstantial evidence against Inspector Lee. "And?" he urged. "What did you find?"

Inspector Woolfe took the flour jar from his coat pocket and put it upon the mantel shelf.

Chief Inspector Jones picked it up and removed its lid.

He stilled at the sight of the money-filled Bow Street Society envelope stuffed within.

"It was on a shelf above the door in his kitchen, sir." Inspector Woolfe watched him pull the envelope free and count the banknotes. "Dr Weeks says he put it there."

Chief Inspector Jones looked up sharply. "I beg your pardon?" He stared at him in bewilderment. "I thought he and John were friends?"

"They are, but I think Inspector Lee's got something on him."

Chief Inspector Jones set down the jar and envelope. "Blackmail?"

"Yeah, but not for money." Inspector Woolfe took a large envelope from the inside of his coat and held it out to his senior officer. "This is the statement Dr Weeks wrote and signed that says he stole the envelope from Miss Trent's office at the Bow Street Society, filled it with money, and put it into the flour jar in Inspector Conway's house. According to Dr Weeks in his statement, he did it because his testimony at Conway's hearing with the discipline board had almost cost him his commission with the Yard."

"That doesn't make sense," Chief Inspector Jones said, unconvinced as he accepted and opened the envelope. "Dr Weeks chose to walk out."

"I know, but whatever Inspector Lee has on him, it's bad enough to make Dr Weeks want to throw himself on his sword, instead of letting whatever it is come out." Inspector Woolfe turned to face Chief Inspector Jones and, with a renewed confidence in his demeanour and determination in his voice, he continued, "Dr Weeks' willingness to make a statement putting all the blame at his own door also says two things to me. First, he wants to protect Conway, his mate. Second, he wants to protect Inspector Lee. The only reason he'd want to do that is to stop Inspector Lee from exposing whatever it is he's got on him."

"In your opinion, which of them put the money in the flour jar?"

"Lee," Inspector Woolfe replied in a heartbeat. "It wouldn't have been hard to, either. Conway doesn't lock his door."

Chief Inspector Jones' expression was grave as he released a soft hum. Turning away a moment later, he moved slowly toward the door as he ran through in his mind everything he'd been told. "If it is as you suggest, and Inspector Lee is not only attempting to entrap Conway but is also blackmailing Dr Weeks in the process, this runs deeper than simple revenge for a perceived wrong." He faced Inspector Woolfe. "Has Inspector Lee intimated to you his reasons for wanting Conway out of the way?"

"He was angered by the board's decision to let Conway return to duty. I think he thought, like the rest of us, he would be dismissed from the service."

"He has expressed no personal hatred for Conway?"

Inspector Woolfe gave a soft grunt that may have been a failed attempt at a laugh. "He hates anyone without money, the arrogant bastard." He flinched at the unflattering slip of the tongue made to his senior officer. "Sorry, sir."

Chief Inspector Jones was lost in thought, however.

Taking Dr Weeks' statement from the envelope as he returned to Inspector Woolfe, he stood by the fire and read it.

"I'll deal with this from here on in," he said once he'd finished. "You're not to breathe a word of it to anyone, not even Inspector Conway." He gathered up the envelope and flour jar.

"Yes, sir," Inspector Woolfe reluctantly agreed, suddenly fearing he'd made a terrible mistake.

THIRTY-TWO

The clock on the mantel shelf struck nine as the fire
dampened the early morning chill in the Society's parlour.
An earthy mustiness also emanated from the tree and
decorations, making the room feel less cosy than normal.
Although the sky was smothered by grey clouds, the light
coming through the window was sufficient to make
igniting the gas lamps unnecessary. With half of his face in
shadow, Mr Elliott sat on the sofa with a disconcerted
expression as Miss Trent relayed the previous night's
events.

"He threatened your person with a knife, unlawfully
held you prisoner, stole the knife from the kitchen, and
unlawfully entered Mr Maxwell's former home. Yet, you
still thought it appropriate to not only bring him here but
allow him to stay overnight with little more than Mr
Maxwell for protection," Mr Elliott adopted a hard tone. "I
would've escorted him to the nearest police station."

"He was frightened and grief stricken. I was never in
any real danger," Miss Trent stated from where she stood
to the left of the fireplace. "I cooked him a hearty
breakfast, but he left it largely untouched. I think he's still
disturbed by the whole ordeal."

"Where is he now?"

"In the waiting room."

"There is a waiting room?"

Miss Trent gave a weak smile. "Yes, but unused."

Mr Elliott stood. "Let's go to him."

Miss Trent led the way from the parlour, across the
hallway, and into the first room on the left. Sparsely
furnished with a few mismatched chairs, its floorboards
were bare, scratched, and sun faded. Its walls were
covered in plum-coloured paper with a dark-purple rose
and vine print. As with the parlour, its wall-mounted gas
lamps were unlit. The incessant noise of Bow Street

drifted through the window whilst a fire snapped and crackled within the hearth.

Mr Baldwin, whom had been pacing the floor, strode over to Miss Trent and Mr Elliott the moment they entered. "How long you goin' to keep me 'ere for?"

"As long as necessary." Mr Elliott arranged three chairs in the room's centre. "Sit."

"You can't keep me 'ere," Mr Baldwin insisted.

Miss Trent put a hand upon his arm, prompting him to look at her. In a gentle voice, she said, "We only want to help you, remember?"

Mr Baldwin gave a small nod. Allowing her to lead him to the middle chair, he sat and glanced at her as she took the chair on the left before him. Mr Elliott took the one on the right and opened his notebook. Mr Baldwin swallowed hard and, leaning forward, rested his elbows upon his knees. He knew he could've easily been facing Inspector Pilker this morning, but the lawyer's reputation for seeing the world in black and white didn't lessen his worry. He straightened and, folding his arms, slouched back in his chair. His knee bounced slightly as he waited for the interrogation to begin.

"Miss Trent has decided not to pursue charges against you for your ill-treatment of her last night," Mr Elliott announced in a cool tone.

Mr Baldwin's features lifted with obvious relief. "Thanks."

Miss Trent smiled.

"Therefore," Mr Elliott continued. "We'll begin with your reason for running away when approached by Mr Snyder and Mr Skinner outside the *Gaslight Gazette*."

"I was scared," Mr Baldwin replied. "I thought you lot had me down as the one who done in Christian."

"Because Mr Skinner said we knew you'd searched the body?" Mr Elliott enquired.

Mr Baldwin lowered his arms and, holding his knees, leaned forward. "Yeah, but I didn't."

Mr Elliott's features tightened as he challenged, "You were seen doing it."

Mr Baldwin sat bolt upright. "Who by?" He looked between them. "They're lying."

"The bookmaker; Mr E.P. Westcott," Mr Elliott replied.

Mr Baldwin scowled. "*That* rat? He scarpered as soon as I saw him!"

"You admit to being at the warehouse?" Mr Elliott enquired.

Mr Baldwin's head jerked back. "What?" His complexion paled. "No."

Mr Elliott closed his notebook and stood.

Mr Baldwin watched him with increasing concern. "Where you goin'?"

"To the police." Mr Elliott went to the door.

Mr Baldwin's eyes widened, and he stood. "You can't do that!" He cast a desperate glance at Miss Trent. "*You* said you wanted to help me!"

"We do." Miss Trent stood as Mr Elliott lingered by the door. "But we can't if you don't tell us anything, Oswald."

Mr Baldwin glanced between them. With genuine fear in his voice and eyes, he insisted, "But I *can't*! Do you know what they'd do if I peached on 'em?" He threw an arm toward the window. "Look at what they done to Christian!"

Mr Elliott returned to the room's centre. "Who?"

Mr Baldwin took a step back. "I don't know."

"Oswald, please," Miss Trent urged.

"Then you leave us with little choice." Mr Elliott turned toward the door.

"No!" Mr Baldwin cried, reaching out to him. "*Please*, Mr Elliott. Have a heart."

"Emotion has no place in legal matters," Mr Elliott stated.

Mr Baldwin's face contorted into a fierce glare. "You bastard!"

Miss Trent moved in front of Mr Baldwin and placed her hands upon his arms. "Oswald, please, rethink what you're saying. They shan't hear from us where we got their names from, and we'll do everything in our power to protect you."

Mr Baldwin bowed his head.

Miss Trent bent forward and peered up at his face. "Think of Christian. He deserves justice, doesn't he?"

Mr Baldwin lifted and turned his head away. "Yeah."

Miss Trent straightened and side-stepped to keep her gaze fixed upon his. "Help us to help you."

Mr Baldwin's mouth formed a hard line as he looked to Mr Elliott who said, "The choice is yours."

Mr Baldwin turned his head and stared out the window. After several moments of consideration, he looked to Miss Trent. "Fine." He cast a warning glance between them. "But if owt happens to me, it's *your* fault."

Miss Trent gave a warm smile and guided him back to his seat. "Thank you, Oswald."

Mr Baldwin mumbled, "You're welcome," and sat.

Removing two sketches from his notebook as he joined them, Mr Elliott held them up once they were settled. "Are these the men you fear?"

Mr Baldwin's face blanched, and he gave a small nod.

"This is Mr Noah O'Hanigan, a boxer, and his manager, Mr Amias Winfield." Mr Elliott lifted each sketch in turn. "Why do you suspect they murdered Mr Grosse?"

Mr Baldwin folded his arms tightly against his chest. "Winfield told O'Hanigan to do this," he gestured to his bruised face, "after O'Hanigan beat Christian. I didn't know their names, then, but Winfield must of remembered me from before, because he said sumthin' about me working for Christian."

"Where did the assault take place?" Mr Elliott enquired.

Mr Baldwin bowed his head but remained silent.

"Was it at the warehouse?" Mr Elliott pressed.

Mr Baldwin gave a minute nod.

"Was it during the set-to?" Mr Elliott enquired.

Mr Baldwin took in a deep breath and released it as a drawn-out sigh. He quietly replied, "Yeah, it was." He lifted his head but broke eye contact with Mr Elliott a second after making it. He looked to Miss Trent instead. "I didn't know what was going to happen."

Miss Trent offered a reassuring smile. "I know."

"Were these men familiar to you before they assaulted you and Mr Grosse?" Mr Elliott enquired, making a note of Mr Baldwin's answers.

Miss Trent placed a reassuring hand upon Mr Baldwin's arm.

"No, but now that you've said it, O'Hanigan was the name of the bloke Christian said was havin' it off with his wife," Mr Baldwin replied, grateful for Miss Trent's presence.

"When did he tell you that?" Mr Elliott enquired.

"The day I went to see him, the day when Winfield almost knocked me down," Mr Baldwin replied. "He said O'Hanigan's manager had come by to give him an earful about tellin' Farley not to let him join his club. I asked Christian why he'd do sumin' like that, and he said it was because O'Hanigan was havin' it off with his missus."

Mr Elliott noted this. "Returning to the question of whether you searched Mr Grosse's body." He lifted his gaze and caught the disgust in Mr Baldwin's face. "Did you?"

Mr Baldwin gave a curt nod as he bowed his head again.

"What were you looking for?" Mr Elliott enquired.

"The notebook," Mr Baldwin mumbled.

"Did you find it?" Mr Elliott enquired.

Mr Baldwin gave a curt shake of his head.

"Did you take anything else?" Mr Elliott enquired.

Mr Baldwin frowned and, lowering his arms, held the edges of his chair as he shifted his weight upon it.

Resuming his former position, he looked to Miss Trent and insisted, "I took his things so Westcott wouldn't."

"Where did you take them?" Miss Trent enquired.

"His office," Mr Baldwin replied.

"Were you the one who forced the door?" Mr Elliott enquired.

Mr Baldwin frowned. With a regretful tone, he replied, "I don't have a key." He glanced at Mr Elliott. "Workin' for the *Gazette*, you get to know a few characters. One of them showed me how to jemmy a door."

Mr Elliott turned back a page in his notebook and added 'housebreaking' to the list of charges Mr Baldwin could potentially face should the police decide to commit him to the magistrates' court. Reluctant to risk losing Mr Baldwin's cooperation by making him aware of this possibility, Mr Elliott decided to keep his own counsel about it. Instead, he changed the subject. "Did you search Mr Grosse's office for the notebook?"

Mr Baldwin's frown deepened.

Mr Elliott looked at him with expectant eyes. When no response was forthcoming, he pressed, "Did you?"

Mr Baldwin sighed. "Yeah."

"Did you find it?" Mr Elliott enquired.

"No." Mr Baldwin glanced at Miss Trent.

"But you were disturbed," Mr Elliott stated.

Recalling the shout he'd heard through the wall of someone threatening to fetch a constable, Mr Baldwin felt a tightening of his gut and a swirling sensation in his stomach. Swallowing to try to ease his resulting nausea and pounding heart, he mumbled, "Yeah."

"And broke a window when you panicked," Mr Elliott stated.

Mr Baldwin glanced at his bandaged hand as his heartrate and nausea increased.

Catching the look, Mr Elliott added, "Precisely." He noted the revelation. "How did you come to be at the warehouse?"

When Mr Elliott didn't scold him for breaking the window, Mr Baldwin felt his nausea subside. "I told you: I saw Christian at the *Key & Lion* the night he was done in."

Mr Elliott watched him with expectant eyes.

"I asked him where the set-to was happenin', but he wouldn't tell me," Mr Baldwin added.

"That still doesn't answer my question," Mr Elliott challenged.

Mr Baldwin slipped his tongue over his dry lips as he considered his answer. "Toby, Mr Sparrow's Pot Boy, told me for a few coins."

"Why wouldn't Mr Grosse tell you?" Miss Trent enquired. "If you were friends."

"We was," Mr Baldwin said. "But he'd told Jeffers from *Sporting Life* he could write the story and wasn't goin' to break his word." He averted his gaze and mumbled, "It was the biggest bloody story of my life."

"Was Mr Grosse aware of your presence at the warehouse?" Mr Elliott enquired.

Mr Baldwin frowned. "He wasn't happy to see me."

Mr Elliott noted this. "When were you assaulted?"

Mr Baldwin lowered his head and stared at the floor as he replayed the night's events in his mind. His expression steadily became more pained as he did so. Rubbing the side of his face a moment later, he covered his mouth as he recalled Mr Grosse's smashed skull. "Erm…" He lowered his hand and, taking a deep breath, folded his arms again. "The set-to had started when I got there. After findin' Christian, I watched it with him. A few rounds in, I went to say sumin' to him, but he wasn't there, so I went lookin' for him. That's when O'Hanigan beat him and then me."

Mr Elliott and Miss Trent allowed Mr Baldwin a few moments to compose himself.

"And then what happened, Oswald?" the latter gently enquired.

Mr Baldwin looked sullen. "I was on the ground for a bit, to make sure O'Hanigan and Winfield was gone, and then went to find Christian." He downcast his eyes and fell silent for several moments. Eventually, in a quiet voice subdued by grief, he said, "He was behind the crates… He was dead."

"And that is when you searched for the notebook," Mr Elliott stated.

Mr Baldwin gave a jerky nod.

Mr Elliott noted this. "Who was in the set-to?"

"Erm…" Mr Baldwin rested his chin in his hand as he looked past Mr Elliott at the floor. "Joe Rake was for the *Nimble Crow*, and Daniel White was for the *Key & Lion*."

"Mr Farley and Mr Sparrow deny all knowledge of the fight," Mr Elliott stated.

Mr Baldwin looked at him sharply. "Well, they would, wouldn't they?"

"Why?" Miss Trent enquired.

"Because everyone knows it's because of them Christian was done in where he was," Mr Baldwin replied.

"How?" Mr Elliott enquired.

"Christian arranged the set-to," Mr Baldwin replied.

"I still don't quite follow you," Mr Elliott said with a genuine hint of confusion in his voice. "We were informed that Mr Sparrow and Mr Farley don't see eye to eye on boxing."

"That's right," Mr Baldwin said. "They've been at each other's throats for years because of it."

"So, how did Mr Grosse persuade them to supply fighters for his bout at the warehouse?" Mr Elliott enquired.

"He didn't," Mr Baldwin replied.

"But you said it was Christian who arranged the bout," Mr Elliott said, irritated.

"He did," Mr Baldwin said.

"But *how*?" Mr Elliott urged, his frustration evident in his voice.

"Oh," Mr Baldwin said, the penny finally dropping. "Christian and me was at the *Key & Lion*, drinkin' with Duncan—Mr Sparrow—when Farley walked in bold as brass. He told Duncan his new pug, Joe Rake, had taken up the mittens. There would of been a fight there and then if Christian hadn't told them he'd arrange a set-to between the best pugs from the *Key & Lion* and *Nimble Crow* to bury the hatchet once and for all."

"*Thank* you," Mr Elliott said through an exasperated sigh.

"Have Mr Sparrow and Mr Farley ever been friends?" Miss Trent enquired.

"I heard they was years back," Mr Baldwin replied. "They do know how to wind each other up."

Satisfied they'd garnered all they could about events at the warehouse—for the time being, at least—Mr Elliott returned to his notes from his first conversation with the journalist. "Have you remembered the 'something else' Mr Grosse mentioned regarding Mr Deon Erskine?"

Mr Baldwin lowered his head as he searched his memory. "I think so… yeah, that was it." He lifted his head. "I told him I'd help find him, but he said there was no need because he'd already gotten an address for him here in London."

"Did he say where it was?" Mr Elliott enquired.

Mr Baldwin frowned. "No. Sorry."

"And Mr Erskine isn't listed in the *Post Office Directory*," Miss Trent interjected.

"Is there owt else?" Mr Baldwin looked between them. "I've got to get to work."

"Nothing further," Mr Elliott replied.

Mr Baldwin stood.

"For the moment," Mr Elliott added.

Mr Baldwin frowned.

Miss Trent stood. "We'd like to place an advertisement in the *Gaslight Gazette* inviting Mr Winfield to come forward. Could you take the copy with you, please?"

Mr Baldwin cast an uneasy glance between them. "Yeah, but it's not come from me."

"Thank you." Miss Trent smiled. "Mr Snyder will drive you to Fleet Street."

* * *

Miss Hicks hummed softly as she pinned the remaining strand of hair atop her head and wiped her face with the corner of a damp cloth. Puckering her lips as she looked in the mirror, she wiped around her mouth before kissing the air. She stood and, reaching behind her, tightened the strings of her scarlet-red dress to accentuate her waist and push up her bosom. The latter was already tightly compacted by her corset but since Miss Trent had agreed to her trying for work at the *Key & Lion*, she wanted to ensure she made the 'right' impression. Running her hands down her sides, she admired her reflection with a broad smile. "Polly Hicks, you're beautiful."

A loud snort from the adjacent room pulled her gaze to its door, momentarily distracting her. Rather than investigate, though, she completed her preparations by putting on her heeled boots and faded, dark-brown, knee-length coat. Once done, she resumed her humming as she went into the other room, walked around the sofa, and proceeded to search the pockets of the sleeping Dr Weeks lying upon it. She pouted when she found just a few shillings but soon remembered where his banknotes were kept.

The rooms in which Dr Weeks lived, and Miss Hicks regularly visited, occupied the second floor of the building belonging to the owner of *R.G. Dunn Pawnbrokers* on the ground floor. Located on St. John Street, London, it was, unsurprisingly, within staggering distance of the *Coach & Horses* public house, one of Dr Weeks' favourite haunts. The rooms comprised of a spacious lounge-come-study-come-laboratory and a decent-sized bedroom.

Despite its size, the lounge was packed with furniture (sofa, bureau, bookcases, armchair, and several tables of varying shapes and sizes). Piles of books on anatomy, emerging scientific techniques, and pseudoscience cluttered every surface, whilst dog-eared journals, including the *British Medical Journal* and *Lancet*, were scattered across the floor and tucked into every conceivable nook and cranny.

Glass jars, beakers, and bowls had also been set up with gas burners, pipes, and other strange-looking pieces of apparatus on the largest of the tables standing beside the bureau. Naturally, empty gin, whiskey, and wine bottles littered the room, along with Dr Weeks' and Miss Hicks' clothes. She'd tried to tidy the place once but had received an earful from the surgeon for her trouble. According to him, it was "organised chaos." She didn't mind since maintaining a home had never interested her. He'd also bought a dressing table and separate wardrobe for her, along with beautiful clothes to fill it with, so she could permit him his eccentricities.

Going to the window overlooking St. John Street, she dislodged the wooden floorboard directly underneath and retrieved a small, wooden tea box. Taking several banknotes from it, she paused before taking several more. "A girl's gotta eat," she muttered as she stuffed the notes down her cleavage and returned the box to its hiding place.

Dr Weeks, who'd slept throughout, lay upon his side on the sofa with his right arm dangling over its edge. On the floor beneath his hand was an empty gin bottle. Although it was a sight she'd come to expect to see whilst staying with him, the increase in its frequency was a small cause of concern for her. This had been the second time in less than a week. The fleeting thought that she should wake him and demand to know what was going on passed through her mind. A glance at the clock told her she didn't have the time, though, if she wanted to get to the *Key & Lion* for when it opened. She laid a blanket over him and, holding her hand in front of his lips to make sure he was still breathing, left him to sleep it off.

* * *

The cold morning light hurt Inspector Conway's tired eyes as he read aloud his notes from the previous night's meetings with his undercover officers. Although he'd assigned two of them to the *Nimble Crow* and *Key & Lion* as promised, he purposefully omitted these from his dictation. Standing behind his desk with the window at his back, he also spoke just slowly enough for Sergeant Caulfield to keep up. Aside from his limbs feeling like dead weights due to the fatigue, his chest and back also ached. Thoughts of his bed weren't far from his mind.

A knock on the door forced him to set them aside, however.

"Come in," he called, flipping his notebook closed and putting it down. He'd already decided to hand over whoever it was to Sergeant Caulfield to deal with. Yet, the face of his visitor obliged him to rethink his plan. "Caleb, what you doin' here?"

The two exchanged a firm handshake.

"Thought I'd show my face," Inspector Woolfe replied, casting an awkward glance at Sergeant Caulfield.

"That's all for now, lad," Inspector Conway said.

"Yes, sir," Sergeant Caulfield said with a brief bow of his head. As he passed Inspector Woolfe, he mumbled a polite "Good morning, sir," before closing the door to give them some privacy.

"I was about to go 'ome for some sleep," Inspector Conway said. "You look like you could do with some, too."

Inspector Woolfe rubbed his bloodshot eyes. "Yeah. I will." He cast a cursory glance over the room as he walked toward the window, gripped by a brief coughing fit. Clearing his throat, he tossed a lozenge into his mouth. "I thought you was downstairs with the rest of them."

Inspector Conway averted his gaze as he tidied his desk. "I was."

"What changed?" Inspector Woolfe watched him, feeling a knot forming in his stomach as he contemplated whether it was his late-night visit to Chief Inspector Jones that had upset the apple cart.

Inspector Conway hesitated before putting his notebook in his drawer and locking it. "I almost punched Lee." He rested his hands upon the desk and leaned his weight upon them. "The bastard got my back up." He cast a sidelong glance at Inspector Woolfe. "I shouldn't of done it." He straightened and took his overcoat from the back of his chair.

Inspector Woolfe frowned deeply as he realised Inspector Lee had been telling the truth about that part. *Could he have been telling the truth about the bribe, too?* He wondered but immediately dismissed it with a subtle shake of his head. *No*, he told himself. *Conway's not like that*. Pushing all thoughts of the allegation aside, since it appeared as though Chief Inspector Jones hadn't acted upon it yet, he picked up Inspector Conway's hat from the desk and held it out to him. "That warrants a hot breakfast, if you're hungry?"

Inspector Conway momentarily stared at him, taken aback, before accepting his hat. "Yeah, I'm hungry." He carried his hat as he went to the door but soon halted to look back at him. "I thought you and Lee was mates now?"

Inspector Woolfe gave a grunt of disgust. "That arrogant sonofabitch? Don't make me laugh."

The corner of Inspector Conway's mouth lifted. "I was worried you'd gone soft."

Inspector Woolfe opened the door. "Just get your arse moving before I die of starvation."

Inspector Conway chuckled as he left the office ahead of him.

THIRTY-THREE

It had taken Mr Skinner longer than planned to find Cricketfield Road. Hackney and Lower Clapton in particular, wasn't somewhere he'd visited. Having taken the train to Victoria Park Station, he'd hired a cab from the queue on Riseholme Street. Upon enquiring with its driver, he'd discovered the Salvation Army Congress Hall was within walking distance of his destination. Therefore, he'd paid to go as far as Linscott Road where he'd alighted and completed his journey on foot. A brief delay caused by a wrong turn had obliged him to seek directions from a local, however.

By the time he pushed open the door to the *Nimble Crow*, the cold had turned his cheeks and nose bright red. Feeling its warm air wash over him as he entered, he ventured further in and cast a cursory glance over the main bar room. Noting the four doors on the balcony at the room's far end, he was a little perturbed by the lack of visible exits on the ground floor. Knowing that most public houses had doors to the cellar and rear yard at the very least, he presumed their locations were hidden by the stairs.

He glanced to his left and right as he approached the bar. The establishment was sparsely occupied with only two or three customers sitting at the tables near to the fires. Looking away, he was compelled to do a double-take when he thought he'd caught one of them—a man in his early thirties with a small, brown moustache and goatee—watching him. The second look confirmed he was simply enjoying some mulled wine, however. Dismissing it as his mind playing tricks on him due to the intensity of the situation, he headed to the left side of the bar to avoid being served anytime soon.

His years as the Mirrells' bodyguard had taught him many things. One of which was the importance of observing your surroundings to identify potential dangers, escape routes, friends, and foes. Whilst it was true the Mirrells' chosen locations were quiet and respectable establishments, his seafaring days had shown him trouble could rear its ugly head at any time and place.

A few minutes passed. The longer he observed, the more he allowed himself to relax. The pub's customers seemed to belong to the middle classes or higher. He doubted he'd encounter any violent bruisers here. He glanced at the man with the goatee and could've sworn he'd caught him watching again. Yet, a second look confirmed he was still just enjoying a quiet drink. *A writer, maybe?* Mr Skinner mused. *Or someone who just likes watching the world go by.* Dismissing these thoughts as irrelevant, he looked up at the balcony. Earlier, Mr Snyder had mentioned the boxing club's gymnasium was upstairs.

"Good morning, sir," a well-dressed man greeted in a contrived upper-class accent as he came around to Mr Skinner's side of the bar.

The men cast appraising glances over each other.

Recalling Mr Snyder's comment about being asked to visit a cheaper pub, Mr Skinner had been careful to dress in such a way that would allow him to avoid the same fate. In other words, he'd chosen an attire consisting of his best tailor-made navy-blue frockcoat over light-brown waistcoat and trousers, and a perfectly pressed white shirt and cravat beneath. The black leather of his riding boots had been polished to a shine to complement the silver handle of the ebony cane tucked under his arm. In short, he had the appearance of a man who possessed enough money to be considered comfortable rather than rich.

"Good mornin'," Mr Skinner replied. He paused to note the man's reaction to his accent. When his emotionless expression remained unchanged, Mr Skinner enquired, "Are you 'Long-Armed Farley?'"

The man puffed out his chest and squared his shoulders. "I am, sir, and you are?"

Mr Skinner offered his natural hand. "Callahan Skinner. I'm interested in joinin' your boxin' club."

Mr Farley gave his hand a firm shake. "Have you spent much time in the ring?"

"A little," Mr Skinner replied. "I was in the Navy."

Mr Farley's voice adopted a hint of disapproval. "Bareknuckle, then."

"Yes, but it was just a way for my shipmates to break me in so to speak. On my first voyage, the captain weighed anchor near a secluded beach and had his best boxer put me through my paces." Mr Skinner smiled. "I'm happy to say I won."

"Had you toed the scratch before going to sea?"

"Once or twice." Mr Skinner gave a one-sided shoulder shrug. "But an argument with a cannon ended both my boxing and seafaring days in one hit." He put his iron hand down upon the bar with a dull thud and rolled up the sleeves of his frockcoat and shirt. Beneath was the prosthetic's iron cage-like frame surrounding his stump and the thick, leather straps keeping it in place. "I want to keep up my strength and stamina. I thought an exercise regimen, under the instruction of Long-Arm Farley, would be just the t'ing."

Mr Farley smiled broadly as he puffed out his chest once more. "It certainly would, sir, as long as you're willing and able to put in the required time, effort, and dedication." In a nonchalant voice, he enquired, "May I ask what it is you do now for employment?"

"I'm a private bodyguard to Captain and Lady Mirrell."

Mr Farley's eyebrows lifted. "*Really*?" His broad smile returned, lifting his features and brightening his eyes. "Then it is my duty and absolute pleasure to welcome you to the *Lower Clapton Boxing Club*, sir." He offered his hand.

Mr Skinner squeezed it firmly. "When can we start?"

"Now if you'd like."

Mr Skinner smiled. He would enjoy this.

* * *

"You'd be an ornament on any man's shelf," Mr Sparrow complimented as he stood with Miss Hicks in the back hall of the *Key & Lion*. Resting his hand against the wall behind her, he lightly pressed his chest against her breasts. "Or bar." Fixing his gaze upon hers, he put the knuckles of his free hand against her cheek before sliding them down to her neck. Slowly rubbing its side, his breathing became heavier when the heel of his hand briefly touched her bare chest. In a soft voice, he added, "You're hired."

"Thank you, sir." Miss Hicks smiled and placed her hand upon his rubbing one. "Shall I ge' to pourin'?"

Mr Sparrow's gaze dropped to her cleavage, and he wetted his lips. "Ar."

Miss Hicks eased his hand from her person. "May I get past, please, sir?"

Mr Sparrow's eyes shot up, startled. Taking a step back, he hoicked up the waistband of his trousers and cleared his throat as his gaze looked everywhere but at her.

"Thank you, sir." Miss Hicks touched his cheek as she passed but softly exhaled when she entered the relative safety of the bar. Hearing the door to the yard close behind her, she suspected Mr Sparrow had gone outside to cool down. The thought gave her further cause to relax and, with a flash of a smile and a glance at the price list, she served her first customer.

* * *

Pinning the lace with his iron fingers, Mr Skinner tightened the knot with his natural hand and tugged on the shoe to check it was secure. As he stood, he felt the silk of the knee-length drawers touch his bare flesh, a sensation that would take some getting used to. Despite the trusted position he held as the Mirrell's private bodyguard, he could only afford cotton clothing. Mindful of the boxing shoes' smooth soles as he turned, he folded his clothes upon the low bench, put his cane beside his boots on the floor beneath, and hung his frockcoat upon a hook on the wall above.

He glanced at the untidy pile of clothes at the opposite end of the bench. Having noticed them upon entering, he now went through them for any clue of their owner's identity. Not only were they made from coarse, dirty material, they were also frayed and heavily worn in places. The shoes' stitching was also coming away. Satisfied there was nothing more to discover, he took a pair of brown leather gloves from the shelf.

As he opened the door to head to the gymnasium, though, the sight of a woman crossing the balcony to the stairs caused him to halt and close the door ajar. Waiting until she was out of sight, he couldn't help but admire her in the meantime. Her heart-shaped face, petite nose, and hazel eyes reminded him of a love he'd lost. Instinctively glancing at his prosthetic hand as a long-buried sorrow reignited in his breast, he pursed his lips and stepped out onto the balcony. Despising his love for the effect she still had on him after all these years, he made a concerted effort to suppress his sadness whilst reminding himself of why he was there.

Having regained his composure, he strode into the gymnasium.

* * *

Toby dumped the empty glasses upon the bar with a loud clink. "Who're you?"

Miss Hicks jerked her head back at the blunt question before releasing a weak chuckle and putting her hands upon her waist. "'Ello to you, too."

Toby tilted his head back and squinted up at her. "You Sparrow's new old lady?"

Miss Hicks gave a sidelong glance at the door to the hall. With neither sight nor sound of the landlord, still, she folded her arms. "His new barmaid." She twisted the lace trim of her sleeve as she weighed up the threat Toby posed to her undercover task. Mr Snyder had described the lad and his job as the pub's Pot Boy. Nothing he'd said had led her to believe Toby was anything untoward, however. Lowering her arms, she offered a small smile with a softening of her eyes and features. In a gentle voice, she said, "Miss Hicks." She rested her hand upon his forearm. "But you can call me Polly."

Toby pulled his arm away and took a step back, startled by the touch. Casting a wary glance over her, he swallowed hard whilst shifting his weight from one foot to the other and back again. "Since when did you start workin' 'ere?"

"Today." Miss Hicks offered another small smile. "Mr Sparrow wants us to be mates, don't 'e?"

"I dunno." Toby frowned but approached the bar, nonetheless. He downcast his eyes and mumbled, "Maybe." He hooked his fingers onto the bar's edge and stared at them as he, too, weighed up Miss Hicks as a threat. In his case, though, it was the likelihood of her convincing Mr Sparrow to toss him out onto the streets. Stealing a glance at her, he recognised someone who'd had as hard a life as him, if not harder. This fact alone was enough to ease his anxiety over his situation. Yet, the recollection of her gentle hand upon his arm convinced him she was a good person. He lifted his gaze and, spitting into his palm, held out his hand. "Lord Toby Grenville the Third, Esquire, but you can call me Toby."

Miss Hicks chuckled as she gave his soiled hand a firm shake. "My Lord."

Toby pouted at her lack of disgust. "You've worked pubs before."

"All my days." Miss Hicks leaned in close, prompting him to do the same. In a hushed voice, she added, "Was born in one, too."

"I was born in the work 'ouse," Toby admitted. "With nothin' and no one."

Miss Hicks met his gaze with a sympathetic one. "Not anymore."

Toby's eyes momentarily lit up before suspicion descended again. Tilting his head to the side, he folded his arms. "How's that?"

Miss Hicks gave a feeble chuckle. "I'm 'ere to look after you now, ain't I?"

"People don't want owt for nowt."

"You've got nowt to give," Miss Hicks pointed out.

Toby blinked, parted his lips, and closed them again. Furrowing his brow as he looked over her shoulder, he realised he couldn't argue with that. Returning his gaze to her, he enquired, "You doin' this out of the goodness of your 'eart?"

"Yeah, and no." Miss Hicks cast another sidelong glance at the door to the hall before leaning closer to Toby again. In a low voice, she continued, "I need someone to look after me, too. You know, a big, strong bloke. I 'eard this was the place to find 'im."

"You wantin' a bruiser?"

Miss Hicks hummed. "There's set-to's 'ere, ain't there?"

Toby frowned. "Not anymore."

"How come?"

Toby glanced at the cellar door. "Sparrow's filled the place with barrels and crates."

Miss Hicks stood bolt upright as she felt a hand slide over her behind.

"I don't pay you to gossip," Mr Sparrow said into her ear.

Miss Hicks turned her head to find his face mere inches from her own. "Sorry, sir."

Mr Sparrow smiled and put his hand upon her hip. "Good girl."

Miss Hicks gave a weak smile in return and, turning toward the bar, caught the apologetic look from Toby as he hurried away to collect more empty glasses.

"Same again, love," a customer said, putting his ale glass down in front of her. In his mid-twenties, he had short, brown hair, a fair complexion, and hazel eyes. Approximately five foot eight inches tall, he wore a green overcoat with frayed edges, tattered brown trousers and waistcoat, and off-white shirt beneath.

Miss Hicks flashed him a smile as she picked up the glass and poured some ale from the barrel.

THIRTY-FOUR

"Bareknuckle may be what you're accustomed to, but we box under the Queensberry Rules here." Mr Farley's voice boomed around the gymnasium as he stood with his shoulders back, his chest out, and his hands held loosely behind his back.

Sitting in front of him, on the steps leading to the ring, was Mr Skinner who watched him intently. Standing to the Irishman's right was Mr Joe Rake who, like him, wore the boxer's attire of silk drawers and smooth-soled shoes. Yet, unlike Mr Skinner, whose gloves rested in his lap, Mr Rake was wearing his. He was also staring at Mr Skinner with hard eyes instead of listening to their mutual trainer's speech.

"Sparring is encouraged, and matches are permitted as long as they contribute to a member's training," Mr Farley continued. "Otherwise, members are forbidden from participating in prize fights unless they are fought as part of a competition. If you follow the proper rules—in *and* out of the ring—your club membership is assured. Do you understand and accept these terms?"

"Aye," Mr Skinner replied.

"There are no second chances," Mr Farley warned. "Break the rules, and you're out."

"I don't plan to," Mr Skinner said in a resolute tone. Casting a sideways glance at Mr Rake, he enquired from Mr Farley, "When can I get in the ring?"

"Now. If you'd like," Mr Rake replied, driving his gloved fists against each other.

"Oi." Mr Farley glared at him. "Enough of that."

Mr Rake scowled but lowered his arms.

"You're nowhere near ready," Mr Farley told Mr Skinner. "And that contraption of yours isn't permitted, either. Take it off." As Mr Skinner removed the prosthetic and set it down, Mr Farley cast an appraising glance over his chest, stomach, bicep, and thigh muscles. He also noted the burn scars on the right side of his face, neck, and right shoulder. "Your physical condition appears fair. It will be your wind, stamina, and speed which we'll have to work on. How old are you?"

"Thirty-eight," Mr Skinner replied.

Mr Farley gripped Mr Skinner's stump and, tugging it toward him, inspected the thick layer of scar tissue on its end. Digging his fingernail into the flesh in several different places, he watched Mr Skinner's face for any hint of pain or discomfort. "Can you hit with it?"

"I'll give it a go," Mr Skinner replied, his voice retaining its resoluteness.

Mr Farley released the stump and straightened. "Joe, get a two-pound Indian Club."

Mr Rake duly did as he was asked, returning a moment later.

"Joe uses a pair, but one is enough for you," Mr Farley offered the club to Mr Skinner, handle first. Once he'd taken it and felt its weight, Mr Farley pointed at his natural hand. "If you make it into the ring, that will be your attacking arm. Your other could be your defensive, but I doubt it could do much in the way of blocking."

Mr Skinner conceded the point when he glanced at his stump. "I'm more interested in the exercise regimen anyway." He tested the club's weight in his hand. "This isn't very heavy."

"It's heavy enough for someone starting out," Mr Farley rebuked. "It's swung around in a circle with your arm outstretched, like a windmill. We'll start with two-to-four rotations to see how it feels. As soon as you feel pain in your arm or shoulder, we'll do another couple of rotations and stop. Over time, you'll build up the muscles in your bicep, forearm, chest, and back of your shoulder blade, as well as loosen your shoulder joint and strengthen your wrist. That will allow you to do more rotations before feeling any pain. Stand up."

Mr Skinner stood and moved away from the steps to give both himself and the club extra room.

"Put your heels together," Mr Farley instructed, tapping Mr Skinner's left calf. "Turn your toes outward at a fifty-degree angle. That's it." Mr Farley moved around to Mr Skinner's front. "Make sure your body and shoulders are equally squared." Mr Farley eased Mr Skinner's shoulders into position. "Let your arms relax. That's it. Head straight. Chin a little down. Look straight ahead." Mr Farley moved aside. "Swing the club three times."

Mr Skinner kept his arm rigid as he swung it in a full circle once, twice, thrice. Although he felt the pull of its weight in his shoulder joint and left side of his chest, he didn't feel any discomfort or pain.

"Another three," Mr Farley instructed.

Mr Skinner repeated the three rotations, wincing as a jolt of pain shot through his shoulder upon completing the third.

"Twice more," Mr Farley instructed.

Mr Skinner gritted his teeth as the jolt of pain shot through his shoulder with each additional rotation. His body felt the benefit when Mr Farley took the club from him.

"Mr Jeffers is downstairs, dear," a woman's voice called from the doorway.

When he looked across, Mr Skinner not only recognised her as the woman from before, but also saw her sweep her gaze over him. Suddenly feeling exposed, he wrapped his arms around his chest in a feeble attempt to protect his modesty.

Meanwhile, Mr Farley gave no acknowledgement of the improperness of his wife laying eyes upon half-naked men. Instead, he called back instructions to inform Mr Jeffers that he would be with him shortly and allowed his wife to leave without reprimand. Whilst Mr Skinner knew it wasn't his place to pass judgement on the domestic situation of the Farleys, he also knew how shocked the Mirrells—Lady Mirrell, in particular—would've been if they'd witnessed such a thing.

"Vigorous exercise is what you need," Mr Farley told Mr Skinner, causing him to do a double take as an entirely different form of 'exercise' initially entered his mind. Realising to what Mr Farley referred, he gave a small nod and mumbled acknowledgement.

"Exercise makes you sweat, and sweat helps clean out the pores," Mr Farley continued. "A firm rubbing of the skin with a rough towel finishes the job. Do this, and your liver and kidneys will thank you." Mr Farley passed the club to Mr Rake who returned it to the table. "They get rid of the impurities from the inside and those that have come in through your pores. If you don't make yourself sweat— or take a cold plunge in the morning—and do the rub down, your liver and kidneys will become overworked, diseased, or both."

Mr Farley glanced at the stump. "Skipping rope would usually be next, but you can run a few circuits of the gymnasium until I'm back instead." He headed for the door. "Joe, run with him!"

"Yes, Mr Farley," Mr Rake called back, his tone and expression betraying a distinct lack of enthusiasm for the idea. Nevertheless, he jogged away a moment later, prompting Mr Skinner to follow suit. As soon as he drew near, though, Mr Rake increased his speed to ensure he stayed in front. Uninterested in the young boxer's petty game and gladdened by the fact his years spent on the Mirrells' countryside estate had given him some stamina, Mr Skinner stuck to a comfortable speed behind him.

"Who was that woman?" he enquired after they'd completed a couple of circuits around the large room.

"Mrs Farley," Mr Rake replied. "Stay out of her way."

"I plan to. I saw the look she gave me."

Mr Rake slowed to run beside him. "She does that." He glanced at the door as they passed. "If Farley catches you lookin' back, you'll be goin' in the ground, not the ring."

Both men were silent as they ran their third and fourth laps. By the time they embarked upon their fifth, their breathing had become heavier, and droplets of sweat covered their skin.

"He shouldn't let her in here if he doesn't want men lookin' at her," Mr Skinner said, his words punctuated by panting.

"She can do nowt wrong in 'is eyes," Mr Rake replied.

Mr Skinner slowed as he felt his chest burn under the strain. "Has she… done wrong?"

"She's as proper as they come," Mr Rake replied.

Mr Skinner swallowed hard and pushed through the pain to complete his fifth lap. By the time he'd completed the sixth, though, it had become unbearable. Slowing to a stop at the side of the ring, he gripped its lower rope with his natural hand and bent forward whilst panting hard. After a few minutes had passed, during which Mr Rake had completed a further two laps, he'd regained his breath and returned to the steps.

"Want sumin' to drink?" Mr Rake enquired when he eventually joined him.

"Sure t'ing." Mr Skinner picked up his prosthetic and stood. "My round."

Mr Rake's features lit up with a smile. "Thanks!" His smile faded, and he cast a wary glance at the door. In a low voice, he said, "Mr Farley don't like me drinkin' beer, so it's got to be lemonade." When their eyes met, he added, "It's his diet."

"Mine will be a lemonade, too, then." Mr Skinner briefly rested his hand upon Mr Rake's back. "That way, neither of us will get in trouble."

Mr Rake grinned.

* * *

Dr Weeks threw open the door as he entered the *Key & Lion*, ignoring the loud bang as it struck a table. Halting long enough to cast his bloodshot gaze along the bar, he strode over to Miss Hicks as she served a customer.

Without taking his eyes off her, he placed himself so close to the customer, they were obliged to step aside. Oblivious to the consequence of his rudeness, Dr Weeks leaned over the bar. "What the hell are ya doin'?"

Miss Hicks took the money offered by her customer. "Workin'."

Dr Weeks narrowed his eyes. "I can see that, darlin'. When did ya start?"

"Today." Miss Hicks flashed her customer a smile. When she turned toward Dr Weeks, though, she stilled. His usually fair complexion was bright red and slicked with sweat, his jaw was covered in dark stubble, and his hair was as dishevelled as his clothes. At any other time, she wouldn't have cared what he looked like as long as he was in a good mood. With the continuation of her undercover task dependent upon the continuation of Mr Sparrow's good opinion, though, she was wary of angering him. Casting a sidelong glance at the landlord, she was relieved to see he was talking to some customers in the corner. She hurried out from behind the bar and, grabbing Dr Weeks by the arm, tried to pull him back toward the door. "Get 'ome and make yourself decent."

Dr Weeks yanked his arm free. "Ge' off!"

Miss Hicks stepped into his personal space and pointed at him, thereby compelling him to lean his head and shoulders back. With hard eyes and sharp tone, she hissed, "*Don't* show me up, Perce!" She lowered her hand. "I've got work to do, and *you're* not gonna ruin it for me, do you hear?"

"What kinda work?"

"It don't matter." Miss Hicks folded her arms. "Anyway, what do you care? As long as there's drink on the go."

Dr Weeks glared at her. "That's bullshit. I love the bones of ya and this place." He lowered his voice. "It ain't safe, darlin'."

"You've never been 'ere before!"

"No, but I ain't blind either."

"Just blind drunk?" Miss Hicks sardonically enquired.

Dr Weeks' glare returned. "What was wrong with the damn railway bar, anyway?"

"Nowt."

He reached for her. "Then ya can go back."

Miss Hicks moved away. "I said '*no*,' Perce! What part of that's not goin' through your bloody head?"

A heaviness formed in Dr Weeks' chest at the aggressive refusal. Feeling a tightening of his throat at the same time, he inwardly scolded himself for being so weak. Lifting his hand to reach for her, but changing his mind and lowering it again at the last moment, he said in a feeble voice, "Polly, darlin'. Come 'ome."

"I will." Miss Hicks looked at him with hard eyes. "At closin' time." She lowered her arms and strode back behind the bar. Upon hearing him following her, though, she plucked a bottle of beer from the shelf and thrust it against his chest. "Go *away,* Perce!"

Dr Weeks grimaced as he caught the bottle with both hands, his eyes filled with hurt. Feeling the heaviness in his chest intensify at the same time, followed by the tell-tale sting of tears, he bowed his head and briefly considered leaving the bottle on the bar. The oblivion, and thereby escape from reality it promised, proved too irresistible, however.

Clutching it tightly, he turned and left the pub, his feelings of self-loathing and guilt growing with every step.

* * *

"Joseph, you have to eat," Miss Trent said through the locked bedroom door.

"I… I'm not hungry," Mr Maxwell's quiet voice replied from within.

"At least come downstairs," Miss Trent urged. "I'll make you a cup of sweet tea."

"N-No, th-thank you."

"But—" Yet, the sound of someone knocking upon the front door interrupted her. Releasing a soft sigh, she lifted her skirts and hurried downstairs. Glancing into the parlour at Dr Colbert and Mr Elliott sitting therein, she opened the front door and stepped back.

Standing on the porch was a six-foot-tall man with a thick, dark-grey beard and moustache. His piercing green eyes gazed at her from beneath a broad-brimmed, dark-brown Panama hat. For several moments, the two sized one another up.

Eventually, he removed his hat and, in a softly spoken, broad, New York City accent, said, "I'm Amias Winfield. I hear you want to talk with me."

THIRTY-FIVE

Having built a sweat during his run, Mr Skinner took Mr Farley's advice and rubbed his skin down with a rough towel. Mr Rake, who did the same, was dressed by the time Mr Skinner was finished, however. Not wishing to delay the quenching of his friend's thirst, Mr Skinner gave him the money for their drinks and told him he'd join him downstairs in a few. Ever since the loss of his hand, the act of dressing had become laborious. Whilst he'd learnt a few tricks to overcome most difficulties, it inevitably took him longer than before. Hence why almost fifteen minutes had passed by the time he was fully clothed. With a last inspection of his appearance in the mirror and swift retrieval of his cane, he finally headed for the door.

"A one-handed boxer isn't something you see every day," Mr Farley's voice said from the other side, prompting Mr Skinner to pause with his hand on the doorknob. When he didn't hear any approaching footsteps, he gently turned it, eased the door open ajar, and peered through the gap. Mr Farley stood by the stairs. Beside him was a man wearing a black bowler hat who cast a worried glance over the otherwise empty balcony.

In his late thirties, the man was approximately five feet eleven inches tall with a lean build. The teardrop shape of his eye sockets gave his narrow face a melancholic air, thereby complementing the grey tinge of his fair complexion. In stark contrast, his hazel eyes were bright with emotion as he insisted in a hushed voice, "Don't change the subject. I have to know—"

"I've given my answer, Jeffers," Mr Farley interrupted in a low, yet menacing voice.

Mr Jeffers swallowed hard. "We—"

"There is no 'we,' not in this."

The remaining colour drained from Mr Jeffers' face. "But—"

Mr Farley entered Mr Jeffers' personal space. "*We* were happy to leave it where it was. *You* took it, so, *you* can dispose of it."

Mr Jeffers parted his lips.

"We don't care how or where," Mr Farley said. "Only that you do it."

"Very well." Mr Jeffers' voice echoed the dejection in his face and eyes.

Mr Skinner opened the door wide and strode toward them. "Mr Farley?"

The landlord turned, revealing a broad smile. "Mr Skinner, there you are."

Mr Skinner offered his natural hand. "Thank you again, for your instruction; it was very enlightenin'."

"I'm glad to hear it," Mr Farley said, giving his hand a firm shake. "You will be accepting my offer of membership, then?"

"Consider it done," Mr Skinner replied.

Mr Farley beamed.

"Could I trouble you for some more instruction tomorrow?" Mr Skinner enquired.

"It's no trouble at all, sir," Mr Farley replied.

Mr Jeffers peered down his nose at Mr Skinner's iron hand. "And precisely *how* will you box one handed?"

"I'm a determined man, sir," Mr Skinner stated in a firm tone.

"This is Mr Ian Jeffers from *Sporting Life*, Mr Skinner," Mr Farley introduced.

"A fine publication," Mr Skinner remarked.

"I think so," Mr Jeffers said.

"But I don't want to be in it," Mr Skinner added.

Mr Jeffers peered down his nose at Mr Skinner's hand again. "I only write about proper boxers." Upon passing Mr Farley on his way to the stairs, he added, "I'll be in touch."

* * *

Thin whisps of smoke poured from Mr Winfield's hand-rolled cigarette as he held it away from his lips. With his elbow resting upon the sofa's arm, the American sat flush against its rear cushion with his other hand holding his hat against its stomach. "The refusal of my fighter's membership to the *Lower Clapton Boxing Club* was down to Grosse." He took a pull from his cigarette and, exhaling its smoke, watched Mr Elliott through its dissipating clouds. "I was within my right to express my displeasure at his actions."

"Verbally, yes. Which, I might add, you did prior to meeting Mr Grosse at the docks," Mr Elliott said. He sat in Miss Trent's armchair, his notebook open upon his knee. "But by ordering Mr O'Hanigan to beat him and Mr Baldwin, you were committing a crime."

"I call it justice," Mr Winfield said. "I'm sorry if that offends your straitlaced, British sensibilities." He took another pull from his cigarette and crushed it out in the ashtray.

"It offends my obligation to the law," Mr Elliott firmly stated. "And to Mr Grosse."

"And mine," Dr Colbert interjected from his position to the left of the fire. Sitting upon a chair borrowed from the kitchen, he did his best to ignore the ache in his lower back. "You said you were within your right to express your displeasure at what Mr Grosse had done. Wasn't Mr Grosse also within his right to express his displeasure at Mr O'Hanigan's shameful behaviour with his wife by persuading Mr Farley not to accept his application for club membership?"

"No." Mr Winfield narrowed his eyes.

"Why?" Mr Elliott enquired.

"Because there's no room for women in the ring." Mr Winfield glared at him.

Dr Colbert frowned, confused.

Upon seeing this, Mr Elliott enquired from Mr Winfield, "You believe Mr O'Hanigan's involvement with

Mrs Grosse shouldn't have had any bearing on his involvement with the sport?"

"In one," Mr Winfield replied.

"But it did, and now Mr Grosse is dead," Mr Elliott said. "Murdered."

Mr Winfield smirked. "Not by me."

"Or Mr O'Hanigan?" Dr Colbert enquired.

Mr Winfield's smile faded. "That I don't know." His gaze shifted back to Mr Elliott. "He might've done it for her." He glanced between them as he added firmly, "But not for me. I got my pound of flesh."

Mr Elliott consulted his previous notes. "Mr Grosse possessed a notebook containing details of all the fights he'd witnessed or been involved with. It's said to also include the names of the managers and backers of the boxers, as well as those of the boxers themselves. Were you aware of its existence?"

Mr Winfield gave a wry smile. "Sure, I knew."

"Have you got it?" Dr Colbert enquired.

"No," Mr Winfield replied.

"Do you know who might?" Mr Elliott enquired.

"Ask that friend of his—Mr Baldwin," Mr Winfield replied.

"He claims to not have it," Mr Elliott said.

"Then I can't help you," Mr Winfield said.

"How valuable is the information contained within it?" Mr Elliott enquired.

"That depends," Mr Winfield replied.

"On?" Mr Elliott enquired.

"Who wants it," Mr Winfield replied.

"Do you want it?" Dr Colbert enquired.

"No," Mr Winfield replied curtly.

"Why not?" Mr Elliott enquired.

"I don't fix fights," Mr Winfield replied.

Mr Elliott remained silent, waiting for the American to elaborate. Unfortunately, Dr Colbert wasn't so patient. In a heartbeat, he enquired, "Who fixed the fights?"

Mr Winfield stared at him. "Grosse."

Dr Colbert took a moment to calm his annoyance. "Yes. Anyone else?"

Mr Winfield narrowed his eyes. "How should I know? I've never seen the damn book."

"A fact you seem to share with countless others," Mr Elliott remarked, casting a warning glance at his fellow Bow Streeter. Upon seeing the calming effect his words also had on Mr Winfield, he continued, "There was a telegram in Mr Grosse's office about the boxer Deon Erskine. Is the name familiar to you?"

"It should be," Mr Winfield replied. "I was his manager."

* * *

Miss Hicks took a sip of brandy and glanced at the clock above the bar. Aside from the lively conversations she'd had with the regulars, she'd spent the evening watching the clock's hands go around. The absence of any set-tos meant few patrons ventured away from the fire, and there was little hope of any new ones arriving. Many of those she'd spoken to earlier were now either slouched over their table asleep or had been nursing the same pint for the past hour. Even Mr Sparrow had withdrawn his attention from her in favour of reading yesterday's *Gaslight Gazette*. It had soon dawned upon her that undercover work might not be as exciting as she'd hoped it would be.

Furthermore, she wasn't sure if her Percy would be waiting outside at closing. It was something he'd always done when she'd worked at the railway bar, but she feared their argument earlier might've convinced him to stay away. All she'd tried to do was keep him safe, as he obviously hadn't known about the Society's plan to watch Mr Sparrow and Mr Farley. If she'd let him stay, he might've tried to 'defend her honour' against Mr Sparrow's wandering hands. Her Perce couldn't fight when he was sober, let alone drunk. Besides, she was used to getting such attention from the publicans she worked for; it was part of being a barmaid. So was walking the streets in search of a cab whilst trying to fend off the unwanted attentions of drunken men, however. If Perce weren't there at closing, she'd have to face them alone. She pouted.

"Who was that bloke you gave the beer to?" Toby enquired, broom in hand.

Miss Hicks looked across the bar at him, recalling their earlier conversation about bruisers. "A mate."

Toby leaned the broom sideways, away from his body, and put his weight upon his other foot. "Thought as much. He, er…" He glanced over his shoulder before leaning toward her and lowering his voice, "is under the thumb of the drink, ain't 'e?"

Miss Hicks considered her answer. Perce enjoyed drinking more than most, but she'd never thought of him as a drunk. "It helps him sleep."

"What do you get for givin' it to 'im?" Toby enquired.

"He looks after me," Miss Hicks replied in a heartbeat. Realising how she felt about him could be as basic as needing somewhere safe to sleep, she considered if that were true. He was young, handsome, and bewilderingly clever. He was also a considerate and gentle lover who treated her like a goddess. Naturally, she was humbled and flattered by his unconditional love and devotion.

Before they'd met, she hadn't dared hope a man like him would be attracted to a woman like her. As it was, they were happy—in their own way. The lack of a ring made their relationship more exciting rather than less, and she wasn't keen to change that anytime soon. *Does that mean I don't love him?* She wondered even as her heart revealed the answer. Where an ocean of affection should've roared, a narrow stream of fondness bubbled. Where devotion should've burned, a small flame of selfish need flickered. It was a need to make Dr Weeks happy for the sole purpose of keeping a roof over her head. If, in the beginning, she'd hoped she'd come to love him in time, it hadn't happened yet. *It still might,* she thought, unconvinced. *But needing his love and support to keep on living is just as important as needing it to feel alive, isn't it? Maybe more so.* She felt a mixture of disappointment and dissatisfaction swirl within her breast as she imagined the rest of her life with Dr Weeks. *Survival is important, but is it worth it when your life's as miserable as a damp, Sunday afternoon?*

Wishing to dismiss these depressing thoughts, she parted her lips to change the subject. Yet, the opening of the door distracted her before she could speak. Thinking it was Perce with his tail between his legs, she forced a smile to give him the warm welcome he deserved. When she saw the newcomer's face, though, she felt her stomach leap into her chest. It wasn't her Perce but someone far more exciting—the boxer from Miss Dexter's sketch, Mr Noah O'Hanigan.

* * *

"Deon wasn't a great boxer," Mr Winfield began, laying his hat beside him on the sofa. "He wasn't even a half-decent brawler." He settled back against the cushions. "After he'd lost three fights in a row, I let him go."

"To the United States of America?" Dr Colbert enquired, hopeful.

Mr Winfield looked at him and sneered, "That's the last place he'd have gone."

"Why?" Mr Elliott enquired.

Mr Winfield returned his gaze to Mr Elliott before casting an incredulous glance between them. "Deon could face a man twice his size in the ring without flinching. Put him near the sea, though, and he'd go to pieces. I had no hope of him getting on a boat to the States."

"Yet, he is rumoured to have done so," Mr Elliott pointed out.

"*Rumours,*" Mr Winfield scoffed.

"The telegram I mentioned was from the *Amateur Athletic Union of the United States of America*," Mr Elliott said. "It was in answer to an enquiry from Mr Grosse about Mr Erskine. That would suggest Mr Grosse thought there was some credence to the rumours."

"Yeah? And what did this 'telegram' say?" Mr Winfield enquired in a cynical tone.

"That they had no record of him," Mr Elliott replied.

Mr Winfield briefly lifted his hand. "There you go."

"When was the last time you saw Mr Erskine?" Mr Elliott enquired.

Mr Winfield looked to the fire as he searched his memory. "Five years ago, at the pub where they fight without the gloves."

"Five years is a long time," Mr Elliott pointed out. "Sufficient for a man to overcome his fear of the sea—if he was determined enough."

Mr Winfield smirked and wagged his finger at him. "You've got a good point there, boy." He lowered his hand as his smile faded. "But not one that can be applied to Erskine. Hell, he wasn't determined enough to go without the drink for the sake of his career. There's no way…" He placed a hand over his heart whilst holding up his other with an open palm. "Aside from an intervention from God, he would've gotten rid of his fear."

"Anything is possible," Mr Elliott coolly stated.

"Not with Erskine," Mr Winfield countered.

"Have you heard from him in those five years?" Dr Colbert enquired.

"Not a whisper," Mr Winfield replied. "But I don't expect to; our business is done."

"Do you have Mr Erskine's last known address?" Mr Elliott enquired.

Mr Winfield shook his head. "Like I said, our business is done."

"Could you tell him we wish to speak to him, if you do hear from him, that is?" Dr Colbert requested.

"Sure," Mr Winfield replied. "Why not."

"We'd also like to speak with Mr O'Hanigan at the earliest opportunity," Mr Elliott said. "Could you arrange it, please?"

"He can't tell you anything more than me," Mr Winfield said.

"Perhaps not, but we still need to speak with him," Mr Elliott said.

Mr Winfield eyed him with suspicion. Nevertheless, he said, "Sure, I'll tell him. If I see him."

Mr Elliott frowned. "I thought you were his manager."

"I am," Mr Winfield said. "That doesn't make me his keeper, though."

"Doesn't he have appointments with you to do exercising and the like?" Dr Colbert ventured.

Mr Winfield's eyes and voice cooled. "He does." He glanced between them. "I'll tell him the next time I see him. That's all I'll promise."

"That's enough," Mr Elliott said. "Thank you."

* * *

Mr O'Hanigan slowly ran an appraising look over Miss Hicks' body, his gaze momentarily lingering upon her breasts, before making eye contact. Having realised he was the man Miss Webster had seen with Mrs Grosse, Miss Hicks had run her eyes over him at the same time. The tension in his shirt's sleeves had led her to admire his unusually large biceps, followed by his broad chest and thick neck. The deformation of his knuckles, ears, and nose from years of boxing seemed to add to his physical charm. To her, it hinted at an inner resilience and courage that was distinctly lacking in Dr Weeks. *This one's a proper bruiser,* she thought. *I wouldn't have to worry about drunken men hassling me at closing if I were on his arm.*

Putting one hand on the bar and the other upon her waist, Miss Hicks leaned forward to allow him a better view of her bosom. Casting a noticeable glance over him, she ran the tip of her tongue over her lips. "Good evenin', sir."

Mr O'Hanigan's green eyes twinkled with delight as his features slowly lifted with his growing smile. In a broad Belfast accent, he said, "It is now."

Miss Hicks lowered her head and, lifting her eyes to meet his, pushed a strand of hair behind her ear as she smiled. "What can I get for you?"

Mr O'Hanigan's smile grew further, still, as possibilities flooded his mind, none of which included alcohol. "Pint of ale."

Miss Hicks turned and, retrieving a glass from the shelf, looked over her shoulder at him as she poured some ale from the barrel. Returning her gaze to the tap at the last moment, she stopped the flow just in time. A brief roll of her eyes at her own stupidity later, she served him his drink and took the necessary coin.

Mr O'Hanigan clasped his hand around hers as soon as the money was in her palm. "What time do you finish, wee girl?"

"Closing." Miss Hicks gently withdrew her hand.

"Do you have someone to walk you home?"

Miss Hicks inwardly leapt for joy. Recalling that Perce may still arrive, though, she decided to hedge her bets. "You can come back later and find out if you'd like?"

Mr O'Hanigan grinned. "That I would."

"The widow thrown you out, has she?" Mr Sparrow enquired in a cool tone as he joined Miss Hicks behind the bar.

"*I* left *her*," Mr O'Hanigan replied.

"No more money in it?" Mr Sparrow chided.

Mr O'Hanigan straightened to his full five feet ten inches height. "I don't know that's anyt'ing to do with you."

"Christian was a mate," Mr Sparrow said. "You and that whore made a fool of him."

Mr O'Hanigan looked at Miss Hicks and smiled as he said, "I just gave her what she wanted."

Mr Sparrow suddenly snatched Mr O'Hanigan by the scruff of his shirt and yanked him forward. Obliged to stand on the balls of his feet as a result, Mr O'Hanigan also gripped the bar's edge to prevent Mr Sparrow from pulling him any farther.

"You're not welcome here," Mr Sparrow snarled and released him with a shove. "Get out."

Mr O'Hanigan straightened his shirt and looked to Miss Hicks.

Determined to secure a late-night guardian one way or another, she subtly lowered her head and coiled a strand of hair around her finger whilst offering him a small smile.

To Mr O'Hanigan, her behaviour was the same as an unspoken invitation from Mrs Grosse. It was enough to convince him to behave. Draining his glass, he cast one last glare at Mr Sparrow and left the pub.

"You're not to serve him again," Mr Sparrow warned Miss Hicks. "If he comes back, fetch me."

"Yes, Mr Sparrow," she meekly agreed, all whilst secretly hoping he would.

THIRTY-SIX

Tapping the canvas with the tip of her paintbrush, Miss Dexter briefly stepped back before applying increasingly larger splodges of paint with a heavy hand. Pulling the paint across the canvas in an ugly smear, she tossed the brush aside and turned her back upon the sabotaged piece. Thinking she heard someone pass by her door, she wondered if it could be Mr Maxwell. Compelled by a deep-rooted need to see him, she strode forward, only to divert to the fireplace at the last moment.

"Don't be foolish, Georgina." She wrung her hands and bowed her head. "You know no good would come of it." Yet, the memory of Mr Maxwell kissing her all those months ago replayed in her mind, reminding her of the love she could neither deny nor destroy. It was ever present, like a heartbeat, and like her heart, she didn't want it to stop. *But I must*, she thought. *It would be immoral and... Paris is waiting for me and... he has hurt me so many times before*. A pained expression formed as she remembered how he'd ended their engagement. She now knew why he'd done so, and she both understood and sympathised with it, but the hurt and questions remained. *Had I not been worth fighting for? Should I have seen the pain in him? Is it truly love between us if my intuition cannot recognise when he is in need of my help?*

The muffled sound of Miss Trent and Mr Snyder's voices downstairs pulled her from her thoughts. The darkness beyond her window was another reminder that she ought to return home to her Ma-Ma and Pa-Pa. She was too distracted to work anyway. *Distracted by thoughts of him...* Mr Maxwell's face filled her mind's eye.

She extinguished the lamps and hurried from the room.

Halfway along the landing, she heard someone knocking on the front door. Halting at once, she held the rail and peered down into the hallway. Miss Trent was already unbolting and unlocking the door. The woman she admitted wore an ankle-length, black velvet cloak. When she pushed down its hood, a mass of naturally frizzy, strawberry-blond hair was revealed.

"I wish to speak with Miss Rebecca Trent at once," the woman demanded.

Miss Trent closed the door. "I'm she, and you are?"

"In desperate need of the Society's assistance," the woman replied. "Mr Voigt has *evicted* me with *nothing* but the clothes on my back!"

"You are Mrs Eunice Grosse," Miss Trent said with distaste.

Mrs Grosse scowled at the tone. "I know what the Society's opinion of me is. Your Miss Webster made it *perfectly* clear. Unfortunately…" She pulled the cloak tighter about herself. "I've nowhere else to turn in London." She crossed the hallway and, looking up the stairs, caught sight of Miss Dexter. She turned upon the clerk. "Are your clients often spied upon, Miss Trent?"

"Never." Miss Trent joined her and saw Miss Dexter hurrying down the stairs toward them. "This is Miss Georgina Dexter, an artist and Bow Street Society member. She has a studio here."

Miss Dexter halted at the foot of the stairs. "Begging your pardon, ma'am."

Miss Trent turned cold eyes to Mrs Grosse. "I appreciate you're in distress, but I don't tolerate rudeness toward our members."

"But you'll tolerate your members' rudeness toward others," Mrs Grosse countered.

Miss Trent put her hands upon her hips. "*Nor* do I accept lodgers. We are not a charity for the homeless and destitute."

"Clearly," Mrs Grosse said in a sardonic tone.

"If there is nothing else, I must ask you to leave," Miss Trent said. "We're too busy investigating your husband's murder to waste time on idle conversation."

Mrs Grosse glared at her. "You're casting me out?"

Miss Trent gave a defiant lift of her chin. "If you wish to see it that way, yes."

Mrs Grosse's glare faltered, momentarily exposing the fear beneath. "I shan't inconvenience you for long," she said in a quivering voice. "All I require is a bed for the night and a railway ticket to Bournemouth in the morning. My sister has invited me to stay with her."

"Is Inspector Pilker aware of your intention to leave London?" Miss Trent probed.

"No," Mrs Grosse dismissed. "All policemen are beastly."

"We're obliged to inform him," Miss Trent said. "*If* we agree to help you, that is."

"Why would you not?!" Mrs Grosse cried. "*I* am a lady in *distress*!"

"Of your own making," Miss Trent retorted.

Mrs Grosse stared at her. "Yes, but…" She gave a dismissive shake of her head. "That is *beside* the point! The Bow Street Society claims to help people who cannot be helped by the police. *I* am one of those people!"

Miss Trent glanced at Miss Dexter's concerned expression. As much as she hated to admit it, Mrs Grosse was right. "Very well," Miss Trent agreed in a terse voice. "Miss Dexter, would you bring us some tea?"

Miss Dexter gave a shallow bob of her body. "Yes, of course."

"This way, please." Miss Trent led Mrs Grosse to the parlour.

* * *

Miss Hicks rubbed her upper arms and shifted her weight from one foot to the other as she shivered outside the *Key & Lion*. The place had become so quiet, Mr Sparrow had allowed her to leave early. Although she'd known it was playing against the odds, she'd hoped Dr Weeks would be waiting for her, ready to make amends for earlier. As it was, her time spent outside was fast approaching thirty minutes, and there was still no sign of him. Mr O'Hanigan hadn't arrived, either. Realising neither of her plans had worked, she released a soft, dejected sigh.

The pub's door opened, causing her to move aside and exchange glances with the customer in the green overcoat. Watching him as he walked down the street, she decided it wasn't a good idea to linger any longer. Soon, the rest of the drunkards would be filtering out, and she didn't want to be around when that happened. She wrapped her arms tightly about herself and walked in the opposite direction in search of a cab.

"What's a lovely wee girl like you doin' wanderin' the streets at night alone?" Mr O'Hanigan's voice enquired from out of nowhere. Halting in her tracks, Miss Hicks darted her gaze this way and that but couldn't see him. Hearing a scrape of a shoe behind her, she turned sharply but again, saw no one. Mr O'Hanigan's voice sounded again. This time it was so close, she could feel his breath on the back of her neck. "I asked you a question."

Miss Hicks turned and felt her breasts press against his chest as they came toe to toe. Lifting her head to gaze into his eyes, she felt both relieved and nervous to see him. It was obvious he could protect them both but equally obvious he could overpower her if he wished. *But would I need much overpowering?* She wondered, wetting her lips. *He's a red-blooded warrior compared to Perce; a poetic lover who's only brave enough to use a knife on a dead body.* She softly replied, "Trying to find a cab 'ome." She brushed her fingers against his. "What's a handsome man like you doin' wanderin' the streets, scarin' the life out of women?"

Mr O'Hanigan grinned.

Suddenly, Miss Hicks felt his large hands upon her arms, followed by the sensation of being pulled sideways and back. Realising he'd guided her into a narrow passageway, she allowed him to hold her against its cold, brick wall as their eyes met once more. For a prolonged moment, they stayed like that, her heartrate increasing along with her breathing as her earlier thoughts about him swamped her mind. *Not much overpowering at all*, she thought as she felt her arousal intensify at the thought of what was to come.

At the same time, he kept a firm hold of her but not so hard it was uncomfortable. The twinkle of lust was also in his eyes as he, too, remembered what his first reaction to her had been. Feeling the familiar stirring between his legs, he slipped his hand between hers as he pinned her with his body and captured her lips with his. A soft moan escaped from her as she both welcomed and surrendered to his boldness.

Satisfied she was willing, the customer in the green overcoat retreated around the corner of the passageway's entrance and lit a cigarette. As he took his first pull from it, quiet panting and grunting drifted from the passageway. *The inspector's not gonna like this*, he thought with dread.

* * *

Leaving the kitchen backwards, Miss Dexter carefully turned with the tray of tea things once she was clear of the door. Thoughts of Mr Maxwell flitted through her mind as she passed the stairs but were dismissed upon her entering the parlour. Giving a polite smile to Mrs Grosse sitting on the sofa, she set the tray down upon the low table in front of her. When the sound of more knocking reached them, she picked up the teapot whilst Miss Trent went to answer the front door.

"So, you're an artist," Mrs Grosse said, watching her pour. "Do you have any talent?"

"I've been told I do." Miss Dexter felt her cheeks warm.

"Do you believe them?"

Miss Dexter filled their cups as she considered her answer. Setting the teapot down, she replied, "Yes. I think so." She offered a polite smile. "I hope you have an enjoyable time in Bournemouth. I've heard it's a lovely place."

Mrs Grosse's lips parted as she stared at her, taken aback by her kind words. "Thank you." She returned her smile. "I hope your talent finds the recognition it deserves."

Miss Dexter's smile grew, filling her face with warmth.

"It was the postman," Miss Trent announced as she returned. Upon seeing her teacup had been filled, she gave Miss Dexter an appreciative smile. "Thank you."

"You're both welcome," Miss Dexter said and left the room.

Taking a seat in her usual armchair, Miss Trent added cream and sugar to her tea. "I've given your request some consideration, Mrs Grosse, and you're correct: one of the many aims of the Bow Street Society is to help those who can't be helped elsewhere. Therefore, I'll make up a bed for tonight and provide the monies for a railway ticket to Bournemouth. Mr Snyder, a cabman and Society member, will take you to the station."

Mrs Grosse put down her cup and smiled broadly.

"*However*," Miss Trent continued in a firm tone, "I'd like you to be honest with us."

Mrs Grosse's smile vanished. Straightening upon the sofa, she glanced at the door, the window, and the mantel clock before returning her gaze to the clerk. "I think that's reasonable. I presume you're referring to Christian?"

"I am."

Mrs Grosse took a sip of tea. "I told Miss Webster and Hicks all I know."

"Questions remain, however."

Mrs Grosse replaced her cup upon its saucer. "Such as?"

Miss Trent scrutinised her face. "Such as: did you murder him?"

Mrs Grosse's emotionless expression remained. "No."

Miss Trent maintained her scrutiny. "Did Mr O'Hanigan?"

Mrs Grosse's lips briefly parted and closed. "No."

Miss Trent caught the tell-tale sign of hesitation. "Why did you hesitate?"

Mrs Grosse took another sip of tea. "Because *I* didn't ask him to murder Christian, *but* he could've decided to do so *without* my influence."

"Did he?"

Mrs Grosse dabbed her mouth with a handkerchief. "I have absolutely *no* idea."

"Of course, you don't," Miss Trent said with blatant cynicism.

Mrs Grosse pointed to the door. "Could my bed be made up now? I'm rather tired."

"Not yet." Miss Trent took a sip of tea to ease her annoyance at the woman. "If, hypothetically speaking, Mr O'Hanigan had murdered your husband, what was his motive? It clearly wasn't love, or you'd be at his fireside now, instead of ours. Was it for money? You were surprised to discover your husband hadn't left a will. Were you and Mr O'Hanigan hoping to marry with the money and house you'd expected to inherit?"

Sorrow seeped into Mrs Grosse's eyes. "It would be nice to say that was the case but… no." She downcast her eyes and released a soft sigh. "Noah was only interested in what was immediately for the taking. When I told him I'd received nothing from Christian's estate and had been evicted from the house by his uncle, he told me I wasn't his problem any longer and left." She drank the remainder of her tea and stared at the leaves in the bottom of the cup. With an intense sadness, she said, "He didn't even love me enough to commit murder."

Shocked and infuriated by the statement in equal measure, Miss Trent's grip tightened upon her cup as she took a large mouthful of tea to quell the almost overwhelming urge to tell Mrs Grosse *exactly* what she thought of her. Unable to destroy it completely, though, she muttered, "Inexcusable."

THIRTY-SEVEN

"I want this again." Mr O'Hanigan held Miss Hicks' waist. "Soon."

"Me, too," Miss Hicks purred, running her finger down his cheek and across his lips.

"When?" His thumbs rubbed her hips through her skirts.

"Tomorrow night." She straightened his shirt and ran her hands over his chest. Sliding them up and over his shoulders, she wrapped her arms around his neck. *A little fun, that's all it is,* she told herself. *Perce isn't going to find out, so where's the harm?*

"I can't wait," he said.

"Nor me," Miss Hicks purred.

He tightly held her behind as their lips met in a final passionate kiss.

* * *

Miss Dexter fastened her coat and tucked in her scarf. Beside her, Mr Snyder was putting on his heavy cloak and collecting his hat from the stand. At the same time, Miss Trent descended the stairs, having shown Mrs Grosse her bed for the night. The grandfather clock struck nine as Miss Trent reached the others with tired eyes.

"I've put her in a bedroom on the second floor," she announced. "Given her disgust upon seeing the bed, I doubt she'll be staying beyond tonight."

"Beggars can't be choosers," Mr Snyder remarked.

"Neither can adulteresses," Miss Trent added.

Miss Dexter toyed with the lapel of her coat as she quietly enquired, "Did you see Mr Maxwell at all?"

"I'm afraid not," Miss Trent sadly replied.

Miss Dexter bowed her head.

"Don't worry." Miss Trent rubbed Miss Dexter's arm. "I'll coax him out of his bedroom with a hearty breakfast."

She smiled weakly. "Either that, or I'll send in Mrs Grosse."

Miss Dexter looked up sharply with a gasp.

"I'm joking," Miss Trent said with a gentle chuckle.

Miss Dexter's cheeks turned red. "Oh. How silly of me."

"I think it's time we got you 'ome, lass," Mr Snyder said to her. "You look like you could do with a good night's rest."

"Yes, I think you're right." Miss Dexter offered a small smile. "Thank you, Sam. Goodnight, Miss Trent."

"Goodnight," Miss Trent said. Catching sight of a small, brown package on the side table, she picked it up and joined the others by the front door.

"What's that?" Mr Snyder enquired, pointing at the package.

"I don't know," Miss Trent replied. "It arrived in the evening post." She tore the paper and stilled as the dark-blue cover of a tattered notebook was revealed.

Miss Dexter lifted her hand to her mouth. "Is that…?"

Miss Trent pulled away the remaining paper and, tucking it under her arm, opened the notebook. Each of its double-page spreads had columns detailing innumerable boxing matches, including the date they were held, their location, their start and end times, and the total number of rounds fought. Crucially, the names of the boxers, managers, referees, seconds, and bottle-holders were also listed. Miss Trent skimmed through several of the pages until she came to a pair of mismatched ones. Strips of jagged paper also ran down the centre fold, suggesting some pages had been torn from the binding. "Unbelievably, it would seem so." She gave it to Mr Snyder. "What do you think?"

Mr Snyder examined several of the pages. "It looks like it could be his, yeah." He put his thumb beside some of the entries. "There's initials here: 'KL' and 'NC.' Could be the *Key & Lion* and *Nimble Crow*." He turned to the last entry. "This one's got both KL and NC by it. Joe Rake and

Daniel White was the fighters. Thomas Blunt was the referee. Duncan Sparrow is down as White's manager, and Ken Farley is down as Rake's. The set-to was at 'warehouse, West India Dock.'"

Miss Dexter felt her blood run cold. "Where poor Mr Grosse was murdered."

"Is there any mention of Deon Erskine?" Miss Trent enquired.

Mr Snyder spent several moments searching the pages. "Nah." He stopped at the jagged pieces of paper in the centre fold. "But someone's torn these pages out. He could of been on them."

Miss Trent took the brown paper from under her arm and examined its postmark. "Miss Webster might be able to determine where the package was posted from." She lowered the paper and stared at the notebook. "But why send it to us? If the information within is so valuable, why would they suddenly decide to surrender it?" She frowned. "Especially if whoever sent it was also responsible for Mr Grosse's death."

"Maybe they wasn't," Mr Snyder said. "Maybe they got the notebook off his body and got scared when his murder was in the 'paper the next mornin'. They could of sent it to us so the coppers wouldn't find them with it and think they'd done him in."

"Perhaps," Miss Trent said.

Miss Dexter shivered.

* * *

The cold wind chilled Chief Inspector Jones' face as the hansom cab drove through Hackney's darkened streets. Pulling his burgundy scarf over his mouth and nose to both warm and hide them, he went through the plan in his mind. The chances of encountering any problems were small, since he was confident no one was home. In all residential areas, there was the ever-present possibility of a curious neighbour intervening. Given the class of residents on

Ballance Road, though, he doubted such a thing would occur tonight. Yet, even if it did, he had a perfectly valid reason for being there: he was Inspector Conway's friend. Feeling himself being pulled to the right as the cab turned the corner, Chief Inspector Jones checked his bowler hat and gloves were secure. A brief dip into his overcoat's pocket also reassured him its contents were still there.

He alighted from the cab once it had slowed to a halt outside Inspector Conway's house and paid the driver a few extra coins to wait for his return. As he'd suspected, the place was in darkness. Nonetheless, he knocked on the door, waited a few moments, and knocked again. The tension in his body eased when he became satisfied Inspector Conway was away from home.

Exhaling softly, he tried the handle and frowned when it turned. Opening the door and stepping inside, he thought, *Inspector Woolfe's statement was also correct. Inspector Lee wouldn't have had any difficulty gaining entry.* He made a mental note to discuss domestic security with his friend at the earliest opportunity.

He closed the door and listened.

Silence.

As he went down the hallway and into the kitchen, he had the passing realisation that he'd never visited Inspector Conway's house as much as he had since he'd set up the Bow Street Society. It wasn't as if he'd never been welcomed. More a case of Inspector Conway working every waking hour; a situation that wasn't conducive for social entertaining. Nevertheless, he was pleased to find the house in a reasonable state of cleanliness, even if signs of the fast-approaching festivities were nowhere to be seen.

The kitchen, like the rest of the house, was in pitch blackness. Reluctant to ignite the lamp in case its light was seen by a neighbour, Chief Inspector Jones reached out with both hands and crept forward. He grunted softly when he subsequently kneed the table.

On a shelf above the door, he thought, recalling Inspector Woolfe's description. After allowing his eyes to adjust to the darkness, he glanced at the back door and the one he'd come through. Given the latter was the only one with a shelf, he assumed it to be the one.

He reached into his pocket and paused, suddenly questioning if he was doing the right thing. Thoughts of Inspectors Conway, Woolfe, and Lee swirled through his mind. Out of all of them, Inspector Conway was the only one he trusted with his life. *The only one I have trusted with my life*, he told himself. *Not only literally but professionally, too.* Inspector Conway knew everything about his connection to the Bow Street Society. Not only this, but he had kept that secret with unerring loyalty. *It's ridiculous to think he would risk our exposure for a few coins*, Chief Inspector Jones realised.

He took the flour pot from his pocket and, making a final check of its empty interior, returned it to the shelf.

THIRTY-EIGHT

Having spent longer than planned briefing Miss Trent, Mr Skinner was late arriving at the *Nimble Crow*. Alighting from his cab whilst it still moved, he paid the driver and crossed the pavement to the door. As he pushed against its handle, though, his chest collided with its stained-glass window, causing the entire door to shake. Taking a half-step back, he pushed a second time but again, the door refused to budge. He consulted his pocket watch and found it was almost thirty minutes after the public house's usual opening time. Slipping the watch into his waistcoat, he rubbed his stubble-covered jaw and peered through the large plate-glass window to the right of the door.

The electrical lamps above the bar were lit, and fires burned in the hearths. Yet, the room was deserted. Hearing a groan of disappointment behind him, he stepped away from the door and saw the man with the goatee standing by the pavement's edge. *When did he get here?* Mr Skinner mused, having not heard his approach.

"Is it closed?" the man enquired.

"Looks to be." Mr Skinner glanced through the window. "But the fires are lit and ev'ryt'ing."

The man pursed his lips and hummed. "Maybe there's been a family drama." As he consulted his pocket watch, Mr Skinner cast a cursory glance over his washed-out blue suit, waistcoat, and tie. They were clean and pressed to perfection. *Either he can afford to get his t'ings laundered for him, or he's married,* Mr Skinner mused. The glint of a gold ring on the man's wedding finger as he returned his watch to his pocket confirmed the latter.

"Probably better to come back at lunchtime, eh?" the man said and walked away.

Returning to the door, Mr Skinner struck its wood several times with his iron hand. Waiting a few moments, he knocked again but louder. A further look through the window initially seemed to confirm that the place was unoccupied. Movement on the balcony a second later made him rethink this, however.

Stepping closer to the glass, he squinted past the fine layer of grime to see Mr Rake descend the stairs and stride toward him. When he heard him slide back the bolts, Mr Skinner stepped back and waited.

Mr Rake opened the door. "Mr Farley ain't 'ere."

"Where is he?" Mr Skinner enquired.

"Out."

"When is he comin' back?"

"Don't know."

Mr Skinner cast a glance over the pub's façade. "Must be serious for him to close."

Mr Rake smirked. "That's so blokes don't talk to his missus when he's not 'ere."

Mr Skinner leaned his shoulder against the remaining locked door. "You're here."

Mr Rake's smile vanished. "I ain't goin' to try owt, am I? Besides, I'm trainin' upstairs."

Mr Skinner scratched his cheek. "I was hopin' to do the same. Can you let me in?"

Mr Rake glanced over his and Mr Skinner's shoulders. Opening the door wide, he stepped outside to look up and down the street. Seeing no one—including Mr Farley—he returned inside. "Get your arse inside."

Down the street, the man with the goatee poked his head around the corner of a shop's doorway and watched Mr Skinner enter the pub. Returning to his hiding place, he took a small pencil from his breast pocket, wiped its tip against his tongue, and wrote the latest circumstance in a notebook concealed within his palm.

"Thanks," Mr Skinner said once the door was bolted. "I owe you a pint."

"If he asks, it wasn't me," Mr Rake said. "It's more than my bloody life's worth."

"You can trust me."

"Can we?" Mrs Farley enquired from the left of the bar.

* * *

"Oh *God*," Miss Trent said as she simultaneously put a hand upon her stomach and turned away. With her features contorted in disgust, she took a few steps toward the window before suddenly dropping her arm and spinning around to face Inspector Conway again. "Is he *certain* it was Miss Hicks?"

Standing before her desk, he held his hat at his side and a troubled look in his eyes. "Yeah. He'd followed her from the pub."

"In a *passageway*, where *anyone* could've caught them, with *Mr O'Hanigan*, no less; a *suspect* in Mr Grosse's *murder*!" Miss Trent released a sound of revulsion. "What on *Earth* was she thinking of?"

"Sex." Inspector Conway tossed his hat onto the desk. "And nowt else."

Miss Trent held her forehead. "That… *woman*!" She allowed her arm to drop to her side. "She could've ruined our entire investigation, and then there's poor Dr Weeks! Does she know what this will do to him?"

"If she did, she wouldn't of done it."

"True." Miss Trent's expression became dejected. "Does he know?"

"Nah. He's not goin' to, either."

Miss Trent stared at him, stunned. "He's got to be told, John."

Inspector Conway sat on the chair before her desk.

"You can't keep this from him," Miss Trent said, standing in front of him.

Inspector Conway looked up at her. "It would only send him to the drink."

"*Fine*." Miss Trent strode behind her desk. "I'll speak to Miss Hicks instead." She sat and pulled her chair up to the desk. "Her behaviour *won't* be tolerated in this Society." She reached for her pen, but Inspector Conway snatched it from the ink stand.

"Wait," he warned.

"She knew the rules, John, but chose to ignore them."

"You can't toss her out of the Society. Not yet."

"And why not?" Miss Trent challenged. "She's shown herself to be both immoral and unreliable. Traits which could get her, Mr O'Hanigan, or both, seriously injured—or worse."

"You wanted her to get the trust of the Fancy and she has."

"*Not* like this, I didn't!"

Inspector Conway lowered his voice. "Think about it, Rebecca. Now that she's got O'Hanigan's trust, he could confess to her about doing in Grosse or tell her who did."

Miss Trent slowly shook her head in disbelief. "I can't believe I'm hearing this."

"If you toss her out of the Society, who's the first bloke she's goin' to run to?"

Miss Trent pursed her lips and, exhaling deeply through her nose, turned her head away. If she'd been asked that before, she would've given Dr Weeks as her answer in a heartbeat. Yet, Polly's outrageous liaison with Mr O'Hanigan had cast that certainty into doubt. Feeling vexed by the realisation that Inspector Conway's suggestion was the likeliest, she curtly enquired, "What do you suggest we do?"

"We let her get on with it," Inspector Conway replied. "See where it goes."

"What you're suggesting is not only immoral, John, but dangerous."

"You already put her in danger when you put her in the *Key & Lion*."

Miss Trent's eyes momentarily widened. "On *your* advice!"

Inspector Conway's gaze hardened. "If you want Grosse's murderer, you've got to take risks."

"Even if it means losing our friendship with Dr Weeks?" Miss Trent countered.

Inspector Conway averted his gaze to the window.

"If he finds out—" Miss Trent began.

"He won't," Inspector Conway interrupted firmly, as his gaze snapped back to her.

"But if he does, it will destroy him," Miss Trent said with a morose tone.

The same sadness entered Inspector Conway's eyes as he softly replied, "I know."

Miss Trent's voice became a little strained with emotion as she enquired, "Do you still think I should let Miss Hicks carry on with Mr O'Hanigan?"

Inspector Conway lowered his chin and fell silent as he stared at the desk's edge for several long moments. Eventually, he replied, "Yeah." He met her gaze. "There's no other way."

"Very well." Miss Trent swallowed her sadness. "But I won't lie to Dr Weeks. If he asks about Miss Hicks and Mr O'Hanigan, I'll tell him the truth."

"Fair enough." Inspector Conway held out her pen.

Miss Trent took it and placed it back on the ink stand.

* * *

Standing beside the bar, Mrs Farley regarded Mr Skinner with cold eyes. Nevertheless, he was struck by the glow of her skin in the warmth of the electrical lamplight. Finding it difficult to feel affronted by her question as a result, he spoke with a gentle tone. "Yes, you can."

Mr Rake quietly added, "Mr Skinner's a member of the club."

"I'm aware of that." Mrs Farley kept her unblinking gaze upon Mr Skinner as she walked toward him. Her demeanour reminded him of a spider closing in on a fly.

Mr Rake hurried past them, muttering, "I've gotta get back."

Listening as he ran up the stairs behind her, Mrs Farley waited until she'd heard the door to the gymnasium close before speaking. "You're also a member of the Bow Street Society. The group who, I've been told, are investigating Mr Grosse's murder."

"Are they?"

"You know they are."

"Do I?"

Mrs Farley glared at him. "Whatever the Bow Street Society *thinks* it knows about my husband is *wrong*. Furthermore, *you* are wasting your time. Leave." She lifted her chin. "Unless you wish to incur my husband's wrath? To *trap* him? Are those your intentions? If so, I must warn you that I'm willing to lay down my life to stop you from succeeding."

"And I must warn you, Mrs Farley, that I don't like people who think they can intimidate me." Although his tone was firm, Mr Skinner's voice nevertheless held a hint of warmth. "I've not hidden my membership to the Bow Street Society; your old man's never asked. Also, since you don't seem to know how it works; the Society doesn't put all its members onto its cases. I don't know if it's investigating Mr Grosse's murder because I've not been put on it."

"Your interest in my husband's boxing club is simply coincidental, is it?" Mrs Farley sardonically enquired.

"Yes," Mr Skinner firmly replied.

"Poppy cock!" Mrs Farley scoffed.

"Believe whatever you want, but it won't change the fact I'm tellin' the truth."

Mrs Farley's glare intensified as Mr Skinner walked away from her. "My husband shall hear of this."

Mr Skinner stopped at the foot of the stairs to look back at her. "Tell him."

Mrs Farley folded her arms.

Feeling her eyes boring into him as he climbed the stairs, Mr Skinner was already formulating his response to any potential confrontation he may have with Mr Farley. If the Navy had taught him nothing else, it had taught him that preparation was everything.

THIRTY-NINE

The ticking of the clock felt deafening in the otherwise still pub as Miss Hicks toyed with a piece of scrap paper on the bar. With her elbows resting on its top, she paid little heed to her cleavage being on display. Due to the regulars being either passed out or well on their way there. The man in the old green overcoat continued to glance at her every now and again but hadn't approached or made any suggestive remarks. In short, he seemed harmless enough.

Unlike Noah O'Hanigan. A heat swept over her as she recalled the previous night, particularly his hands and… She straightened and smoothed down her dress whilst pushing the memory from her mind. Yet, the more she tried, the more she dwelt on it, and the hotter she became. It was like a fire she couldn't extinguish.

Running her hand through her hair, she tried to distract herself by picturing Dr Weeks. Unfortunately, she'd been disappointed to find him passed out on the sofa when she'd returned home. If he could've been roused, he would've given her the perfect end to an exciting night. As it was, she'd been left feeling unfulfilled. *There'll be other times, though,* she realised with a smirk.

Mr O'Hanigan had been as good as his word and walked her as far as St. John Street. A spur-of-the-moment story about her not wanting to awaken her elderly mother had convinced him to depart before they're reached *R.G. Dunn Pawnbrokers*, however. The thought of sneaking him inside when Dr Weeks wasn't home caused her arousal to reignite. Yet, the thought of arriving with Mr O'Hanigan when Dr Weeks was there not only intensified her arousal but led her to consider the possibility of enjoying them together. Her face flushed bright red as heat erupted from her core.

Loud knocking violently pulled her from her thoughts.

When it sounded again, she realised it was coming from the door to the yard. Intrigued by who it was, but also keen to disguise her eavesdropping, she tidied the shelf by the door leading from the bar to the back hall and listened.

The yard door opened, followed by a quiet greeting from Mr Sparrow, and several pairs of feet walking into the parlour. Upon hearing its door close, she slipped into the back hall and waited in case Toby decided to pursue her. When a few moments had passed with no sign of the potboy, she crept along the hall and put her ear to the parlour door.

The first male voice she heard wasn't one she recognised. It sounded quite upper class, however. "You said to get rid of it, Farley, and that you didn't care how. *That* is what you said!"

"Not by sending it to *them,* Jeffers!" A second male voice replied that she assumed belonged to 'Farley.' *The landlord of the Nimble Crow,* she thought.

"You're overreacting," Mr Jeffers said. "The Bow Street Society *aren't* the police. They can't *do* anything."

"They can give it to the police!" Mr Farley shouted.

"I tore out the pages with Erskine's name," Mr Jeffers said. "The notebook can't be used as evidence without them."

"They're not *blind*! They'll notice they're missing!" Mr Farley shouted.

"Jeffers is right; both the Society and the coppers can't point the finger at us without the pages on Erskine," Mr Sparrow insisted. "We need to hold our nerve, or none of us will escape the hangman."

"Our heads wouldn't be in the noose if it wasn't for *him*," Mr Jeffers said.

"You agreed to all this," Mr Farley retorted.

"And I wish to *God* I hadn't," Mr Jeffers replied in a desperate voice.

Miss Hicks withdrew from the door with a racing heart. Had she heard what she thought she'd heard? *Becky's got to be told*, she thought. Lifting her skirts, she crept out into the yard before running down the service alleyway and into the street to find a cab.

* * *

"Get out," Inspector Woolfe snarled.

"I thought the sergeant was mistaken when he said you'd refused to see me." Inspector Lee stepped inside and closed the door. "Retreat isn't a foible of yours." He cast a disapproving glance over Inspector Woolfe's dishevelled appearance. "Although many things are." Inspector Lee removed his gloves and, taking off his hat, put them inside as he approached Inspector Woolfe's desk.

"Deaf arrogance is one of yours," Inspector Woolfe retorted.

Inspector Lee wiped the vacant chair with his handkerchief and sat. "I take it you didn't like what you found at Inspector Conway's house?"

Inspector Woolfe pulled his bushy eyebrows together in a fierce scowl.

Inspector Lee inspected his fingernails. "Out of curiosity, what did you find?"

"What you put there," Inspector Woolfe snarled.

Inspector Lee's gaze flicked to him. "I beg your pardon?"

"You heard me."

Inspector Lee put his hand upon his chest. "*I* didn't put it there."

"So, a Bow Street Society envelope stuffed with banknotes just magically appeared in his flour jar, did it?"

Inspector Lee's gaze cooled as he lowered his hand. "You *know* how it got there."

Inspector Woolfe lowered and shook his head.

"Admit it, Caleb. You were wrong about Conway. As were we all."

"Nah." Inspector Woolfe glared at Inspector Lee. "I know it was you, and I'm going to prove it." He stood. "Until then, we're done, Gideon. Me and Colbert are going

348

to find out the name of Miss Trent's employer on our own."

"Conway's downfall will also be yours if you're not careful."

Inspector Woolfe's eyes narrowed. "Is that a threat?"

"No. Merely a prediction." Inspector Lee stood and, tucking his hat under his arm, took his time in putting on his gloves. "But you know where I am should you suddenly see sense."

"I'd rather die first." Inspector Woolfe jerked his head toward the door. "Get out."

"Don't say I didn't warn you," Inspector Lee said, allowing his hard gaze to linger upon his fellow inspector before strolling from the room.

* * *

Hanging his great cloak and hat upon the stand in the Society's hallway, Mr Snyder wiped his reddened nose with the back of his hand and gave a loud sniff. "Mrs Grosse made her train to Bournemouth," he informed Miss Trent beside him. "But only after Inspector Pilker had had a word."

"He wasn't pleased when I spoke to him on the telephone this morning." Miss Trent tilted her head. "Was she still a suspect at the end of their conversation?"

"I don't know; he wouldn't let me stay."

"How did she seem afterward?"

Mr Snyder scratched his cheek as he considered his answer. "Relieved and happy to be leaving London." He smiled. "But we all get like that sometimes."

"We do." Miss Trent drew in a slow, deep breath that she softly exhaled. "Especially now."

Mr Snyder glanced up. "Has he not come out yet?"

Miss Trent frowned and shook her head whilst rubbing her temple. "Nothing interests him, Sam. I'm starting to get worried—more than before."

"He'll come around, lass. He just needs time, that's all."

Miss Trent gave a feeble smile. "I hope so." She took in another deep breath. "Anyway." She led him into the meeting room where Miss Webster sat with a crumpled piece of brown paper on the table in front of her. "Miss Webster thinks she might have identified where the parcel was posted from."

Miss Webster's eyes were warm as she lifted her head to greet the cabman. "Good afternoon, Mr Snyder." She turned and held up the paper. "Yes, the postal office on Fleet Street. The obliteration marking the stamp includes the initials F.S. and E.C., or Fleet Street and Eastern Central. That is, the Eastern Central postal district." She placed her thumb beside the number within the obliteration. "And this is one of the numbers used for postal items processed in the E.C. district." She laid the paper in the middle of the table as Mr Snyder and Miss Trent sat opposite. "Mr Baldwin could've easily left the *Gaslight Gazette's* office to post the notebook to Miss Trent."

Miss Trent hummed. "I'm not sure myself. I'd like to think I've gained Mr Baldwin's trust since our chat at Mr Maxwell's house. He could've easily given it to me in person."

Mr Snyder rested his clasped hands upon his stomach. "There's more 'papers than the *Gazette* on Fleet Street." He tilted his head back as he rubbed his beard in thought. "Including *Sporting Life*." He laid one arm across his stomach and, leaning upon it with his other elbow, rested his chin in his hand. "Mr Grosse had that in his office and didn't Mr Baldwin say sumin' about another bloke writing about the set-to at the warehouse?"

Miss Trent consulted her notebook. "Yes, here it is. Mr Ian Jeffers, journalist with the *Sporting Life* newspaper. Mr Baldwin thought that, as Mr Grosse's friend, he should've been chosen to write the story instead of him."

"Mr Baldwin could've posted the notebook from Fleet Street to implicate Mr Jeffers in Mr Grosse's murder," Miss Webster suggested.

Mr Snyder gave a slow nod. "Maybe."

Miss Trent frowned. "I'm still not convinced. Mr Baldwin was angered by not being chosen, but he seemed far angrier at Mr Grosse's murder."

Mr Snyder and Miss Webster's eyes glazed over as they considered Miss Trent's argument and pondered Mr Jeffers' potential role in Mr Grosse's murder. A moment later, though, the sound of knocking pulled them from their reverie.

"That might be Mr Voigt." Miss Trent stood. "I told him Mrs Grosse was leaving for Bournemouth." She left the room and crossed over to the front door. Unbolting and unlocking it within seconds, she was taken aback when Miss Hicks rushed inside. "Polly, what are you—?"

"I know who done in Mr Grosse."

"*What*?" Miss Trent closed the door. "*Who*?"

Miss Hicks walked around the hallway, changing directions multiple times, as she repeatedly ran her hands through her hair and touched her face. "Mr Farley, or Mr Sparrow. But Mr Jeffers was there, too… And pages… Sumin' about Erskine." She stopped abruptly and, pushing her fingers into her hair, held her head. "I scarpered after what I heard."

Miss Trent crossed over to her. "What did you hear?"

"*Them*! Arguing!" Miss Hicks paced at the foot of the stairs. "Mr Farley was angry because Mr Jeffers had sent sumin' here, but Mr Jeffers said the Society couldn't do owt because it's not coppers, but Mr Farley said we're not blind, and Mr Sparrow said they've got to hold their nerve to escape the hangman."

"Everythin' okay?" Mr Snyder enquired from the meeting room door.

"No, it bloody well isn't!" Miss Hicks hugged herself tightly as she glared at him.

Miss Webster softly tutted at the language. Standing behind Mr Snyder, she'd also been drawn out by Miss Hicks' raised voice.

"Don't you tut at me!" Miss Hicks yelled, advancing upon her fellow Bow Streeter.

"I think we *all* need to calm down," Miss Trent ordered, blocking her path.

Miss Hicks continued to glare at Miss Webster over the clerk's shoulder but made no further move toward her. "I've been scared half out of my wits! I don't need a *toff* playin' the high and mighty!"

"Dr Weeks managed to stay sober, did he?" Miss Webster sardonically enquired.

"That's *enough*," Miss Trent warned, casting a hard look between the two. "Miss Hicks, tell me again, what you overheard. Was it at the *Key & Lion*?"

Feeling her heart pounding in her chest, Miss Hicks took several deep breaths, followed by a hard swallow, as she tried to calm her fear. The proximity of Miss Trent and Mr Snyder also offered some comfort, even if she wanted to slap Miss Webster, still. "Mr Farley, Mr Sparrow, and Mr Jeffers talkin' about Erskine and the hangman."

"They also mentioned the notebook," Miss Trent interjected.

"What did they say?" Miss Webster enquired, careful to keep her voice calm.

Miss Hicks' features tightened as she looked at the secretary. "Mr Jeffers was the one who sent it to Becky. He took out the pages about Mr Erskine, too."

Mr Snyder, Miss Trent, and Miss Webster exchanged glances.

"Was Mr Grosse mentioned by name?" Miss Trent enquired.

Miss Hicks held her head as she tilted her head downward and searched her memory. Eventually, she replied, "No." Her eyes widened, and her brows lifted as she looked between them. "So, they might not of done in Mr Grosse after all?" She held out her open palm. "They could of just got the notebook from his body, couldn't they?"

"It's possible," Miss Webster agreed.

"I think we ought to have words with Mr Jeffers," Mr Snyder suggested.

"But he'll know who told you!" Miss Hicks cried.

"Did he, or any of the others, see you listening in on their conversation?" Miss Trent enquired.

"No, the door was closed," Miss Hicks replied.

"You should have nothing to worry about then," Miss Trent said.

Miss Hicks stared at her. "I ain't going back there, Becky. Not for all the bloody tea in China!"

Miss Trent frowned. "You've got to, Polly. Mr Sparrow might get suspicious. Besides," she put a gentle hand on her arm, "you're not going to be alone."

Miss Hicks glanced at Mr Snyder. "But they know he's a member of the Society."

"Not Sam," Miss Trent said.

"Who?" Miss Hicks enquired, confused.

Miss Trent looked around at their expectant eyes. After a moment's consideration, she knew she couldn't keep the secret any longer. "Conway's man."

"Conway's got a copper at the *Key & Lion*?" Mr Snyder enquired, surprised.

"He's undercover," Miss Trent replied.

"The bloke in the old green coat," Miss Hicks mused aloud.

"I don't know what he looks like," Miss Trent said. "Only that he's been keeping an eye on you since you started working there." Miss Trent watched Miss Hicks avert her gaze as she considered the possibility that he might've also seen her with Mr O'Hanigan. Deciding to leave that conversation for another day, though, Miss Trent went on, "You'll be safe as long as he's around. In the meantime, Mr Snyder, Miss Webster, and Mr Elliott will speak to Mr Jeffers about the notebook once he returns to the *Sporting Life* office." She raised her hand as

Miss Hicks parted her lips to protest. "The postal mark on the parcel proves it was sent from Fleet Street, so, we won't have to reveal what you overheard unless it's absolutely necessary."

Miss Hicks visibly relaxed. "Good." She gave an appreciative smile. "I'd best be getting back."

"I'll drop you off on the way," Mr Snyder said.

"I'll send word to Mr Elliott," Miss Trent added.

"What should we do in the unlikely circumstance of Mr Jeffers confessing to Mr Grosse's murder?" Miss Webster enquired.

"Escort him to the nearest police station," Miss Trent replied. "There's very little else we can do without the authority of the law."

FORTY

"*Excelsior Baths*, Bethnal Green. Elijah Maidment's Special Night. Success of Lovell, Barnard, Sid Phillips, and Stoneblake in six-round contests," a man in his mid-forties read aloud from that day's edition of *Sporting Life*. He was surrounded by a group of middle and working-class men who were either listening or peering through the large window of that publication's office. Located at 148, Fleet Street, four doors down from the office of the *Sportsman* newspaper, its display included photographs of champion boxers with bloodied gloves and posters announcing the current headlines. The man continued, "a dense fog prevailed throughout the East End last evening (Wednesday), and although it lifted toward the time announced for the commencement of hostilities—"

"What's this, a bloody weather forecast?" one man jibed. "Get to the fight!"

A murmur of agreement rose from the group.

The man with the newspaper mumbled his way through the next few lines before continuing in a louder voice, "Lovell and Honeywood were first… 'Neither proved "flyers," but nevertheless in their own style, fought well throughout'—"

"They were awful, in other words," a middle-class man remarked.

"Who won?" the weather forecast jibe man enquired.

The man with the newspaper read the next line. "Honeywood."

Mixed murmurings of disappointment and indifference rose from the group.

At the same time, the Society's hansom cab slowed to a stop nearby, and Mr Elliott and Miss Webster alighted. Whilst the former had a brief discussion with Mr Snyder, the latter slipped her gloved hands into a muffler and looked past the group at the window. As moments passed, she caught the curious glances of the men out of the corner of her eye.

"Excuse us, gentlemen," Mr Elliott said to the crowd as he approached.

"'Ere, she can't go in there!" the weather forecast jibe man cried upon seeing Miss Webster at the lawyer's side.

"I *beg* your pardon?" Miss Webster challenged. "I shall go wherever I like."

"Your concern is appreciated but unnecessary," Mr Elliott said, addressing the man.

"Just lookin' out for the lady, sir." The man doffed his hat and stepped aside.

Miss Webster halted to give him a piece of her mind but was immediately pulled inside by Mr Elliott. Tugging her arm free the moment they'd passed through the door, she glared at him and said, "How *dare* you prevent me from speaking."

"It wouldn't have ended well," Mr Elliott stated in his usual monotone.

"For him, certainly." She moved into the lawyer's personal space. "It's men like *you* who are suffocating womenkind."

Mr Elliott's features tensed. "I take offence to that."

"As you should," Miss Webster retorted.

"Pardon me," a man's voice said to their left, prompting them to turn their heads.

Approximately five feet eight inches tall, he had short, dark-brown hair combed back across his scalp, a long, narrow face, and warm, dark-green eyes behind a pair of brass-rimmed spectacles. Printing ink covered his long, slender fingers and the white apron tied around his waist. Beneath, he wore a brown waistcoat over a white shirt and brown trousers. His brown tie was tucked into his shirt, presumably to prevent it from being accidentally dipped into the ink. "I'm Mr Longbeam. May I help you at all?"

Miss Webster strode over to the counter behind which he stood. "We wish to speak with Mr Ian Jeffers. We understand he's a writer here."

Mr Longbeam's gaze flicked to Mr Elliott. "Which name should I give?"

"Miss Agnes Webster and Mr Gregory Elliott." Miss Webster leaned sideways to block Mr Elliott from Mr Longbeam's view. "Please."

Mr Elliott reached around her to give his card to Mr Longbeam.

"One moment, sir," Mr Longbeam said, taking the card with him as he went upstairs.

Meanwhile, Miss Webster twisted her torso to glare at her fellow Bow Streeter. "Am I suddenly invisible?"

"Here you are," Mr Elliott replied. "Unfortunately."

"In that case, you aren't helping matters," Miss Webster quipped as she walked away to examine the boxing and horse racing advertisements which covered the walls.

"Good afternoon, sir. I'm Mr Ian Jeffers. Mr Longbeam said you wished to speak with me?" Mr Jeffers enquired after descending the stairs and approaching the counter with his hand outstretched a few moments later. Mr Elliott's card was in his other.

"Yes, I'm Mr Gregory Elliott, and this is—"

"Miss Agnes Webster, personal secretary to Lady Katheryne Owston," Miss Webster interrupted as she strode forward. "We are here as members of the Bow Street Society."

Mr Jeffers' eyebrows lifted. Blinking rapidly as he glanced down at Mr Elliott's card, he quietly said, "But your card states you're a lawyer, sir. If I'd have known you were a member of the Bow Street Society—" He suddenly put it down and pushed it across the counter before taking a step back with a shake of his head. "I'm afraid I can't speak with you." He turned away. "Goodbye."

"We know you sent Mr Grosse's notebook to us," Miss Webster called after him.

Mr Jeffers halted at once and cast a wide-eyed stare across his shoulder at her.

"The mark on the postage stamp proves it." Miss Webster took the brown paper from her pocket and laid it out upon the counter.

Mr Jeffers covered his mouth as he slowly turned toward it. Keeping his distance from the counter, though, he fixed his gaze upon the mark as she pointed it out.

"These initials represent Fleet Street, and this number corresponds to the postal office here," Miss Webster explained.

Mr Jeffers lifted his gaze and looked between them as he lowered his hand. In a subdued voice, he said, "That doesn't prove I sent it."

"True," Mr Elliott said. "But your reaction speaks volumes."

"Oh *God*," Mr Jeffers cried, covering his mouth as he turned away.

"Is there somewhere private we may speak?" Mr Elliott enquired.

Mr Jeffers kept his hand clapped over his mouth as he swallowed hard and stared at the stairs. Breathing hard at the same time, he was clearly in a state of some distress.

"We can only help you if you cooperate with us," Mr Elliott said.

Mr Jeffers pulled his hand away as he turned his head. "Help me? How?"

"By giving you the benefit of my legal counsel," Mr Elliott replied.

Mr Jeffers' gaze darted between them. "Who said I required it?"

"You have," Mr Elliott replied. "By the fear in your eyes."

Mr Jeffers turned his back upon them and walked toward the rear of the building, only to return a moment later. With unblinking eyes, he insisted, "I didn't murder anyone."

"But you did send Mr Grosse's notebook to us," Miss Webster said.

Mr Jeffers swallowed hard. "Yes."

"How did you come to have it?" Mr Elliott enquired.

"I took it," Mr Jeffers replied in a quiet voice.

"From his body?" Mr Elliott probed.

The colour drained from Mr Jeffers' face. "Yes."

"Some pages were torn out. Do you have them?" Miss Webster enquired.

Mr Jeffers looked at her sharply. "How did you…?"

"I saw the torn paper in the notebook's binding," Miss Webster replied.

Mr Jeffers considered the answer as Mr Farley's voice echoed in his mind: *They're not blind! They'll notice they're missing!* A wave of nausea came over him, compelling him to sit upon Mr Longbeam's chair. Gripping the counter's edge at the same time, he took several deep breaths to quell the urge to empty his stomach. *The Society and the coppers can't point the finger at us without the pages on Erskine,* Mr Sparrow's voice echoed in his mind, prompting Mr Jeffers to think, *But I didn't do it.* He looked up at Mr Elliott and, in a tentative voice, enquired, "If I cooperate with you… if I tell you all that I know… do you give me your word you will be secret with me?"

"We are obliged to inform the police of anything we discover," Mr Elliott replied.

Mr Jeffers bowed his head.

"But you have my word that I'll do my utmost to help you," Mr Elliott added.

Mr Jeffers slowly lifted his head.

"You have mine, too," Miss Webster said.

Mr Jeffers looked between them and, bowing his head, considered his options.

"The pages… are about a boxer called Deon Erskine," Mr Jeffers eventually revealed.

"May we see them?" Miss Webster enquired.

Mr Jeffers gripped the counter's edge to steady himself as he stood. "They're locked in my desk upstairs, but I can tell you what they contain."

"We shall have to see them, still, but go on," Mr Elliott said.

"I understand." Mr Jeffers swallowed hard. "His fights… for the most part. Also… an address."

"Will you take us there?" Mr Elliott enquired. "We have a cab waiting outside."

Mr Jeffers' eyebrows raised again. "Take you…? Now?"

"After you've retrieved the pages, of course," Miss Webster replied.

"For what purpose?" Mr Jeffers challenged. "Erskine hasn't been there in years."

"We prefer to leave no stone unturned," Miss Webster replied.

"The pages, Mr Jeffers," Mr Elliott urged.

Mr Jeffers' complexion turned ashen. "Very well… I shan't be a moment."

* * *

Miss Hicks put the freshly poured pint of ale before the man in the green overcoat and took his payment. Watching him sideways as she put the coins into the cash register, she tried to imagine him in a policeman's uniform. Yet, his unshaven chin, dishevelled hair, and lean frame made it difficult.

"Have I got sumin' on my face?" he enquired.

Taken off guard by the sudden question, Miss Hicks momentarily froze. "What?"

"I said, 'have I got sumin' on my face?'" he repeated.

"Oh." Miss Hicks returned to him. "No. Sorry."

The man picked up his pint and, casting a glance over his shoulder, went back to his chair by the fire. Whether he suspected she had guessed his identity or found him attractive, she couldn't say. Regardless of which it was, she felt safer with him there.

Toby put some empty glasses on the bar. "Where did you scarper off to?"

"When?"

"Before. You was 'ere one minute, gone the next."

Miss Hicks put her hand upon her hip and flicked her hair. "Needed some fresh air, didn't I?" She cast a glance around the near-deserted pub. "It was as quiet as the grave, so I took my chance." She wet her lips. "Did, uh, Mr Sparrow notice I was gone?"

"Nah." Toby leaned back against the bar with his elbows upon its edge. "Don't know what's wrong with the guv'nor, but 'e ain't been right since Mr Farley and Mr Jeffers left."

Miss Hicks' stomach clenched. "When was that?"

Toby looked up and over his shoulder at her. "After you scarpered." He glanced over her. "If you wasn't my China, I'd of said you'd gone to peach on 'em."

Miss Hicks folded her arms. "I *ain't* a peach."

"You scarpered quick enough." Toby looked across the bar room.

"What could I of peached on them about anyway? They're just mates, right?"

Toby looked up and over his shoulder at her again. "Don't be daft."

Miss Hicks put her hand on her waist and, putting her other upon the bar, leaned forward. "Why was he letting him in here, then?" Standing bolt upright as large hands slid over her hips, she felt a man's crotch and chest press against her. His warm breath also brushed against her bare neck as its stale-beer scent filled her nostrils.

"If you ask nicely, I might tell you," Mr Sparrow said close to her ear.

Miss Hicks looked to the man in the green overcoat.

He didn't move.

Meanwhile, Toby had turned toward the bar at the sight of his employer.

Miss Hicks forced a smile. "Sorry, sir. It's none of my business."

"No." Mr Sparrow released her and, stepping back, gave her behind a firm slap. "It's not." As he walked away, Miss Hicks pursed her lips to prevent the sigh of relief from escaping. *A lot of good you are*, she thought, casting a scowl at the undercover policeman who immediately averted his gaze. *Yeah, look away*, she thought.

"See?" Toby enquired in a quiet voice. "The guv'nor ain't right."

"He seemed himself to me," Miss Hicks drily remarked.

Toby shook his head. "Nah, sumin's on his mind." He pulled a folded piece of paper from his pocket and presented it to her. "I nearly forgot. A messenger boy brought this for you before." As she took it, he added, "I've not read it." He gave a weak smile. "Can't read."

Miss Hicks gave him a sympathetic look. "Maybe I'll teach you."

Toby's eyes lit up. "Would you?"

"Owt for a mate," Miss Hicks replied.

Toby was practically bouncing as he went in search of more glasses.

Unfolding the note, Miss Hicks read the signature at its end. It was from Dr Weeks. She released a soft sigh as she thought, *Work, again.* Skimming over the rest of the note's contents, she gathered he wouldn't be home until the morning. She didn't read the reason because she knew it would be the usual one. Screwing up the note, she came out from behind the bar and tossed it into the fire to prevent others from reading it. Obliged to pass by the table of the man in the overcoat as she did, she made a point of not looking at him. *Bloody coppers. Useless, the lot of them.*

* * *

The room was long and narrow with a window at one end, a door at the other, and a meagre chimney breast and hearth on the right-hand side. Its low ceiling was dark cream, whilst its walls were covered in a dark-brown paper. The former was grubby, and the latter was peeling and sun faded. The exposed floorboards were uneven underfoot, creaky, and riddled with woodworm in places. Finally, the few items of furniture consisted of a washstand, chest of drawers, and a single, wooden bed. The last had a leg missing, so, a soap box had been placed under that corner. To Mr Elliott's mind, the place was only marginally more cheerful than a prison cell. Fortunately, its landlady was upbeat, hospitable, and eager to please.

Walking past the hearth, Mr Elliott peered through the window at the yard below. The room was on the second floor of a lodging house on Crozier Terrace in Hackney. A stone's throw from the Hackney Union Workhouse, the street's residents hadn't yet reached the depths of criminality but were close.

Mr Jeffers, Miss Webster, and Mrs Dwight, the landlady, were gathered by the open doorway leading into the equally dim corridor. Mr Jeffers turned his bowler hat as he held it against his stomach, his eyes fixed upon Mr Elliott. Meanwhile, Miss Webster had been careful to place herself where a swift exit would be obstructed. Mrs Dwight, on the other hand, seemed blissfully unaware of the tension between her three visitors.

In her early fifties, she had plaited long, dark-grey hair coiled into a bun at the base of her skull. Her rounded face, chocolate-brown eyes, and button nose gave her a jovial appearance despite her malnourished frame and old, tattered, dark-blue dress.

"It's not much, but I keep it clean," Mrs Dwight said in a proud tone.

"When did Mr Erskine leave?" Mr Elliott enquired.

"Five years ago," Mrs Dwight replied. She rested her clasped hands against her skirts and briefly pressed her chin against her chest. "Mind you," she lifted her head, "I couldn't get it let for a good month after."

"Why?" Miss Webster enquired.

Mr Jeffers tightened his grip upon his bowler hat and turned away.

"He left all his things," Mrs Dwight replied. "Never sent for them, and that wasn't like Mr Erskine."

Mr Elliott returned to the group. "Did he mention any family to you?"

"Never," Mrs Dwight replied.

"What of his friends?" Mr Elliott enquired.

"Mr Sparrow was the only one he ever talked of," Mrs Dwight replied. "But that was to be expected."

"Why?" Mr Elliott enquired.

Mrs Dwight glanced down. "Well… he did the doings for him, didn't he? Down in that cellar of his."

"Mr Erskine fought in the bareknuckle fights at the *Key & Lion*, is what she means," Mr Jeffers said, his voice fraught with tension. He met Mr Elliott's gaze. "Before he went to America."

Mrs Dwight chuckled and, putting her fingers to her lips, chuckled again. "Forgive me, sir."

Mr Jeffers clenched his jaw.

"Have we amused you?" Miss Webster enquired, affronted.

"No, miss." Mrs Dwight smiled. "It's just, when sir said Mr Erskine had gone to America, I couldn't help but chuckle."

"Because Mr Erskine was afraid of the sea," Mr Elliott stated.

When Mrs Dwight confirmed it to be true, Mr Jeffers retreated to the window.

"Did a Mr Christian Grosse ever ask you about Mr Erskine?" Miss Webster enquired.

"He did," Mrs Dwight replied. "A few days before he was done in, the poor soul."

"We found a photograph of Mr Erskine in his," Miss Webster consulted her notebook, "'toeing-the-scratch' boxing stance amongst Mr Grosse's belongings. Did you give it to him?"

Mrs Dwight put her hand upon Miss Webster's arm. "It's funny you should bring that up, miss, as that's what I was wanting to say before. Mr Erskine adored that photograph. He said it reminded him of better days. When he went off and left it behind like that, I knew it wasn't like him. I told as much to Mr Grosse when I gave it him."

Mr Jeffers paled.

"One last question," Miss Webster said. "Can you recall the last time you saw Mr Erskine?"

"Dear me." Mrs Dwight put her hand to her cheek and turned her head away as she spent several moments searching her memory. "I think so... yes." Her eyes were bright with recollection as she met Miss Webster's gaze again. "He'd been to work laying his bricks and was going out for a drink. To the *Key & Lion* it must of been."

Mr Jeffers' complexion turned ashen.

"Thank you, Mrs Dwight," Miss Webster said.

"You're welcome, miss, sirs," Mrs Dwight said. "I'm happy to do what I can, when I can." She flashed them a smile and left.

The moment she had gone, Mr Elliott looked to Mr Jeffers. "There is more to this than a missing notebook."

Mr Jeffers turned away.

"Tell us," Mr Elliott urged.

Mr Jeffers repeatedly shook his head as he paced before the window. "I never murdered anyone." He cast a hard glance at the lawyer, "I shan't book my appointment with the hangman."

"You might not have a choice," Mr Elliott coolly stated.

Mr Jeffers halted. "I beg your pardon?"

Mr Elliott approached him. "If you were aware another planned to murder Mr Grosse at the warehouse, the court would consider you equally guilty of the crime."

Mr Jeffers' jaw dropped. "But I... it wasn't... I *never*..."

"This is the brevity of the situation you're in," Mr Elliott warned. "I've promised you the benefit of my legal counsel, but its advantages are limited if you insist upon concealing vital information."

Mr Jeffers slowly lowered and sat on the edge of the bed. Tightly gripping its frame, he quietly enquired, "Is there no other way?"

"None," Mr Elliott replied. "The time has come to tell the whole truth."

Mr Jeffers stood. Feeling a rolling sensation in his stomach, he unlatched and opened the window wide to take in a lungful of air. He considered climbing out, but the sight of the sheer drop to the yard obliged him to dismiss the idea. *The drop beneath a noose is just as terrifying,* he thought. *If what Mr Elliott says is true, the hangman awaits me whether I speak or not. Unburdening the secret could prove advantageous in the long term, though.* He took in another lungful of air and turned to the Bow Streeters. "It has, but I want you to make a promise first."

Mr Elliott and Miss Webster cast sideways glances at one another.

FORTY-ONE

"Before we begin, Mr Jeffers, I must caution you that whatever you say could be used as evidence against you," Inspector Pilker warned.

Sitting beside him at the table was a uniformed police constable with pen, inkwell, and paper. Behind them was a solid wooden door leading into the busy corridor of New Scotland Yard. Meanwhile, Mr Elliott and Mr Jeffers sat opposite the constable and inspector respectively. A large window behind them overlooked an area of greenery adjacent to the Victoria Embankment and River Thames. The afternoon sun hung low in the sky.

"Do you understand?" Inspector Pilker enquired.

"Yes." Mr Jeffers kept his hands tightly clasped upon the table.

"I must also caution you, Inspector, that my client's statement comes with certain conditions," Mr Elliott said.

"I thought it might," Inspector Pilker remarked in a cool tone. "What are they?"

"Firstly, he would like it to be noted that he is here voluntarily," Mr Elliott replied.

Inspector Pilker nodded to the constable who wrote it down. "And the second?"

"Immunity from prosecution in exchange for his testimony," Mr Elliott replied.

"You want to turn Queen's evidence?" Inspector Pilker enquired.

"I do," Mr Jeffers replied.

"Against whom?" Inspector Pilker enquired.

Mr Jeffers looked to Mr Elliott who replied, "Mr Grosse's murderers."

Inspector Pilker's expression remained emotionless. "The word of one man isn't sufficient to prosecute a murder case, as I'm sure you're aware, Mr Elliott." He glanced at the tattered blue notebook on the table. "Particularly the word of a suspected thief."

Mr Jeffers turned desperate eyes to the Bow Streeter. "I told you he wouldn't—"

"Calm yourself," Mr Elliott interrupted, his gaze fixed upon Inspector Pilker.

Mr Jeffers bowed his head and dry-washed his hands.

"I concede that Mr Jeffers' testimony isn't sufficient on its own," Mr Elliott said. "But I guarantee it shall lead to the physical evidence required to secure a prosecution."

Inspector Pilker looked between them. "I shall have to speak to the prosecutor at court."

"We understand that," Mr Elliott said. "All I ask at the moment is for reassurance that the Metropolitan Police will not pursue a prosecution against my client."

Inspector Pilker straightened in his chair and, picking up the tattered notebook, flipped through several of its pages whilst pondering the proposition. Finally, he set the notebook aside. "I agree to your terms."

Mr Jeffers' face lit up with a smile.

"Under the understanding that I can't prevent the crown's prosecutor from pursuing charges if he deems it appropriate," Inspector Pilker warned.

Mr Jeffers' face fell, and he looked to Mr Elliott for assistance. The lawyer cupped his hand against his client's ear and, leaning in close, whispered a brief explanation. As he pulled back, Mr Jeffers' expression was grim. Nevertheless, he aired no disagreement when Mr Elliott told Inspector Pilker, "We understand."

"Good." Inspector Pilker picked up the notebook and torn pages. "Let's begin." He glanced at his constable. Upon seeing his pen poised, he set the items before Mr Jeffers and enquired, "Whom did these belong to?"

Mr Jeffers stared at them. "Mr Christian Grosse."

"Are the pages from the notebook?" Inspector Pilker enquired.

Mr Jeffers gave a small nod.

"Who tore them out?" Inspector Pilker enquired.

"I did," Mr Jeffers mumbled.

"Why?" Inspector Pilker enquired as his constable wrote furiously at his side.

Mr Jeffers pushed the pages aside and sat back in his chair. "They contain information about a boxer named Deon Erskine. I tore them out to prevent the Bow Street Society from seeing it." He cast a sideways glance at Mr Elliott. "I didn't think there was any way they could trace the parcel back to me."

"Nor did I," Inspector Pilker stated, turning hard eyes to the Bow Streeter. Following Mr Elliott's brief explanation of Miss Webster using the markings on the postage stamp to trace the parcel back to the Fleet Street post office, he enquired from Mr Jeffers, "Where did you find the notebook?"

Mr Jeffers swallowed hard. "On Mr Grosse's body. It… it was in his breast pocket."

"Why did you send it to the Bow Street Society?" Inspector Pilker enquired.

"Because it connected me to Mr Grosse's murder," Mr Jeffers replied.

"Why take it at all?" Inspector Pilker enquired.

"Because it contains *highly* valuable information," Mr Jeffers replied, irritated by the policeman's tone. "Especially to the right bidder. The wage of a journalist, even one as respected as I, isn't high. I could've retired several times over on the monies those gents would've paid to keep their names dissociated from the brutality of boxing."

"Blackmail?" Inspector Pilker suggested with a tilt of his head.

"No," Mr Jeffers replied. "I had no intention of publishing anything in the notebook. If the gents wanted to make payment to guarantee no one else would, I would've seen to it the notebook never saw the light of day."

Inspector Pilker held up the loose pages. "Mr Deon Erskine wasn't a gentleman, though. His manager, Mr Amias Winfield, is openly involved in boxing. What did you hope to gain by holding back these pages?"

Mr Jeffers bowed his head in a jerky movement. Swallowing hard as his complexion paled, he quietly replied, "My life."

Inspector Pilker leaned forward with his ear turned toward him. "I beg your pardon?"

"My life!" Mr Jeffers cried, forcing the policeman back.

Inspector Pilker glared at him. "Why was your life in danger?"

Mr Jeffers shifted his weight upon his chair as a profound sorrow entered his eyes. "Because I was there when—" He drew his elbows in and held his clasped hands close to his chest as he bowed his head low. "Mr Sparrow and Mr Farley murdered Mr Grosse."

FORTY-TWO

The sun slid behind some clouds, thereby making the interview room gloomier than before. Whilst the constable stood to turn up the gas lamps, Inspector Pilker's gaze bore into the top of Mr Jeffers' head. His expression remained emotionless, however. Hearing the scrape of the constable's chair as he sat and resumed his writing, Inspector Pilker straightened and sat back in his own. "Tell us, in your own words, exactly what happened."

"The set-to at the warehouse was planned," Mr Jeffers said. "Mr Sparrow, Mr Farley, and me orchestrated the confrontation at the *Key & Lion* in the hope Mr Grosse would rise to the bait and organise the bout." He rubbed his knuckles hard as his gaze turned inward to the events of that night. "He did… His loyalty to Mr Sparrow wouldn't allow him to see his friend hurt."

He put his forehead in one hand whilst the other clenched into a fist. "Mr Grosse arranged the venue and the boxers. Me, Mr Sparrow, and Mr Farley waited until the fight was a few rounds in before going in search of him. Mr Winfield and Mr O'Hanigan had gotten to him first. We hid behind some crates and waited until Mr O'Hanigan had finished beating him. Mr Grosse staggered around in something of a daze for a while afterwards. Then… Mr Sparrow and Mr Farley…" He clenched his eyes shut and, disgusted, said, "Oh *God*."

"We have to know all of the details," Inspector Pilker urged.

Mr Jeffers brought his other hand up to hold his head as his lips visibly trembled. "Mr Sparrow spoke to Mr Grosse… Mr Farley hit him from behind… Mr Grosse fell… Mr Farley hit him again… and stopped…" Mr Jeffers took in a deep, shuddering breath. "Mr Grosse was dead."

"Is that when you took the notebook?" Inspector Pilker enquired.

Mr Jeffers gave a curt nod. "They didn't want me to. I couldn't leave it, not when I knew what… what it was rumoured to contain."

"What did Mr Farley use to hit Mr Grosse with?" Inspector Pilker enquired.

"He called it a 'life preserver,'" Mr Jeffers replied. "It was a piece of wooden cane… with a large ball of lead at the end."

"Where is it now?" Inspector Pilker enquired.

"I don't know. Mr Farley must still have it," Mr Jeffers quietly replied.

"What happened next?" Inspector Pilker enquired.

Mr Jeffers lifted his head and clasped his hands in front of his face. "Uh, we left, I think."

"Did you inflict any injuries upon Mr Grosse?" Inspector Pilker enquired.

"*No.*" Mr Jeffers met his gaze. "I wanted no part in it."

Inspector Pilker glanced sideways at Mr Elliott as he considered the validity of Mr Jeffers' story. It certainly fit with what they knew about Mr Grosse's death. Yet, many key questions remained unanswered. Questions which he doubted Mr Jeffers would answer truthfully. Deciding to test his theory, he assumed a calm tone as he enquired, "Why did Mr Sparrow and Mr Farley murder Mr Grosse? Why did you agree to accompany them?"

Mr Jeffers looked to Mr Elliott for guidance.

"Please, answer the questions," the lawyer said.

Mr Jeffers gave a curt nod and, swallowing hard, bowed his head and held his clasped hands upon the table, close to his body, once more. "Mr Grosse was writing a book about boxing in London. He was planning to include Deon Erskine. He'd asked Mr Sparrow and Mr Farley about him. They told him the story we'd agreed upon: Erskine had gone to the United States of America to continue his boxing career. At first, Mr Grosse accepted this. But Mr Sparrow saw a telegram tucked in Mr Grosse's notebook, saying there wasn't a record of Mr

Erskine fighting over there. Mr Grosse had also said in passing that he'd found an address in London for Mr Erskine." Mr Jeffers lowered his head further. "Mr Grosse, without knowing it, was getting too close to the truth. If he'd found out, we'd all be for the gallows."

Inspector Pilker leaned forward. "Found out what, precisely?"

Mr Jeffers looked the policeman straight in the eye. "That Deon Erskine is buried under the cellar at the *Key & Lion*."

FORTY-THREE

Miss Dexter knitted her fingers against her skirts and stood close to Miss Trent outside Mr Maxwell's bedroom. The pitter-patter of rain against the windows of the unoccupied rooms came through their open doorways, filling the sparse landing with a gentle rhythm. As she focused upon it, Miss Dexter felt the intensity of her nervousness and concern ease a little. She hoped that Mr Maxwell was soothed by it, too. Yet, the longer Miss Trent's knocks went unanswered, the more doubtful of this Miss Dexter became.

"I think there's been quite enough of this," Miss Trent said. Taking a double page of the *Gaslight Gazette* from her pocket, she unfolded it and slipped it under the door. "A trick Mr Locke taught me," she explained at Miss Dexter's perplexed expression. Crouching before the lock, she inserted another key and wiggled it around until they heard the clang of the other fall onto the floor. Putting the first away, she carefully pulled the newspaper out from under the door to reveal the second key lying upon it.

"How very clever!" Miss Dexter gasped in astonishment.

Miss Trent picked up the key and used it to unlock the door. Standing, she opened the door wide and strode inside with Miss Dexter hurrying along closely behind. The room was in complete darkness; even the fire had burnt out. Igniting a gas lamp and turning it up to its full strength, Miss Trent turned to look upon Mr Maxwell's pathetic, prone form in the bed. Meanwhile, Miss Dexter had rushed over and knelt at its side.

"It's time to get up, get washed, get dressed, and eat," Miss Trent announced.

Mr Maxwell turned over to face the wall.

"Please, Joseph," Miss Dexter urged, deeply concerned. "For me?"

"Would you prepare a bath, please, Miss Dexter?" Miss Trent enquired.

"Yes, of course." Miss Dexter stood and, hurrying to the door, momentarily stopped to cast another worried look back at Mr Maxwell.

Miss Trent stood by the bed and folded her arms.

"Leave me be," Mr Maxwell mumbled.

"I shan't."

Mr Maxwell curled up into the foetal position and wrapped his arms around his head.

"You can't stay in here," Miss Trent stated. "Oliver's trial ends tomorrow."

"I don't care," Mr Maxwell mumbled.

"We both know that's not true." Miss Trent tugged the blanket off, pulling him onto his back in the process. His face was covered in dark-red stubble whilst dark circles marred the pale complexion around his eyes. His hair also appeared matted. Dropping the blanket, Miss Trent pulled him by the arm toward the edge of the bed. "Get up. *Now*."

Mr Maxwell's other arm flailed wildly. "I don't want to!"

"We all have to do things we don't want to at times," Miss Trent dismissed, taking hold of his wrists and pulling him onto his feet. Switching back to holding one arm, she led him across the room to the chair by the hearth and stood him before it. She put her hands on his shoulders and, pushing downward, obliged him to sit. "I'm going to get another fire going and find some clean clothes. Miss Dexter is preparing a bath." She cleared out the remnants of the old fire and built a pile of fresh coal and kindling within the hearth that she promptly ignited with a match.

"I don't know what's happened to send you back to this dark place but, quite honestly, I'm tired of worrying sick about you all hours of the day and night." Miss Trent wiped her hands upon her apron. "I've enough to occupy my thoughts with the Society without you adding to it." She found some clean trousers, shirt, and waistcoat and laid them out upon the bed. "I'm going to help Miss

Dexter. If I find you in that bed when I come back, there'll be words."

Mr Maxwell frowned, but he knew they were only trying to help. "I… I understand."

Miss Trent's expression softened. "I shan't be long."

* * *

"Mr Jeffers claims he was drinking after hours with Mr Sparrow, Mr Erskine, and Mr Farley at the *Key & Lion* when a heated argument began about which was superior, gloved or bareknuckle boxing," Inspector Pilker informed Chief Inspector Jones.

Standing in the latter's office with the transcript of the interview in his hands, Inspector Pilker glanced between it and his senior officer behind the desk. Following the completion of his interrogation, Mr Jeffers had been placed into protective custody. Mr Elliott had insisted upon accompanying Inspector Pilker, however; a request he'd initially refused. Yet, Mr Elliott's revelation that the Society had a plan to locate the evidence required to secure a conviction persuaded him to change his mind. He wanted the meddlers to neither interfere nor create bad publicity for himself, his investigation, or the Metropolitan Police. Allowing them to run around, unchecked, would risk them all.

"Mr Farley accused Mr Erskine and Mr Sparrow of being brutes for refusing the gloves," Inspector Pilker continued. "Mr Erskine and Mr Sparrow, in turn, accused Mr Farley of 'going soft' for taking up the mittens. Mr Jeffers alleges Mr Farley was insulted by this and challenged Mr Erskine to a no-glove bout in the ring in the pub's cellar."

Chief Inspector Jones recalled Miss Trent informing him of Inspector Conway's last bout in the place. This, in turn, led to the image of the burning file appearing in his mind's eye. Maintaining an emotionless expression despite this, he sat back in his chair and steepled his fingers.

"Mr Erskine, who'd faltered in the ring in his recent bouts, swiftly lost to Mr Farley," Inspector Pilker continued. "Mr Jeffers claims that, when he left the cellar to use the privy, Mr Erskine was 'licking his wounds,' Mr Farley was 'boasting of his skill,' and Mr Sparrow was 'offering more drinks.' When he returned a few minutes later, though, Mr Erskine was 'lying on his back upon the floor, his eyes wide open,' with Mr Farley 'standing over him, slapping his face, and demanding he wake up.' Mr Sparrow was 'bent over the pair, insisting Mr Erskine couldn't be dead.'"

"What did Mr Jeffers say he did then?" Chief Inspector Jones enquired.

"He demanded to know what had happened, but neither man volunteered an answer," Mr Elliott replied. "He said they were clearly in a state of shock."

Inspector Pilker glared at the Bow Streeter as he continued, "According to Mr Jeffers, 'Mr Farley asked Mr Sparrow what they were going to do.' To which, Mr Sparrow suggested fetching a police constable. Mr Farley 'descended into utter panic, stating that the police would think they murdered Mr Erskine and send them to the hangman.' Mr Jeffers insisted he'd 'had no part in it,' but Mr Farley told him 'he was there' and so was 'in as much trouble as them.' At this point, Mr Jeffers alleges, Mr Sparrow suggested burying Mr Erskine's body under the cellar. Mr Jeffers told him 'People would notice he was missing,' but Mr Farley countered this with 'not if we tell them he went to America.' Mr Jeffers claims to have been unconvinced by the plan but, 'seeing no other way out,' had 'gone along with it.'"

"And his reason for assisting with Mr Grosse's murder?" Chief Inspector Jones enquired.

"The same," Inspector Pilker replied.

"When do you intend to arrest the others?" Chief Inspector Jones enquired.

"It's not as simple as that, sir." Inspector Pilker put the transcript down in front of him. "Mr Jeffers has given his statement in exchange for immunity from prosecution."

Chief Inspector Jones' gaze slid to Mr Elliott. "Under your advice, I presume."

"Without turning Queen's evidence, Mr Jeffers is vulnerable to prosecution under the law of common purpose," Mr Elliott said. "I was merely protecting my client's best interests."

"What evidence do you have to corroborate Mr Jeffers' story?" Chief Inspector Jones enquired from his subordinate.

Inspector Pilker frowned. "None. At the moment."

"But the Bow Street Society has a plan to find it," Mr Elliott said.

"Perhaps it does," Chief Inspector Jones said. "But neither it nor you have any authority here."

"We don't presume to," Mr Elliott stated.

"Have you located the murder weapon?" Chief Inspector Jones enquired.

Inspector Pilker's frown deepened. "Mr Jeffers thinks Mr Farley may still have it."

Chief Inspector Jones picked up the transcript and read its remainder. "When do you intend to search the cellar?"

"If I may outline the Society's plan, Chief Inspector?" Mr Elliott requested. "It concerns the search for both Mr Erskine's body and the murder weapon."

Chief Inspector Jones lowered the transcript. "Very well."

"Sir…" Inspector Pilker moved closer to his senior officer. "I strongly urge you to consider prohibiting any further involvement of the Bow Street Society in this investigation."

"I want to hear what they have to say," Chief Inspector Jones said in a firm tone.

Inspector Pilker retreated and went to the window to hide his annoyance.

"The Society intends to distract Mr Sparrow and Mr Farley elsewhere whilst their establishments are searched," Mr Elliott said.

"Tomorrow is Christmas Eve," Chief Inspector Jones reminded him. "Both establishments will be closed on Christmas Day. In short, there is precious little time to do what you propose."

"We're aware of that and have factored it into our plan," Mr Elliott said.

Chief Inspector Jones glanced at Inspector Pilker who continued to look out of the window. "We're listening."

"It's reasonable to presume both men would prefer to take money from their high-spirited customers than attend a boxing match on Christmas Eve," Mr Elliott continued. "Unless it was a once-in-a-lifetime opportunity to see a rematch between the Whitechapel Ox and Bulldog."

"Whitechapel Ox and Bulldog…" Chief Inspector Jones mused aloud as he searched his memory. He looked up sharply. "But aren't they…?" He looked to his subordinate for confirmation.

"Yes, sir," Inspector Pilker replied. "Mr Sam Snyder and Inspector John Conway."

FORTY-FOUR

The night air was freezing. Yet, a warmth flooded Miss Hicks' body. Her bare fingers were numb. Yet, they ached to touch another. Stroking her arm in the meantime, she stood with her back to the wall as she watched the passageway's entrance. Only a few minutes had passed since she'd left the pub, but it felt like a lifetime. Her mind whirled with thoughts of the previous night and what could've held up Noah. Although she was loathed to admit it, she knew the longer she waited, the more likely it was he wouldn't come. She'd given him what he'd wanted, after all. Feeling increasingly foolish, she contemplated visiting Dr Weeks at work. He'd be pleased to see her, at least.

"Penny for 'em."

A smile lifted Miss Hicks' face and brightened her eyes the moment she saw him. "Noah. You came."

"I said I was." Mr O'Hanigan wrapped his large arms around her.

Miss Hicks embraced him in return. "You did. I'm sorry."

"How sorry?"

"*Very* sorry." She closed her eyes and savoured the taste of his lips as they kissed.

He held her chin. "Will you show me?"

She gazed into his eyes. "Yes."

He gently rubbed her cheek with his thumb. "At your place?"

She pulled her head away. "But my mum, she'll be sleeping."

He held her cheeks and slowly teased her lips with his. "I'll be quiet."

She released a soft, shuddering breath as her heart raced. "How quiet?"

He grinned. "*Very* quiet."

She snaked her tongue across her lips as she considered his suggestion. Dr Weeks had been summoned to God knows where to cut up God knows what. Experience told her he was unlikely to return before dawn. They'd have the entire place to themselves. *I'll sneak Noah out before first light*, she thought. *No one need ever know.* She knitted her fingers with his. "I've money for a cab."

His grin grew into a broad smile as he allowed her to lead him from the passageway.

* * *

"I don't like being backed into a corner, Rebecca," Chief Inspector Jones said.

"Does anyone?" Miss Trent countered.

"Nor do I like Mr Elliott's visits to the Yard." Chief Inspector Jones crossed to the window. The courtyard below was quiet as the odd fragment of muffled conversation drifted up from the chop house downstairs. Although located a stone's throw from the Bank of England, the establishment and surrounding area were deserted at this time of night. "I can only tolerate his arrogance for so long."

"I share your concern, Richard, I do." Miss Trent joined him at the window. "But there's no other way to guarantee Mr Sparrow and Mr Farley's absences from their pubs."

Chief Inspector Jones lowered his voice. "It's only been a matter of days since John's last fight. You've seen what state he's in. He's not as young as he was, either." His expression turned sombre. "After everything we've put him through, too… It's not right."

"What isn't?" Inspector Conway enquired.

Chief Inspector Jones and Miss Trent turned to find him standing in the doorway.

"Come in and close the door," the former replied, moving away from the window.

Inspector Conway did as he was instructed and, removing his hat, tossed it onto the table in the middle of the otherwise bare room and sat.

"How are you?" Chief Inspector Jones cast an appraising look over Inspector Conway whilst taking the chair opposite him.

"Can't complain." Inspector Conway glanced at Miss Trent as she sat to the right of Chief Inspector Jones, close to the fire. Catching the sombre look in her eyes, he shifted his gaze to his senior officer and noticed the same in his. "What's the matter?" He sat forward and rested a bent arm upon the table. "Has sumin' happened to Hicks or Skinner?"

"No," Miss Trent replied. "They're both safe."

"Sumin's happened," Inspector Conway insisted.

"Not yet, it hasn't," Chief Inspector Jones said. "Whether it does… well, it rather depends on you."

Inspector Conway furrowed his brow. "How's that?"

"We need you to help us secure evidence that proves the guilt of Mr Grosse's murderers," Miss Trent replied. "But it would mean putting yourself in harm's way."

"I do that anyway," Inspector Conway stated.

"Not like this," Chief Inspector Jones remarked.

Inspector Conway pulled his arm off the table and sat back against his chair. Looking between them, his expression reflected the seriousness of his tone. "What do you want me to do?"

"We need to distract Mr Sparrow and Mr Farley whilst the police search their pubs," Miss Trent began. "The only way to do that is to lure them away with something they couldn't resist. Naturally, boxing came to mind."

Inspector Conway looked between them as he suspected what was coming.

"Mr Sparrow and Mr Farley wouldn't want to miss a bout. Especially, if it was a rematch between the Whitechapel Ox and the Bulldog, albeit one fought under the Queensberry Rules," Miss Trent said.

"I'm against the idea," Chief Inspector Jones stated.

"But it's the only way," Miss Trent pointed out.

"Even so, you're under no obligation to agree, John," Chief Inspector Jones said.

Inspector Conway looked between them. Turning his head away, he took his time in placing a cigarette between his lips and lighting it with a match. Standing immediately afterward, he went over to the fireplace and tossed the match into the bottom of the hearth before exhaling a large cloud of smoke. Coughing a few times as a result, he rested the heel of his cigarette-holding hand on the mantel shelf and held his broken ribs whilst taking in a slow, deep breath. Releasing another cough with an obvious wince, he straightened and put the heel of his free hand upon the mantel shelf, too. Turning his gaze inward, he considered his decision. "How many rounds?"

"The fight will end once we receive word from the search parties," Miss Trent said.

Chief Inspector Jones frowned deeply. "Which means it could be a long one."

Inspector Conway took another pull of his cigarette as he crossed the room to the window. "What does Sam say?"

"He's willing if you are," Miss Trent replied.

Inspector Conway looked out at the building opposite as he took a final pull from his cigarette. Exhaling the smoke, he turned to the others. "What are you gonna do if I'm not?"

Miss Trent cast a concerned glance at Chief Inspector Jones. "We'd find something else to lure Mr Sparrow and Mr Farley away from their pubs."

"Like what?" Inspector Conway tossed his cigarette into the fire on his way back to the table. "Boxin' is what they live and breathe." He sat. "I'll do it."

Chief Inspector Jones pursed his lips and exhaled loudly through his nose. "Have you seen yourself lately? The *state* you're in?"

"I feel it," Inspector Conway replied.

"So, *why* worsen it by going back into the ring?" Chief Inspector Jones demanded.

"Because Grosse deserves justice," Inspector Conway replied firmly.

"Not at the cost of your life, John," Chief Inspector Jones countered.

"That's not your decision to make, Richard," Inspector Conway softly replied.

Chief Inspector Jones' features softened as his eyes filled with worry. "I hope you know what you're doing."

Miss Trent put her hand on Chief Inspector Jones' arm. "Sam hasn't boxed in years, and they're friends besides." She withdrew her hand. "And Dr Weeks will be there to provide medical assistance."

Inspector Conway gave a weak chuckle. "God help us."

Chief Inspector Jones remained unconvinced. "I second that sentiment."

"I'll survive. I always have," Inspector Conway reassured. From Miss Trent, he enquired, "Where's this set-to happening?"

* * *

"*Shh*," Miss Hicks warned Mr O'Hanigan, her finger pressed against her lips, as they entered the narrow, unlit passageway at the side of *R.G. Dunn Pawnbrokers*. With his hand in hers, she crept past the dark windows to the separate door reserved for her and Dr Weeks' use. Well, mainly Dr Weeks', on account of his unsociable working hours. Taking the latch key from where she'd tucked it between her breasts, she unlocked the door as quietly as she could and led Mr O'Hanigan up the creaky stairs beyond. When they finally made it into the cluttered lounge, she released the breath she'd been holding and lit the kerosene lamp on Dr Weeks' desk.

"This is yours?" Mr O'Hanigan glanced over the scientific instruments, piles of journals, and empty bottles.

His tone held a hint of concern, whilst his eyes were suspicious.

"No." Miss Hicks clasped her hands behind her back and, lowering her head, looked up at him with sheepish eyes as she closed the distance between them. "It's my lover's. He's a surgeon."

Mr O'Hanigan turned toward the door.

"*Don't* go." Miss Hicks threw her arms around his waist to stay him. She gently rubbed his chest and gazed into his annoyed eyes with needful ones of her own. "It don't bother you that I've got another bloke, does it?" She offered a weak smile. "You were Eunice Grosse's lover—"

Mr O'Hanigan took a firm grip of her shoulders. "Who told you that?"

Miss Hicks wet her lips. "It don't matter. All that matters is you was, wasn't you?"

Mr O'Hanigan released a deep sigh. "Yeah."

Miss Hicks stroked his cheek. "She was married." She touched his lips. "I'm not." She leaned up and kissed him softly. Keeping her lips close to his, she whispered, "And my Perce won't be 'ome until mornin'."

Mr O'Hanigan spun around with her and pushed her back against the door.

Miss Hicks' face flushed bright pink as, with a swiftly rising and falling chest, she fixed him with a lustful gaze. "Our secret, yeah?"

Mr O'Hanigan pressed his body against hers, thereby making her feel his need. In a voice made rough by its breathlessness, he replied, "Our secret."

FORTY-FIVE

It was the following evening, and the *Excelsior Hall* on the corner of Florida Street and Mansford Street was at full capacity. Veteran members of the Fancy sat shoulder to shoulder with regulars of the *Key & Lion* and *Nimble Crow* around a raised twenty-four-foot ring. Strategically placed amongst them were plain-clothed police officers belonging to the Mob Squad, New Scotland Yard, and a few of the divisions. Inspector Lee and Sergeant Gutman were there representing T (or Kensington) Division.

Although they weren't formally involved in the Grosse case, they'd been recommended by Inspector Pilker to Chief Inspector Jones who, as the most senior officer, was the operation's lead. All of the officers present had been personally selected and briefed by Chief Inspector Jones with the assistance of Inspectors Pilker and Conway. Their task was to maintain surveillance of Mr Sparrow and Mr Farley until Chief Inspector Jones gave the signal for their arrests. Detailed descriptions of both men had been supplied for everyone to commit to memory.

As he sat with Sergeant Gutman to the right of the ring, Inspector Lee cast an appraising glance over his surroundings. Serving the residents of Bethnal Green, the *Excelsior Hall* housed a swimming pool during the summer months. When the days grew colder, the pool was covered to create a large, open space for concerts, meetings, and boxing matches. According to Sergeant Gutman, this was the same ring used for a contest of the manly sport a few nights prior. Thus, it appeared the *Excelsior Hall* was a natural choice when considering which venue would make their prey feel safe.

A haze of tobacco smoke, combined with the din of innumerable conversations, filled the room to create an oppressive atmosphere. It wasn't how Inspector Lee would've usually spent his Christmas Eve, but the lure of seeing Snyder and Conway beat each other to a pulp had proven too great to resist. His plan to remove the Head of the Mob Squad from his position, whilst simultaneously tarnishing the Bow Street Society's reputation, had failed to bear fruit. Whether it was a case of Inspector Woolfe's loyalty being unbreakable was unclear. Either way, though, their short-lived cooperation had ended, and with it had gone Inspector Lee's connection to Dr Colbert. He'd have to think of another way to destroy the irksome meddlers.

"I saw 'em first time 'round," a toothless man boasted behind Inspector Lee.

"Who won?" the man's neighbour enquired.

"The Ox," the toothless man replied. "It's been many a year since 'e toed the scratch."

"And the Bulldog's been on good form," the neighbour remarked.

Inspector Lee's ears metaphorically pricked up at this. Leaning his head back a little, he did his best to drown out the other noise and focus on the two men's conversation.

"But he's still got the bruises from 'is last bout," the toothless man pointed out. "One punch to them ribs, and it'll be over."

Recalling the bruises on Inspector Conway's face when they'd last met, Inspector Lee wondered if the grizzled policeman had been honest with his senior officers about their origin. Making a mental note of it, he knew nothing could be proved by bruises alone. He also doubted these men, or others like them, would readily peach on one they considered their own. Nevertheless, the knowledge may prove useful in the future.

When the men's conversation moved onto boxers he'd never heard of, Inspector Lee turned his attention to the seating directly opposite. The first two rows had been reserved for members of the Bow Street Society, much to the chagrin of the Metropolitan Police officers present. Yet, the meddlers were allegedly entitled to a seat on account of Mr Snyder being in the fight. Rumour also had it that the operation was their idea and that a few of them were assisting Inspectors Pilker and Woolfe with the searches of the *Key & Lion* and *Nimble Crow*. If true, it was a slap in the face of every officer there.

Recognising only a couple of faces in the Society's designated rows, Inspector Lee committed the rest to memory. They could be members he'd not had the displeasure of meeting. Those he knew were Mr Joseph Maxwell and Mr Virgil Verity. The former had earlier attended the final day of his father's trial. Unsurprisingly, Oliver Maxwell had been found guilty of the murder of Mrs Poppy Maxwell. The questions of whether he'd driven Mrs Sybil Maxwell to suicide or attempted to murder Joseph had proven difficult to prove. Therefore, Oliver had been found not guilty on the counts of manslaughter and attempted murder. Yet, regardless of this, the judge had donned the black cap and sentenced Oliver to the ultimate fate. Rather than execute him on the blessed day of Christmas, though, it was assumed his sentence would be carried out in the new year.

It had been back in October, during the Cosgrove case, when Inspector Lee had first met Mr Verity. In his sixties, the spiritualist and retired schoolmaster had a shrewd eye and vigour despite his outwardly frail appearance. His immense beard and moustache were a washed-out white colour, whilst his hair was silver. All were neatly combed to give him a distinguished air echoed in his great overcoat, brown scarf, and black gloves. Inspector Lee watched as Mr Verity talked at Mr Maxwell with a flurry of hand gestures aimed toward the ring.

Running his gaze along the rows a few moments later, Inspector Lee noticed Miss Trent was conspicuous by her absence. She, unlike others of her sex, had been given special leave to attend tonight's bout. According to Inspector Pilker, Chief Inspector Jones had authorised it in the hope of showing the public that the police were willing and able to assist them in whatever way they could. It was an admirable effort, but one Inspector Lee doubted would succeed. By the end of tonight, the police would've arrested two of the most respected members of the Fancy. Inspector Lee scanned the faces of the crowd surrounding the Society members, but Miss Trent remained elusive. He concluded she must be giving a few final words of encouragement to Mr Snyder in the changing area.

From the corner of his eye, Inspector Lee caught sight of Dr Weeks approaching the judges' table. The Canadian had been selected to provide medical treatment to the boxers. Amusement briefly touched Inspector Lee's heart as he imagined Dr Weeks' reaction to a living patient. The thought of Inspector Conway being one of them swiftly reminded him of his failed plan, however. Feeling his amusement swept away by anger as a result, he resolved to confront Dr Weeks over his suspected part in the failure at the earliest opportunity. Fortunately, he didn't have long to wait.

After speaking with the judges for a few minutes, Dr Weeks made his way through the crowd toward the public conveniences. Inspector Lee immediately got to his feet and, making his own way around the ring, quickened his pace as Dr Weeks disappeared. Following him into the damp-smelling room a moment later, he momentarily paused upon seeing him at the urinal. When it became evident Dr Weeks hadn't paid his arrival any heed, Inspector Lee allowed the door to close with a thud.

Looking over his shoulder, Dr Weeks' face blanched the moment he saw Inspector Lee's face.

"You seem frightened." Inspector Lee walked toward him, prompting Dr Weeks to hurriedly tuck himself back in and fasten his trousers.

"I don't like fellas creepin' up on me when I'm takin' a piss," Dr Weeks rebuked.

"You haven't got anything I haven't seen before," Inspector Lee dryly replied as he further closed the distance between them. "I'm pleased I've caught you alone, though." He moved closer still. "We've got something very important to discuss."

"I ain't got a damn thing to say to ya." Dr Weeks moved back toward the wall.

"But you have." Inspector Lee followed and held the tip of his walking cane against Dr Weeks' stomach. "Inspector Woolfe believes I put a Bow Street Society envelope in Inspector Conway's house." His eyes cooled. "Why do you think that is?"

Dr Weeks pressed himself against the wall. "I don't know."

Inspector Lee pushed the tip of his cane into Dr Weeks' stomach, causing him to wince in discomfort. "Are you quite certain of that?"

Dr Weeks gripped the cane and tried to push against it. Inspector Lee proved stronger, however. Squinting and going red in the face as he nevertheless tried to apply as much pressure as possible, he growled, "*Damn* sure!"

Inspector Lee pushed hard against the cane.

"*Argh!*" Dr Weeks cried as pain shot through his stomach. "I swear to *God* I ain't said anythin' to him!"

Inspector Lee maintained his pressure upon the cane as he leaned closer. "Don't play games with me, Doctor. You shan't win."

"I ain't!"

Inspector Lee briefly applied some additional pressure to the cane before releasing it completely and stepping back. Dr Weeks immediately stumbled forward with a harsh grunt and firm grip of his stomach. Watching him as he stood, doubled over in pain, Inspector Lee said, "This is the only warning you'll get."

Dr Weeks looked up with terror in his eyes.

FORTY-SIX

"This is taking too long," Inspector Pilker remarked softly. Leaning with his hands upon the left-hand sill of the bay window, his nose almost touched the cold glass as he watched the corner of Church Road. Four Metropolitan Police constables in civilian attire sat in the pitch-black parlour behind him.

Adjacent to Nesbit Street, the house served their need for a discreet base for their surveillance. Its owners had been persuaded to vacate to a hotel for the night after Inspector Pilker had given his personal reassurance that their neighbours wouldn't see hide nor hair of them. Hence the darkness. He'd also been careful to send just one plain-clothed officer to keep watch outside the *Key & Lion*. His orders were to return to the house the moment Mr Sparrow left for Bethnal Green. Inspector Pilker and his men had been waiting for thirty minutes and counting. "Baines, go and see if there has been any movement."

"Yes, sir," a mature male voice replied from the darkness.

Listening to his quiet departure, Inspector Pilker watched his silhouette pass by the window a moment later.

* * *

At precisely the same time, Inspector Woolfe watched the *Nimble Crow* from the house directly opposite. From his vantage point in the first-floor bedroom, he could see much of the bar through the pub's left-hand window. With the sash window raised a couple of inches, he could also hear the conversations of anyone passing through the main door. Like Inspector Pilker, he also had four Metropolitan Police constables in civilian attire waiting with him.

Unlike his colleague, though, he'd taken advantage of the homeowner's generous hospitality by having her make some tea for him and his men. From what he could gather from his brief conversation with her, Miss Simms was a middle-aged spinster who had benefited from her late father's will to become financially independent. As a result, she lived alone but in comfort. Inspector Woolfe suspected their impromptu visit and request to use her guest bedroom had come as a welcome distraction on an otherwise lonely Christmas Eve.

Catching movement by the bar, he saw Mr Elliott emerge from the door and head down Cricketfield Road, in search of a cab. According to the written instructions from Chief Inspector Jones, it had been agreed to keep direct contact between the police and the Bow Street Society members to a minimum. Something Inspector Woolfe was more than happy to do in light of recent events. Taking a mouthful of tea and releasing a small cough, he settled down to wait for Mr Farley to depart for Bethnal Green.

* * *

Straddling a low bench in the middle of the changing room, Sergeant Caulfield struggled to block out the sound of the crowd as he wrapped Inspector Conway's hands. Although there was a solid door and short corridor between them and the main room, the rumble of voices was unmistakeable. It put the already apprehensive Sergeant Caulfield further on edge.

"What you thinking, lad?" Inspector Conway enquired in a calming tone.

"That I wish they'd be quiet." Sergeant Caulfield gave a feeble smile as he briefly met his eyes.

Similar to his colleagues, Sergeant Caulfield wore plain clothes consisting of dark-blue trousers, waistcoat, and tie. He'd rolled up the sleeves of his off-white shirt and tucked them tightly against the fold of his elbows to avoid any blood splatter soiling the material. Meanwhile, Inspector Conway wore the smooth-soled shoes, knee-length silk drawers, and dark-green jersey of a competitive boxer.

The door opened, and Chief Inspector Jones entered.

"I'll finish this off," Inspector Conway told Sergeant Caulfield. "You make sure the water's sorted."

"Yes, sir." Sergeant Caulfield stood and, stepping over the bench, hurried from the room.

"He's nervous," Inspector Conway explained once he'd gone.

"He's not the only one," Chief Inspector Jones mumbled as he took in Inspector Conway's bruised face.

"How's Sam?" Inspector Conway slipped on a tan leather glove.

Knowing the damage it could do to a man's face, Chief Inspector Jones averted his gaze and walked to the bench's far end. "He's fine, I think. Rebecca is with him." He looked at his friend and, upon seeing him trying to fasten the glove with one hand, straddled the bench and took over the task. "More importantly, how are you?"

"Ready to get in that ring."

Chief Inspector Jones turned anxious eyes upon him. "It's not too late to back out."

Inspector Conway gave a loose shake of his head. "Nah."

Chief Inspector Jones leaned forward as he urged, "No one would think any less of you."

"*I'd* think less of me."

"But look at the state you're in."

"Richard—"

"It's *suicide*, John!"

They fixed each other with concerned, unblinking eyes for several moments.

It was Chief Inspector Jones who broke the stalemate first. Briefly bowing his head, he said, "Look, I know your stubbornness and pride forbid you from throwing in the towel, but *neither* will mean anything if you're six feet under."

"It's good to hear you've got faith in me."

"I'm being serious, John."

"Me, too."

Chief Inspector Jones stood and walked away from the bench. "I can't force you to back out." He turned toward him. "But I want you to remember that I was against this from the start."

Inspector Conway tied off the lace of the first glove and slipped on the second. "Why did you agree to it, then?"

Chief Inspector Jones frowned deeply and, with a soft sigh, returned to the bench. "I couldn't see any other way forward." He pulled Inspector Conway's gloved hand into his lap and tied the laces.

As a heavy silence descended between them, Inspector Conway decided to change tact. "What does the Yard think of us working with the Society on this?"

"It knows that it's the Society assisting *us* on this," Chief Inspector Jones replied in a hard tone.

"What's the difference?"

"Dishonourable dismissal." Tying off the laces, Chief Inspector Jones allowed Inspector Conway to withdraw his hand. "I was obliged to make Assistant Commissioner Terrell aware of your part in this operation. He wasn't pleased to hear a serving officer will be seen participating in a boxing match but understood the need for such measures. The fact you will be fighting under the Queensberry Rules also went in your favour."

"Does he know about—?"

"No," Chief Inspector Jones firmly interrupted. "And nor will he." At Inspector Conway's questioning look, he admitted, "I burnt the file."

Worry entered Inspector Conway's eyes. "It's not like you to break the rules."

Chief Inspector Jones' expression softened. "Sometimes we have to take unorthodox steps to do what is right. A great man taught me that."

"We'll have to have a drink with him sometime."

Chief Inspector Jones softly chuckled as he stood and gave him a pat on the back. "Good luck, John."

FORTY-SEVEN

"Look lively, lads," Inspector Pilker ordered as the silhouettes of two men and a woman came into view from around the corner.

Moving away from the window when the trio entered the house, he immediately recognised Miss Hicks and Constables Baines and Smith upon their arrival in the parlour. With spades in hand, the remaining policemen gathered around Inspector Pilker as Constable Smith announced, "Mr Sparrow closed the pub and took Toby off to Bethnal Green in a cab."

Inspector Pilker looked to Miss Hicks. "Is that what they told you?"

"It is. I would of gone with 'em, only women ain't allowed by the ring. So…" She moved closer to him, "I thought I'd come with you lot." She put a hand on his shoulder and flashed him a smile. "The back door is on the latch."

Inspector Pilker shrugged off her hand and headed for the door. "Baines, escort Miss Hicks back to Bow Street."

"*Oi*, I done all the work," Miss Hicks scolded, going after him.

Inspector Pilker stopped and sardonically retorted, "You poured a few pints."

Miss Hicks pointed at him. "Don't take that tone with *me*, copper! I could of got hurt doin' what I done!" She cast a glare at the others. "You're only 'ere 'cause of what *I* overheard." She pushed past Inspector Pilker. "I'm goin' back to that pub and you can't stop me!"

Inspector Pilker grabbed her by the arms and dragged her back. "Baines!"

"Ge' off!" Miss Hicks yelled as she tried to struggle free to no avail.

"Handcuff her. Gag her. I don't care. Just get her away from here," Inspector Pilker ordered, shoving her toward Constable Baines who swiftly assumed a firm grip on her.

"Yes, sir." Constable Baines dragged her deeper into the parlour as Inspector Pilker and the others filed outside. "Come on, now, miss, don't make me put the derbies on you."

"Pilker you *swine*!" Miss Hicks yelled as she finally surrendered to the inevitable. "Weeks is goin' to hear about *this*!" *Noah, too,* she thought. "You'll wish you wasn't *born*!"

* * *

Mr Skinner swallowed his ale and licked his lips. The *Nimble Crow* was unusually quiet for Christmas Eve, a fact that hadn't gone unnoticed by its landlord. He'd watched with increasing confusion as, one by one, his customers had drained their glasses and hurried off over the course of the afternoon and early evening. Rather than enquire where the fire was, though, Mr Farley instead sold drinks at a reduced price to convince them to stay. Alas, few took advantage of the offer. Furthermore, those who did, soon joined their friends in departing soon after. Mr Farley wasn't pleased.

During Mr Elliott's visit earlier, Mr Skinner had made a point of discussing the Conway and Snyder fight within earshot of Mr Farley. Yet, despite this, the landlord had failed to seek answers from Mr Skinner once Mr Elliott had left. Instead, he'd loitered by the bar, in a state of flux, whilst occasionally casting uncertain glances at him.

Fearing the Society's plan was about to fall apart despite his efforts, and success of Mr Snyder's whisper campaign amongst the Fancy about the fight, Mr Skinner drained his glass. This act spurred something in Mr Farley though as, no sooner had Mr Skinner put the empty glass down on the table, did he see the landlord approach with an excitable look in his eyes.

"May I have a word in your ear, sir?" Mr Farley enquired in a hushed voice.

"Sure t'ing," Mr Skinner replied. "Pull up a pew."

Mr Farley placed a stool close to Mr Skinner's and sat. With one elbow upon the table's edge, he leaned into Mr Skinner's personal space and enquired in the same hushed voice, "Is it true? What I overheard your friend tell you earlier, about the set-to between Snyder and Conway; is it true?"

Mr Skinner smiled. "Ev'ry word of it."

Mrs Farley approached the table and picked up the empty glass.

Mr Farley's eyes glowed with excitement. "When? Could you get me in?"

Mrs Farley stilled at the eagerness in her husband's voice. Looking between them, she felt a fluttering sensation in her stomach as she realised Mr Skinner was attempting to lure her husband away from the pub. "Where are you going, dear?"

Mr Farley and Mr Skinner ignored her.

Mrs Farley put the glass down and sat beside her husband. Putting a tentative hand upon his arm, she meekly began, "It's Christmas Eve—"

Mr Farley shushed his wife and enquired from Mr Skinner, "Could you?"

Mr Skinner cast a wary glance at Mrs Farley. "Sure, I could."

Mr Farley's face lit up with excitement. "When is it happening?"

"In under an hour," Mr Skinner replied. "At the *Excelsior Hall* in Bethnal Green."

"But we have Midnight Mass—" Mrs Farley said, her eyes bright with panic.

"Forget Midnight Mass," Mr Farley dismissed. "This is more important."

"But *Ken*—!" Mrs Grosse cried, gripping his arm.

"Unhand me, woman," Mr Farley ordered, pulling himself free.

When he stood and went behind the bar, she swiftly followed with wide, desperate eyes. "*Please*, listen to me," she begged, but he instead rang the bell for last orders.

Glancing out the window as he made his own preparations to leave, Mr Skinner noticed the man with the goatee-beard watching him from his seat by the fire. Thinking it was his agitated mind playing tricks on him, Mr Skinner looked to Mr Farley and back again. The man with the goatee-beard continued to watch him.

"Drink up, gents!" Mr Farley cried, gathering up the empty glasses.

Mrs Grosse hurried along behind him, wringing her hands.

"What is *wrong* with you, Rosa?" Mr Farley demanded after a time.

Mrs Grosse cast a terrified glance at Mr Skinner. "You can't go with him, Ken."

"Goodnight, gents!" Mr Farley called as all but the man with the goatee-beard left.

"We'd best be going if we want to get good seats," Mr Skinner urged.

"Wait a minute, sir," Mr Farley said with a lift of his hand. "What do you mean, Rosa?"

Mrs Farley wrung her hands some more. "You can't trust him, Ken. He's a member of the Bow Street Society. They mean to put the blame for Mr Grosse's murder on you."

Mr Farley stilled, and Mr Skinner held his breath.

The man with the goatee-beard stood.

Feeling her panic intensify at her husband's lack of response, Mrs Grosse pressed, "Ken?"

"Be quiet, woman!" Mr Farley snapped.

Mrs Grosse stared at him, stunned, as he turned and walked away.

"Maybe I ought to go—" Mr Skinner began, taking a step back toward the door.

Mr Farley turned sharply. "You're not going anywhere, lad!" He looked to his wife, "Rosa, get upstairs."

Mrs Farley hesitated.

"Do as I say!" Mr Farley bellowed.

Mrs Farley immediately ran across the room and up the stairs, her hand pressed against her mouth to stifle the sob that threatened to escape.

"I'm sorry, sir, but we're closed," Mr Farley informed the man with the goatee who exchanged concerned glances with Mr Skinner. "We have some business to discuss."

The man with the goatee didn't move.

"Goodnight, sir," Mr Skinner urged, not wanting anyone to get caught in the crossfire.

Although reluctant to go against his orders to protect the Bow Streeter, the man with the goatee knew it wasn't a good idea to rile the disturbed landlord further with his continued presence. He left the pub and went to Miss Simms' house.

"Who are you?" Inspector Woolfe enquired when he was eventually admitted to Miss Simms' guest bedroom.

"Sergeant Donald Croft of the Mob Squad, sir," the man with the goatee replied as he produced his warrant card. "Acting under the orders of Inspector Conway."

Inspector Woolfe narrowed his eyes at the revelation. "What orders?"

"To protect Mr Callahan Skinner, sir," Sergeant Croft replied.

Inspector Woolfe glanced out of the window. "Why aren't you still in the pub?"

A grave expression formed on Sergeant Croft's face. "Mr Farley was about to close to go to the fight when his wife told him Mr Skinner was a member of the Bow Street Society. I tried to stay, but both Mr Farley and Mr Skinner insisted I go."

"Get to Bethnal Green and tell Chief Inspector Jones what's happened," Inspector Woolfe ordered.

"Yes, sir," Sergeant Croft replied. Upon seeing Inspector Woolfe heading for the door also, he enquired, "Where are you going?"

"I'm going to get into that pub," Inspector Woolfe replied and strode from the room.

* * *

Mr Sparrow soaked up the atmosphere in the *Excelsior Hall* as he waited with excited anticipation. A part of him was disappointed his pub had missed out on hosting the fight but given its significance, he appreciated why the grander venue had been chosen. Having recognised a few in the crowd, he'd stopped on his way to his seat to have a brief conversation with them. Now settled with Toby at his side, he switched between checking the time on his pocket watch and checking for any signs of life at the changing rooms' doors.

On the other side of the room, Miss Trent, Mr Maxwell, and Mr Verity listened to Mr Elliott as he recounted his conversation with Mr Skinner at the *Nimble Crow*. Coming to its end, Mr Elliott added, "There was no reason to suspect Mr Farley hadn't taken the bait."

"So, why isn't he here with Mr Skinner?" Miss Trent enquired, concerned.

"Maybe Mr Farley needed time to clear the pub," Mr Verity suggested in a northeast of England accent. "It's doing well compared to the *Key & Lion*."

"Pardon me, miss," a man in his mid-thirties said into Miss Trent's ear. Approximately five feet eight inches tall, he had unkempt, mousy-brown hair, hazel eyes, and a grubby complexion. His attire consisted of a brown overcoat, dark-grey trousers, off-white shirt, and tweed cap.

Recognising him as Sergeant Dwyer, Miss Trent assumed a nonchalant demeanour as she replied, "Yes?"

"I've been instructed to tell you that it's time," Dwyer said in a low voice.

Miss Trent felt her heart sink. She would've preferred to wait for the arrival of Mr Skinner and Mr Farley, but they were already running thirty minutes behind schedule. Any longer and they risked Mr Sparrow becoming impatient, suspicious, or both. With a sombre expression, she thanked Dwyer for the information and watched him return to his seat on Mr Sparrow's left. On Mr Sparrow's right, beside Toby, sat Chief Inspector Jones.

Mr Roger Harlow, a portly gentleman in his late forties with a charcoal-coloured moustache and black hair, climbed into the ring. Appointed by the judges as referee for this bout, he wore a long-sleeved, light-blue shirt beneath a black waistcoat with dark-grey trousers. Standing in the middle of the ring, he raised his arm above his head and waited for the noise to ease. Once satisfied he would be heard, he filled his lungs and projected his voice across the space. "Gentlemen, may I have your attention, *please*?!"

The crowd's focus turned toward the ring, prompting the last few conversations to fade away.

"Welcome to this special boxing event," Mr Harlow continued, his voice effortlessly filling the room. "I'm Mr Roger Harlow, your referee for tonight, and these are your judges: Messieurs Weston, Boxshall, and Pendleton." A brief wave from Mr Pendleton garnered no reaction from the crowd. "And now it's time to meet the fighters. In the blue corner, weighing in at a hair's breadth above eleven stone, I give you John 'The Bulldog' Conway!"

A cacophony of applause, cheering, insults, and booing erupted from the crowd as the door to the changing room opened, and Inspector Conway emerged. Walking down the aisle to the ring, he was careful to give its edges a wide berth due to several spectators attempting to grab him as he passed. Sergeant Caulfield followed closely behind with a bucket of water and sponge in one hand and a bottle of water in the other. Both men's expressions were serious as they climbed the steps and entered the ring, but Sergeant Caulfield appeared to be the tenser of the two.

"In the red corner, weighing in at just under ten stone," Mr Harlow continued. "I give you Sam 'The Whitechapel Ox' Snyder!"

Raucous applause exploded from the crowd as several leapt to their feet.

Meanwhile, Mr Maxwell peered over the heads of those in front as the door to the other changing room opened, and Mr Snyder emerged. Mr Elliott, who regarded boxing as nothing more than an excuse for violence, watched with cold stoicism as Mr Snyder walked down the aisle, shaking the hands of those he passed. Dr Colbert, who carried the bucket of water, sponge, and bottle of water, followed at a short distance to give his fellow Bow Streeter the space to enjoy his warm reception. Throughout, Miss Trent had tried to concentrate on each fighter's entrance, but her thoughts inevitably returned to Mr Skinner and what could've happened.

"Who do you think will win, sir?" Sergeant Gutman enquired from Inspector Lee.

"Snyder, if he's ruthless." Inspector Lee exhaled the smoke from his cigarette.

As Mr Snyder and Dr Colbert climbed the stairs and entered the ring, Dr Weeks paced at its side. Wild imaginings of what could happen, both to Inspector Conway and himself, vied for space in his mind, causing his stomach to do somersaults. Retrieving the hip flask from his pocket, he cast a nervous glance at the judges before taking a hefty swig of whiskey.

"Seconds, leave the ring," Mr Harlow instructed Sergeant Caulfield and Dr Colbert. To Mr Snyder and Inspector Conway, he invited, "Join me over here, please, gents."

Shielding his mouth with his hand, Chief Inspector Jones softly enquired from Sergeant Dwyer, "Has there been any word?"

"None," Dwyer replied.

Chief Inspector Jones frowned. This didn't bode well for Mr Skinner *or* their joint operation.

"You know the rules," Mr Harlow said. "I want a good, clean fight. Touch gloves."

Snyder and Conway bumped gloves.

Mr Harlow lifted and threw down his arm in time with the ding of the bell.

The remainder of the crowd leapt to its feet in raucous cheering and jeering.

The fight had begun.

FORTY-EIGHT

"Sit." Mr Farley pulled a stool out from under the table and set it down by the fire.

Mr Skinner gave him a wide berth as he crossed the room and sat.

"It's a shame." Mr Farley set down another stool opposite Mr Skinner's and sat. "I would've enjoyed the rematch between Snyder and Conway."

"There's still time."

"Not now." Mr Farley's features slackened. "Not anymore."

Mr Skinner studied Mr Farley closely. His anger had subsided, but Mr Skinner knew it could return at the flip of a coin. "Because of what your wife said?"

"Because of who you are," Mr Farley countered with a hard edge to his tone.

"Me and the Society weren't trying to trap you."

"But you *were* trying to coax me away from the pub?"

Mr Skinner considered his response. On balance, he thought honesty held the least likelihood of incurring Mr Farley's wrath. "Yes."

"Why?"

"To search it."

Mr Farley became very still. If the revelation had alarmed him, it wasn't showing on his face. Instead, he maintained an emotionless expression as he enquired, "What for?"

"I t'ink you know."

Mr Farley's mouth formed a hard line before he averted his gaze and stood. Walking over to the fireplace, he rested a hand upon its mantel shelf as he looked at the flames within its hearth. "You wouldn't have found anything."

Mr Skinner had his doubts. "We're searching the *Key & Lion*, too."

Mr Farley's gaze snapped back to the Bow Streeter.

* * *

As promised, the back door into the *Key & Lion* opened
when Inspector Pilker pushed it. Slipping inside, he poked
his head into the parlour and crept down the hall to the bar.
Both rooms were unoccupied and in complete darkness.
Doing a thorough sweep of the ground floor to be certain
they were empty, though, he finally returned to his men
waiting in the yard.

"The door to the cellar is in the bar at the end of the
hall," he informed them. "There's no one home, but that
doesn't give us license to dawdle."

"Yes, sir," Constable Smith assented.

"On your way," Inspector Pilker ordered, stepping
aside to allow them through.

Once they were inside, he released the latch and
closed the door. *Just in case Miss Hicks finds her way here
after all*, he thought.

* * *

Mr Snyder staggered backward following successive
punches to his face and jaw. With his head swimming
from the pain of a broken nose, he struggled to see past the
swelling in his left eye socket. The roar of the crowd also
became muffled. Side-stepping to the left and right whilst
shielding his face behind his gloved fists, he fought to
regain his focus as Inspector Conway moved around him.

Catching sudden movement out the corner of his eye,
Mr Snyder ducked his head and lifted his fists to block
Inspector Conway's jab. Swinging out afterward, Mr
Snyder aimed for the side of Inspector Conway's head but
only hit air as the policeman weaved out of harm's way.
Grunting when Inspector Conway drove his fist into his
ribs, Mr Snyder took a sharp step back whilst trying to
catch his breath.

"Why are you holding back?" Inspector Conway
growled as he stalked him around the ring.

"Not as young… as I was," Mr Snyder replied, panting hard.

"Hit him!" someone yelled from the crowd.

"Ge' 'im in the ivories!" another added.

Inspector Conway attempted to punch the right then left sides of Mr Snyder's head. Sending both off course with deftly timed blocks with his gloves, Mr Snyder swung for Inspector Conway's jaw. Finding his target this time, he followed it up with a punch to the opposite side of Inspector Conway's chest.

A cheer erupted from the crowd as Inspector Conway staggered sideways from the force of the blow. Mr Snyder went after him but waited as he regained his footing. With agony etched upon his face, Inspector Conway visibly struggled to take a deep breath. Worried that one of Inspector Conway's broken ribs may have punctured his lung, Mr Snyder was relieved to hear the ding of the bell, signalling the end of the round.

"John?" Mr Snyder enquired, deeply concerned.

"I'm okay," Inspector Conway wheezed, returning to his corner.

Waiting for him was an anxious Dr Weeks. "What is it? Yer ribs?"

Inspector Conway gave a jerky nod and dropped onto his stool with a grunt. Mr Snyder watched from across the ring as Dr Weeks applied pressure to various parts of Conway's chest. When one caused him to wince sharply, Mr Snyder flinched at the same time.

"Can ya breathe?" Dr Weeks enquired as he fixed Inspector Conway with worried eyes.

"Yeah," Inspector Conway replied, releasing a cough the moment he tried to take a deep breath.

"You don't look good, sir," Sergeant Caulfield interjected.

"I ain't losing after one round," Inspector Conway growled and dragged himself to his feet.

* * *

Constable Smith and his colleagues grunted and wheezed as they rolled empty barrels aside and stacked crates at the cellar's edge to clear the floor. Retrieving their spades from against the wall, they looked to Inspector Pilker for further instruction.

From his raised position on the stairs, he had a largely unobscured view of the cellar. Whilst most of the spots he saw were old bloodstains, possibly from bareknuckle matches, there was one in the far corner that caught his eye. Much larger than the others in length and width, it was also oblong in shape. *The outline of a grave?* Pointing to it, he ordered, "Start over there first."

* * *

"Where's Duncan?" Mr Farley enquired as his mind reeled from the revelation.

"At the fight."

With a glazed look, Mr Farley retreated from the fireplace and went behind the bar. Keeping a close eye on his every move, and noting where his hands were, Mr Skinner was uncertain whether the club was the only weapon Mr Farley owned. Although confident he could defend himself against it, he knew his chances of survival were much smaller if Mr Farley produced a gun. Shifting his weight to the stool's edge to easily duck under the table if needed, he kept his voice to an even tone. "Do you want to tell me what happened?"

Mr Farley released a brief, lacklustre laugh. "I know I've been hit around the head a few times, but I'm not daft yet." He poured a large measure of whiskey and drank half in one swallow.

Meanwhile, Inspector Woolfe had managed the difficult task of accessing the pub's rear yard. After spending several minutes trying to locate the entrance to the service alleyway in the near pitch blackness, he'd struggled to identify the pub's gate for the same reason. When he'd eventually found that, he was annoyed to discover it was locked from the inside. As a result, he'd been obliged to make an unflattering climb over the wall; a reminder that he wasn't getting any younger.

Resting against the damp brickwork as he caught his breath, he rubbed his heavily scraped palms over his fur coat to cool the burning. At the same time, he pondered how to get inside the pub without alerting its occupants. Obviously, knocking on the back door was out of the question. So, too, was climbing through a window, as none on the ground floor were wide enough to accommodate his frame.

The one in the central panel of the back door could be quietly broken if he muffled the sound with his fur coat, however. Inspector Woolfe stepped away from the wall and, picking up a large stone as he crossed the yard, peered through the glass.

Mr Farley had left the key in the lock.

Giving a broad, yellow, tooth-filled smile, Inspector Woolfe covered the window with his coat and struck the glass with the stone until it cracked. Pushing it through with his fur-covered fist, he reached inside and turned the key with a quiet click.

* * *

"Sir, I think I've found something!" Constable Smith declared as the tip of his spade struck something in the dirt.

Inspector Pilker and the others rushed over and gathered around the hole.

Constable Smith continued to dig with the spade but was soon obliged to switch to his hands. Kneeling in the hole, he clawed away at the dirt until a glimpse of dark-purple material caused him to halt. Glancing up at his colleagues' tense expressions, he continued his careful excavation with shaking hands. Within moments, the skeletal remains of a human being were exposed.

Constable Smith clambered to his feet at the sight. Fighting to hold down the contents of his stomach, he mumbled, "I... I think I've found him, sir."

Inspector Pilker gripped Constable Smith's shoulder and stared down at the remains with wide-eyed delight. "I think so, too, Constable." He smiled. "I think so, too."

FORTY-NINE

A room the size of a matchbox lay beyond the door from the yard. Hooks on the wall to Inspector Woolfe's right held a man's winter coat and scarf. A pair of sturdy-looking black leather boots stood beneath. On the opposite side of the space, directly in front of him, was a step leading to a solid wooden door. The muffled sound of a lone voice drifted through it, causing Inspector Woolfe to stop and listen. Although he recognised it as male, its words were indistinguishable. The sound also was coming from afar. He crept onto the step and eased the door ajar.

Bright, electrical lamplight assaulted his vision the instant he peered through it. Jerking his head back with a wince, he blinked several times before squinting as he cautiously peered through the gap once more. After allowing his eyes to adjust, he saw the opulent, yet deserted interior of the pub's main bar area. The underside of a flight of stairs stood across from his hiding place. Beyond this lay the bar itself with a long, barrel-lined counter running down its centre.

"Remember who you're talking to," Mr Skinner said. "I'm not a copper."

Inspector Woolfe opened the door a fraction wider and saw Mr Skinner sitting by the fire.

Mr Farley topped up his glass and returned to his stool. "But you're from the Bow Street Society. I've read in the newspaper how they've worked with the police."

Inspector Woolfe slowly opened the door wide and crept out.

Catching a glimpse of Inspector Woolfe as he hid behind the stairs, Mr Skinner was both surprised and reassured by the policeman's presence. The knowledge he had some support also bolstered his resolve to coax the truth from Mr Farley. "The coppers despise the ground we walk on. They're not going to believe anyt'ing I say."

Mr Farley drank some whiskey as he contemplated how much he could trust him.

"Unlike Mr Sparrow," Mr Skinner added.

"Duncan isn't a peach," Mr Farley said resolutely.

"A man will sacrifice his own mother if it saves him from the gallows," Mr Skinner pointed out. "And that's where Mr Sparrow will be if the coppers find what we t'ink they will in the *Key & Lion's* cellar."

Mr Farley drained his glass and set it down with a thud. "It was an accident." He fixed Mr Skinner with a rigid gaze. "He hit his head. It wasn't meant to happen."

Mr Skinner leaned forward and lowered his voice. "Deon Erskine... or Christian Grosse?"

A pained expression formed upon Mr Farley's face. "Both." He turned his head toward the fire. "We were drinking after hours at the *Key & Lion*; me, Duncan, Deon, and Ian. The conversation got onto boxing, as it often did, and me and Deon had fisticuffs. I bested him, the drunken bastard, and that should've been the end of it." He bowed his head as regret etched itself upon his face. "But Deon wouldn't let it be." He glanced up the stairs behind him. "He said some vile things about Rosa." His voice became quiet. "I'm a boxer; I can control my anger, but, that night, the drink dulled my restraint, and I lost my temper." He turned his head back toward the table but kept it bowed. "I hit him. He fell and... he must've hit his head on the floor because he wouldn't get up."

"Why did you bury him under the cellar?" Mr Skinner enquired.

Mr Farley's gaze snapped back to him. "I panicked— we all did." His eyes darted in all directions, careful to avoid Mr Skinner, as, in a voice tinged with desperation, he continued, "I said we ought to bury him. Duncan said people would miss him. I said we could tell them he'd gone to America." He rested his hand upon the table and leaned toward Mr Skinner, "Bareknuckle was kept up over there for a time." He briefly averted his gaze as he muttered, "I forgot he was bloody afraid of the water."

"You said Mr Grosse's death wasn't meant to happen either," Mr Skinner said. "Why was that?"

Mr Farley's face turned ashen as he plucked his glass from the table and went back behind the bar. As he poured himself a double whiskey, he replied in a voice laced with regret, "People believed our story about Erskine. It didn't make sense, but people believed it." He gripped the glass tightly against his stomach and stared into its depths. "Then Christian decided he wanted to put him in his book." He gave a small shake of his head. "He'd been working on it for years." He lifted the glass to his lips. "he'll never finish it now."

"Did Mr Grosse find out what happened to Mr Erskine?" Mr Skinner enquired.

Mr Farley shook his head and took a mouthful of whiskey. "But he was getting close." He glanced down the bar. "He was standing just there when he asked me about him. It felt like someone had walked over my grave." He took another mouthful of whiskey. "I told him the story, about Erskine going to America, and he seemed to accept it. When I told Duncan what had happened, though, he said Christian had been asking about Erskine at the *Key & Lion*, too. He said Christian mentioned he had an address in London for Erskine, and Duncan saw a telegram from America in Christian's notebook. It was just a matter of time before Christian stumbled upon the truth."

An intense sorrow filled Mr Farley's face and eyes. "None of us wanted to do him in." His voice faltered as it became strained with emotion. "He was a good man… and a loyal friend." His eyes became damp. "But we had no choice."

Deciding he'd heard enough, Inspector Woolfe straightened to his full height with the intention of making them aware of his presence. Hearing a floorboard creak behind him, though, he turned to see a fist hurtling toward his face. With no time to react, he felt its impact against his nose, followed by an explosion of pain. Forced off balance at the same time, he stumbled back and fell against the underside of the stairs. His head struck the wood, and he saw the floor hurtling toward him. Next, oblivion.

Mr Rake retreated as Inspector Woolfe fell at his feet. "Mr Farley!"

Feeling concerned for both himself and the policeman, Mr Skinner hesitated before following Mr Farley to the scene.

"He was hiding under the stairs," Mr Rake explained once they'd joined him.

Mr Farley glared at the boxer. "How long have you been here?"

"Not long, sir," Mr Rake replied, taken aback. "I'd just come up from the cellar."

Remembering that he'd asked the boxer to move some crates down there, Mr Farley conceded he was probably telling the truth. He returned his attention to Inspector Woolfe's prone form. "Who is he?"

"I don't know, sir," Mr Rake replied.

Mr Farley looked to Mr Skinner with hard, expectant eyes.

Mr Skinner considered denying all knowledge of Inspector Woolfe's identity and presence. Yet, he swiftly dismissed the idea as pointless since a search of Inspector Woolfe's coat would reveal his warrant card. "He's Detective Inspector Caleb Woolfe of the Metropolitan Police."

Mr Farley's hands clenched at his sides. "You *knew* he was there, didn't you? That line about the police not believing anything you say was a lie!"

Mr Farley advanced upon Mr Skinner, prompting the latter to pull his Webley Mark 1 revolver from its concealed shoulder holster. Halting the moment he saw it, Mr Farley snarled, "Only a *coward* would hide behind a gun."

Keeping the revolver aimed firmly at Mr Farley's gut, Mr Skinner said, "Joe, there are some coppers in the house opposite."

Mr Rake cast an anxious glance between the men.

"*Go*," Mr Skinner ordered.

Mr Rake exploded into a run and rushed out the back door.

"You'll never make it in the ring," Mr Farley said, taking a step closer to Mr Skinner.

"That's far enough," Mr Skinner warned, aiming the revolver a little higher.

"Cripples can't be boxers." Mr Farley moved closer still.

Mr Skinner's features contorted into a fierce glare. "What did you call me?"

"You heard!" Mr Farley cried as he lunged for the revolver.

Mr Rake stopped in the road as a shot suddenly rang out.

FIFTY

Feeling as if a large pebble had struck him above the elbow of his natural arm, Mr Skinner yanked the revolver from Mr Farley and swung at his head with his iron hand. The prosthetic struck the landlord's temple, knocking him unconscious and sending him to the floor. It was only when he stood over him that Mr Skinner felt an intense burning sensation spread throughout his limb. A glance at the growing patch of blood on his sleeve confirmed his fear—he'd been shot.

"*Ken!*" Mrs Farley shrieked from the stairs before rushing to her husband's side. "What did you do to him?!"

"Not'ing worse than what he was going to do to me." Mr Skinner pressed the bent fingers of his iron hand against his wound, but the blood continued to flow.

A groan sounded from Inspector Woolfe.

"You deserved it!" Mrs Farley cried as tears poured down her face.

"Your husband's a murderer," Mr Skinner told her.

Mrs Farley vehemently shook her head. "No. *No*, I *don't* believe it!"

Inspector Woolfe slowly rolled onto his side and tentatively touched his face. In a heavy voice, he growled, "The bastard's broken my nose."

Mr Skinner leaned against the bannisters as the pain in his arm intensified.

Suddenly, the back door flew open, and Mr Rake ran inside, followed by the constables from Miss Simms' house.

"What kept you, lads?" Mr Skinner enquired as his face turned clammy and pale.

"You're hurt," Mr Rake observed with deep concern.

"Mr Farley set off my revolver," Mr Skinner explained. "I need to stem the bleeding, but my fake hand's bent. Can you get my handkerchief from my breast pocket and tie it around my arm, please?"

Mr Rake immediately did as he was asked.

Meanwhile, the constables helped Inspector Woolfe to his feet.

"Start searching," Inspector Woolfe ordered once he sat on a stool. "That life preserver's here somewhere."

"You're wasting your time," Mrs Farley warned.

Inspector Woolfe narrowed his eyes. "Hewer!"

"Yes, sir?" Constable Hewer replied from across the room.

"Escort Mrs Farley to the Maria, then come back for her husband," Inspector Woolfe ordered.

"Yes, sir." Constable Hewer took her gently by the arm. "Come with me, please, ma'am."

"Ken's solicitor will ensure we're freed by the morning," Mrs Farley informed Inspector Woolfe as she went with the constable.

"Must be love," Inspector Woolfe muttered.

As the remaining constables searched the bar area and gymnasium, along with the Farley's private rooms, Mr Rake headed for the stairs.

"Where are you going?" Inspector Woolfe challenged.

"To get bandages for your nose and his arm." Mr Rake pointed over his shoulder at the changing room door.

Inspector Woolfe grunted. "Go on but come straight back. You're under arrest."

"What for?" Mr Rake demanded, taken aback.

Inspector Woolfe indicated his broken nose.

"I didn't know you was a copper," Mr Rake insisted.

"It doesn't matter," Inspector Woolfe said. "It's still assault."

"He fetched help when he didn't have to," Mr Skinner pointed out. "Couldn't you turn a blind eye just this once?"

Mr Rake looked at Inspector Woolfe with hopeful eyes. "Please, sir. I can't go to prison. What'll happen to my old mum? I'm all she's got."

Inspector Woolfe tried to stay angry with Mr Rake but couldn't manage it. "Fine, but *just* this once."

Mr Rake smile broadly. "Thank you, sir."

Inspector Woolfe gave another grunt as he thought, *Maybe I'm going soft in my old age.* Seeing Constable Hewer enter via the back door, he lifted Mr Farley from the floor and held him upright. "Make yourself useful before you get those bandages," he told Mr Rake. "Help Constable Hewer carry this one to the Maria."

"Yes, sir!" Mr Rake exclaimed, eagerly putting Mr Farley's arm around his neck.

* * *

The noise of the crowd rang in Mr Snyder's ears as his head spun from Inspector Conway's latest punch. Swaying as well, he struggled to keep his hands up when Inspector Conway came close for another onslaught of rapid punches. Somehow managing to block most of them, Mr Snyder swung out wildly with his fists. Still disoriented, though, he stumbled whilst striking air as Inspector Conway sluggishly weaved out of harm's way.

Meanwhile, the freezing night air numbed Miss Trent's cheeks and turned the tip of Chief Inspector Jones nose pink as they emerged from the *Excelsior Hall*. Having been induced to abandon their respective positions by the arrival of Constable Smith and Sergeant Croft, they now listened as they recounted the latest happenings at the *Key & Lion* and *Nimble Crow*.

"Inspector Pilker is certain they're human bones?" Chief Inspector Jones enquired from Constable Smith.

"A doctor will have to confirm it but yes, sir," Constable Smith replied.

"Do you know if Mr Skinner found the murder weapon?" Miss Trent enquired from Sergeant Croft who looked to Chief Inspector Jones for guidance.

"Please, answer her question," Chief Inspector Jones authorised.

"I don't think so, miss," Sergeant Croft replied.

"Inspector Woolfe is a competent officer. He'll ensure Mr Skinner's safety," Chief Inspector Jones reassured

Miss Trent. "In the meantime, Mr Sparrow must be arrested in light of your discovery, Smith."

"Now, sir?" Constable Smith enquired.

"Yes, now," Chief Inspector Jones firmly replied.

As Chief Inspector Jones, Miss Trent, Constable Smith, and Sergeant Croft went inside, they heard a collective yell erupt from the crowd. They stayed at the back of the room and watched as Mr Snyder delivered blows to Inspector Conway's stomach and head. Winded and driven sideways as a result, Inspector Conway landed on the ropes before falling to the canvas. With most spectators on their feet, including Mr Sparrow and Toby, the crowd broke out into raucous boos, jeers, and demands for Inspector Conway to get up.

"John, can ya hear me?" Dr Weeks enquired from outside the ring.

Inspector Conway fought to get a lungful of air as he sat up on one elbow.

"It ain't worth it!" Dr Weeks insisted. "Ya gotta toss in the towel!"

Inspector Conway gave a jerky shake of his head.

Seeing how rapt Mr Sparrow and Toby were by the drama unfolding in the ring, Chief Inspector Jones tapped Constable Smith on the arm and pointed to their prey. The constable made his way down the aisle and along the row to Sergeant Dwyer. After a brief word in his fellow officer's ear, Constable Smith grabbed Toby by the arm and dragged him from his seat.

"Ge' off!" Toby yelled.

Angered by the rough manhandling of his employee, Mr Sparrow attempted to snatch Constable Smith by the scruff of his shirt. The young constable proved too wily for him, however. With a loud curse, Mr Sparrow went to go after him, only to feel a hand upon his shoulder. Close to his ear, he heard Dwyer say, "Mr Duncan Sparrow, I'm arresting you on suspicion of the manslaughter of Mr Deon Erskine and the murder of Mr Christian Grosse. I'm also arresting you on suspicion of conspiring to murder Mr

Christian Grosse. I must caution you that anything you say may be used as evidence against you in court." Dwyer forced Mr Sparrow back into his seat and handcuffed the landlord's wrist to his own.

Seeing the handcuffs between Sergeant Dwyer and Mr Sparrow's wrists, Mr Snyder called to Inspector Conway from his corner. "Sparrow's been arrested!"

"Did ya hear that?" Dr Weeks enquired, but Inspector Conway was already using the ropes to pull himself to his feet. "*John*, don't be a damn fool!"

Yet, Inspector Conway either didn't hear or chose to ignore him, for a moment later he was staggering back to the centre of the ring. In response, Mr Snyder raised his gloved fists and side-stepped left and right until Inspector Conway reached him. At which point he lowered his guard and became immobile, thereby allowing Inspector Conway to land two consecutive punches on his jaw and head. Allowing his body to go with the force, he fell onto his back upon the canvas.

More booing and jeers erupted from the crowd.

Anxious that he could be seriously hurt, Miss Trent stared at Mr Snyder. Mr Maxwell, Mr Verity, and Mr Elliott did the same. A second later, the ding of the bell signalled the end of the round, prompting Inspector Conway to stagger back to his corner. Dr Weeks and Dr Colbert immediately clambered into the ring. As the latter dragged Mr Snyder back to his corner, the former knelt before Inspector Conway.

"John?" Dr Weeks put his face close to Conway's.

Inspector Conway's breaths were now short, high-pitched wheezes.

Meanwhile, Dr Colbert poured water over Mr Snyder's head, rousing him.

"Time!" Mr Harlow called.

Inspector Conway gripped the ropes, ready to drag himself back to his feet.

Dr Weeks put his hands on his arms, holding him down. "I can't let ya."

Inspector Conway stared at him with a mixture of anger and surprise.

"Ya go back out there, ya ain't comin' back," Dr Weeks warned.

Mr Snyder stood with Dr Colbert's assistance and returned to the centre of the ring.

"The victory ain't worth yer life," Dr Weeks said.

Inspector Conway tried to take a deep breath but couldn't. Coughing violently instead, he knew it was over. He released the ropes and fell forward against Dr Weeks. As the surgeon supported him, Mr Harlow counted down the last few seconds Inspector Conway had to return to the centre of the ring. When he inevitably didn't, Mr Harlow gripped Mr Snyder's wrist and declared him the victory— much to the delight of the crowd.

* * *

Over an hour had passed, and Inspector Woolfe and his constables were nearing the end of their search. Having exhausted the obvious places first, they'd next looked in the obscure ones. Namely, inside the chimney breasts, on top of the rafters, and under the floorboards. When none yielded the strange-looking club, Inspector Woolfe begrudgingly wondered if Mrs Farley had been right. Standing by the pub's front doors, he ate a cough lozenge and ran his gaze over the interior. There were no hidden doors, no loose bricks, no tiles without mortar, nothing. Contemplating having a brandy to ease the pain in his face, he looked to the bar.

The bar... he pondered. Its intricately carved panels were like nothing he'd ever seen. *Probably custom made*, he thought. As he went over his limited knowledge of carpentry, he realised the panels' carver couldn't have completed the work in situ due to the awkwardness of the angle. Therefore, they must've been created in the carpenter's workshop and brought to the pub, which meant they were just nailed to a frame. *With a cavity inside,* Inspector Woolfe thought. "Hewer, search the bar."

"Pardon, sir?" Constable Hewer enquired, confused.

"Do it," Inspector Woolfe ordered. When the constable moved to go behind the bar, though, he pointed to the panels. "Check what's *inside*, constable."

Constable Hewer hurried back out and, crouching in front of the panels, tried to move each one in turn. When he poked his fingertips under the frame of the third, it popped out into his hands, and a long object wrapped in a hessian sack toppled out from the cavity behind. Inspector Woolfe plucked the sack from the floor and, with Mr Rake, Mr Skinner, Constable Hewer, and the other constables following, carried it to the bar. He turned the sack upside down, and a wooden cane with a large ball of lead tied to its end dropped onto the bar with a loud thud. A dark red stained covered the ball.

Inspector Woolfe gave a broad, yellow, tooth-filled smile. "Well done, lad." He pulled Constable Hewer against him in a sideways embrace. "You've found it!"

EPILOGUE

Early January 1897

BRUTAL BOXERS
DENY MURDER

Mr Duncan Sparrow, publican of the *Key & Lion*, and Mr Kenrick Farley, publican of the *Nimble Crow* and proprietor of the *Lower Clapton Boxing Club*, today entered 'not guilty' pleas at their hearing in the Central Criminal Court at the Old Bailey. Both men are accused of the manslaughter of Mr Deon Erskine, a boxer, five years ago, and the murder of Mr Christian Grosse, a private enquiry agent, before Christmas.

They were sensationally apprehended during a joint operation between the Metropolitan Police and the Bow Street Society. Detective Chief Inspector Richard Jones, who led the operation, and the Society's clerk, Miss Rebecca Trent, have declined to comment.

Mr Sparrow and Mr Farley were remanded in custody following the hearing. Their

trial is scheduled to begin in
March.

"Relations with the police are going to be even more
strained after this," Miss Trent remarked, lowering the
Gaslight Gazette. Sitting by the Snyder's fire, she had a
stomach full of shepard's pie, courtesy of Louise, Sam's
wife. She and Sam occupied the armchairs opposite Miss
Trent's, whilst the five Snyder daughters were talking
loudly amongst themselves in the adjacent bedroom.

Aged forty-six, Mrs Snyder was five feet tall with a
stout build and broad upper arms which hinted at her role
as the primary cook, 'maid,' and laundress in the family.
Her plaited, pale-yellow hair rested against her shoulder,
whilst her mottled cheeks boasted a natural, rosy glow.
She wore a thick, woollen dark-red shawl over a light-red,
long-sleeved cotton dress. The apron she habitually wore
was draped over one of the mismatched chairs tucked
beneath the wonky, square table in the middle of the room.

Despite the passage of two weeks since the boxing
match, Mr Snyder's face remained heavily bruised. He
also winced each time he moved on account of his bruised
chest and sides. Unsurprisingly, he'd only moved from his
armchair to his bed and vice versa, during this period. In a
voice muffled by a cut lip, he said, "It can't be helped,
lass."

Miss Trent hummed, knowing he was probably right.

"How's Mr Skinner now?" Mr Snyder enquired.

"Better," Miss Trent replied. "He's avoided an
infection in the wound."

"The doctor getting the bullet out in one piece was
probably what done it," Mr Snyder mused aloud. "Is Miss
Hicks back at the railway bar?"

Although annoyed by the mere mention of Polly's
name, Miss Trent managed to keep her expression
emotionless. "I think so. Toby's working there, too. As a
pot boy."

"Poor lad." Mr Snyder's tone turned sombre. "Wonder what'll happen to him if Mr Sparrow goes to the gallows."

"He'll be fine." Miss Trent gave a reassuring smile. "The Society will make sure of it."

"Enough about grisly murders, pot boys, and cantankerous policemen." Louise took the *Gaslight Gazette* from Miss Trent and set it aside. "How was your aunt when you visited at Christmas?"

Miss Trent was initially grateful to Louise for the distraction from her worries about the Society. Yet, when she enquired after her Aunt Dorothea, Miss Trent felt a weight form in the pit of her stomach. She offered a weak smile that failed to reach her eyes. "She's well."

"And the rest," Louise coaxed.

Miss Trent's smile warmed. She should've known she couldn't hide anything from the Snyders. "She *was* well and pleased to see me." Her smile faded, and she momentarily cast her gaze downward. "Relieved, too." A melancholy entered her expression and voice as she continued, "We spoke at great length about my parents. About…" She paused to take in a shallow, shuddering breath, "what happened. She's agreed to support my petition to have my father moved to consecrated ground."

"I still can't believe it," Mr Snyder said.

"I thought my aunt might've told you, given that you're one of her oldest friends," Miss Trent admitted. "But," she frowned, "the shame was too much for her to bear, I suppose."

"Still, things are out in the open now." Louise patted Miss Trent's hand. "Where they ought to be."

Miss Trent offered a feeble smile as her gaze returned to Chief Inspector Jones' name in the *Gaslight Gazette*. Thinking about how complicated things had become between the Society and police, she felt genuine fear on behalf of her friend. What had begun as a noble endeavour—namely, the creation of the Society—could easily ruin his reputation, his professional career—his entire life, even. Especially now that the press perceived the Society as equal to the police, if not superior. *No*, she thought. *That is one truth that shouldn't be brought out into the open.*

* * *

Dr Weeks clenched his jaw and grunted as he pulled on the bandages as hard as he could. Pinning them with his knee, he took the safety pin from between his teeth and reached to secure them. Inspector Conway moved at the last moment, though, causing both the bandages and Dr Weeks' knee to slip. He also dropped the safety pin in the process. "Damn it, John, ya gotta hold *still*!"

"You try having a bloke sit on your back when you've got broken ribs," Inspector Conway retorted. Sitting on a chair in his kitchen, he bent forward with his folded arms resting upon his lap. His heavily bruised torso was unclothed to enable Dr Weeks to change the bandages binding his ribs, or that had been his intention. The additional weight of the Canadian's knee sent bolts of pain through Inspector Conway's chest each time he breathed in.

Dr Weeks crouched and retrieved the pin from where it had landed under the table.

"I'd rather be straddlin' Polly's back," Dr Weeks remarked as he stood.

Feeling a pang of guilt at the mention of that name, Inspector Conway bowed his head.

Having failed to notice the change in his friend's demeanour, Dr Weeks put the pin back between his teeth and gripped the bandages. "Don't *move* this time, d'ya hear?"

Inspector Conway released a soft grunt of acknowledgement, grateful for the change in subject.

He'd been bored out of his mind over these past two weeks. Chief Inspector Jones had forbidden him from returning to work despite Inspector Conway's insistence that he was fine. Even Christmas with his mum and brother had done little to lift Inspector Conway's spirits. A couple more days of inactivity, that's all he had to endure. After which he could go back to work with Chief Inspector Jones' blessing. He'd had no choice but to agree to his senior officer's terms, as it was either that or risk being put back in front of the disciplinary board for insubordination.

Pulling the bandages tight, Dr Weeks used the safety pin to secure them. "Yer done," he announced through a sigh of relief and passed Inspector Conway his shirt.

"*Jesus*, Weeks, could you get them any tighter?" Inspector Conway winced as he slipped his arm into his shirt's sleeve. "I can barely bloody breathe."

"Yer lucky ya didn't puncture a lung," Dr Weeks scolded.

Knocking sounded from the hallway.

"Are ya expectin' anyone?" Dr Weeks enquired.

Inspector Conway shook his head.

Dr Weeks left the kitchen and, striding to the front door, muttered under his breath, "Probably some Christians wantin' donations for the baby Jesus—" He stilled the moment he opened the door and saw who it was. "Chief Inspector…" The thought that he'd come to arrest him for planting the envelope in Inspector Conway's house exploded into his mind. Yet, J Chief Inspector Jones' smile and all-round jovial reaction to his presence put paid to this fear. Dr Weeks opened the door wide. "Come in. John's in the kitchen."

"Thank you, Doctor." Chief Inspector Jones removed his bowler hat as he stepped inside. Hanging it on a hook on the wall, he removed his coat and scarf and hung these on the adjacent hook. With Dr Weeks following, he strolled down the hallway and into the kitchen. "Good afternoon, John." He offered his hand. "I see you're on the mend."

"Hello, Richard," Inspector Conway squeezed Chief Inspector Jones' hand. "Yeah…" He gestured to the surgeon. "Weeks' taken good care of me."

"It must be quite the novelty for you, Doctor." Chief Inspector Jones smiled with a playful twinkle in his eyes. "Tending to a patient with a pulse."

"I'm only doin' it 'cause he's a friend," Dr Weeks rebuked.

"And I, for one, appreciate all that you've done for him," Chief Inspector Jones said with sincerity.

Unsure how to take the compliment, Dr Weeks mumbled, "Yer welcome."

Hoping to have lured Dr Weeks into a false sense of security, Chief Inspector Jones watched his face closely as he said, "Actually, I'm glad I've caught you both. I wanted to discuss Inspector Lee."

The colour drained from Dr Weeks' face.

"What about him?" Inspector Conway enquired.

Chief Inspector Jones sat. "I'm making him the new head of the Mob Squad."

Dr Weeks' stomach did a somersault.

Inspector Conway stared at Chief Inspector Jones, stunned. His shock swiftly gave way to anger. "What about me?"

Feeling as if he were about to empty his stomach at any moment, Dr Weeks hurried to the door. "I gotta get back to work."

"Oi—" Inspector Conway began, but Dr Weeks disappeared.

When he heard the slamming of the front door a moment later, Chief Inspector Jones was convinced Inspector Woolfe's suspicions were correct. Inspector Lee *did* have a hold on Dr Weeks. The surgeon's blatant fear and swift departure proved it.

Oblivious to all of it, Inspector Conway glared at his senior officer. "Are you drunk?"

"Certainly not."

"You must of gone mad, then."

"I'm neither drunk nor mad."

Inspector Conway took a moment to calm his growing anger. Nevertheless, there was a definite edge to his voice as he enquired, "So, what the bloody hell are you playing at, Richard? Lee's the one who's been investigating the Society, or have you forgotten?"

"Not at all."

A pained expression passed over Inspector Conway's face. "Do you think I'm past it?"

Chief Inspector Jones' brows lifted in unison. "*No*, John."

"*What*, then?" Inspector Conway growled. "Sumin's made you demote me."

"Not demoted, but reassigned."

"To *what*?" Inspector Conway demanded, feeling his anger rise again.

"Where, actually," Chief Inspector Jones replied. "I'm reassigning you to E Division."

"*Bow Street*? But—" He stopped when an idea struck him. "Nah." He shook his head. "You wouldn't be that daft."

"I beg your pardon?" Chief Inspector Jones enquired, affronted.

"Putting Lee in charge of keeping a close eye on the Society so you can keep a close eye on Lee."

Chief Inspector Jones smiled. "Not me, John. *You.*"

Inspector Conway frowned deeply. "What about Woolfe?"

"He's too loyal to you to suspect anything," Chief Inspector Jones replied. "Besides, I think Woolfe would rather like to see Inspector Lee removed from the Met. He despises him as much as you do."

"Does Rebecca know?"

Chief Inspector Jones hesitated. "No. Inspector Lee is less likely to suspect a conspiracy if her reaction to his new assignment is genuine."

"She's not goin' to like that."

"What she doesn't know won't hurt her." Chief Inspector Jones glanced at the flour pot on the shelf.

* * *

It was early the next morning when a cab slowed to a stop outside the Bow Street Society's house. The low winter's sun shone into the cab's interior, compelling Mr Maxwell and Miss Dexter to shield their eyes. Both felt emotionally and physically exhausted after witnessing Oliver's final moments on the scaffold. Although it had only been a matter of weeks since that terrible business had begun, it felt as though its end had taken forever in coming. Now that it had, neither Mr Maxwell nor Miss Dexter felt the relief they'd hoped for. Instead, there was just an emptiness tinged with sadness, as if mourning the loss of something they'd never truly had.

Opening the cab's doors, Mr Maxwell alighted before taking Miss Dexter by the hand to assist her in doing the same. Once they both stood on the pavement, he reluctantly released her. "Th-thank you for coming with me, Georgina. I… I don't think I could've faced him on my own."

Miss Dexter gave his hand a gentle squeeze. "Yes, you could've." Reluctantly releasing him, she turned away to avoid looking at him when she broke her news. Feeling a fluttering sensation in her stomach at the same time, she inwardly reminded herself that it was for the best. "Joseph… I have something to tell you. I should've told you before Christmas but I… I couldn't find the right words."

"Wh-what is it?" Mr Maxwell's face filled with worry. "I'll do anything to help."

Miss Dexter turned sad eyes upon him. "Including letting me go?"

Mr Maxwell felt a sudden clenching in his chest. "L-Letting you…? B-But… Georgina… I *love* you."

"And I you," Miss Dexter softly admitted. "But Lady Owston has invited me to Paris, and I… I've accepted."

Time seemed to slow down as Mr Maxwell's senses dulled. *Paris?* he thought. *But that's in France. How will I cope with her so far away? How will I live?* His mind conjured up a memory of his brother Dermid sitting on his bed, telling him about America. *New York City,* he thought. *Yes… that's it. That's what I'll do.*

"I have to do this. For me," Miss Dexter said. "I don't know when I'll get another opportunity." She smiled weakly. "I'll be back in a month."

Mr Maxwell took her hands in his and held them close to his heart. "I-I understand, Georgina. R-Really, I do." He kissed her knuckles. "I wish you the very best in life." His eyes became sad. "And-and if that isn't me… so be it."

Miss Dexter squeezed his hands. "If we're meant to be, fate will find a way."

"Y-Yes, I… I suppose it will." Mr Maxwell gave a feeble smile.

Miss Dexter pulled away. "Goodbye, Joseph."

Mr Maxwell felt a lump form in his throat. "G-Goodbye… Georgina."

Miss Dexter kissed him softly upon the cheek and hurried inside.

Enjoyed the book?
Please consider writing a review

Discover more at www.bowstreetsociety.com

Notes from the author

Spoiler Alert

The events of *The Case of the Pugilist's Ploy* occur almost immediately after the resolution of Poppy's murder case in *The Case of the Maxwell Murder*. The only exceptions to this are the events described in this book's epilogue, which occur immediately after those described in the epilogue of *The Case of the Maxwell Murder*. Both epilogues occur in early January 1897. I rewound the timeline for the bulk of *The Case of the Pugilist's Ploy* because I wanted to explore the aftermath of Poppy's murder, Sybil's suicide, Oliver's arrest, and Inspector Conway's disciplinary board hearing. The books are very character driven, and, so, I didn't want to deny my readers the opportunity to see how events had impacted their favourite characters' lives.

The Manly Art

When I created Mr Snyder's character profile, I included a former career in bareknuckle boxing in his backstory. This was partly to give the group a tough protector type, and partly to lay the foundation for a future mystery surrounding the sport. Given Inspector Conway's working-class background and reputation for being a tough man, it made sense to give him the same past experience of bareknuckle boxing.

    With all of this in mind, and the fact they're similar in age, it was natural to assume they would've crossed paths in the ring. As stated in the *Notes from the author* in the previous book, this past connection was touched upon in *The Case of the Spectral Shot* when Miss Trent reminds Inspector Conway that he knows Mr Snyder can take care of himself. To which the latter unconsciously rubs his jaw.

Needless to say, I couldn't resist the temptation to pit Mr Snyder and Inspector Conway against each other in the ring in this book. This was because I was intrigued to see how it would unfold and who would win. I also knew it was unlikely there would be another opportunity to put Metropolitan Police officers and Bow Street Society members in one place with each group being fully aware of the other's presence. If the books were ever to be dramatized, I think this scene is one that would translate well from text to screen.

My bible whilst writing about boxing in *The Case of the Pugilist's Ploy* was *Art of Boxing and Manual of Training Illustrated* by ex-Champion Lightweight of America and England, William "Billy" Edwards. An eBook of the work written in 1888, it also features lithographs of Billy and his friend and former ring opponent, Arthur Chambers, demonstrating various poses and moves.

Like many veterans of the time, Billy had engaged in both bareknuckle (prize ring) and gloved fights. He also shared his fellow veterans' view of boxing as a science and art. Therefore, it's unsurprising that the manual is written from this standpoint. As an author striving to depict late nineteenth century boxing as accurately as possible, its descriptions and explanations of the basics of boxing, training equipment, exercise regimen, diet, competition/training attire, and rules were invaluable. The depictions of these elements in *The Case of the Pugilist's Ploy*, were based upon Billy Edwards' descriptions and explanations, along with a couple of others sources (see the **Sources of Reference** section).

Yet, Billy's manual also helped me go beyond the mere practicalities of the sport. In his introduction to the book, he gave me a glimpse into the contemporary attitudes toward boxing during a time of great change. Particularly, how former bareknuckle boxers had to adapt to continue their careers when prize fights were being actively repressed by the authorities.

There are two parts of his manual which, in my opinion, best illustrate these points. The first is the inclusion of the three sets of rules boxers of the time were aware of: the London Prize Ring Rules (covering bareknuckle bouts), the Marquis of Queensberry Rules (covering gloved matches), and the newly introduced "American Fair-Play Rules." It's fascinating to note that the London Prize Ring Rules acknowledged, and made arrangements for, the strong possibility of a police raid:

> That in the event of a
> magisterial or other
> interference, or in case
> of darkness coming on, the
> referee [or stakeholder in
> case no referee has been
> chose] shall have the
> power to name the time and
> place for the next
> meeting, if possible on
> the same day, or as soon
> after as may be. In naming
> the second or third place,
> the nearest spot shall be
> selected to the original
> place of fighting where
> there is a chance of its
> being fought out.

The second part of the manual I think encapsulates the attitude of the average boxer at the time comes from Billy's introduction. In it, he states:

> In the first place, then,
> be it said that although it
> is an admitted fact that
> the good old palmy days of

the P. R. [Prize Ring] have
passed away, and lusty
manhood is no longer
allowed, by law, to exhibit
to his fellow-man, in their
most perfect and scientific
developed character, those
grand attributes of
physical power, strength,
nerve, pluck, endurance,
determination, and courage,
that we all profess to
admire, and the lack of
which we resent as a stigma
unworthy to be borne,
still, I am glad to say
that there yet remains a
very large majority of
right-minded people who
approve and support the Art
of Boxing as a wholesome
and legitimate means of
physical recreation and
exercise, enjoyed for the
purpose of benefiting our
bodily health and
condition.

As Billy states above, there was a resentment toward the
repression of prize fighting by the law amongst former
practitioners. This is an attitude that's certainly shared by
Mr Sparrow in the book. Yet, by 1896, there was growing
support amongst boxers for the Marquis of Queensberry
Rules as a means of "legitimising" the sport at a time when
many detractors were campaigning for all forms to be
banned. To them, there was nothing scientific or noble
about what was, essentially, assault by consent.

Mr Farley is a strong advocate for the Queensberry Rules for this very reason. In his mind, the survival of the sport depends upon *all* fighters making the transition. Like Billy Edwards, Mr Sparrow, Mr Snyder, and Inspector Conway, Mr Farley had previously fought in the prize ring. Also, like Billy Edwards, though, he has adapted to the new way of using boxing as a means of maintaining good health and peak physical condition.

His former career in the prize ring is alluded to in the book when he recognises Mr Joe Rake as a prize fighter from his knuckles. Due to the lack of gloves, prize fighters' knuckles were often heavily swollen and battered. According to Billy Edwards' manual, the knuckles of those starting their boxing training could "get a little raw or rubbed." Therefore, he recommends "a few applications of weak tannic acid solution, or rosin, or good strong pickle out of the salt-pork barrel" to "soon make the hands and knuckles tough."

In *The Case of the Pugilist's Ploy*, it's revealed Mr Skinner engaged in bareknuckle boxing whilst in Her Majesty's Royal Navy, a fact Mr Farley also picks up on. This revelation is based upon a passage in Billy Edwards' *Art of Boxing* in which he states that "young [Arthur] Chambers had ample opportunities whilst afloat to become initiated into the mysteries of the fistic art, for it is even still a good old custom in the navy, during fair and pleasant weather, to allow the blue-jackets to skylark during the second dog-watch, which is between four and six o'clock in the evening."

Other works which assisted me in creating an accurate depiction of late nineteenth century boxing were: W. Russel Gray's nonfiction essay *For Whom the Bell Tolled: The Decline of British Prize Fighting in the Victorian Era* and Peter Lovesey's fiction book, *The Detective Wore Silk Drawers: The Second Sergeant Cribb Mystery*. I highly recommend both to those interested in the history of boxing and how its shaped the modern era of the sport.

Exploring Bow Street Society's London

As with previous books, many of the locations in *The Case of the Pugilist's Ploy* are real. These include Nesbit Street, Glyn Street, and Homerton High Street in Hackney, Cricketfield Road in Lower Clapton, the Excelsior Hall in Bethnal Green, and the offices of *Sporting Life* in Fleet Street. Fictitious locations include the *Key & Lion* and *Nimble Crow* public houses. The *Lower Clapton Boxing Club* is also fictitious. According to *Dickens's Dictionary of London* from 1879, the real *Clapton Boxing Club* was based at the *Swan Hotel*. Therefore, the name of my fictitious club is in homage to the real club. In *Dickens's Dictionary of London*, he states that:

> With a, perhaps
> unconscious, touch of
> humour, the club has
> adopted scarlet as its
> distinctive colour—
> delicately suggestive of
> the "claret" which is
> occasionally 'tapped' at
> its meetings.

In the same volume, Charles Dickens records the real-life *West London Boxing Club* meeting at the *Bedford Head* (a public house) on Maiden Lane, Strand. Therefore, I based my fictional boxing club in a public house (*Nimble Crow*) in homage to this real-life club.

The descriptions of *New Scotland Yard*'s exterior and interior were based upon contemporary photographs captured around 1896, and floorplans of the ground and first floors drawn by architect, Norman Shaw, in 1888. The originals of the floorplans are held by the Royal Institute of British Architects (RIBA) Drawings & Archives Collections. Its curator, Fiona Orsini, was kind enough to provide photographs for me to use as points of reference. It's fascinating to note that only one of the building's current two structures stood in 1896. Construction of the second started around 1896/1897. As I couldn't determine the precise year through my research, I omitted any reference to an adjacent construction site in my description.

The visit to Tonbridge, Kent

My descriptions of the geography, locations, construction work, newspaper, and police divisions and uniform, in Tonbridge, Kent, are wholly accurate to how they would've been in 1896. This is because they are based upon contemporary photographs, floorplans (in the case of the police station), and guides, and modern internet sources, given to me by Pam Mills [MA], author of *Prevention, Detection & Keepers of the Peace: Policing Tonbridge, a Division of Kent County Constabulary. The first 50 years and more.* (Tunbridge Wells; Heronswood press Ltd, 2022). Pam also double checked the historical accuracy of the book by reading what I'd written about Tonbridge and telling me what I needed to correct. All this, alongside the sources which I'd found myself (see the **Sources of Reference** section) are why the descriptions connected to Tonbridge are as accurate as they are.

The Metropolitan Police and the West India Docks' Import Dock

In chapter eleven, Dr Weeks reveals Mr Grosse's body was discovered by an officer of the West India Docks' Import Dock's private police force, Mr Zechariah Ellis. He'd then reported his discovery to a patrolling constable of the Metropolitan Police's K (or Stepney) Division. Until 1908, security across all of the London Docks was managed by five separate companies, each with its own private police force. These were: *London and St*

Katharine's, Surrey Commercial, *India and Millwall*, the *Royals* (covering the Royal Albert, Royal Victoria, and King George V Docks), and *Tilbury*. In 1908, the newly formed *Port of London Authority (PLA)* created the *Port of London Authority Police Force*. As I couldn't determine for certain which of the five companies covered the West India Docks' Import Dock in 1896, I omitted this reference from my description.

It's all in the delivery

Crime fiction aficionados familiar with the standard phrasing of a caution given to prisoners by police officers will have noticed a discrepancy in the phrasing used by Inspector Pilker and Sergeant Dwyer. This is because there wasn't an official standard for this essential piece of policing prior to 1906. According to Richard Cowley in his book, *A History of the British Police* (The History Press, Stroud, 2011), prior to 1906:

```
Various forms of the
caution had been used, from
'Be careful, it will be
used against you on your
trial if you are committed
by the Magistrates' to 'You
need not say anything
unless you like, whatever
you say will be used
against you', and all the
variations in between.
```

Language, specifically slang, allowed me to add texture to my portrayal of the boxing world in the late nineteenth century. Pugilist (or Pug) and pugilism to describe boxers and boxing respectively are widely recognised terms within the boxing fraternity even today. Other pieces of slang and boxing terms used in *The Case of the Pugilist's Ploy* were drawn from:

Billy Edwards' *Art of Boxing and Manual of Training Illustrated* (Independently published, 2021) (originally written 1888)

J. Redding Ware's *The Victorian Dictionary of Slang & Phrase* (Bodleian Library, University of Oxford, 2013) (originally published 1909)

Rev. E. Cobham Brewer, LL.D's *A Dictionary of Phrase and Fable* (Cassell and Company Ltd, London, Toronto, Melbourne and Sydney, 1894 edition)

Peter Lovesey's *The Detective Wore Silk Drawers: The Second Sergeant Cribb Mystery* (Sphere, 2013)

Those pieces of slang and boxing terms used are:

Battle monies
Bottle holder
Face his man/Face their man
The fancy
First blood
Knock-out
Knocked into a cocked hat/Knocked into the middle of next week
Mittens
Sauce-box
Seconds
Set-tos
Sharp's the word—and quick's the motion
Stakeholder

Mr Sparrow's slang is used in the West Midlands, specifically Birmingham, where he is originally from. These are "aggin'," "cack-handed," "nause," "righ' lampin'," "couple or three," "having a benny," "myther," and "ar."

If you'd like to discover more about the Bow Street Society, including its members, please visit the official website at www.bowstreetsociety.com. Finally, please consider writing a review if you enjoyed this book, and thank you for your continued support.

~ T.G. Campbell, *November 2022*

MORE BOW STREET SOCIETY

All titles are available from Amazon NOW

OW STREET SOCIETY

The Case of The Curious Client

T.G. Campbell

(Bow Street Society Mystery, #1)

WINNER OF FRESH LIFESTYLE MAGAZINE BOOK AWARD APRIL 2017

In *The Case of The Curious Client,* the Bow Street Society is hired by Mr Thaddeus Dorsey to locate a missing friend he knows only as 'Palmer' after he fails to keep a late night appointment with him. With their client's own credibility cast into doubt mere minutes after they meet him though, the Society is forced to consider whether they've been sent on a wild goose chase. That is until events take a dark turn and the Society has to race against time not only to solve the case, but to also save the very life of their client…

(Bow Street Society Mystery, #2)

In this sequel to *The Case of The Curious Client,* the Bow Street Society is privately commissioned to investigate the murder of a woman whose mutilated body was discovered in the doorway of the London Crystal Palace Bazaar on Oxford Street. Scandal, lies, intrigue, and murder all await the Society as they explore the consumerist hub of the Victorian Era & its surrounding areas, glimpse the upper classes' sordid underbelly, and make a shocking discovery no one could've predicted...

(Bow Street Society Mystery, 3)

When Miss Trent is paid a late night visit by a masked stranger the Bow Street Society is plunged into its most bizarre case to date. New faces join returning members as they encounter unsolved murders, the contentious world of spiritualism, and mounting hostility from the Metropolitan Police. Can the Society exorcise the ghosts of the past to uncover the truth, or will it, too, be lured into an early grave…?

BOW STREET SOCIETY

The Case of
The Toxic Tonic

T.G. Campbell

(Bow Street Society Mystery, #4)

When the Bow Street Society is called upon to assist the
Women's International Maybrick Association, it's
assumed the commission will be a short-lived one. Yet, a
visit to the *Walmsley Hotel* in London's prestigious west
end only serves to deepen the Society's involvement. In an
establishment that offers exquisite surroundings,
comfortable suites, and death, the Bow Street Society must
work alongside Scotland Yard to expose a cold-blooded
murderer. Meanwhile, two inspectors secretly work to
solve the mystery of not only Miss Rebecca Trent's past
but the creation of the Society itself...

(Bow Street Society Mystery, #5)

A month has passed since the dramatic events at the Walmsley Hotel, but both the Bow Street Society and Scotland Yard continue to reel from their repercussions. Guilt-ridden over the Society's part in the suspension of Inspector Conway, Miss Trent is doing all she can to help whilst maintaining the veil of secrecy around their mutual friend. Yet even they hadn't foreseen the tragedy that is about to occur. A tragedy that will shock the Bow Street Society to its core...

SOURCES OF REFERENCE

Research has been conducted into the historical period *The Case of The Pugilist's Ploy* is set in. Aspects covered in this research include: the state of boxing in the last twenty years of the nineteenth century, Tonbridge in Kent, and numerous real-life locations. Though not directly referenced in this book, the research was used to form the basis of narrative descriptions and some character dialogue. I've therefore strived to cite each source used within my research here. Each citation includes the source's origin, the source's author, and which part of *The Case of The Pugilist's Ploy* the source is connected to. All rights connected to the following sources remain with their respective authors and publishers.

BOOKS

Edwards, William, <u>Billy Edwards'</u> <u>Art of Boxing and Manual of Training Illustrated</u> (Independently published, 2021) (originally written 1888)
Rough, disfigured knuckles of pugilists Mr Grosse has admired.
The terms "set-tos," "scratch," and "facing their man" in Chapter 3.
Using "punishment" as a synonym for dealing punches.
Description of a boxer's "mark."
The terms "draw" and the ploy referenced.
Using the left fist to attack and the right fist to defend.
The term "seconds" and the boxers returning to their corners between rounds.
The prize-fight boxing referee calling "time." The prize-fight boxing referee allowing eight seconds for a boxer to return to the "scratch" before declaring their opponent the winner. The terms "stakeholder" and "battle monies" in Chapter 3.
The size of a Queensberry Rules boxing ring.

The names, locations, and descriptions of the club weights, dumb-bells, bags' weights, rope, and construction, and the flying-bags in the Lower Clapton Boxing Club's gymnasium.

The term "toed the scratch" and the description of the correct position.

Description of remnants of ring in warehouse.

Penning opponent in corner and stance opponent takes to defend himself: "in-fighting."

The use of the term "wind" to refer to breathing.

Benefits of swinging an Indian Club

Correct way of standing when swinging Indian Clubs

Benefits of sweating, cold water plunges, and rubbings with the towel

Inspector Conway's boxing attire at the Excelsior Hall match.

Ware, J. Redding, <u>The Victorian Dictionary of Slang & Phrase</u> (Bodleian Library, University of Oxford, 2013) (originally published 1909)

The term "sauce-box," meaning mouth, in Chapter 3.

The term "jemmy."

The use of the word "barney" to refer to an argument.

LL.D., Cobham Brewer, Rev. E., <u>A Dictionary of Phrase and Fable</u> (Cassell and Company Ltd, London, Toronto, Melbourne and Sydney, 1894 edition)

The term "fast gents" in Chapter 1.

The terms "the fancy," "set-tos," and "knock-out" in Chapter 3.

The phrase "sharp's the word—and quick's the motion!"

The phrase "To be knocked into a cocked hat, or into the middle of next week."

Lovesey, Peter <u>The Detective Wore Silk Drawers: The Second Sergeant Cribb Mystery</u> (Sphere, 2013)

The terms "pugs" and "first blood" in Chapter 3.

Bradshaw's Rail Times for Great Britain and Ireland: December 1895 (Middleton Press)
The time of the train taken by Inspector Woolfe from London to Tonbridge, Kent.

Cowley, Richard. **A History of the British Police** (The History Press, Stroud, 2011)
The absence of a standardised caution given by the police to a prisoner. Before October 1906 – "Previously, various forms of the caution had been used, from 'Be careful, it will be used against you on your trial if you are committed by the Magistrates' to 'You need not say anything unless you like, whatever you say will be used against you', and all the variations in between."

Bell, Neil R A, and Wood, Adam **SIR HOWARD VINCENT'S POLICE CODE: 1889** (Mango Books, 2015)
The absence of a standardised caution given by the police to a prisoner.

Gray, W. Russel, **For Whom the Bell Tolled: The Decline of British Prize Fighting in the Victorian Era** (Journal of Popular Culture, 1987)
Regulations of Railways Act of 1868 put a stop to people travelling out of London for prize fights.

Anderson, Jack, **Pugilistic Prosecutions: Prize Fighting and ahe Courts an Nineteenth Century Britain** (School of Law, Queen's University Belfast)
Mr Elliott's explanation about the illegality of prize fighting

McDowall, F.S.A., SCOT., William, The Mind in the Face: An Introduction to the Study of Physiognomy, (L.N. Fowler, London, c.1885)
Mr Skinner's nose and chin suggesting clean habits.
A high and massive brow being a physical sign of wisdom and intelligence.
Physical features, wisdom, and intelligence being degraded by vice.

Daniels, J.H. A History of British Postmarks (London, 1898)
Miss Webster's analysis of the stamp and obliteration/postmark.

Mattison, Dr J.B., The Treatment of Opium Addiction (Originally published in 1885)
The size, preparation, and frequency of the Sodium Bromide treatment Dr Lynette Locke is giving to her husband Percy. Also, the side effects Percy is experiencing. Namely, his drowsiness followed by a profound slumber (and its timing), his inability to stay awake for long periods, and his aversion to exercise. Although the side effects of loss of appetite and an aversion to washing and conversing aren't named in Mattison's work, one would think they'd be natural consequences of a patient wanting to sleep all of the time.

Thomas, M.D., A. E., A Practical Guide for Making Post-Mortem Examinations for the Study of Morbid Anatomy, with directions for embalming the dead and for the preservation of specimens of Morbid Anatomy (Boericke & Tapel, New York and Philadelphia, 1873)
The description of the base of skull fracture being caused by the blow on top of the skull based upon the line "it will sometimes be discovered that fracture exists at a point opposite to that point which the blow was received… or, received on the top of the skull, fracture may result at the base." Signs of death.

Gray, Henry, 1825-1861; Spitzka, Edward Anthony, 1876-1922 <u>Anatomy, descriptive and applied</u> (Published 1913)
https://archive.org/details/anatomydescript00gray
Use of the terms "inner table" and "outer table" in reference to the skull

WEBSITES

Record HO 45/9709/A50934 <u>POLICE - METROPOLITAN: Employment of lift attendants in uniform at New Scotland Yard sanctioned. Insurance of lifts not approved</u> (1890 – 95) *from the catalogue description on the* <u>National Archives</u> *website* https://discovery.nationalarchives.gov.uk/details/r/C47 41630?descriptiontype=Full&ref=HO+45/9709/A50934
The presence of a uniformed lift attendant at New Scotland Yard,

<u>Homburg</u> *article by Admin on the* <u>Vintage Fashion Guild</u> *website. Dated: February 25th 2017* https://vintagefashionguild.org/hat-resource/homburg/
The uniqueness of Mr Grosse's Homburg hat. According to the article, the hat was popular amongst residents of Homburg, Germany, in the 1880s but didn't become fashionable in England until the second decade of the twentieth century.

<u>Brummie Slang Words, Phrases & Accent (a Local's Guide)</u> *article on the* <u>BRB – Gone Somewhere Epic</u> website
https://brbgonesomewhereepic.com/brummie-slang/
The terms "nausea," "righ' lampin'," "couple or three," and "ar."

Timeline *on the* **Tonbridge Historical Society** *website.*
http://www.tonbridgehistory.org.uk/history/timeline.ht
m
The name of Tonbridge Junction train station. According to this timeline, the station was renamed to this in 1852.

Extract from **Tonbridge for the Resident, the Holiday Maker and the Angler,** **by W. Stanley Martin and B. Prescott Row (price sixpence),** *written in 1896 from* **Tonbridge Historical Society** *website*
http://www.tonbridgehistory.org.uk/photos/the-high-street--1/index.html
The reputation of, and the quotation cited regarding, the Rose and Crown Hotel on High Street, Tonbridge. Demolition and construction work on the west side of the High Street, widening of High Street, and the demolition of old cottages in Tonbridge.

The Rose and Crown Hotel *entry on the* **Tonbridge Historical Society** *website.*
www.tonbridgehistory.org.uk/places/the-rose-and-crown.htm
The reference to the hotel's windows overlooking the High Street in Tonbridge.

The Kent Constabulary entry on the British Police History website
https://british-police-history.uk/m_show_nav.cgi?force=kent_county&tab=0&nav=alpha&type=n
The Kent County Constabulary having the heraldic horse rampant on its crest

Death by Blunt Force Trauma article on the Officer website
https://www.officer.com/investigations/article/10249149/death-by-blunt-force-trauma
Reaction of blunt force trauma to the skull

Rigor Mortis *article on the* **Science Direct** *website*
https://www.sciencedirect.com/topics/medicine-and-dentistry/rigor-mortis
Rigor mortis setting in between 2 – 6 hours after death.

'The West India Docks: The docks', in Survey of London: Volumes 43 and 44, Poplar, Blackwall and Isle of Dogs, ed. Hermione Hobhouse (London, 1994), pp. 268-281. British History Online http://www.british-history.ac.uk/survey-london/vols43-4/pp268-281 **[accessed 12 November 2022].**
The disuse of the warehouse and general fortunes of the West India Docks' Import Dock.

Remembering the Port of London Authority Police Force article on the **Isle of Dogs Life** website
https://isleofdogslife.wordpress.com/2019/11/15/remembering-the-port-of-london-authority-police-force/
The West India Docks' Import Dock having its own private police force and the five companies responsible for security across all of the London Docks named in the 'Notes from the author' section.

History of Amateur Boxing article on the **Team USA** website
https://www.teamusa.org/usa-boxing/about-us/history-of-amateur-boxing
The Amateur Athletic Union of the United States of America and their records starting in 1888.

The History of Cremations article on the **Urns with Love** website
https://www.urnswithlove.co.uk/blogs/news/72467333-the-history-of-cremations
The reference to urn-burials by Miss Dexter.

Birth, Marriage & Death Records in Ontario *article on the* **Ontario Ancestors** *website.*
https://ogs.on.ca/resources/birth-marriage-death-records-in-ontario/#:~:text=Before%20that%20time%2C%20births%2C%20marriages,before%20it%20was%20widely%20followed.
Registration of Dr Weeks' birth in a parish record and births formally registered from 1869 onwards (but not widely followed for a few years).

A Comprehensive Guide to Brummie Slang *article on* **The Culture Trip** *website*
https://theculturetrip.com/europe/united-kingdom/england/articles/a-comprehensive-guide-to-brummie-slang/
The terms "cack-handed," "aggin'," "having a benny," "myther," and "ar" used by Mr Sparrow.

Boxing Dictionary *section of the* **Title Boxing** *website*
https://www.titleboxing.com/boxing-dictionary
The term "card."

History of Boxing Equipment *article on the* **Title Boxing** *website*
https://www.titleboxing.com/history-of-boxing-equipment
The smooth soles of the shoes worn in the boxing ring.

British Postmarks Catalogue
https://www.rpsl.org.uk/gplstatic/BL_CrawfordDocs/016668998.pdf
Miss Webster's analysis of the stamp and obliteration/postmark

Sporting Life entry on the **British Newspaper Archives** website,
https://www.britishnewspaperarchive.co.uk/titles/sporting-life
Location and name of Sporting Life newspaper. "1859–1915 The Sporting Life" and "Sporting Life, published in London, started as a biweekly publication that became a daily publication in 1883. During its first year of publication, it was called Penny Bell's Life and Sporting News. The following year, the paper changed its name to Sporting Life."

Sporting Life - Thursday 17 December 1896 from the **British Newspaper Archive** website
https://www.britishnewspaperarchive.co.uk/viewer/bl/0000893/18961217/061/0004
Article man reading outside of Sporting Life office is loosely based on this one.
The fact the Excelsior Hall was used for competitive boxing matches during December.

Fleet Street in seven centuries; being a history of the growth of London beyond the walls into the Western Liberty, and of Fleet Street to our time. With a foreword by Sir William Purdie Treloar. Drawings by T.R. Way [and others] (Published: 1912)
http://archive.org/details/fleetstreetinsevOObell
Group gathered around the window of the Sporting Life office on Fleet Street.
The proximity of the Sporting Life office to that of the Sportsman publication.
Contents of the display in the window of the Sporting Life office, including photographs of champion boxers with bloodied gloves.

Excelsior Hall *article on the* **East End Memories** *website*
http://www.eastend-
memories.org/excelsior/excelsior_2.htm /
Name of the hall, its location, and fact swimming pools were covered over during the winter months for concerts and meetings

What does being shot actually feel like? *article on the* **Today I Found Out** *website*
http://www.todayifoundout.com/index.php/2019/04/wh
at-does-being-shot-actually-feel-like/
Mr Skinner's physical sensations and reactions to being shot.

Walter Hunt: Safety Pin CONSUMER DEVICES *article on the* **Lemelson-MIT Program (LMIT)** *website*
https://lemelson.mit.edu/resources/walter-
hunt#:~:text=Mechanic%20and%20independent%20i
nventor%20Walter,the%20safety%20pin%20in%2018
49
Use of a safety pin by Dr Weeks. It was invented in 1849.

* * *

Lee Jackson's *The Victorian Dictionary*
http://www.victorianlondon.org/index-2012.htm
The following sources are all taken from The Victorian Dictionary website

Rowe, Richard, Life in the London Streets Chapter 10: At a Coffee Stall (1881)
The red-hot coals of the base of the urn on the coffee stall Inspector Conway visits. Also, the use of Earthenware cups, the adulteration of coffee with chicory, and the fact coffee stalls are only pitched at night.

Wright, Thomas The Pinch of Poverty, by The Riverside Visitor Chapter 14: "All Hot!" (1892)
The appearance of the coffee stall and urn is based upon a sketch in this work.

Mayhew, Henry London Labour and the London Poor: OF COFFEE-STALL KEEPERS (1851, 1861-2)
The reference of who visited the stall and when is based upon this line from Mayhew's work: "some of the stall-keepers make their appearance at twelve at night, and some not till three or four in the morning. Those that come out at midnight, are for the accommodation of the 'night-walkers', 'fast gentlemen' and loose girls; and those that come out in the morning, are for the accommodation of the working men."
The references to the purchasing of ham sandwiches from the coffee stall, the thinness of the bread, and the quality of the meat is based upon this line from Mayhew's work: line "It is usually cut up in slices little thicker than paper. The bread is usually 'second bread.'"

Dickens (Jr.), Charles, "Boxing" Dickens's Dictionary of London, 1879
According to Dickens, the headquarters of the real-life Clapton Boxing Club was at the Swan Hotel, Upper Clapton. The name of the fictional Lower Clapton Boxing Club was chosen in homage to this real-life club. Also, according to Dickens, the real-life West London Boxing Club met at the Bedford Head (a public house) on Maiden Lane, Strand. The venue of the fictional Lower Clapton Boxing Club (Nimble Crow public house) was chosen in homage tot his real-life club. Amateur Boxing Association, its year of formation, and its role.

Dickens (Jr.), Charles, "Newspapers" Dickens's Dictionary of London, 1879
Location and name of Sporting Life newspaper: "SPORTING LIFE, 1d., 148, Fleet street. Sport"

Robinson, W., Remation and Urn Burial or the Cemeteries of the Future (Cassell & Company Limited, London, Paris, New York & Melbourne, 1889)
The term "urn-burial."

PHYSIOLOGY OF THE LONDON IDLER. CHAPTER VI. CONCERNING THE GENT. (Punch, 1842)
The sketch from this article used as basis for evidence of customers smoking in the shop.
Tabitha's description is loosely based on the woman serving behind the counter depicted in this sketch.

George R. Sims (ed.), Living London, (1902)
Customers of East End fish and chip shops drowning their chips in vinegar and the fried fish shop.

Cunningham, Peter, Hand-Book of London, (1850)
Smells at the West India Docks (not the bodily odour or musty clothes, though)

MAPS AND FLOORPLANS

Booth, Charles Booth's Maps of London Poverty East and West 1889 (reproduced by Old House Books) *purchased from* **Shire Books http://www.shirebooks.co.uk/old_house_books/**
The classification of Cricketfield Road and the close proximity of Lower Clapton to Hackney.
The classification of College Street, Hackney.
The proximity of College Street to Homerton High Street, Hackney. Location of Mr Grosse's house based upon classification of Glyn Road. Location description and the subsequent route Inspector Conway and Miss Trent take, and the landmarks they see, after leaving the fried fish shop. Class of residents on Crozier Terrace and the street's proximity to the Hackney Union Workhouse

Shaw, Norman, <u>METROPOLITAN POLICE; NEW CENTRAL OFFICES</u> Ground and First Floors (1888) courtesy of Fiona Orsini, curator at the Royal Institute of British Architects (RIBA) Drawings & Archives Collections.
Layout of the interior of New Scotland Yard's ground and first floors. Also, the windows and private lavatory in Chief Inspector Jones's office.
Layout of interview room and location within New Scotland Yard building

Exterior, floorplans, and front elevation of the proposed police station at Tonbridge supplied by **Pam Mills [MA], author of <u>Prevention, Detection & Keepers of the Peace: Policing Tonbridge, a Division of Kent County Constabulary. The first 50 years and more</u>. (Tunbridge Wells; Heronswood press Ltd, 2022)** *with explanatory note.*
External appearance and internal layout of the Tonbridge Division police station, and layout of its yard.

EXPLANATORY NOTES & ASSISTANCE

The following were provided by **Pam Mills [MA], author of <u>Prevention, Detection & Keepers of the Peace: Policing Tonbridge, a Division of Kent County Constabulary. The first 50 years and more</u>. (Tunbridge Wells; Heronswood press Ltd, 2022):**
Pedestrian exit for Tonbridge Junction train station was on Station Approach. This is also the main door opposite the telegraph office.
The name of the Tonbridge Division of Kent County Constabulary and the existence and location of the newly formed detective branch at Wrens Cross, Maidstone.
Arrangements made between the superintendent at Bow Street and the superintendent at the detective branch at Wrens Cross, Maidstone, for Inspector Woolfe to have the assistance of a detective officer.

The founding of Tonbridge Free Press in 1869 and the location of its office on the High Street in Tonbridge.

PHOTOGRAPHS, PAINTINGS, AND SKETCHES

PHOTOGRAPH: <u>View into Tonbridge</u> taken by Allwork Bros. courtesy of Roger Lewis *supplied by* **Pam Mills [MA],** *author of* <u>**Prevention, Detection & Keepers of the Peace: Policing Tonbridge, a Division of Kent County Constabulary. The first 50 years and more**</u>**. (Tunbridge Wells; Heronswood press Ltd, 2022)** *with explanatory note.*
The crowded nature of the thoroughfare outside of Tonbridge Junction train station and the location of the telegraph office opposite the station.

PHOTOGRAPH: <u>Pembury Road</u> *photograph supplied by* **Pam Mills [MA],** *author of* <u>**Prevention, Detection & Keepers of the Peace: Policing Tonbridge, a Division of Kent County Constabulary. The first 50 years and more**</u>**. (Tunbridge Wells; Heronswood press Ltd, 2022)** *with explanatory note.*
The location of the Tonbridge Division train station on Pembury Road.

PHOTOGRAPH: <u>Tonbridge Division Police Station</u> *photograph supplied by* **Pam Mills [MA],** *author of* <u>**Prevention, Detection & Keepers of the Peace: Policing Tonbridge, a Division of Kent County Constabulary. The first 50 years and more**</u>**. (Tunbridge Wells; Heronswood press Ltd, 2022)** *with explanatory note.*
External appearance of the police station and layout of the yard

PHOTOGRAPH: <u>Tonbridge Division Police Station</u> *(March, 1899) photograph supplied by* **Pam Mills [MA], author of** <u>Prevention, Detection & Keepers of the Peace: Policing Tonbridge, a Division of Kent County Constabulary. The first 50 years and more</u>. **(Tunbridge Wells; Heronswood press Ltd, 2022)** *from Frank Chapman's book with explanatory note.*
External appearance of the police station and layout of the yard. Also, the overall description of Sergeant Hunnicutt's uniform.

PHOTOGRAPH: Tobacconist's Shop in the Victorian Walk at the Museum of London's London Wall site.
Description of humidors, cabinets, pillars, and shelves in Linton's Tobacconists.

WATERCOLOUR PAINTING: <u>A view of Tunbridge, Kent</u>*, painted in 1788 by Paul Sandby on the* <u>Artsy website.</u>
https://www.artsy.net/artwork/paul-sandby-a-view-of-tunbridge-kent
The watercolour of Tonbridge, Kent, hanging in the Rose and Crown Hotel.

INK SKETCH: <u>The Sporting Life Building, 148 Fleet Street, London</u> *painted in 1891 by Joseph Pennell as shown on the* <u>Court Gallery</u> *website*
https://www.courtgallery.com/exhibitions/80/works/art works10413/
Group gathered around the window of the Sporting Life office on Fleet Street.

* * *

City of London: London Metropolitan Archives
https://www.londonpicturearchive.org.uk
The following citations are from the above source:

PHOTOGRAPH: *Record No: 65988* <u>Entrance to Victoria Park Station in Riseholme Street</u> **(Photograph taken in 1899) Catalogue No: SC_PHL_01_119_75_18279**
The location of Victoria Park Station and the inclusion of Broad Street Station in City of London as a destination from Victoria Park Station.

PHOTOGRAPH: *Record No: 36675* <u>Broad Street Station</u> **(Photograph taken c. 1890) Catalogue No: M0013072CL**
Catching a hansom cab outside Broad Street Station.

INFORMATION SHEETS

Hunter, Michael, <u>The Victorian Villas of Hackney: A Hackney Society Publication</u> (1981) http://www.hackneysociety.org/documents/Victorian_V illas_1981.pdf
House description based upon photograph of 97, Glyn Road in this information sheet.

<u>Regina *v.* John Swindall and James Osborne</u> (Heard before Lord Chief Barron Pollock on March 23rd 1846)
Mr Elliott's explanation of the piece of case law regarding the law of common purpose.

Printed in Great Britain
by Amazon

14117766R00267